Kidnapping Fate
A Luna Stone Series
Aurora Lunaire

Wicked Whispers Publishing

Cover Art by Arsalan Ali

Editing by Aiman Mengal

For more information visit: www.auroralunaire.com

To my incredible family and friends—thank you for standing by me through every twist and turn of this indie author journey. To my wonderful beta readers, your honest feedback and encouragement made these stories stronger. And to my amazing editor, Aiman Mengal, your guidance and sharp eye brought my words to life. I couldn't have done this without each of you.

Content Warning

Your safety and comfort as a reader matter deeply to me. This story contains sensitive themes that may be distressing. I believe in being transparent so you know what to expect because while I want to tell powerful, emotional stories, I also want you to have a safe and pleasant reading experience.

This book includes references to:
- Kidnapping

- Murder

- Death

- Pregnancy loss / Death

- Infanticide

- Rape (mentioned, not described in detail)

Please take care of yourself while reading, and remember it's always okay to step away or return when you feel ready.

Contents

Prologue

20 years ago

A lpha Beto sat behind his desk at his company, Luna Enterprise, watching his Beta and best friend Marcos's walk back.

"Man, calm down. The girls are just having lunch," Alpha Beto said, trying to ease the tension rolling off his beta. But Beta Marcos wasn't so easily reassured. His jaw tightened, his hands restless as he leaned against the office desk.

"I have a bad feeling," Marcos murmured, his voice low and strained. "I shouldn't have let her out of my sight. She's so close to having the baby."

Beto sighed, his tone softening. "My friend, stop worrying. You should be excited! You're about to be a father. Sofía and Andrés are going to have a new playmate."

The words tugged a faint smile from Marcos, but the unease still lingered in his dark eyes. Refusing to let himself be idle, he dove back into their work, channeling his nervous energy into the steady hum of Luna Enterprise.

The hours passed slowly, each second dragging on as Alpha Beto and Beta Marcos worked through the day. Just when it seemed like Marcos might finally be able to push his worries aside, his phone rang.

He snatched up his phone, his heart lodging in his throat. The voice of one of the lead warriors crackled through the line, tight with urgency.

"Beta Marcos, we were ambushed. They... they've taken Delilah."

For a moment, Marcos couldn't move, couldn't breathe. His world stopped. Beto, with his shifter hearing, heard the whole conversation; without a second thought, the Luna stone alpha started barking commands. Beto's loud voice snapped Marcos out of his frozen state, and together they tore from their office, gathering their warriors as they raced toward Dalilah's last known location.

The scene was nothing short of carnage. Guards lay scattered across the ground, their lifeless eyes staring into the abyss. The few who survived were gravely wounded, their breathing shallow and desperate. Blood soaked the earth, and Delilah was nowhere to be found.

Hours passed as they searched, following every scent, every trace yet no luck. When they finally found her, it was worse than Marcos could have imagined.

Marco could smell his true mate. That delicate mix of lavender and bergamot teased his senses as he approached the place where they'd found her. Yet, something was wrong. Deeply wrong.

Her scent, once soothing and unmistakably hers, was now drowned out by the sharp, metallic sting of blood. The copper tang grew stronger with each step, wrapping around him like a noose.

When he reached the door, the only thing separating him from Delilah, her scent had vanished entirely. All that remained was blood and dread.

With trembling fingers and fear gripping his heart, Marco pushed the door open.

And his world shattered.

Delilah lay broken on the floor, soaked in crimson and barely breathing. Her once-vibrant spirit now flickered like a dying flame. His wolf howled inside him, a soundless cry of rage and heartbreak. But it was her eyes that destroyed him—hollow, vacant, lost.

She didn't need to say the words. He saw it in her. He felt it in the bond.

Their child was gone.

Her abdomen had been torn open, and there was nothing left inside but devastation.

Marcos fell to his knees, pulling Delilah into his arms as if he could shield her from the pain, from the cruel reality that had stolen everything from them. Her breath was shallow, her skin pale, her blood staining his hands.

"Delilah," he whispered, his voice cracking as he pressed his forehead to hers. "Stay with me. Please, stay with me."

Her eyelids fluttered open, her gaze locking onto his. Her lips trembled as she tried to smile, but the effort was too much. "The baby..." she breathed, her voice a fragile whisper. "I'm so sorry."

"No, no, don't say that," he begged, clutching her tighter. "You have nothing to be sorry for. This isn't the end, Delilah. You're going to be okay. We'll get through this. Together."

Tears welled in her eyes as she reached up to touch his face, her hand trembling against his cheek. "I promised....to be with you forever... I'm so sorry. "

He shook his head violently, fresh tears streaming down his face. "Don't. Don't talk like that. You're strong. You're the strongest person I know. You can fight this."

Her tears spilled over, her fingers tracing his jaw as if memorizing every detail. "I love you, Marcos. You made me so happy, gave me a love I never thought I'd have. But now... you have to let me go."

"I can't," he rasped, his voice breaking. "You're my mate. My heart. My everything. I can't do this without you."

"Yes, you can," she whispered, her voice growing fainter. "Promise me you'll fight. Protect the pack. Avenge us. Make them pay... For our baby."

"I promise," he swore, his chest heaving as he held her closer. "I'll make them regret this. Every last one of them. I'll avenge you. I swear it."

A faint smile touched her lips, but her eyes were dulling, her breaths growing shallow. "Always remember, I love you... Always..."

Her hand slipped from his face, falling limply to her side as her body stilled. Marcos froze, his anguish boiling over into a howl so raw, so primal, it seemed to shake the very earth.

Marcos knelt for what felt like an eternity, cradling Delilah's lifeless body, his grief a storm, brewing into something darker and violent. With a low, guttural growl, he laid her gently on the blood-soaked ground, brushing her hair away from her face one last time.

Then he rose and walked toward the warriors assigned to his mate. His walk was slow, trembling, and dangerous. His hand shot out, grabbing the nearest injured guard by the throat and slamming him hard against a tree. Bark cracked. Bone might've, too.

Marco's eyes had changed. They were gone feral with the unmistakable gleam of his wolf pushing to the surface. Claws burst from his fingertips, piercing the man's skin as blood welled beneath his grip. But his hand trembled.

Not from weakness.

From restraint.

The war inside him raged. His wolf clawing, demanding vengeance, begging to be unleashed. But Marco held on, barely. His jaw clenched, body taut with fury, every muscle coiled as he fought to stay in control.

"Tell me what happened!" Marcos snarled, his voice a mix of human and beast.

The guard coughed, his voice weak but desperate to explain. "W-we were ambushed... out of nowhere. The attack was... they came at us from all sides. At first, we couldn't tell who it was... until the Luna—" He grimaced, pain etched across his face, but he forced the words out. "She recognized one of the men. Black Stone Pack."

Marcos froze for a moment, his mind consumed by the name. His grip faltered just enough for the warrior to gasp in air.

"Black Stone," Marcos repeated, his voice a venomous growl. "George." He released the guard, letting him crumple to the ground as Marcos turned to Alpha Beto. His eyes burned with the fire of a man with nothing left to lose. "We're going to destroy them."

Beto, equally enraged but trying to temper his emotions, nodded grimly. "We'll assemble the warriors."

For five years, the Luna Stone Pack waged war on the Black Stone Pack. It was no simple clash of wolves, it was a bloodbath. The ferocity of the Luna Stone's vengeance nearly exposed paranormal world to humans on more than one occasion. But to Marcos, it didn't matter. Nothing mattered except making George pay for what he'd done.

The Black Stone Pack fought back, but they were no match for the full force of the Luna Stone Pack. Marcos led his warriors into battle after battle, his feral rage a driving force that struck fear into even the most seasoned of George's soldiers. Beto tried to keep the pack balanced, to temper the chaos, but even he was consumed by the thirst for justice.

Despite the carnage, George remained elusive, his cowardice keeping him in the shadows while his pack fell apart.

The Council of Shifters finally intervened, their patience exhausted. The ancient governing body convened, and representatives of other packs demanded an immediate end to the war. Marcos stood before them, his eyes hollow but blazing with unyielding fury.

"George killed my mate. My child. And you want me to let him walk free?"

The council leader, a towering shifter with an air of authority, fixed Marcos with a cold stare. "You've offered no concrete evidence tying him directly to the attack. What we have are statements, and a trail of destruction that now threatens to expose us all. This war ends now, Beta Marcos. It's what's best for the paranormal community."

The only lead we had connecting Alpha George to the Luna Stone Pack was a she-wolf who once served their Luna. She had been seduced by the Beta of Black Stone Pack, coaxed into revealing sensitive information details like the Luna's schedule and movements. But just days after her confession, her body was found in a run-down motel miles from the pack lands. Dead. Silenced.

In the end, Alpha George had covered his tracks well. Too well. No evidence, no witnesses. Nothing that could tie him directly to her murder. And Alpha Beto knew it.

As the Council adjourned and the room slowly emptied, Beto approached Marcos in a hushed, solemn tone. "It's over... for now," he said quietly. "But George isn't invincible. Sooner or later, he'll make a mistake."

Reluctantly, Luna Stone agreed to a ceasefire. The war ended, leaving Black Stone crippled and George in hiding, his pack a mere shadow of what it once was. But for Marcos, there was no closure, no peace.

The wind whispered through the towering pines that guarded Marcos's secluded cabin, a hidden refuge deep in the forest—far from the pack, from duty, from memories he couldn't bear to relive.

Alpha Beto trudged up the uneven path, Leo squirming on one hip while a curious three-year-old Andrés clung stubbornly to his leg. Sofía, not much older but sharp-eyed and silent, trailed behind them like a small sentinel.

He knocked hard on the weather-worn door, the sound cracking through the quiet. No answer.

Again, louder this time. "Marcos!" Beto barked. "I know you're in there. Open the damn door, or I'll break it down."

A beat. Then another.

Finally, the door creaked open. Marcos stood in the threshold like a ghost of the man Beto once knew. His eyes were hollow, his hair unkempt, jaw dark with days-old stubble. No greeting. No protest. Just a silent retreat as he stepped aside and let them in.

The air inside was thick. Smelling of stale wood, fading embers, and the raw scent of a man who'd stopped being part of the world. The space was bare, save for a single photo of Delilah on the mantle. She smiled in it. Marcos didn't even look at it anymore.

Beto set Leo down and took a long, steady breath before speaking. "This ends today."

Marcos said nothing. He just dropped into a chair, arms crossed, shoulders hunched like a man bearing the weight of too many yesterdays.

"You've shut everyone out," Beto continued, voice low but iron-hard. "You think this is what she wanted? You disappearing into the woods, waiting to die while the rest of us keep breathing around the hole she left behind?"

Still nothing. No flicker of acknowledgment. Just that quiet, dangerous stillness.

"I know it hurts," Beto said, stepping closer. "But we all lost her, Marcos. She was like a sister. And you were—are—my brother."

A muscle ticked in Marcos's jaw. That was the first sign of life.

"You don't get to vanish. Not when there are people who still need you." Beto's tone sharpened. "You think this pain makes you special? That no one else misses her? That you're the only one who'd trade anything to have her back? You're not."

Marcos's knuckles whitened where they gripped the armrest. But he still didn't break.

So Beto twisted the knife.

"My kids ask about you every goddamn day. Do you know that? Andrés still thinks you're his hero."

Right on cue, tiny footsteps padded across the room. Andrés approached, gaze wide and solemn as he looked up at the man he'd only ever seen as strong.

He reached out and tugged on Marcos's sleeve. "Uncle Marcos?"

The man didn't flinch, but his breath caught.

"Mama says you're sad." The boy's voice was barely a whisper. "But I miss you."

Marcos finally looked at him. The curls. The eyes. The hope.

Andres smiled, unsure. "If you come back, I promise to be good."

That did it.

A low, ragged sound tore from Marcos's throat, like something primal finally giving way. He dropped his head into his hands, his body trembling with the weight of everything he'd tried so hard to keep buried. When he finally reached for the boy, it wasn't in strength—it was surrender.

He pulled Andres into his lap and held him like a lifeline, tears falling silently down his cheeks.

Beto stepped forward and rested a hand on his shoulder, his voice quiet now—gentle, grounded.

"You don't have to carry this alone anymore."

Chapter 1

MAYA

In moments like this, I can't help but wonder—what did I ever do to the Moon Goddess to deserve a life like mine?

I stared at my hands, clenched tightly in my lap, tuning out the sound of my father's voice. His words blurred into background noise, just another storm I had no power to stop. From an early age, I'd learned that silence was safer. That arguing never changed anything. He never cared...not about my thoughts, and certainly not about my feelings.

He was a cold-hearted man, incapable of love. The only things I ever received from him were bruises and orders, never affection. Never warmth. Just pain, laced with power and control.

"Maya. Maya. Maya, are you fucking listening to me?" His voice cracked through my haze like a whip, seconds before his palm did the same to my cheek.

My head whipped to the side, my skin stinging, but I didn't cry out. I'd stopped doing that years ago.

He dove right back into his usual rant, throwing out the same bitter accusations I'd heard a hundred times before. In his eyes, I wasn't a daughter. I was a tool. My only worth came from securing a mate powerful enough to benefit the pack. I wasn't a person to him, just a bargaining chip born to be traded, used, and discarded for political gain.

But the problem with his brilliant plan? No one wanted to align with a pack known for its corruption, theft, and bloodshed.

And the saddest part of it all? Most of our pack were good people, innocent wolves born into a nightmare they never asked for.

They deserved better. We all did. But with my father in control, peace wasn't going to happen, and I was stuck, trapped in my own home with no way out.

If I'm honest, the only thing good that ever existed in this cursed pack was my mother. Our Luna.

She was warmth in a world of ice. The only reason I knew what love felt like. Her embrace, her soft voice, the way her eyes sparkled even in the darkest moments... those memories were the only balm to my battered soul. She showed me what a parent's love could be real and unconditional.

But that light was extinguished four years ago, and since then... it had been nothing but hell. Pure, unrelenting hell under my father's rule.

The crash made me flinch, the sound of something heavy shattering against the wall echoing through the room. I stood still, tense, watching as my father marched toward me. His face was flushed with rage, jaw clenched so tightly I thought his teeth might crack.

He stopped inches from me, towering over me, his chest heaving.

"You think you're better than us now? Just 'cause I let you leave for college?" he bellowed. "You're not. You're only good for one thing—and that's doing what the hell you're told."

The fury in his voice made my stomach twist. I tried to shrink into myself, but it was no use. His hand lashed out, seizing my face, squeezing my cheeks together so hard I could already feel the bruises forming beneath his grip.

"Look at me when I'm talking to you, you ungrateful little shit," he growled, spittle hitting my face. "Do I need to remind you who's in charge here?"

"No, Alpha George," I whispered, eyes fixed to the ground. I knew better than to meet his gaze. There was nothing my father hated more than being challenged, especially by a female, especially by me.

He released my face with a scoff, but the reprieve was short-lived. His fingers brushed my cheek, not gently but possessively. The touch made my stomach turn.

"You look just like your mother," he murmured, his voice low, almost admiring.

My heart stopped. That was the first time I'd ever heard him say that. I didn't believe it. I never felt like I resembled either of them. I used to joke, in the privacy of my own thoughts, that I must have been left on their doorstep by mistake. That I didn't belong. That maybe the Moon Goddess herself had misplaced me.

He smiled then, slow and cold, as he turned away, pacing across his office like a predator preparing to pounce. "Time you started acting like the daughter of an Alpha."

"What do you mean?" I asked, voice trembling

"What do I mean?" he repeated with mock sweetness. "Simple. Everything we've done—the schooling, the training, all of it—it's finally about to pay off."

He made his way back to his desk and sank into his leather chair, the air thick with finality.

"It's time you became useful."

My heart thudded violently in my chest.

"You can't mean..." I choked on the words, fear thickening my voice. He can't mean what I think he means.

"Oh, but I do." His grin deepened, eyes gleaming with twisted satisfaction. "You're getting mated, Maya. I've found the perfect future alpha. You'll mate him, and in return, we gain an alliance with a strong pack."

"Do I know this alpha I'm to be mated with?" I asked, doing my best to mask the storm of anger and disgust twisting in my gut.

"Of course," my father replied with a smug smile, as if this news should please me. "Do you think I'd hand you off to just anyone? You'll be mated to Mike once he takes over his nephew's pack and officially becomes the next Alpha of Crescent Moon. Through you, we'll finally solidify that alliance."

The room tilted. My vision narrowed.

Mike.

Mike was an older man, probably in his fifties, and the uncle of the current Alpha of Crescent Moon. I could only assume he planned to challenge his nephew for the title after all, you only become alpha by blood... or by force.

Now it made sense why he'd been spending so much time around our pack and getting close to my father.

I never liked him. Neither did my wolf.

There was something off about him. The way he looked at me... like I was something he wanted to own. The way his tongue would slide over his lips when he thought no one was watching.

He made my skin crawl.

"But Mike is twice my age," I whispered, horror creeping up my spine, but I tried to keep my cool.

"He could be my father. You can't tie me to a man like him. Do you even know what he does to women?"

Fear crept into my voice before I could stop it.

Everyone knew about Mike. The bruised she-wolves who disappeared. The rumors no one dared say out loud.

He wasn't just cruel; he was dangerous.

Whenever he visited, people kept their wives and daughters out of sight. And still, no one did a damn thing.

Alpha George stood slowly, his movements calm but deliberate.

He came around the desk and leaned against it, arms crossed, staring down at me like he was about to hand down a sentence I already knew I couldn't fight.

"I can," he said darkly, "and I will."

His voice was low, full of conviction, like the weight of his word was law carved in bloodstone.

"You know your purpose, Maya. You were born to serve this pack—my pack. You owe it to us... to me... to ensure our survival. And that means mating Mike and sealing the alliance that will finally elevate Black Stone from the gutter."

I felt my wolf stir inside me, furious and ready to shred through the skin of the man standing in front of me. Her growl echoed deep within my chest, vibrating against my bones. I was being sold—traded like cattle. Not for love. But for power. For greed.

But I couldn't speak that truth aloud.

Not with my father's eyes locked on me, sharp and un-relenting, like he could cut me down with just a look.

So I did what I'd always done—I lowered my eyes and swallowed the scream clawing at my throat. My fingers curled into the fabric of my dress, nails biting into my palms as I forced myself to nod.

"Yes, Father."

My voice sounded distant. Hollow. Like it belonged to someone else entirely.

Inside, my wolf whimpered. Not from pain but from restraint. From the unbearable weight of silence. She was furious, restless, pacing beneath my skin like a caged animal sensing a slaughter. But I kept her down. I had to.

Because the truth was, I was terrified.

Terrified of what he'd do if I disobeyed.

My father stood, satisfaction tightening the cruel line of his mouth. He moved around the desk and came to stand in front of me again. I didn't flinch when he touched my hair, though every cell in my body recoiled. His touch was not fatherly—it never had been. There was no warmth. Only possession.

"You've always been a burden that I never wanted," he said with mock affection. "Do this one thing for me... and you will finally have a purpose."

Meaning?

What meaning was there in becoming another man's property?

What meaning existed in lying beneath a monster like Mike, letting him mark me, touch me, claim me—just because it would benefit my father?

But I didn't speak.

I couldn't.

Not with his breath brushing my cheek. Not when I could still feel the echo of his slap burning across my skin. My mother was gone. No one else would protect me. And no one would dare to stand against him—not even me.

"Next month," he said simply. "You'll be presented to Mike during the full moon. Be ready."

I gave him another stiff nod, my lips pressed tightly together to keep the tremble from slipping out

A knock at the door interrupted our conversation.

"Alpha, Mike from Crescent Moon pack is here to see you," said one of the warriors.

17

I looked at my father with pure terror. Goddess, I do not want to see this man.

"Calm down, he is not here to see you. I will be busy tonight; have dinner in your room and do not leave the house. You may go," he added, dismissing me like I was nothing more than a servant.

I turned and walked out of his office, spine rigid, steps carefully measured—because showing weakness would only make things worse.

But the moment the heavy door clicked shut behind me, I exhaled a breath I hadn't realized I'd been holding.

I kept walking—down the hall, past the guards, past the wolves who avoided my gaze, as because the last male that looked at me paid with his life.

Only when I reached the privacy of my bedroom did I let the tears fall.

I curled into myself on the edge of the bed, burying my face in my hands as silent sobs wracked through me. My wolf was still there, still pacing. But now her growl was low and mournful, full of sorrow.

I sat there, unmoving, staring at the floor as the last of my tears dried on my cheeks. My body felt numb, but my heart... my heart was splintering into too many pieces to count.

One month.

In one month, I would be handed to a man who made my skin crawl. A man twice my age. A man whose eyes devoured me like a predator sizing up his next kill. My wolf shuddered just at the thought of his touch.

I gripped the edge of the bed, knuckles turning white.

Why? Why couldn't the Moon Goddess have taken him instead of her?

My throat tightened painfully, and the ache in my chest deepened until it felt like I couldn't breathe.

"I wish you were here, Mom," I whispered, my voice barely audible, even to myself. "I don't know what to do now that you're gone."

If she were here, none of this would be happening. She would've stood in front of me like a shield, defying Father with that quiet strength she carried. She would've taken my trembling hands in hers, brushed the hair from my face, and told me I wasn't alone.

But she was gone. Her scent, once so familiar and comforting, had long since faded from the walls of this house. The light she brought into this cruel, suffocating world had been extinguished, and the darkness crept in like rot.

All I could do was curl beneath the blankets that no longer brought comfort, clutching a pillow like it might anchor me to the pieces of myself I was trying so desperately to hold together.

I wished for my mother.

I prayed to the Moon Goddess for strength.

A knock at the door jolted me from an unintentional nap.

One of the maids stepped in, silent and wary, her eyes never quite meeting mine. She placed a tray of food on the table and murmured, "Alpha's orders—you're to eat in your room and not set foot outside the house."

Then she was gone, as quickly and quietly as she came.

Dinner felt more like a command than a comfort, but I ate it anyway, knowing refusing would only give my father another reason to rage. Afterward, I slipped into the shower, hoping the hot water would rinse away the dread clinging to my skin.

But peace wouldn't come.

My mind kept circling back to the same grim thought: in just one month, I would be mated... sharing a house, a bed, and a life with Mike.

My stomach twisted.

The image of his cold hands on my body made my skin crawl. I pressed my forehead against the cool tile wall, trying to breathe, trying to not cry. The steam thickened around me, masking the silent tears that still slipped down my cheeks.

That was when I heard it.

Boom.

A loud crack echoed in the distance. I flinched, but didn't think much of it. Warrior training sometimes involved explosive wards—they liked to show off.

Then came another.

And a third.

Something wasn't right.

I rinsed the soap from my hair with quick hands and stumbled out of the shower, wrapping a towel around my wet body as I rushed to the window.

The backyard was still, quiet—but my wolf's ears perked at the sound of growling and clashing from the front of the estate.

My pulse quickened.

I padded across the wooden floor, still dripping, and pulled back the heavy curtain from the front window.

What I saw stole the breath from my lungs.

A male wolf—not one of ours—was in the middle of a brutal fight with my father's guards.

And he was winning.

Easily.

I couldn't tear my eyes away. He was massive—larger than any male I'd ever seen, though that didn't say much. I'd only ever known the wolves of Black Stone. But this one... this one was different.

Sweat and blood clung to his tan skin, the sharp lines of his body moving with a kind of deadly grace. Every flex of his body was power incarnate, muscles moving with such lethal grace it was almost... hypnotic. My fingers twitched, aching to trace the curves of his arms, the hard ridges of his chest.

What the hell was wrong with me?

I shook my head, snapping myself out of the daze.

He wasn't just fighting. He was coming for the house.

Panic surged through me.

I dashed to the dresser, throwing on the first clothes I could find—black leggings and a loose tee. My wet hair clung to my back, and water dripped down my neck as I grabbed the heavy porcelain vase from my nightstand and backed into the corner of my room.

My breath came shallow.

Please don't come in here, I begged silently. Please don't find me.

But if he did... I wasn't going down without a fight.

Even if part of me, deep in the wild place where my wolf stirred... didn't fear him.

Chapter 2

ANDRÉS

The dense forest surrounding the Black Stone Pack's territory was eerily silent, save for the occasional rustle of leaves in the night breeze. I crouched low behind a bush, my sharp eyes scanning the area as I waited for the signal. My muscles were tense, coiled like a spring, ready to unleash my strength the moment it was needed.

My sister Sofía was out there, held captive by Alpha George—a man who had underestimated the wrath of the Luna Stone Pack. I clenched my fists, my sharp claws itching to tear through anyone standing in the way of her freedom.

"Stay sharp, Andrés," Leo's voice came through the comms. "Estrella and I are almost through their system. Once the loop starts, we'll have an hour to make this quick."

"Understood," I murmured, my voice steady, though my heart was a storm of emotions. I couldn't afford to let my mind wander. Sofía was counting on me.

While I waited, a bitter thought kept clawing its way to the surface.

If it weren't for Mason... none of this would've happened.

I know it's wrong to think it. But I can't help it.

If Sofía hadn't mated him, hadn't gotten swept up in that damn fated bond, she would be safe. Home. With us.

But no.

Instead, she was ripped from her life, from our territory, and now we were the ones risking everything to save her.

The so-called sacred bond had become her curse.

Fated mates. The words made my lip curl.

I never believed in all that fairytale bullshit. Everyone acts like it's some divine gift from the Moon Goddess. Destiny. Love. Completion.

All I see is weakness.

People lose their minds for a mate. They give up logic. Power. Freedom.

Sofía was one of the strongest people I knew—and yet even she hadn't been able to resist the pull. Now look where it got her.

And the worst part?

Part of me knows it's only a matter of time before it happens to me.

And when that day comes... I pray I have the strength to resist it.

Moments later, the signal came. A faint double chirp in my earpiece. The plan was in motion. I moved swiftly; my movements silent but deadly. My team followed, spreading out to set the explosives along the perimeter of the Black Stone Pack's main camp. I encountered warriors, but I dispatched them efficiently, my knife a blur as it found its mark in their throats.

One guard lunged at me, but I sidestepped, my hand gripping the man's wrist and twisting it until I heard the satisfying crack of bones. With a quick strike to the temple, the guard fell limp to the ground. I didn't even pause, moving onto the next target.

As we reached the last parameter, Mason's voice crackled in his ear. "Detonate on my mark."

My finger was hovering over the trigger. A few seconds passed before Mason's voice came through. "Now."

The ground shook as the explosives detonated, fire and smoke erupting in the distance. Chaos ensued as the Black Stone Pack scrambled to respond. My team and I surged forward, the element of surprise giving us the upper hand.

I was in my element, cutting through warriors like a blade through water. I parried an attack from my left, using the momentum to drive my knife into the attacker's chest. Another came at me with a club, but I ducked low, sweeping the man's legs out from under him before delivering a swift, deadly blow to his throat.

Then it hit me, a scent unlike anything I had ever encountered. Honeysuckle and citrus, fresh and sweet, wrapped around me like a comforting embrace. It was so intoxicating it made me falter mid-step.

My wolf roared to life, clawing at me from the inside.

Mate.

The single word echoed in my mind, igniting a hunger I couldn't explain.

I stumbled, momentarily forgetting about the mission, the chaos around me. I needed to find the source of that scent. My body moved on instinct, following the trail of honeysuckle and citrus as if it were the only thing that mattered.

My wolf growled impatiently. I didn't know why this was happening, but every fiber of my being demanded me to find whoever was at the end of that scent. It wasn't just a distraction. It was a calling.

The trail of honeysuckle and citrus led me through the camp, cutting through the chaos and carnage as if it were guiding me like an invisible thread. My senses sharpened, my vision narrowed, and everything else faded into the background. All that mattered was reaching the source of that scent.

Then I saw it—a hidden house tucked behind thick trees, guarded by Black Stone warriors. The windows glowed faintly from within. As I crouched in the shadows, my eyes locked on a figure in one of the windows.

She was breathtaking. A young woman with fiery red hair cascading in damp waves over her shoulders. She had just stepped out of the shower, her towel clinging to her body, barely covering her curves. My breath hitched as the towel slipped, giving me a glimpse of her side—a smooth stretch of skin, perfectly shaped breasts with soft rose-petal pink nipples that made my wolf howl in appreciation.

Mate. My wolf's roar was deafening now, taking over every rational thought I had. I lost control, something that hadn't happened since my teenage years. With a primal growl, I charged forward, my sole focus on reaching her.

The guards saw me coming and readied their weapons, but they were no match. I was a blur of motion, my claws cutting through the air as I dispatched the first warrior with a clean strike to the throat. The second lunged at me, but I ducked, slamming my elbow into the man's ribs before driving my claws deep into his side. Blood sprayed across the ground, but I didn't stop.

More warriors emerged from the shadows, their growls warning me to back off. I smirked, my wolf relishing the challenge.

One warrior charged me with a heavy axe, swinging it in a wide arc. I sidestepped, grabbing the man's wrist and twisting until he dropped the weapon. A quick jab to the solar plexus left the warrior gasping for air before I finished him with a sharp twist of his neck.

Two more came at me simultaneously. One swung a spear while the other lunged with claws extended. I rolled between them, coming up behind the first and slashing the back of his knees. As the man fell, I grabbed the spear and drove it into the second warrior's chest with a savage roar.

When the last body hit the ground, I stood amidst the carnage, my breathing heavy. Blood dripped from my claws, pooling around my boots. The scent was stronger now, pulling me toward the house.

I approached the door, my claws retracting as I forced myself to calm down. Taking a deep breath, I pushed the door open slowly, my heart pounding in anticipation. The room was dimly lit, empty except for the lingering scent that drove me wild.

And then—crash!

Pain exploded at the back of my skull, a sharp, ringing crack as something slammed into me. I staggered, vision blurring, but my wolf surged forward, snapping me upright before I could hit the ground.

Instinct took over. My hand shot out, catching my attacker's wrist in a crushing grip. I yanked them toward me—only to be met with a fist to the face and a blur of unruly red hair. My wolf snarled in irritation, the sound rumbling low in my chest.

She came at me again, wild and fast, but this time I caught her strike mid-swing, twisting her wrist just enough to hold her still. That's when I saw her.

Her.

The woman from the window.

Sage eyes blazed up at me, sharp with fury, and she twisted in my grasp with surprising strength. She swept my legs out from under me, but I rolled and came up just as quick. This time, I caught her and pinned her, her wrists trapped above her head, my body caging hers.

She snarled, arching and writhing against me, and the friction of her movement sent heat lancing through my veins. My wolf reveled in the fight, in the electric challenge sparking between us.

Her scent was everywhere now—clinging to her hair, her skin... intoxicating. My wolf clawed harder for control. I dipped my head before I could stop myself, inhaling deep at the curve of her neck. My lips brushed her skin, and the shiver that shot through her matched the one tearing through me.

She gasped, and her scent spiked with something new. Desire.

"Get off me, you pervert!" she snarled, bucking beneath me.

Reality snapped back hard, and I pushed away. She scrambled up, cheeks flushed, lips parted, breathing ragged.

I arched a brow, my voice dropping into something rough and low. "Little wolf... is it you who smells so delicious?"

Her blush deepened to a dangerous shade of crimson. She turned her head, avoiding my gaze, but her body betrayed her dilated pupils, quickened breaths, and that scent... Goddess, that scent wrapping around me like smoke.

A slow, wicked grin curled my lips. My mate was fiery, fierce, and unyielding, but her body responded to me as if it already knew.

I tried to hold my wolf back. Tried. But he moved fast, shoving past my restraint. One heartbeat, we were staring at each other. The next, my mouth crashed onto hers.

It wasn't gentle. It was raw and possessive. A claiming kiss that spoke of need more than want. My chest pressed to hers, my heart pounding in sync with hers.

She fought at first, her fists hammering against me. But I caught both wrists easily, pinning them above her head with one hand while the other slid down the curve of her body. Her heat, her softness, her scent. Everything burned through me.

Then… a sound.

A breathy, unguarded moan against my lips. My wolf roared in triumph. I took advantage, deepening the kiss, my tongue sweeping into her mouth to taste her. She was sweet, intoxicating honey and wild. I devoured her like she was the last taste I'd ever have.

For a heartbeat, she melted, her body arching up to meet mine. My wolf howled with victory.

Then the world shattered in white-hot agony.

Pain exploded through my groin, stealing my breath as she drove her knee into me with brutal precision.

"Argh! What the hell?" I groaned, falling to the side and clutching myself, my wolf whining pitifully in the back of my mind. She scrambled to her feet, her fiery hair a wild halo around her flushed face. Before she could run, I managed to grab her ankle and pull her back down to the floor.

I stood quickly, blocking the door before she could make it any farther. My eyes locked on her as she got to her feet, glaring at me with the ferocity of a she-wolf protecting her den.

"Why are you running from me?" I asked, my voice laced with confusion and frustration.

Her reaction was immediate. She looked at me like I'd grown a second head. "Why am I running from you?" she repeated, her voice dripping with incredulity. She started pacing, her movements animated, her cheeks pink, and her lips bruised from our kiss.

"You show up at my house," she began, pointing at me accusingly, "kill my guards, and then you—" she threw her arms in the air—"sexually assault me! And you're asking why I'm running? You fucking psycho!"

Her words hit me like a slap to the face, and for a moment, I just stared at her, dumbfounded. Did she not feel it? The bond, the pull, the overwhelming connection that left me breathless?

I took a step forward, raising my hands in a gesture of peace. "I'm sorry," I said, my voice soft but firm. "I didn't mean to frighten you ...or overstep. I came here looking for my sister. She was kidnapped by your alpha. I walked in because your scent—it called to me. My wolf took over. It's been a long time since that's happened."

Her pacing slowed, her expression shifting from fury to cautious curiosity. I kept going, hoping to reach her.

"I don't normally behave like that. My wolf was just..." The word mate almost slipped out, but I stopped myself just in time. "I'm truly sorry for everything. Can we start over? I'm Andres."

I extended my hand to her, a faint hope blooming in my chest. But she didn't take it. Instead, she crossed her arms, her piercing green eyes narrowing as she studied me.

"Why are you here? Andrés," she said finally, her tone guarded.

I held her gaze, my voice steady. "Like I told you, I'm here to rescue my sister, Sofía. She was kidnapped by Alpha George as part of a plot to hurt the Luna Stone Pack. My pack."

Her arms tightened across her chest, but there was a flicker of something in her eyes—sympathy? Doubt? It was hard to tell. "Alpha George doesn't kidnap people for no reason," she said cautiously. "If your sister is here, there has to be a reason."

"I told you the truth," I said firmly. "My sister was taken to get to Mason, her mate, and our pack's Alpha. I don't know what game your Alpha is playing, but I won't leave here without her."

Her lips pressed into a thin line, and for a moment, she just stared at me. Then she sighed, a resigned expression crossing her face. "If what you're saying is true, you're going to have a hell of a time getting her out of here. Alpha George doesn't keep his prisoners in the regular dungeons. They're held somewhere else ...hidden in this camp."

With a smirk on my face, I said, "Not as hard as you think. You'd be surprised at the things you can do with a little technology." I took a deliberate step closer to her, my eyes locked on hers. "The question I have for you is, why are you defending a psychopath like Alpha George? Are you one of his...pets?"

The word dripped with venom, and just the thought of her with another man sent a surge of anger and jealousy through me. My wolf snarled internally, a possessive growl that I barely managed to keep in check.

Before she could respond, I closed the distance between us. Now face-to-face, I found myself staring into the most defiant sage green eyes I had ever seen.

"Ewww, gross. No," she shot back, her voice sharp with disgust. "It doesn't matter if I believe you or not. I am a

Black Stone wolf; I must defend my Alpha and pack. Loyalty is more important than morality. And if you're from the Luna Stone Pack, then that means we are enemies."

I lifted my hand, brushing a stray curl behind her ear. Her scent hit me like a punch, but I kept my composure, leaning in slightly as I asked, "Are we? Because earlier, your body didn't say we were enemies. Earlier, your body wanted to be my friend. Do you want to be my friend, little wolf?"

Her eyes widened briefly before narrowing in annoyance. She slapped my hand away from her face, her cheeks pink with anger. "You caught me off my game. So don't confuse surprise for anything else. I do not want to be friends with strangers."

"Strangers, huh?" I murmured, tilting my head. "I don't want to be a stranger. I told you who I am, but I didn't get a name from you. Why?"

Frustrated, she crossed her arms, her nails tapping against her elbows. "My name doesn't matter," she spit out.

"Oh, it matters," I said, "It matters a lot. But if you don't want to tell me, it's ok. I will just call you little wolf."

Rolling her eyes, she huffed, "You said you had technology to help you find the hidden dungeon where Alpha George keeps his prisoners. What kind of technology is it?"

My wolf practically purred, sensing an opportunity. I leaned closer, lowering my voice just enough to be teasing but firm. "Let's make a deal. I'll tell you what you want to know if you answer my questions about you—and be honest. One for one."

She stared at me, her lips pressed into a thin line as she weighed her options. Finally, she sighed, tossing her hands in the air. "Okay. Deal."

I couldn't help the victorious smile that spread across my face. My wolf was grinning just as wide. This fiery little wolf was playing right into my hands.

But the second the thought crossed my mind, the satisfaction soured.

What the hell am I doing?

I should've been pulling away—not leaning in. I should've left the second I realized what she was. I should've turned my back and walked the hell out of this territory before I let her settle under my skin like this.

But I didn't.

I couldn't.

The pull was too strong, the scent of her too addictive. My wolf was obsessed, already curling around her like she belonged to us—like she was us. And the worst part?

Part of me didn't want to stop him.

Chapter 3
ANDRÉS

Against my better judgment, I leaned against the wall, arms crossed, forcing a relaxed posture I didn't feel. A wicked smile tugged at my lips before I could stop it.

"So, tell me, little wolf... how old are you?" I asked, keeping my tone light, teasing like this was just a harmless conversation and not the beginning of my downfall.

The words felt foreign on my tongue.

I wasn't the type to smile. I didn't flirt. I didn't chat. And yet, here I was grinning like a damn fool, tossing out questions like we had all the time in the world.

She rolled her eyes at the nickname. "I'm thirty days short of twenty-one," she said with sass, her voice laced with that fiery spark I was beginning to crave.

That makes sense, I thought to myself. She couldn't feel the full pull of the mate bond yet. Wolves typically didn't recognize their mates until they matured at twenty-one.

She was probably feeling something because she was so close to turning, but her wolf couldn't tell her I was her mate. That could be a problem.

It hit me that I wasn't allowed to tell her she was my mate until she turned twenty-one. Shifter law made that explicitly clear. But leaving her here, in this hellhole with a psychopath like Alpha George? Absolutely not. I couldn't. She was my mate, my other half, and I refused to leave without her.

A hand waved in front of my face, jolting me out of my thoughts. "Hello, Earth to weirdo," she said, her tone impatient. "Are you going to answer my question or just keep zoning out? What's this big, bad technology you have that'll help you find your sister?"

I blinked a few times, realizing I'd been lost in my own head. "Oh, right," I said, straightening up. "My sister has a tracking device embedded in her shoulder that tells us where she's located."

She stared at me like I'd grown another head. "Wait a minute," she said, holding up a hand. "You guys tag your she-wolves with GPS devices? What the actual fuck?"

"No," I said, smiling at her reaction. "We don't go around tagging our she-wolves with GPS devices. My sister is the daughter of the Luna Stone Pack's alpha, and she's next in line to take over as alpha herself. My father decided it was necessary for all of us to have tracking devices implanted, just in case lunatics like your alpha tried to kidnap us." I shrugged. "And look, years later, it's working to help rescue her."

She tilted her head, her expression softening slightly as she seemed to process my explanation. "Okay, that makes sense," she admitted reluctantly. "I guess."

I nodded, seizing the opportunity to steer the conversation. "My turn," I said, moving to sit on the edge of her bed. I kept my posture relaxed, trying to make myself seem less like a threat. "Why are you so devoted to the Black Stone Pack? Why are you willing to overlook kidnapping, abuse, and all the other terrible things your corrupt alpha does?"

My approach worked. She hesitated for a moment before walking over and sitting on the far side of the bed, keeping her distance but still closer than before. Baby steps, I told myself.

She took a deep breath, her shoulders tensing before she finally spoke. "You don't understand," she said quietly. "I grew up here, born and raised. Everything I know, everything I am, is because of the Black Stone Pack and..." She paused, her voice faltering. "And my— I mean, Alpha George."

The way she stumbled over his name didn't escape me. There was more to her relationship with this pack, and with George, than she was letting on. I leaned forward slightly, keeping my voice soft but firm. "And what, little wolf?"

Her eyes met mine, and for a moment, I thought she might open up. But then she shook her head, her walls snapping back into place. "It doesn't matter," she said, her voice flat. "What matters is that I'm loyal to my pack."

My wolf growled in frustration, but I kept calm. She was hiding something, and I'd find out what it was—one step at a time.

Before I could respond, she jumped back to her feet, pacing again like a restless storm. Her fiery hair whipped around her as she pointed at me, her tone sharp. "Wait a damn minute—you said your father thought it was important that you guys were chipped. Then you said your sister was the daughter of the Luna Stone Pack. That means..." Her eyes widened slightly. "You're the son of the alpha?"

A smirk pulled at one side of my mouth. "Is that your question, little wolf?"

She rolled her eyes dramatically, crossing her arms. "Ugh, yes, that's my question."

I couldn't stop the grin from spreading wider. "Very well. Yes, I am the second-born of Alpha Beto of the Luna Stone Pack. I'm next in line to become CFO of Luna Enterprises and an advisor to the next Alpha of Luna Stone, my big sister, Sofia. Who, by the way, is still being kept here against her will by your alpha."

She stiffened slightly at my words, but instead of responding, she abruptly said, "Then go rescue her! Why are you wasting time talking to me?"

I stood, closing the distance between us in a few long strides. Her eyes widened slightly as I loomed over her, my chest nearly level with her face. It struck me again how small she was, petite and fiery, a contradiction of soft curves and sharp edges. It was adorable.

"I want to rescue her," I said, my voice low and steady, "but there's something about you that doesn't allow me to leave you behind."

Her breath hitched as I reached out, running my fingers through a lock of her vibrant red hair. My wolf growled softly in approval, urging me closer. The urge to taste her lips again was overwhelming, a pull I couldn't resist.

She bit her lower lip, and it was my undoing. Without thinking, I cupped her face, my thumb brushing over her lip to pull it free. Her lips were soft, warm, and the small sound she made sent a bolt of heat straight through me.

"I wish I could bite that lip," I murmured, my voice barely above a whisper.

Her green eyes darkened, and for a split second, I thought she might lean into me. But she stiffened instead, her cheeks flushing as she pulled away slightly.

I let her go, my thumb lingering on her lips for just a moment longer. "But I won't. Not unless you want me to."

She stared at me, her eyes filled with uncertainty, and I held my breath, hoping—praying—she'd give me the green light. The need to devour her lips again, to taste her, was a fire roaring inside me. She hesitated but then took a small step closer, her lips just a whisper away from mine.

Before they could touch, the door burst open.

"Andres—" a Crescent Moon warrior said, his voice urgent, but he froze when he saw us. "Oh, sorry, I didn't know you were with someone." He cleared his throat awkwardly, shifting his weight. "They found your sister. The team is regrouping in the center of the camp. They're looking for you."

I growled low in my throat, my wolf irritated at the interruption. "I'll be there shortly. Leave us alone."

The warrior nodded quickly, stepping back and shutting the door behind him, leaving me alone once more with my beautiful mate. The tension between us thickened as I turned back to her, stepping closer until there was barely a breath of space between us. I reached out, gently tilting her chin up so her sage-green eyes met mine.

"Little wolf," I murmured, my voice soft but firm, "I was hoping to have more time to talk, but we have to go."

Her eyes blinked rapidly, her confusion clear as she took a cautious step back. "Go? Go where?"

I clenched my jaw, swallowing the growl rising in my throat. She wasn't coming willingly—not yet—and every part of me screamed to grab her and run. But I couldn't force her. Could I?

"We're leaving this place," I said, my tone leaving no room for argument. "You're coming with me to Luna Stone."

Her eyes widened, and she crossed her arms defensively. "Excuse me? I'm not going anywhere with you. This is my home."

"This is a hellhole," I countered, my voice rising slightly. "And after we are done with your alpha, I am not sure what would be left of this pack."

"I can't just leave. Everything I know is here," she snapped, her voice full of frustration.

See, this is why I hate fated mates. She didn't want to come with me, but the damn bond made it impossible for me to walk away.

Leaving her behind wasn't an option—not with Alpha George, not in this fucked-up pack.

Even if she hated me for it... I'd find a way to get her out.

"I'm not asking," I said firmly, stepping closer until she was pressed against the wall. "I won't leave you here. You're coming with me."

She glared up at me, her defiance shining bright. "And if I say no?"

I leaned in, close enough that our breaths mingled, but I kept my hands at my sides. "I hope you say yes," I said softly, my voice full of quiet confidence. "Because deep down, you know you don't belong here. You belong with me."

Her expression flickered, uncertainty warring with the fire in her eyes. I could tell she was struggling.

I softened my tone, brushing a strand of hair away from her face. "Come with me, little wolf. Let me show you a better life."

For a moment, she just stared at me, her chest rising and falling quickly. Then, to my surprise, she let out a soft sigh and said, "If I go with you...what happens to me?"

I smiled, my wolf practically purring at her words. "You'll be safe. Protected. And maybe...you'll finally see where you really belong."

We stared at each other for a second, the silence charged with unspoken tension. I could almost see her coming to terms with what I was saying, the way her gaze softened and her posture relaxed. For a moment, I thought she was ready to come with me willingly.

Then, without warning, she spun and delivered a high kick straight to my chest. The impact sent me stumbling back, catching me off guard. She bolted toward the door, but I recovered quickly, blocking her exit and pinning her path with my body.

"Little wolf, that hurt," I said, my voice low and edged with irritation. "Do not be difficult."

She pushed on my chest, rolled her eyes, her defiance burning bright. "It was meant to hurt, jackass."

I couldn't help the slight smirk tugging at my lips. "So much hostility," I teased, my voice dropping into a softer tone as I stepped closer. "Why are you fighting me so hard?"

"Why?" she snapped, glaring up at me. "Because you're a lunatic who barged into my home, killed my packmates, and then started bossing me around like I'm supposed to just...follow you!"

Her words hit hard, but I stayed calm, my hands held slightly up to show her I wasn't a threat. "I did what I had to do to find my sister. You know as well as I do that Alpha George isn't a man who plays fair. If I hadn't taken action, Sofia wouldn't stand a chance."

"Loyalty above morals," she shot back, though there was a flicker of something in her eyes—doubt, maybe? Fear?

"That is the most cult thing I have ever heard. Without morals, then who are we but mere beasts. We are more than that," I said sincerely, my voice softening further. "You're strong, she wolf, and your loyalty is amazing. You would make any alpha proud to have you part of their pack. But you don't have a good alpha, so why is his loyalty worth your morality, your integrity or your conscience?" I said while moving slowly and deliberately.

"You just don't understand. I cannot leave," she said, looking at her hands

"Don't make this harder than it has to be," I said gently. "I don't want to force you, little wolf. But I will keep you safe, whether you like it or not."

She looked up, her jaw tightening. "You're impossible, you know that?"

"I've been told," I replied with a grin. "Now, are you coming with me, or do I have to throw you over my shoulder and carry you out of here?"

Her glare could have set me on fire, but the blush creeping up her neck betrayed her. "You wouldn't dare."

I raised an eyebrow. "Try me."

For a moment, we stood there, locked in a silent standoff. Then she let out a frustrated growl and muttered, "Fine. I'll go. But this doesn't mean I trust you."

"That's fair," I said, stepping aside to let her move toward the door. "You don't have to trust me yet. But you will."

She shot me a glare over her shoulder, but she didn't argue

We walked out of the room into the dimly lit hallway, the air thick with tension. I kept my eyes on my little wolf, not trusting her for a second. Every step she took, every subtle shift of her body, I tracked. This was too easy. She wasn't coming willingly—not entirely. She was planning something; I could feel it in the way her muscles tensed and her head tilted slightly, as if listening for an opportunity to strike.

As we descended the stairs, she made her move. One moment she was walking calmly, and the next, she launched herself forward, leaping toward the bottom of the staircase headfirst. I froze for half a heartbeat as she shifted mid-air, her body morphing into an incredible auburn wolf.

She was stunning, her fur a rich, fiery color that shimmered in the faint light. She was slightly larger than the average she-wolf, her form sleek yet powerful, but still smaller than my wolf. For a moment, I couldn't help but admire her—then she bolted, racing out of the house and into the camp.

I chased after her, my instincts roaring to life. She was fast, her movements graceful and sure, and she gave me a hell of a chase. But it wasn't enough to make me shift. My wolf urged me to let him out, to run her down as his equal, but I held back, my human form more than capable of catching her.

I lunged forward, grabbing her by the tail and yanking her hard. She let out a startled yelp as I pinned her to the ground, my body covering hers. My hand clamped firmly around her throat, holding her still as she writhed beneath me.

"Shift," I commanded, my voice low and firm.

She growled, her teeth snapping inches from my face in defiance. I tightened my grip on her throat, my patience thinning. "Shift, little wolf," I repeated, my tone sharper this time.

Still, she resisted, her body twisting and fighting beneath me. Her fiery spirit was admirable, but I had reached my limit. My wolf was done playing games, and so was I. Summoning my Alpha, I let the full weight of my command ripple through the air as I shouted, "Shift!"

The ground seemed to tremble with the force of my command. My little wolf whimpered, the sound cutting through me, but I held firm. Her body quivered beneath me as she obeyed, her form shimmering and shrinking back into her human self.

The shift left her completely bare beneath me, and I couldn't help the way my eyes roamed over her. She was stunning. Her skin was flawless, soft curves and strength combined in perfect harmony. My wolf growled in approval, and it took every ounce of self-control I had not to let my hands roam over her soft skin. She was a work of art, a goddess made flesh—and she was mine.

Then her voice snapped me out of it. "You used your Alpha command on me," she whispered, her tone trembling with a mix of shock and anger.

I blinked, her words breaking through the haze of admiration. She stared up at me with wide, furious eyes, her cheeks flushed, whether from anger or embarrassment, I couldn't tell.

"You forced me to shift back," she continued, her voice sharper now, her hands fisting at her sides.

I stood, lifting her up by her arm so she was on her feet, and met her gaze with steady resolve. "Yes, I did," I said evenly, my voice cold and unwavering. "Do not get it confused. I may not be the next Alpha, but I am every bit as much an Alpha as my sister and brother. The Alpha lineage in my family is strong, and you'd better understand this: with me, there are no negotiations. I get what I want one way or another."

Her lips parted as if to argue, but no words came out. She simply stared at me, her fiery defiance momentarily dimmed by the weight of my authority.

I pulled off my shirt, the cool night air brushing against my skin, and draped it over her shoulders, covering her. The fabric hung loose on her smaller frame, but it shielded her from my eyes—and the eyes of anyone else who might dare to look.

Without waiting for her response, I bent down, grabbed her, and hoisted her over my shoulder like a sack of potatoes—just as I'd warned her I would if she kept fighting me.

She thrashed weakly, her fists pounding against my back. "Put me down, you caveman!" she yelled, her voice muffled by her hair falling in front of her face.

I smirked and slapped her backside, ignoring her protests as I strode back toward the center of the camp where my team was waiting. "You'll thank me later, little wolf," I said, my tone smug. "One way or another."

Chapter 4

MAYA

Darkness clung to me like a second skin. My head throbbed in dull, relentless pulses, and my throat burned as though I had swallowed glass. A groan tried to slip past my lips, but it couldn't. My mouth was tapped. I pried my eyes open, the world around me swimming in and out of focus. Panic slithered through my veins when I tried to move—only to find that I couldn't.

My hands. My legs.

Bound.

The cold bite of restraints wrapped around my wrists and ankles, holding me in place. My heart pounded against my ribs as I struggled against them, but the rough material only dug deeper, sending a sharp sting up my arms. My breath came in short gasps as I blinked into the dim interior surrounding me. The world outside the small, tinted windows was nothing but a blur of darkness and streaks of light.

I was in a vehicle.

That realization sent a fresh wave of terror through me, and my chest heaved as panic clawed its way up my throat, my eyes stinging with tears as I glanced around the moving vehicle, strapped down, helpless, not knowing where they were taking me or who had taken me.

My heart pounded so hard it hurt, and then, like a crack splitting through ice, the dam in my mind gave way, and the memories surged back in a flood: the argument with my father, the fight, the man, the hands grabbing me... sharp, disjointed flashes that slammed into me all at once, leaving me gasping for air.

I remembered everything now. It had probably been hours since he'd tied and thrown me into the back of this SUV like I was nothing more than a piece of cargo.

The SUV jolted over a pothole, and I shifted uncomfortably, trying to find some way to ease the ache in my back. My mind wandered, replaying the events that had turned my entire life upside down. How did I get here, kidnapped and tied up in the back of an SUV.

The worst part is how my body reacted to that man. Andrés provoked my body in a way I had never experienced. I was not used to it.

The way he looked at me, touched me... it sent shivers down my spine, both thrilling and terrifying. How could someone make me feel so exposed, so vulnerable, yet so alive?

The memories of those stolen kisses burned my cheeks and caused a warmth in between my legs that angered me. I had no business feeling this way, especially for a stranger.

I closed my eyes, trying to shut out the overwhelming emotions threatening to consume me, forcing myself to focus on what I'd left behind. I wouldn't pretend to miss everything, certainly not my father but there were parts of that life I'd always carry with me. The familiar faces of the packmates I'd grown up with... and sweet, gentle Mildred, the nanny who helped raise me. After my mother died, she was the only warmth left in that cold house, the only one who ever showed me real love.

My jaw tightened at the memory of what I'd overheard in the pack house. My father, reckless as always, had decided to kidnap the daughter of Luna Stone Pack's alpha, Sofía. Andrés' sister. I hadn't known her personally, but I'd known that my father had someone captive in our territory. This wasn't some minor pack squabble; my father had done an act of war.

And now, here I was tied up in a SUV. Taken by the very wolf sent to rescue his sister, caught in the crossfire of my father's dangerous games. I took a deep breath, forcing myself to focus.

As much as my father deserved whatever punishment was coming his way, it didn't mean Andrés had the right to kidnap me, throw me over his shoulder, and act as if he had every right to decide where I go or what I do.

The memory of meeting Andrés for the first time flashed in my mind, unbidden and infuriatingly vivid. His dark, commanding eyes had locked onto mine, and for a moment, I'd forgotten to breathe. Then there was his scent: rich, intoxicating, filled with something primal that made every nerve in my body ignite. Even now, I could feel the pull, the way my skin had prickled under his gaze, as if my body was attuned to him in a way I couldn't understand.

No other wolf had ever made me feel that way; no other man had ever come close.

I shook my head, trying to banish the thought. I couldn't let myself feel that. I won't. I had to think of my so-called purity, the one thing my father had demanded of me above all else. His twisted belief that my value lay in remaining untouched was something I'd carried like a curse. To him, I wasn't a person; I was a bargaining chip, a pawn in his schemes. My worth was measured by the alliances he thought he could buy with my "purity."

Resentment churned low in my stomach, bitter and relentless. I hate how he reduced me to something so meaningless. And worse, I hate how every time I tried to break free, to live for myself, he'd made others pay the price.

I remember the night I dared to go on a simple date. Just a quiet evening with a boy from the pack who had shown me kindness. My father's retaliation was swift and brutal. He'd beaten the boy to a pulp, leaving him broken and bleeding in the packhouse courtyard. Then he'd gone further, raping the boy's mother as a lesson, making sure I knew that every act of defiance would come with a cost.

"This is your fault," he'd said coldly, his voice void of emotion. "Every time you disobey me, someone else pays the price. You will stay pure, or others will suffer. Your worth lies in what you can bring to this pack."

Those words had chained me, wrapping around my mind and body like iron shackles. They isolated me, turned me into a ghost of myself, too afraid to even look twice at anyone, too afraid to let anyone close. I'd locked my heart and my body away, building walls high enough that no one dared to cross them.

Until Andrés.

From the moment I laid eyes on him, he had awakened something inside me that I had not known existed. It was like I no longer had control over my own body.

I had wanted him gone. I had wanted him far away so I could breathe again, so I could feel in control. And yet... my body had wanted him close. My body had craved the heat of him next to me, the strength in his touch, the way his voice had made my skin tingle and my heart race. My body had reacted to him in a way I couldn't rationalize. It was as if every part of me had been pulled toward him, drawn by something stronger than logic or willpower. How had that been possible? This man had been a stranger, one who had taken me away from the only home I had ever known.

And that had terrified me more than anything my father had ever done.

The car came to an abrupt stop, jolting me out of my thoughts and forcing me to focus on the present. I looked around, taking in our surroundings. It seemed like we were in some sort of park. RVs were parked in neat rows, and cabins dotted the distance, their warm lights glowing faintly in the twilight.

Andrés glanced at me through the rearview mirror, his dark eyes meeting mine with that infuriating mix of authority and calm. I stared back, refusing to let him intimidate me. What the hell is he doing now?

He turned in his seat to face me, his expression unreadable. "I'll be back. I'm getting us a cabin. Do not leave or call attention to yourself. It won't end well."

Before I could respond, not that I could say much with the tape still covering my mouth, he opened the door and climbed out, shutting it behind him with an air of finality. He walked toward a building in front of us, which I could only assume was the front desk.

I let out a muffled huff of frustration and lay back down. This was ridiculous. Kidnapping me was one thing, but now we were stopping at some secluded cabin park for the night? What was his plan? Keep me tied up in some dingy cabin until he figured out what to do with me? I kicked the seat in front of me in a small act of defiance, but it didn't make me feel any better.

Some time passed before I saw him again, walking out of the building with boxes and bags in his hands. He climbed back into the SUV without a word and started driving, the tension in the vehicle heavy as ever. We traveled deeper into the woods, the narrow dirt road winding away from the rest of the cabins. Trees loomed on either side, their branches casting eerie shadows in the fading light.

Finally, after what felt like forever, the car slowed to a stop in front of a lonely, isolated cabin. It was tucked away, barely noticeable among the thick forest surrounding it. My stomach twisted as I realized how remote we were. No

RVs, no other cabins nearby—just this one, hidden and secluded.

And all I could think was, I'm going to spend the night alone in a remote cabin with a man.

Goddess help me.

Andrés got out of the SUV without a word, his movements quick and deliberate. Before I could even process what he was doing, he was at my door, opening it with a determined expression. Without asking or waiting for my cooperation, he grabbed me, clearly intent on hauling me out of the car like a sack of flour.

I tried to protest, squirming against his grip, but my hands were still tied up. He eventually removed the tape from my mouth. "Stop manhandling me and tell me where you're taking me!"

He paused, his jaw tightened and he took a deep breath, as if willing himself to stay patient. "I have been driving for hours, and I need to rest, so stop fighting me. You stubborn little wolf."

I glared at him, defiance bubbling up despite the nervous flutter in my stomach. "I can get myself out. I don't need you manhandling me and getting all touchy-touchy," I shot back, wriggling to free myself as I tried—unsuccessfully—to climb out of the SUV on my own.

He smirked, the infuriating expression making my blood boil. "Oh really?" he drawled, catching one of my flailing limbs with ease. In one swift motion, he pulled me to the edge of the seat, leaving me perched precariously with my knees opened wide while my ankles were still tied up. He placed himself in between my knees, causing our bodies to press far too close.

The proximity made my breath hitch. My knees brushed his hips, and I couldn't ignore the heat radiating off him. He leaned in, his smirk growing wider as he said, "Why would I deny your body my 'touchy-touchy' when your body responds so nicely to it?'"

The words rolled off his tongue slowly, deliberately, as if savoring every syllable. His fingers, warm and firm, trailed a line from my knee to my upper thigh, making my skin tingle. My breath hitched again, louder this time, and I cursed myself for the reaction. Rolling my eyes as hard as I could, I did my best to pretend that his closeness did not affect me.

He didn't stop there. His hands gripped my waist, his touch firm but not rough, and he pulled me closer against him. My body betrayed me completely, a soft, involuntary sound escaping my lips before I could swallow it down.

His grin widened, his eyes darkening as he leaned closer, his voice dropping to a low whisper. "Little wolf," he murmured, "why do you deny your body what we both know you're feeling?"

My heart thundered in my chest as he pressed even closer, his body wedging between my thighs, leaving no space between us. His lips brushed against my ear, his voice sending a shiver down my spine. "We both know what you want," he said softly before nipping my earlobe.

Before I could respond—whether with a scathing retort or an admission I didn't want to give—he placed my tied hands around the back of his neck, with his claws ripped the tapped bonding my ankles together and lifted me effortlessly, "Little wolf, wrap those sexy legs of yours around my waist. I plan on bringing everything in with one trip. His arm grabbed my ass securing me in place, and with his foot, he slammed the SUV door shut.

Having him so close to me caused a knot in the bottom of my stomach and a heat in my core. The heat of his body was causing my core to become hot and slick with desire. Desire that soon enough, he would smell. His hands touching my ass felt so good I almost moaned from the pleasure. His hands only held me for a short time before he picked up the box and bags he got from the front desk.

I groaned in frustration, my cheeks burning. Goddess help me; what was wrong with me? Why was my body responding like this?

Andrés carried me into the cabin effortlessly, his grip firm but not uncomfortable. I tried to ignore the heat radiating from his body as he had me in such a vulnerable position. Once inside, he set me down, and I stumbled slightly, glaring up at him. He didn't even seem fazed, his sharp eyes scanning the room as if everything was perfectly normal.

The cabin, small from the outside, was surprisingly roomy inside. There was a small kitchen with all the essentials, a spacious living room with a worn but comfortable-looking couch, and a staircase leading up to a loft I hadn't yet seen. Near the kitchen was a half-bathroom, but there wasn't a bathtub or shower, which meant the upstairs loft likely held the full bathroom.

I paused, my eyes falling on the single bed upstairs visible from the railing. My stomach dropped. Only one bed? My thoughts immediately went to the worst-case scenario. I turned to Andrés, who was walking behind me, his confident stride making it impossible not to notice the strength in every movement.

"I only see one bed," I said, pointing upstairs, trying to keep my voice steady. "Where am I going to sleep? The sofa?"

Andrés chuckled softly, the sound low and maddening. He stepped closer to me, his finger lifting my chin as he leaned in slightly. His touch sent a jolt of heat down my spine. "You will be sleeping up there in the loft," he said, his voice dripping with finality, "with me, little wolf."

My eyes widened as the implication sank in. "What? No, absolutely not—" I tried to protest, but the words got stuck in my throat. My mind betrayed me, flashing images of how close we'd be, how the bed would barely fit the two of us. Stop it, I scolded myself. He's kidnapped us. He's our enemy. Goddess, get your hormones in check!

I cleared my throat, forcing myself to focus. "I will not sleep in the same bed as you," I said firmly. "I can easily sleep on the sofa."

Andrés smirked, taking a slow, deliberate step forward. His presence was overwhelming, forcing me to instinctively back up. "I'm not leaving you out of my sight, little wolf."

"Then I'll sleep on the floor!" I snapped, desperate for a way to put distance between us.

He took another step closer, his voice a low rumble. "Nope. You need to be close to me. Next to me."

Frustration bubbled up inside me, and I knew it showed on my face. My fists clenched at my sides as I prepared to argue, but before I could say anything, Andrés moved. His hand slipped to the back of my neck, his fingers threading through my hair, gripping tightly enough to tilt my head back.

My breath hitched as our faces were suddenly mere inches apart. I could feel the heat of his breath against my lips, his sharp eyes locking onto mine with an intensity that made my knees weak.

"Little wolf," he said softly, his voice low and commanding, "stop arguing with me. I told you—I get what I want."

The dominance in his tone made my heart race, my body betraying me once again. I swallowed hard, trying to ignore the way my lips tingle, the way my skin burned under his touch. I hated how he made me feel so out of control, so completely at his mercy. But what I hated even more was how much a part of me liked it.

Chapter 5

MAYA

After what felt like an eternity of bickering about where I would sleep, I finally gave up the fight. Exhaustion dragged at my limbs, and more than anything, I needed a break from Andrés.

"Fine," I muttered. "I need to use the bathroom."

Andrés leaned against the counter, arms crossed over his broad chest, watching me like a hawk. "Don't get any ideas, little wolf. I'm tired and have no desire to chase you through the woods tonight. Do as you're told."

I bit back a retort, settling for a sharp nod before heading up the stairs. His piercing gaze burned into my back the entire way, but I refused to look at him. He might be my captor, but I wouldn't give him the satisfaction of seeing me rattled.

The cabin was deceptively welcoming: rustic, warm, stocked with everything I might need, but it was a prison nonetheless. And Andrés was its warden. He might not be locking me in a cell, but the invisible chains of his dominance were just as binding.

I walked up to the loft, finding the bed, a small closet, and a bathroom. Rummaging around, I found clothes my size. The clothes were simple but comfortable, clearly chosen to fit me. Of course, I thought bitterly. He arranged for the cabin manager to have food and clothes ready when we arrived. I hated how meticulous he was, how he left no room for error.

Except one.

A small window in the bathroom. Large enough for someone with a petite frame, like me, to squeeze through.

My pulse quickened as a plan formed in my mind. I had to play it smart, bide my time. I would eat, act compliant, lull him into thinking I was broken. Then, when I went to shower, I'd be gone before he even realized it.

Squaring my shoulders, I descended the stairs, the aroma of food curling through the air and making my stomach grumble in betrayal. Andrés stood at the stove, sleeves rolled up, muscles flexing as he worked with effortless precision.

I shouldn't have watched him. Shouldn't have noticed the way the firelight highlighted the sharp lines of his face or how the steady confidence in his movements made cooking look like something... intimate.

Annoyed with myself, I rolled my shoulders back and raised an eyebrow. "Impressive. You can cook."

He glanced over his shoulder, his lips curving in the faintest smirk. "At the pack, we learn all the skills we need to survive. If I didn't know how to cook, how could I feed myself? Or my family?"

Something in his tone softened at the mention of family, but I ignored it, focusing instead on the pasta he drained with practiced ease. He had that irritating way of making everything look effortless.

"So, what are you making?" I asked, trying to fill the silence that hung awkwardly between us.

"Chicken Alfredo," he replied, raised a brow as he turned back to me, and I quickly rolled my eyes, annoyed that he kept staring at me.

As he plated the food, he poured himself a glass of white wine, then turned toward me, bottle in hand. "Do you want some?"

"I can get it myself," I snapped, reaching for the bottle at the same time he did.

Our hands brushed, and suddenly, warmth surged through me, an electric jolt that zipped up my arm, curling low in my stomach. I gasped, recoiling as if burned, but not before I caught the flicker of something in Andrés's eyes. A recognition. A silent confirmation that he felt it too.

He didn't say anything. Just poured the wine and handed me the glass, his expression unreadable.

We sat in silence as we ate. I wanted to hate the meal, but I couldn't. It was too good. Too warm. Too... comforting. The flavors burst in my mouth, and before I could stop it, a small, pleased sound escaped my lips.

I froze.

Andrés chuckled, low and quiet, as if even he were surprised by the sound.

"Thanks," he said simply, taking another bite.

For a brief moment, something between us shifted. The sharp edges of animosity dulled, just enough to let something else seep through.

But then he kept staring.

His honey-brown eyes locked onto me with unsettling intensity, and after a few minutes, I dropped my fork with an irritated sigh. "What?"

Andrés's smirk deepened, infuriatingly confident. "I like to look at what's mine."

Heat flared in my chest, a mix of anger and something I refused to name. "I am not yours."

The smirk faded. His jaw tightened, and for the first time, he looked almost... scary. "You can deny it all you want, little wolf, but you are. And I'll keep you safe. Whether you like it or not."

"I didn't ask to be saved," I said finally, my voice softer but still defiant.

His expression darkened, his brows furrowing as his jaw tightened. "Your home wasn't safe," he said quietly, "I took you because your home is with me. I can keep you safe."

His words struck a nerve, and I looked down at my plate, suddenly unsure of what to say. I hated how his words made me feel. Desired and wanted.

I pushed away from the table. "I'm done. I'm taking a shower and going to bed."

Andrés said nothing as I climbed the stairs.

The moment I reached the bathroom, I turned on the shower, letting the water mask any sounds I made. I stripped quickly, leaving the clothes behind to avoid suspicion, then moved toward the window.

It was smaller than I would've liked, but I could make it work. My heart pounded as I maneuvered through, carefully shifting my weight so I wouldn't fall. My upper body slipped through easily, but my hips, damn them, got stuck.

I gritted my teeth and wiggled, shoving at the frame, my breath coming fast.

Then... a sound. A rustle of movement. A shift in the air.

My stomach dropped.

No. It's just your imagination.

With one final shove, I broke free, tumbling out of the window. The shift came instinctively, my wolf landing gracefully on all fours.

Yes. Piece of cake.

I crouched low in the brush, ears twitching as I scanned my surroundings. But my wolf hesitated, her gaze flicking back toward the cabin.

No, I told her. We're leaving.

But her reluctance made something cold settle in my chest.

My wolf eyes fixated on the silhouette of Andrés in the kitchen.

What the hell? No, you big heifer, we're leaving! I don't care how hot, sexy, or —I shook my head furiously. No! We are not thinking about how delicious he looks right now. We are escaping!

It took far too much effort to convince her, but eventually, she started running, her paws kicking up dirt as we sprinted away from the cabin. Relief washed over me as the forest swallowed us up. Thank the goddess, I thought.

I ran.

The night air rushed past me, cool and crisp, but I barely noticed it. My wolf's paws pounded against the forest floor, my heartbeat thrumming in my ears as I pushed myself faster, farther.

I was escaping. I was free.

Then.

A massive weight crashed into my side, sending me flying. I hit the dirt with a sharp yelp, rolling until I dug my claws into the earth to stop myself.

A low, menacing growl vibrated through the air.

I whipped around, chest heaving.

A pair of dark brown eyes stared me down, glowing with fury beneath the moonlight.

Andrés.

His towering black wolf stepped from the shadows, fur bristling, dominance pouring off him in suffocating waves. His gaze locked onto mine, pinning me in place without a single word.

My wolf tensed beneath his scrutiny, instincts warring between fight and flight.

Shift.

The order wasn't spoken, but I felt it. The weight of his command pressed into me, demanding obedience.

I bared my teeth in response. No.

His wolf exhaled sharply, irritation flickering in those cold, calculating eyes.

Shift.

I snarled, lowering my stance in clear defiance. My fur bristled, my claws digging into the dirt. He wanted me to obey?

Normally, I would. But not here, not now. I had to go home. My pack was attacked and I did not know what happened to my people. To my nanny.

Then, in a single fluid motion, he shifted.

His wolf's body reshaped and twisted, fur melting into smooth, tanned skin. In seconds, the massive predator was gone, replaced by a man, broad, powerful, entirely too confident.

And completely, shamelessly naked.

Moonlight bathed his skin, casting sharp shadows over the ridges of his muscles. His dark hair was tousled, his strong jaw set with frustration, and those eyes burned into mine.

"Little wolf," he said, voice low, warning. "Shift back. Now."

I curled my lip in response, lifting my head defiantly.

No.

Then, in a blur of motion, he lunged.

Not to attack.

To grab me.

I dodged at the last second, twisting out of his reach, but he was too damn fast. His arm snapped out, catching my scruff, fingers twisting into my fur. My body jerked as he yanked me forward, pulling me flush against his warm, bare chest.

A violent shiver ran down my spine.

I thrashed, growling, but he didn't let go. His grip was firm, strong, unyielding.

His voice dropped lower, smoother, dangerous. A pulse of raw, alpha power surged from him.

It was like fire, sinking into my bones, forcing my wolf to still. My body locked in place as a single word slammed into me—irresistible, absolute.

"Shift."

I fought it. Goddess, I fought it.

But he was too strong.

The command gripped my soul, clawing through every fiber of my being, dragging me under, my body convulsed, bones twisting, reshaping, my fur shrinking back into smooth, exposed skin. I collapsed onto the cold dirt, human again, my body trembling from the forced shift.

The moment I was fully changed, his grip changed too.

His fingers locked tight in my tangled hair, his breath hot against the back of my neck.

My body shuddered, a mix of rage and humiliation.

Andrés's grip didn't loosen.

Instead, he leaned in, his voice a low, smug murmur against my ear.

"You are mine. And you are not leaving."

A violent tremor ran through me. Not from cold. Not even from fear.

From him.

My chest heaved with angry breaths, he finally let me go, stepping back as I scrambled to my feet.

I turned away from him, trying to cover my naked body.

Andrés, still naked himself, just watched me, eyes dragging over me, like he had all the time in the world.

I glared. "Enjoying the view?"

His smirk was slow, unapologetic. "I'd be lying if I said no."

Heat licked at my skin. I hated him. I loathed him.

And worse?

I hated how my body reacted to him.

Andrés took a step forward, his presence a gravity I couldn't escape.

"Now that you're done with your little rebellion," he murmured, "are you ready to come back willingly, or do I have to throw you over my shoulder?"

My fists clenched. My body ached from the forced shift, my wolf still reeling from the Alpha command. But I wasn't going to make this easy for him.

I tilted my chin up, defiant. "I'd rather die."

Andrés smirked, the look in his eyes infuriatingly patient.

"That's the thing about you, little wolf," he said, voice deep, smooth, dangerous.

"You say things like that," his fingers brushed my jaw, barely there, but enough to send an unwelcome thrill through me, "but your body tells me a very different story."

I jerked away from him, my breath uneven. "Go to hell."

Before I could react, before I could even think of running again, he grabbed me by the waist and threw me over his shoulder effortlessly, like I weighed nothing.

I yelped, furious, pounding my fists against his back. "Put me down, you overgrown brute!"

A sharp smack landed on my bare ass.

I froze, shock slamming through me.

He just

Oh, that bastard.

Andrés chuckled, utterly unbothered by my writhing. "Keep squirming, little wolf. It's cute."

"I hate you!" I shouted, struggling harder.

He sighed, like I was the most exhausting thing in the world. "Sure you do."

Another smack landed on my other bare ass. Then he carried me back toward the cabin, his grip firm spanking my ass, unyielding.

And despite everything, despite my anger, my resistance, my utter hatred for this man, my body still betrayed me. Every time he spanked me, I felt my core clinch and become wetter.

After ten spanks, Andrés carried me through the woods in silence, his body radiating heat against mine.

I hated him. I loathed him.

But more than anything, I hated how my body felt against his, how I was hyper-aware of every shift of his muscles, every breath he took, every painful pleasure that I felt when he smacked my ass.

He didn't set me down until we reached the bathroom in the cabin.

And when he did, it wasn't gentle.

My bare feet hit the cold tile floor, my knees nearly buckling from the exhaustion of the forced shift. I did my best to not show my weakness. I forced my spine straight, my breath still coming hard and fast.

His eyes darkened as they roamed over me, lingering shamelessly on every inch of my body. From my dirt-streaked toes to my exposed, small chest, his gaze devoured me in a way that made my skin tingle.

Normally shifters were not modest, but Andrés didn't even try to hide his desires.

And as much as I hated to admit it, part of me liked it.

His touch. His scent. The way his dominance wrapped around me like an inescapable force.

What had gotten into me? How had I let him dominate me like that? And why did every part of me crave more?

Goddess, what was happening to me? I must fight this.

The sound of the water rushing brought me back from my thoughts. Keeping my arms crossed instinctively, I shielded myself as I entered the shower. Surely, he'd leave and give me some privacy to clean up.

But he didn't.

Instead, Andrés stepped into the shower with me, the heat of his naked body overwhelming the already humid space.

"What are you doing?" I asked, my voice higher-pitched than I intended. I hated how nervous I sounded.

"What does it look like I'm doing?" he replied, his tone edged with irritation. "I'm taking a shower."

"I don't think this is a good idea," I protested weakly, my voice rising slightly as his sheer size seemed to shrink the space around me.

His broad shoulders brushed against the narrow walls, and when he reached for the soap, his elbow grazed my arm, sending a jolt of awareness through me. I flinched at the contact, every nerve in my body hyper aware of his proximity.

And then there was that.

Something brushed against me occasionally, lightly, and I didn't need to look down to know what it was. Heat surged to my cheeks as I pressed myself harder against the wall, desperate to avoid any further contact.

"Relax, little wolf," he murmured, his voice low, as he noticed my discomfort. "This is just a shower. Unless, of course, you want it to be something more."

I glared at him, trying to summon the strength to hold my ground, but my wolf wasn't helping. She was practically purring, thrilled by the closeness and feeding me all sorts of inappropriate thoughts.

"This is ridiculous," I snapped, though my voice wavered. "I can't even move in here without—"

"Without what?" he interrupted, leaning closer. His wet hair dripped onto my shoulder, his lips hovering near my ear. "Without brushing against me? Without feeling me?"

I stared at him, torn between the rational part of me screaming to fight this madness and the primal need that urged me to let go, to surrender my body to him. My wolf growled in approval, urging me to let him have me.

But I couldn't. This man had kidnapped me, and his pack was the enemy of my father. I had no reason to trust him.

Summoning what little strength I had left, I snatched the soap from his hand. "I can bathe myself," I said firmly, though my voice was shaky.

Before I could move, Andrés got closer to me, "Just know that if you need assistance, I am here."

After taking the quickest shower I could imagine I stepped out of the shower but I was stopped by Andrés's big hands on my shoulder. He did not say anything, but he wrapped a soft towel around my body, drying me with meticulous care. When I was dry, he slipped one of his oversized shirts over my head, the fabric falling loosely, brushing against my thighs.

Before I could protest or regain any sense of control, he scooped me up in his arms, carrying me effortlessly to the bed.

I wanted to argue when I realized his intention: he planned to sleep beside me. My lips parted to protest, but the fight drained out of me before the words could form. I had no energy left to fight him. The warmth of his body, and the steady beat of his heart, lulled me into a state of drowsy surrender.

I let my head sink into the pillow, my limbs feeling too heavy to move. Andrés slid into the bed beside me, his strong arm draping possessively over my waist. His presence was suffocating and comforting all at once, a paradox I couldn't begin to unravel.

Sleep overtook me quickly, pulling me into its depths. For a while, I felt safe, cocooned in the quiet of the night and the warmth of his body.

But then, a noise woke me, a soft click that sent a shiver racing down my spine. My eyes fluttered open, and in the dim light of the room, I noticed something cold and unfamiliar around my wrist.

Oh great. Handcuff.

Chapter 6

MAYA

The next morning, I didn't move immediately, unsure of my surroundings until I realized I was no longer bound. Slowly, I sat up and glanced at my wrists. The faint marks from the handcuffs had already faded, leaving no trace of the restraints from the night before. My mind replayed everything: the woods, the shower, and him.

After putting on some clothes, I descended the stairs, following the faint smell of breakfast wafting through the cabin. I found him in the kitchen, his broad shoulders turned to me as he worked over the stove. The sight was almost domestic, a sharp contrast to the wild, commanding man from last night.

"Hey, little wolf," he said, glancing over his shoulder. "How did you sleep?"

I cleared my throat, trying to ignore the heat creeping up my neck. "Good," I said quickly, but I knew the blush blooming across my cheeks betrayed me. My pale skin made it impossible to hide how his presence affected me, and the memory of everything he'd done last night only made it worse.

His smirk widened slightly, but thankfully, he didn't comment. Instead, he turned back to his cooking. "So, are you planning to ever tell me your name?" he asked as he dished up a hearty breakfast.

I was scared to give him my name. As the daughter of alpha George, who knew what he would do to me. My father hurt his sister, and who knows what other things he has done to their pack. "No, you seem to like calling me little wolf."

He growled, "I want to call you mine. Eventually, you're going to have to give me your name."

"I do not know what delusion you have calling me yours, but I will escape and return home," I spat out, not wanting him to get any ideas.

Andrés did not say anything, but based on the clinching of his jaw and the white of his knuckles as he held his fork, I know he did not like that response.

We ate in relative silence, though my mind was far from quiet. Every glance at him brought back the sensation of his hands on me, the sound of his voice when he growled my name. The memories were vivid, clinging to me no matter how hard I tried to shake them.

After breakfast, Andres packed up the cabin, efficiently gathering our belongings for the trip ahead. The SUV was parked outside, and I hesitated as we approached it, the memory of being tied up in the back seat yesterday fresh in my mind.

"Please, can I sit in the passenger seat this time?" I asked, my voice soft, almost pleading.

He stopped, turning to me with a piercing gaze. "I don't want to tie you up, little wolf. But I don't trust you," he said, his tone surprisingly sincere. "I can't risk you yelling for help to the first car we pass."

"I won't do that," I said quickly, my tone earnest. "I promise to behave. I just don't want to be uncomfortable again."

He sighed deeply, running a hand through his dark hair as he considered me. "You promise," he muttered before approaching me to kiss me—but instead, I felt a prick in my neck, my eyes snapped to Andrés'.

"I wish I could trust you," he, says, with an empty needle in his hand.

"What did you do? " I asked, totally freaking out.

"I gave you a strong sedative. It will allow me to drive without having to worry about you trying to escape." he said seriously

"You are an asshole....I hate..." I said before everything went black

After my vision cleared, I realized I was back in the damn SUV's back seat, the stiff leather sticking to my bare arms. The sunlight filtered through the tinted windows, glaring enough to make me squint. Still daytime. Great. At least I hadn't been out for too long—though my body ached like I'd been run over.

"You're awake. Great. I was starting to think I sedated you too much," Andrés said casually, his voice smooth. His piercing gaze flicked back to me through the rearview mirror. "You've been out for a while."

Confusion swirled in my groggy mind, sharpening into panic. "What do you mean I've been out for a while?" My voice cracked, the words sounding too weak.

He gave a light, humorless laugh. "Like I told you before, I couldn't risk you yelling for help at the first car you saw. And knowing you, that's exactly what you would've done. I don't need attention brought to us."

My hands tugged at the coarse rope digging into my wrists. They were tied again, along with my feet, and panic clawed at my chest as I scanned the endless stretch of desert surrounding us. Nothing but miles of sand, rocks, and oppressive heat.

"Where the hell are we?" I demanded, my throat dry.

"Arizona," he answered nonchalantly, his tone far too calm for someone who'd just admitted to drugging me.

My eyes widened in shock. "Arizona? What the fuck are we doing in Arizona? I thought you said we were going to your pack in California!" I hissed, my voice rising as anger began to overshadow my fear.

Andrés' grip tightened on the steering wheel, his jaw clenching briefly. "Plans changed after your little escape attempt the other night," he replied, his tone hardening. "You forced my hand."

"I don't get it," I shot back, my voice trembling with frustration.

He sighed as if he were dealing with a child. "You and I need time to get to know each other before we arrive at the pack. So, we're making a stop at a private property I own here. Isolated. Secluded. Just us."

My stomach twisted into knots, a bitter mix of fear and helplessness rising in my chest. "Why are you doing this?" I cried out, my voice cracking. "I don't want to be here! I just want to go home!"

"Your old pack is not safe. I've told you that already," he replied, his tone softening slightly but still unyielding. "Your home is with me now. That's how it is."

I glanced out the window again, my mind racing as I took in the unforgiving expanse of the desert. It hit me then: there was nowhere to run. Nowhere to hide. My voice came out shaky as I tried to piece everything together. "What do you mean, my escape attempt the other night? That was last night."

A sly smile curved his lips, his eyes glinting with something I couldn't place. "You've been out for two days, mi amor."

I froze, the realization crashing over me like a tidal wave. "Two days?" I repeated, my voice barely a whisper before it rose to a frantic yell. "You drugged me for two days?!"

He glanced at me through the mirror again, his expression cool and unbothered. "I already told you. I couldn't risk you drawing attention to us, especially in human towns. Maybe I gave you a little too much, but it was necessary. In the end, it was for the best."

My heart pounded, rage simmering beneath the surface of my panic. "You're insane," I spat, struggling against the ropes again. "This isn't okay! You can't just—"

"Calm down. We're almost there," he interrupted smoothly, his calm demeanor only fueling my frustration.

Calm down? My breathing grew shallow as the reality of my situation hit me full force. I'd been kidnapped, drugged, tied up like a prisoner—and now I was being carted off to some secluded house in the middle of the Arizona desert. Trapped. Alone. Completely at his mercy.

I bit back a sob, my chest heaving as I stared at the passing landscape. All I could think about was escape, even if the odds were stacked against me. Because if I didn't fight back, I'd lose more than my freedom. I'd lose me.

The rest of the drive was suffocatingly silent, the only sound the hum of the SUV's engine and the occasional crunch of gravel under the tires. I lost track of how many hours passed, the monotony of endless desert blurring together until, finally, we approached a large iron gate.

Andrés leaned out slightly, entered a code on the keypad, and the gate creaked open, revealing a sprawling mansion. The sight stole my breath for a moment—not that I'd let him know it.

He glanced at me with that ever-present smugness, his lips curling into a small smirk. "Welcome to one of our vacation homes, little wolf."

The SUV came to a stop in front of the grand entrance, where two people stood waiting. Before I could fully process their presence, a tall man with salt-and-pepper hair opened my door, bowing slightly. "Andrés, how are you? I trust your travels went well. The master suite is prepared, as are all the items you requested."

"Thank you, Manuel," Andrés said, clapping him on the back with a familiarity that surprised me. Then his voice dropped to a low, commanding tone.

My door was pulled open fully, and Andrés offered me his hand. The possessive gleam in his eyes dared me to refuse. Reluctantly, I let him help me out of the SUV, my wrists still bound, my pride screaming at me to bite his hand instead.

"Let me introduce you to my little wolf. She hasn't graced me with her name yet, but she will soon," he said with a look of pride in his eye.

"Little wolf," he purred, his hand slipping to my lower back, sending a chill down my spine that wasn't entirely from fear. "This is Manuel, my butler, and Lucia, our housekeeper and cook. Whatever you need, simply ask, and they'll take care of it."

Manuel dipped his head respectfully, his expression neutral, while Lucia—a warm, curvy woman in her mid-sixties—offered a kind smile that tugged at something buried deep inside me. She reminded me so much of my nanny back home.

"Andrés," Lucia said in a lilting accent, her tone as sweet as her smile, "shall I help the missus freshen up? Perhaps we can... remove her restraints?"

Her gaze flicked to my bound hands, a flash of pity crossing her face.

Andrés' expression softened marginally, though his tone remained firm. "Yes, prepare her bath. I'll take care of the rest."

Lucia nodded and disappeared into the house, leaving me alone with him and Manuel. The heat of his hand burned through the thin fabric of my shirt as he guided me forward.

The mansion loomed before us, its grandeur almost overwhelming. Everything about it screamed wealth and power, from the towering columns to the shimmering glass doors. Inside, it was even more stunning—a breath-taking mix of sleek modern design and old-world charm. Marble floors gleamed under the golden glow of chande-liers, and floor-to-ceiling windows showcased a view of the desert that could have been pulled straight from a painting.

He straightened and motioned for Manuel to leave us, then gently turned me toward a grand staircase. "Let's get you settled," he said, his voice dripping with faux tender-ness.

As we ascended the stairs, I couldn't help but glance back at the door, my mind racing with futile escape plans. I was trapped.

For now, I'd play along. But no matter how lavish the cage, it was still a cage. And I was determined to find a way out, even if it meant taking Andres down with me.

Andrés led me to his bedroom, and I couldn't help but gawk. The space was massive, with rich, masculine tones—deep greys, dark woods, and navy accents. One entire wall was made of glass, showcasing the endless expanse of desert beyond. The view was stunning, but it only emphasized how far I was from freedom.

The en-suite bathroom was equally impressive. A large claw-foot tub sat at the center, surrounded by polished marble and subtle gold fixtures. Lucia stood near the tub, her hands clasped in front of her, staring out the window as if lost in thought.

"Andrés, the lady's bath is ready," she said, turning to Andrés with a respectful nod. Her voice was warm, almost maternal. "Shall I help her get ready?"

"Yes," Andrés replied briskly, his tone distracted. "I need to make a phone call. I'll be back shortly." He glanced at me briefly, his eyes lingering as if to remind me that escape wasn't an option. Then he turned and left the room without another word.

Lucia gestured for me to come closer, her movements unhurried and calm, as if this were all perfectly normal. I hesitated but eventually stepped forward, feeling the ropes on my wrists and ankles dig into my skin as I moved.

"I added lavender salts and oils," she said kindly. "They'll help calm you and soothe your muscles. I heard y'all traveled all the way from Florida; that's a long drive." She extended a single claw from her finger, slicing through the ropes with a quick, precise motion.

As the bindings fell away, I rubbed my sore wrists, a wave of relief washing over me. "Thank you, Lucia," I said softly, trying to keep my voice steady.

"You're welcome, *mija*." She paused, her warm eyes meeting mine. "I wish you'd give me your name so I know what to call you."

I hesitated, glancing toward the door to make sure Andrés wasn't lingering. "I have my reasons for not wanting him to know my name," I said carefully, offering her a small smile. "But you can call me 'M.'"

Her lips curved into a kind smile. "Very well, Ms. M. Now, let's get you ready for your bath."

She moved to help me out of my clothes, her movements gentle but firm. I felt a twinge of embarrassment but allowed her to guide me into the warm water. The lavender-scented steam surrounded me, and I couldn't help but relax slightly as the tension in my muscles began to melt away.

Lucia started undoing my hair, her fingers working through the tangles with practiced care. When she began wetting it, I protested weakly. "Lucia, I can bathe myself. You don't have to…"

"It's my pleasure," she interrupted gently. "Manuel and I don't get many visitors to the mansion, and certainly not many ladies that Andrés brings here. It would be an honor to care for you."

Her words struck me as odd, but there was a sincerity in her voice that made it hard to refuse. I let her continue, the sensation of her fingers massaging shampoo into my scalp surprisingly soothing. It had been so long since anyone had cared for me like this—since I was a little girl, back before my mother died.

"Lucia," I murmured after a moment, "have you been working for Andrés for a long time?"

"Oh, yes," she said with a chuckle. "Since before he was born. I'm a distant cousin of his grandmother. When we moved here from Puerto Rico, the family gave us these jobs and a place to stay. I used to change Andrés' diapers back in the day."

That caught me off guard, and I couldn't help but laugh softly. "Andrés as a baby? What was he like?"

Lucia's eyes twinkled with nostalgia. "He was always quiet and serious. We used to say he was an old soul in a child's body."

The warmth in her tone made me pause. For a moment, I let myself imagine Andrés as a child, curious and serious, before his edges were hardened by whatever had shaped him into the man he was now. But the thought only deepened my confusion—and my frustration.

I leaned back slightly, watching her as she worked. "Lucia," I began carefully, "why haven't you said anything about how I got here? You saw I was tied up."

Lucia's hands stilled briefly before she resumed rinsing my hair. "Andrés called us while you were on route and explained your situation. I don't agree with how he decided to approach things, *mija*, but I understand why he feels this is the only way to keep you close and safe."

Her words stirred something uneasy in my chest. "But why does he need to keep me close? Why does he need to keep me safe? We just met," I said, my voice flustered and rising slightly.

Lucia met my gaze, her expression unreadable. "Sometimes," she said softly, "we are bound to people before we even understand why. Andrés sees something in you, something worth protecting. Perhaps in time, you'll see it too."

"Lucia, *gracias*. I'll take it from here," Andrés said, his voice smooth as velvet as he strode into the bathroom.

Chapter 7

ANDRÉS

I stared at my phone, the screen illuminated with a barrage of missed texts. My family had shown relentless curiosity, concern and outright frustration spilling into my inbox. Most I ignored, but the message from my father stood out. Not as my dad, but as my alpha.

Call me immediately, the text commanded.

I had avoided it during the drive, too focused on getting to the sanctuary of my Arizona home. The sooner I had her somewhere safe and private, the better. But now that we were finally here, I couldn't put it off any longer. I sat in my office, running a hand through my hair as I braced myself.

The call barely rang before his voice came through, sharp and demanding. "Andrés?"

"Yes, Alpha," I responded coolly, leaning into his tone. If he wanted to pull rank, then fine, I'd treat him as such.

"Andrés," he growled, "don't be a smart ass. You've left me no choice but to address you like this. You weren't answering anyone's texts. Your mother is driving me insane, worried sick about what's going on with you."

I sighed, pinching the bridge of my nose. "Sorry. I'm fine. Everything is fine."

"Bullshit," he snapped. "You took a woman from Black Stone Pack. Tied her up. Threw her in the back seat of an SUV. Are you out of your mind?"

"I didn't throw her," I retorted, gritting my teeth. "I placed her in the car. And tell Sofía to stop being so *chismosa*."

"This isn't a joke, Andrés!" he barked. "We just attacked Black Stone Pack to get your sister back after Alpha George kidnapped her. Now you go and kidnap one of their she-wolves? Do you know how bad that makes us look?"

I inhaled deeply, steadying myself before dropping the bomb. "She's my mate."

Silence. Then, softly, "Your mate?"

"Yes," I said, my voice tight with frustration. "She's my mate. But she's only twenty, papá. She can't sense the bond yet, and I... I tried to talk to her, but she wouldn't listen. She got defensive, shut me out."

"So you took her," he said, his voice a mix of disbelief and exasperation.

"What else was I supposed to do? Walk away from her? I couldn't. My wolf wouldn't let me," I said, frustrated.

My father sighed heavily on the other end, the weight of the situation sinking in. "She's your mate... Oh, *mi hijo*. I don't know what to say."

"I just... I just want time with her," I admitted, my voice low. "Time to get to know her. Time to decide what to do. But my wolf is going crazy. He wants to claim her. He doesn't understand why we can't."

"What do you mean?" my father asked.

I dropped into the worn leather chair by the fireplace, the silence crackling louder than the flames behind me.

"I mean... I never wanted a mate," I admitted, the words feeling heavier than I expected. "Not at all."

He didn't say anything.

"This bond is nothing but a curse," I continued, voice rough. "A way for man to lose their freedom. Look what happened to Sofía. She got kidnapped."

My wolf stirred, restless and growling at the thought. He didn't agree. He wanted her. He needed her. And that was the damn problem.

"Your sister's kidnapping had nothing to do with her mating bond and everything to do with Alpha George's actions," said my father

"My brain doesn't want a mate," I said slowly, dragging my hand down my face, "but my wolf... he won't shut up. The second I saw her, everything inside me flipped. Her scent, her eyes, the way she fought me... I should've walked away, *Papá*. I knew that. I tried."

"But you couldn't," he finished for me.

I nodded, staring at the flames. "I'm not even sure what I'm doing now. She's terrified of me. She doesn't trust me.

She doesn't even feel the bond yet. And I'm here playing this dangerous waiting game. Between fighting the bond that makes me want to claim her and hoping she'll come around."

My father sighed again, the sound older than he was. "The bond isn't about control, Andrés. It's about balance. You may see it as a cage now, but it can also be your freedom, if you let it."

I clenched my jaw. "I don't know if I'm ready to let anything in."

"You should give her a chance," he said gently

"I don't know," I said, raking a hand through my hair again. "She doesn't even recognize the bond. These past three days have been hell. She's fighting it. Fighting me."

My father let out a sympathetic hum. "That must be torture. When will she turn twenty one?"

"In three weeks," I say, taking a deep breath

"So what's your plan?" says my father

"Honestly? I have no fucking idea," I confessed, overwhelmed. "I'm playing this by ear, and I feel like I'm screwing it up at every turn. My wolf and I are not seeing eye to eye. I am losing control."

"Okay," he said, his tone shifting to something more measured. "My suggestion would be to stop being a controlling asshole to her."

I try to object, but before I could get a word out my father interrupted.

"Don't say you're not because I raised you. I know how of a control freak you can be." he takes a deep breath and says, "Stay there with her until after Sofía's mating ceremony. Take that time to court her. Get to know each other. Make her fall in love with you so she can forget the stupidity you did. When is closer to her birthday bring her to the pack so we can all finally meet her."

I sighed, leaning back against my chair. "I don't know."

"Andrés," he said, his tone firm but not unkind, "You cannot run away from your mate. Get to know her. Listen to your wolf."

"Ok," I say, unsure if I mean it.

My father takes a deep breath, "Stay in touch, and I'll let you know once the ceremony is over."

"OK" I reply.

"Andrés," he added, his voice softening, "I know this isn't easy, but I'm excited for you. I can't wait to meet my new daughter."

The words hit me harder than I expected, a knot forming in my chest. "Thanks, *papá*."

The line clicked off, and I sat there for a long moment, staring at the phone in my hand. I had to figure out what I am going to do. Regardless, if I decide to give in to the mating bond I have to fix this mess. I just don't know how.

As I walked back into my room, the heady aroma of lavender mixed with the intoxicating scent of my mate filled the air. My wolf purred in satisfaction, pride swelling in his chest. This was how it should be: her scent everywhere, claiming my space as hers.

I stepped into the bathroom, leaning casually against the doorframe. "Lucia, *gracias*. I'll take it from here," I said, my voice low and commanding.

Lucia, ever respectful, nodded and left without a word, closing the door behind her. My eyes immediately found her my little wolf sitting in my massive tub, wet, naked, and utterly exquisite.

My wolf growled with approval, pushing forward, eager to stake his claim. But for now, I kept him in check, enjoying the view as her gaze flickered to me. I remove my shirt and leave it on the bathroom counter as I make my way to her.

She tried to keep her expression neutral, but her eyes betrayed her, roaming over my body. I didn't miss the way her gaze lingered on my chest, traveled down to my abs, and froze on the V of my hips, just above my undone jeans. I smirked, a wicked thought crossing my mind.

I flexed slightly, my cock shifting under the denim, and sure enough, her eyes darted down. Caught you.

Oh, little wolf, I thought, suppressing a chuckle. Your body wants me. Your wolf wants me. What easy prey.

"You're blushing, little wolf," I teased, my voice dipping into a deep, amused tone. "Are you okay?"

"Yes," she replied quickly, her voice defensive and a little too high-pitched.

Her jaw tightened as she crossed her arms over her chest, trying to maintain some semblance of modesty.

"Maybe because I'm trying to take a bath, and you're looking at me like I'm dinner," she shot back, her tone sharp.

I chuckled low in my chest, the sound vibrating through the air between us. "Your wolf doesn't seem to mind that I'm here. I can sense her excitement."

Her cheeks flushed a deeper shade of red, and she glared at me. "Well, you're sensing wrong. I'd like my privacy so I can finish bathing."

I crouched beside the tub, my eyes locking on hers. "I can't do that," I said, my voice smooth and firm as I reached out, brushing a damp strand of hair from her face.

The touch was light, almost tender, but the jolt of electricity that sparked between us was impossible to ignore. Her breath hitched, and her eyes widened, betraying the effect I had on her.

"You need to leave," she said, though her voice faltered as she leaned back slightly, trying to put distance between us.

I tightened my jaw, her rejection affecting me this time, and let my knuckles skim the surface of the water as I trailed my hand along the rim of the tub. "This is my house. My room. My bath," I said, my tone dropping. "I don't think you're in any position to order me around."

Her breath hitched again, and I could sense her wolf stirring within her, torn between defiance and submission.

Without taking my eyes off her, I began removing the remainder of my clothes. Her eyes widened, and she quickly averted her gaze, but not before I caught the way they lingered for just a moment too long.

"What are you doing?" she demanded, her voice a mix of outrage and something else, something less certain.

"I am going to wash your hair," I said simply, placing my feet into the tub. Water splashed over the edge as I settled her in between my legs.

"I don't need any help," she snapped, her voice rising as her cheeks burned a brighter shade of red. "Lucia already finished—"

Her words cut off with a sharp inhale as I reached forward, pulling her closer. Her back between my legs, the heat of her skin sent a shiver down my spine, and I could feel her trembling slightly, caught between fear and something else.

"Relax," I say, my voice low and rough.

She froze, her breathing shallow as I reached for her hair, gathering it gently in my hands. My fingers worked slowly, massaging her scalp as I lathered the shampoo, my touch firm but careful.

"You don't have to fight me," I murmured, my lips brushing against the shell of her ear. "I'll take care of you. If you just allow me."

Her wolf stirred again, and I could feel her body responding despite her protests.

I leaned in closer, my lips just brushing her ear as I spoke. "I want to know more about you."

She tensed slightly under my touch, but I didn't stop, letting the soothing motion of my hands lull her into relaxation. "Why?" she asked, her voice soft but guarded.

"Why not?" I replied simply.

Her silence was heavy, but she didn't pull away, so I pressed on, my voice gentle. "Tell me about your childhood. What was it like growing up in Black Stone Pack?"

She hesitated, but as my hands moved to rinse the shampoo from her hair, she finally spoke. "It wasn't anything special," she said finally, her tone light but forced. "I grew up in the Black Stone Pack my whole life. I'm an only child, and my father... well, he's strict. I didn't get to see much of the outside world."

I raised an eyebrow, "What do you mean? Did you go to school? College? Did you interact with other supernatural or even humans?"

She hesitated. "No," she admitted. "I never left the pack growing up. I was homeschooled, and even after two years of online college, I had to beg my father to let me attend classes in person."

My jaw tightened, frustration palpable, but I kept my voice steady. "Why?"

She took a deep breath, "Responsibilities got in the way," I said softly. "My father... he has high expectations, and his views on what female wolves should and shouldn't do are... strict."

"Strict how?" I said quietly, my hands resuming their slow movements. I poured water over her hair, careful not to let it run into her eyes, and trying to keep my wolf calm.

"He doesn't think much of she-wolves," she said, bitterness creeping into her voice. "At least, not as individuals. To him, our worth is measured by what we can bring to the table, whether that's through alliances, strength, or... other means."

I let out a low, dangerous growl, my hands tightening on her hair. "So, he treated you like a tool," I said, my voice sharp. "Something to be used when it suited him."

She nodded. "Yes. My training was rigorous combat, pack management, diplomacy, all so I'd be ready when he decided to marry me off. My job was to make a good alliance, to help strengthen the pack."

I flinched despite myself, the raw anger in me setting me on edge.

"Ouch," she complained.

I let her hair loose from my hands, "Sorry." My jaw clenched as I tried to speak.

"The idea that your father saw you as nothing more than a bargaining chip, when you are so much more than that," I said through gritted teeth.

She stayed quiet for a while until I broke the silence, "You're not a tool, little wolf," I said, grabbing her chin and turning her face towards me. "You're not something to be traded or used. And no one will ever treat you like that again."

"Why does it bother you so much?" she asked quietly, unable to stop myself. "You barely know me."

Staring at her sage green eyes, "Because no one deserves to be treated like that," I said simply.

Trying to change the subject, I asked, "So, who taught you how to fight? I know you didn't learn to move like that on your own," I said, while washing her back.

Her body tensed for a moment, "The Alpha taught me," she said.

"Alpha George?" I spat, my lip curling, unable to hide the anger I felt when I heard that name. "Why? If he doesn't see she-wolves as equals, why bother giving you attention?"

"Because he does value us," she said, the bitterness in her voice unmistakable. "But only for what they can offer the pack."

I felt her body stiffen under my touch, and I knew this was a topic she did not want to talk about. "I'm sorry," I said sincerely, my voice low. "I didn't mean to upset you."

She shook her head. "It's fine."

I didn't press further, sensing she did not like to talk about it. Instead, I reached for a soft sponge, lathering it with soap as I let my hands trail lower. "Lean forward. Let me wash your back."

She hesitated, but eventually, she leaned forward in the water, her bare back fully exposed to me. The curve of her spine, the softness of her skin… it was almost too much. My wolf growled, pushing at the edges of my control as I dragged the sponge slowly down her back, over the smooth expanse of her shoulders and the dip of her waist.

The more I touched her, the more her scent thickened in the air, mingling with my own growing arousal. She couldn't hide it—her body was responding to me, just as mine was to her.

"You smell incredible," I murmured, unable to stop the words from slipping out.

Her body tensed slightly, and she turned her head to glance back at me. "Andrés," she said, her voice wavering, "this is… this is too much."

"Too much?" I asked, leaning closer, my chest hovering over her back, sending a shiver through both of us. "Or exactly what it needs to be?"

She turned her face forward again, her breathing uneven. "This is completely inappropriate."

"Shhhh," I whispered against her ear, my lips so close I could feel the heat of her skin. "Stop over-thinking."

I let the sponge trail lower, over the curve of her back, dipping just above the waterline. Her breathing hitched, and I could feel her body trembling slightly under my touch.

Her scent grew stronger, wrapping around me like a drug, and I knew I was walking a thin line. My cock, already hard and aching, pressed against my briefs.

"Little wolf," I growled softly, my voice thick with need, "you say this is too much, but your body... likes it. Your wolf likes it."

She shivered, her body arching slightly, and I couldn't help but smile against her ear.

"Tell me to stop," I murmured, my lips brushing the sensitive spot just below her ear. "If you don't want this, tell me to stop."

But she didn't say a word. Her silence was deafening, her breathing uneven, her body leaning into mine despite her best efforts to stay distant.

Then out of the silence she said, "Stop".

Chapter 8

MAYA

Last night, after the heated bath, Andrés surprised me: he left me alone. He gave me space, let me finish in peace without another touch or teasing remark. I still had to share his bed, but he didn't try anything. Just silence... and the steady warmth of his presence beside me.

Now, I sit frozen in the sunroom, eyes locked on the world beyond the glass. The morning light is soft, but my thoughts are sharp. Last night's conversation cracked something open—memories of grueling training, the crushing weight of expectations. They flooded my mind, ghosts of a life I once thought were mine to endure.

Ten-year old me laid sprawled on the ground, my lip busted, a bruise forming on my cheek. Father loomed over me, his voice a snarl. "Get up, now! Do you think your enemy will care that you're a child? That they'll go easy on you because you're innocent?"

I gritted my teeth, replying, "No, Alpha."

"Then get your ass up and fight!" I staggered to my feet, small fists raised in a fighting stance. For hours, I endured his brutal training sessions, which only grew harsher with time. Yet once my training ended, father dismissed me, retreating to his own affairs. In those hours, I found solace with my mother, Luna Dana, the pack's kind-hearted Luna, often seen as the only light in the pack's darkness. My mother gave me a glimpse of another side to life.

My mom would dab at my busted lip with a soft cloth, her gaze tender. "My sweet girl, I know your father is hard on you. But believe me, he does it to protect you. As the daughter of an Alpha, you'll have many enemies, and you must learn to defend yourself."

I sighed, wincing slightly. "I know, Mom. It just... it hurts. Sometimes, I just want to play. It sucks that I have to do all this because Luna Yolanda is evil and wants to kill me."

My mother took my chin gently, meeting my eyes. "Don't believe everything your father says. Yes, there is evil in the world, and you must be cautious. But Luna Yolanda is not the villain here. Don't let his hatred poison your heart. You are my sunshine in this darkness, and one day, you'll be the light this pack needs."

The sound of footsteps pulled me from my thoughts. Andrés stepped into the room, his eyes on me with a quiet intensity. He studied me for a moment, his head tilting slightly, curiosity etched across his features.

"How were you feeling?" he asked softly, his voice laced with concern.

He closed the space between us with slow, deliberate steps until he was standing in front of me, his hand reaching out to brush a strand of hair from my cheek. The touch was intimate, electric.

"I'm not your enemy, little wolf," he murmured, his fingertips trailing along my jaw, raising my face to look at him. "But you are mine."

My body betrayed me instantly, heat flaring low in my belly, my wolf stirring with excitement, practically purring at his closeness. I grit my teeth, furious at the way my skin tingled beneath his touch, the way my pulse stuttered. I turned my face away sharply, refusing to let him see the war inside me. His gaze lingered on me for another heartbeat before he stepped back.

"I have a business call," he said, his tone shifting to something smoother, more controlled. "Lucia can get you anything you want." And with that, he turned and walked away, leaving behind the thundering rhythm of a desire I couldn't afford to feel.

I have to leave. Now.

If I stayed in this house one more damn day, I'd fall deeper into the trap Andrés was carefully spinning around me. No chains. No threats. Just quiet, dangerous kindness. Soft smiles. Thoughtful gestures. The way his hand lingered a second too long on my back. The way his eyes looked at me like I already belonged to him.

But I wouldn't let myself forget what this really was.

A kidnapping.

He took me from everything I knew, everything I was. And now he thought a few sweet words and familiar comforts would undo that? That I'd melt into his arms because the cage he kept me in was made of velvet?

Hell. No.

Even if my wolf stirred when he was close, even if my body ached when he touched me, I wasn't going to become another tragedy. Another she-wolf falling for the male who stole her freedom.

I rose from the sunroom, heart thudding against my ribs like a war drum. The silence of the desert beyond the glass felt like it was mocking me, reminding me just how far from home I really was.

Even if I found an open door or window, I couldn't just run away. I was in the middle of the desert. I needed a car.

I moved carefully now. Quiet. Deliberate.

Slipping through the halls like a shadow. Every step silent, every corner approached with bated breath. He could be anywhere. Watching. Listening.

And if he caught me now...

No. I wouldn't let that happen.

Door after door, room after room, nothing useful. But then, like the Goddess herself was guiding me, I found the stairs. A chill hung in the air as I descended, and the scent of oil and metal tickled my senses.

I found the garage.

My breath caught.

It was like stepping into a dream or a villain's vault. Sleek black SUVs. A vintage Mustang. Something red and low that looked like it belonged on a track. But the silver beast tucked in the corner? That one called to me.

An Aston Martin.

I only knew the name because the guys at the pack never shut up about it. Said it was the fastest thing on four wheels.

That was the one.

I crept over and whispered a silent prayer to the Moon Goddess as I reached for the handle.

Click.

Open.

A shaky breath escaped me as I slid into the seat, heart racing. And there it was, sitting right there on the dashboard like a gift from the heavens.

The key.

Double jackpot.

I slid it into the ignition and slowly turned. The engine purred to life beneath me, low and deep like a predator awakening. My hands trembled as they wrapped around the wheel. My pulse roared in my ears.

"Okay," I whispered. "Just forward, back, stop. I can figure this out."

My father never let me learn to drive, said it wasn't necessary. He kept warriors around me at all times who drove me around.

But not anymore.

I moved the car slowly at first, inching forward, my eyes scanning the walls for some sort of garage opener. And then I saw it just above me, clipped to the visor.

I reached up, fingers brushing over the small remote, and pressed the button.

The motor above groaned, and the garage door began to rise.

And as the first sliver of sunlight cut through the shadows, something in my chest cracked wide open.

Hope.

Freedom.

I watched, breath caught in my throat, as the door lifted higher and higher, revealing the endless stretch of desert beyond. The moment the sunlight bathed the car, I felt it.

I was almost free.

A breathless laugh escaped my lips.

"Let's see how fast you can fly, silver beauty."

And with trembling fingers, I reached for the gear.

Ready to disappear.

The wheels jerked beneath me as I sped down the narrow desert road, the car swerving left, then right. I gripped the steering wheel like it might disappear, knuckles white, arms stiff.

"Shit," I hissed, correcting the wheel again as I bounced slightly over the edge of the asphalt.

Driving in a straight line was harder than I thought.

Still, the wind howled around me, and the sun blazed ahead, and it didn't matter that I had no idea where I was going—I was moving. I was free.

Up ahead, a tall black gate loomed across the road. My stomach twisted. It marked the edge of Andrés' property. If I could just make it past that, maybe just maybe I'd be beyond his reach.

I floored the gas pedal.

The car surged forward, tires squealing as I gritted my teeth and held the wheel steady. The gate was closed, thick metal bars waiting to stop me. But I wasn't stopping. Not for anything.

Bang!

The front of the car slammed through the gate, metal screaming and snapping as I burst through it, pieces flying in my rearview mirror like confetti.

"I did it!" I screamed, breathless, half laughing, half crying as I powered down the empty road. "I'm out!"

The wind tangled in my hair. The sun kissed my skin. My heart thudded like thunder. It wasn't pretty, and it sure as hell wasn't graceful—but I was doing it. Alone. Free.

I drove.

Swerved a little more than I should've. Nearly clipped a cactus. Missed a stop sign, or maybe it was a rock. Either way, I didn't care. I was a full hour out and still flying.

Until something flashed past me.

A blur of black tore past me so fast, the wheel jumped in my hands. I yelped, jerking to the side. "What the hell..."

My heart was still hammering as the vehicle disappeared and all I saw was empty desert.

I tried to shake it off. Maybe someone else was just driving like a lunatic. I didn't have time to worry about it.

But then, five minutes later, I saw it.

The same car.

Parked sideways across the road, blocking everything.

And standing in front of it, arms crossed, jaw clenched, eyes burning like fire under the afternoon sun

Andrés.

I slammed my foot on the brake. The car skidded, tires screaming against the hot pavement as I stopped just a few yards away.

My breath left me in one ragged exhale.

Shit. Shit.

He was pissed. I could feel it. Rage radiated off him in waves thick and pulsing with dominance. His chest rose and fell like he'd sprinted a mile, his eyes never leaving mine.

Fear wrapped its icy hands around my throat.

I was not going back.

No matter what.

Not even if it meant crashing right through him.

I inhaled sharply and slammed my foot down on the gas.

The engine roared.

And I drove straight toward him.

I didn't slow down. Didn't blink.

I hoped, prayed, he'd move. That I could swerve, ruin his car, and be gone before he could grab me.

But as I got closer... he didn't budge.

He just stood there.

The engine roared beneath me, the speedometer climbing. I kept my eyes locked on Andrés, refusing to flinch.

He wasn't moving.

Move, dammit, I begged silently.

And then he did.

But not the way I expected.

In a blur of supernatural speed, he leapt onto the hood of the car.

I screamed, instinctively slamming on the wheel, but it was too late. He crouched like a beast above me, feral rage etched into every line of his body. Then...

CRACK!

His fist shattered the windshield, glass exploding around me in glittering shards. My scream caught in my throat as his arm shot through the broken window, grabbing the wheel.

"Stop the fucking car!" he roared, voice ragged with fury.

I panicked. My feet kept pushing down on the gas pedal, even as my hands fought the wheel he now held in a bruising grip.

"Let go!" I cried, vision blurring from the wind and broken glass.

But he didn't let go.

With a growl, Andrés shoved his shoulder through the mangled window, forcing his way inside. His arm curled around me, powerful and relentless. In one brutal move, he yanked the emergency brake.

The world flipped.

Metal screamed. The tires shrieked as the car twisted violently, flipping once, twice.

Pain exploded in my body as everything went weightless. Then...

Silence.

Dust settled.

My breath was ragged, shallow. Blood trickled down my arms, tiny cuts stinging like fire. The taste of iron clung to my tongue.

Before I could even register what happened, strong arms were dragging me out through the broken window.

"Ah," I gasped, trying to fight, but every part of me throbbed in pain.

And then I was up against the side of the car, pinned between twisted silver metal and the furious Andres.

He gripped my shoulders, his face inches from mine.

"What the fuck were you thinking?" he growled, voice low, dangerous. "You could've died, jodia loca."

My teeth clenched. "I know what loca means," I spat back. "And I'm not crazy. I'm trying to escape. I don't want to be here. I want to go home."

His eyes blazed. A muscle in his jaw ticked.

"Your home," he growled, "is with me." His voice dropped into something possessive, almost feral. "And I will never let you go."

Before I could scream, before I could throw another punch, he lifted me.

One arm wrapped around my thighs, the other braced against my back as he threw me over his shoulder like I weighed nothing.

"Put me down!" I shouted, pounding my fists into his back.

He didn't even flinch.

From this view, I saw the wrecked Aston Martin behind us. Damn it. That silver beauty didn't deserve that ending.

I also saw the SUVs that had pulled up quietly—his men, no doubt. When the hell had they arrived?

"Let me go!" I screamed again, fury burning hotter than my bruises.

Andrés just let out a growl, low and full of warning. "Stop fighting me, little wolf," he said, almost amused.

Then smack.

His hand landed on my ass, hard and fast.

I gasped.

The sting snapped through me... followed by a warm, rough palm dragging slowly over the ache he left behind.

It made my body jerk, confused between the sharp flash of pain and the slow melt of desire that followed.

Goddess help me... I clenched my thighs.

No. No. He was my captor.

But the warmth from his hand seared through my clothes and down to places I didn't want to acknowledge. My wolf whimpered.

And I hated that part of me, the part that responded.

"Keep squirming like that," he growled, his voice thick with warning and something darker, "and I'll make sure you can sit for a week."

Chapter 9

ANDRÉS

I should've been furious.

She wrecked one of my favorite cars. Risked her life on open roads she didn't know how to navigate. Tried to leave me again.

But all I could feel was the sheer, suffocating fear of losing her.

My mate.

My fucking heart.

That made me the most angry. The fact that, due to this bond, I couldn't stomach the thought of her getting hurt or her leaving me. I had already decided that it would be impossible to fight this bond, but it still angered me the control it had over my emotions.

I carried her inside, her body limp against mine, the scent of blood still clinging to her skin. My wolf was barely contained, snarling inside me, pacing with each heartbeat.

Her breaths were shallow, her jaw clenched in pain, but I knew she was awake. Knew she was fighting the weight of it all just like always.

Her arms and legs were mottled with angry bruises. Her lip was split. But the cuts, thank the Goddess, were already closing. Shifter healing had kicked in. Her skin knit back together slowly but surely. It would take a few hours, a day at most, and she'd be whole again.

I kicked open my bedroom door and laid her down on the bed as gently as I could.

"Stay still," I muttered, brushing the hair from her face.

Her eyes snapped open. Glared at me like I was the monster under her bed.

"Don't touch me."

I ignored her and grabbed a cold compress, pressing it gently to the dark bruise forming along her jaw. She flinched away, but I didn't let go.

"You need to rest. You're in pain," I said, angry that she was so stubborn

"I don't care." She tried to sit up, wincing instantly.

"I do!" I snapped, louder than I meant. My hand trembled as I held the cold compress.

"You're not supposed to hurt." My voice cracked, low and hoarse. "I am supposed to protect you."

She pushed the compress from her face and shoved at my chest, weak but stubborn. "You think I care what you want? You kidnapped me."

"I did it to protect you!" I yell out.

"I never asked for your protection," she snapped, eyes glistening.

I clenched my jaw, my hands shaking as I cleaned the blood from her arm. "You think I want this?" I said through my teeth. "You think I enjoy this uncontrollable pull that I have for you while you look at me like I'm the enemy?"

"You are the enemy!" she bit back, her voice cracking. "You took me. You forced me to stay here. No matter how sweet you pretend to be, you stole me from my pack!"

"I saved you!" I roared. Grabbing her by the chin, "I never pretend to be sweet."

Her eyes filled with angry tears, but she didn't let them fall. "You made me a prisoner."

I stared at her, my chest heaving, my other hands curling into fists.

"If something happened to you..." I swallowed hard, voice thick.

Her gaze flickered, just for a second. And it hurt how fast she looked away again.

"Then maybe you shouldn't have kidnapped me," she whispered coldly.

Silence stretched between us.

I reached for her again, but she slapped my hand away.

"Don't help me. Don't touch me. I don't want your kindness or your care."

I froze, my throat tight.

Fine.

"Have it your way," I said, voice low and dangerous.

I stood, every inch of my body tight with rage and something that felt too close to heartbreak.

"You stay here," I snapped. "And I swear, if you try to run again… I will leave your ass so red, you won't be able to sit for months,"

I didn't wait for a response.

I stormed out of the room and slammed the door behind me, fists clenched, heart breaking with every step I took away from her.

Pacing the hall like a possessed man, dragging a hand through my hair, trying to breathe through the fury and frustration knotting in my chest.

I had pulled her from a wreck. Carried her bleeding and bruised into my home. She could've died trying to run from me. And now, after all of it, she still looked at me like I was the monster in her story.

Maybe I was.

A soft voice pulled me out of the storm swirling in my head.

"You're going about this all wrong."

Lucía.

She stood at the end of the hall, arms crossed, her eyes calm but sharp, always watching. Always knowing too much. Her silver-streaked hair was braided neatly over one shoulder, her expression unreadable.

"Ms. M is young," she said gently, "and her wolf is even younger. She doesn't understand why she's here, or why a stranger suddenly cares so much. She's confused. Lost. Forcing her to accept you? That's not going to work."

I exhaled harshly and leaned against the wall, letting my head fall back.

"She is mine."

"I know that," Lucía said. "But she doesn't. Not in the way you do. Not yet."

I stayed quiet.

"She wants to go back to her pack," she continued. "Maybe letting her visit, see it would help. It might remind her you're not a tyrant."

I let out a humorless laugh. "What pack? Her alpha ran like a coward. Their ranks were shattered. Half of them fled. The others barely survived. I don't even know if there's a pack left to return to."

Lucía shrugged one shoulder. "Then find out."

I looked at her, frowning. "You don't understand. She fights me every step of the way. She's driving me insane."

Lucía's eyes glinted. "She should. There's a fire in that girl, Andrés. Don't let her softness fool you. She may be quiet, but that wolf in her won't let you control her."

I dropped my head into my hands, groaning. "She'll be the death of me."

Lucía walked closer, her tone softening.

"Instead of waiting for the bond to do the work, maybe you should work for her heart."

I lifted my gaze, narrowing my eyes. "What do you think I've been trying to do?"

She gave me a long, disappointed look. "If this is how young men court women these days, I weep for the future."

That earned a low growl from me, but I bit it back.

"You want her?" Lucía said, voice calm but firm. "Win her over. Not with chains. Not with threats. Not even with that brooding scowl of yours."

I raised a brow.

"With care. With patience. And for the love of the goddess, Andrés, listen. Listen to her words. Her silence. Her pain. Earn her trust, not just her submission."

Her words sank in, deeper than I wanted to admit.

I turned away from her, staring down the hall toward my room, toward the girl behind that door.

The one the Moon Goddess had chosen for me.

My mate.

I stared at the door I just slammed, fists still tight at my sides, my wolf pacing just beneath the surface, restless and agitated.

"What the hell am I supposed to do, Lucía?" I asked, my voice low, raw.

She tilted her head slightly, that knowing gleam in her eyes never wavering.

"Give her space," she said gently but firmly. "Let me care for her tonight. She's bruised, angry, and overwhelmed. What she needs right now isn't your dominance—it's time. She needs to hear about you from someone else."

I shook my head, that ache tightening in my chest again. "I need to be by her side. My wolf needs her."

Lucía arched a brow. "Then tell your wolf to stand down. Because right now, your need to be near her is not more important than her need to feel safe. You'll have your time, Andrés. Once she turns twenty-one, once her wolf fully awakens, the bond will hit her like a storm. But until then... back off."

I growled low, frustration burning like fire under my skin, but I knew she was right.

I nodded silently and turned, forcing myself to walk away.

Each step down the hall toward my study felt like a war-like I was peeling myself away from something sacred. But I needed clarity. I needed answers. And maybe, just maybe, a plan that didn't end with my little wolf looking at me like I was the villain in her story.

I closed the door to my study and leaned back against it for a moment, breathing deep.

I pulled out my phone and dialed.

Mason answered on the second ring. "Andrés. I was wondering when you'd call."

"I need to know what the hell happened to Black Stone Pack after I left," I said without preamble, sinking into the chair behind my desk.

There was a pause. Then Mason spoke, quieter than usual. "It's... not good. Turns out a lot of the wolves in that pack were never loyal to Alpha George. They were afraid. Beaten into submission."

"They've been trying to rebuild," he continued. "My brother volunteered to step in temporarily. He's leading while the Council of Shifters figure out the next steps."

Mason's brother was the alpha of Crescent Moon Pack and a great help during the rescue of my sister.

I frowned. "Is the pack stable?"

"Stable-ish," Mason replied. "They want to stay together, but they don't have a real alpha. Not yet. They're holding on with hope and routine. They've got trauma to work through, but there's strength in them. Real strength."

I sat in silence, absorbing every word. It makes sense that he would help out while the council figured out who would take over. The Council of Shifters kept order in the shifter community, made sure we had good relationships with other supernatural, make sure shifters did not break rules and that we never get exposed to the humans.

Maybe... just maybe...

Taking her back there could be a way to show her I was willing to let go of control. That I saw her. Heard her. That I wanted her trust.

"Thank you," I said finally, voice tight.

"No problem," Mason said. "Your dad shared with us your situation with your mate. I wish you good luck in this journey."

After we hung up, I sat back, eyes locked on the ceiling.

Could I really let her go... even just for a visit?

Because the way she looked at me now—like I was a threat, a captor—it gutted me.

And I'd do anything to change that.

⸻

MAYA

I laid there in silence, the soft mattress doing little to ease the aching in my body.

My limbs throbbed with the bruises from the crash, but the worst of the cuts were already fading, my wolf working overtime to heal me. Still, everything hurt, especially the tension coiled so tight inside my chest I could barely breathe.

I hated this room. Hated the way it smelled like him. I hated the way my skin still tingled from where his hands had touched me. I hated how my body remembered everything.

The moment he yanked me out of the car, rage and fear thick between us.

The way he shoved me against the metal, yelling like I was the one breaking his heart.

And Goddess help me...

The way it felt when he spanked me.

I squeezed my thighs together, shame and something darker rolling low in my stomach. The sharp sting of his palm, the heat of his hand when he rubbed it after, and that deep, growling command—Stop fighting me, little wolf—it had done something to me.

And that something terrified me.

Because my mind screamed to run. To hate him. But my body... and my wolf...

They were whispering something else entirely.

He tried to tend to me, and I pushed him away. He looked like I'd gutted him. The way his voice cracked when he said I could've died... the way his hands shook...

Why do you care so much?

I rolled onto my side with a groan, teeth clenched as pain radiated through my ribs.

Then the door creaked open.

Lucía stepped in, soft and slow like she'd been waiting for the storm to pass. She carried a steaming cup of tea and a warm towel over her arm, her gaze assessing me the moment she stepped inside.

"Don't worry," she said gently, "he's not coming back in tonight. I made sure of it."

I didn't respond.

She set the tea beside me and walked to the ensuite bathroom. I could hear water running.

"You need to bathe," she called. "Let me help you."

I wanted to snap. To tell her to get out. But my body hurt too much to argue, and truthfully... I didn't want to be alone.

Lucía returned and helped me to my feet, her hands careful but firm as she supported me into the bath. Warm water kissed my skin, and I nearly moaned at the relief.

As she gently washed away the blood and dirt, she spoke softly.

"Andrés is a good man, you know. Stubborn. Possessive as hell. But good."

I scoffed. "He kidnapped me."

"He saved you," she said, unbothered by my tone. "Your pack was collapsing. Alpha George was a tyrant. Your life would've crumbled with that pack."

"And he just decided that I belonged to him? Like I'm some... prize?" I snapped, glaring at the tiled wall.

Lucía sighed. "You're young. Your wolf hasn't fully matured yet. Once it does, everything Andrés is doing... will make sense."

I clenched my jaw, ignoring the painful throb in my chest. "There's no world where kidnapping someone is okay. No reason that justifies taking away someone's choice."

Lucía paused, brushing a soft towel across my shoulders. "You don't have to agree with how he did it. I wouldn't, either. But don't pretend you haven't seen another side of him."

I said nothing.

But the images came unbidden.

The way his face shattered when he saw me bleeding.

The desperation in his voice when he begged me to stop the car.

The pain in his eyes when I called him the enemy.

"I don't want to see that side of him," I whispered, the words slipping out before I could stop them. "Because if I do... I won't know how to hate him anymore."

Lucía didn't smile. She just nodded, pressing a kiss to the top of my head like a mother would a wounded child.

She helped me into bed, tucked the covers around me, and left the tea steaming on the table.

"You don't have to forgive him," she said at the door. "But don't close your eyes to the truth, either."

Then she was gone.

And I was left staring at the ceiling, heart pounding.

I laid there in the silence, the room dark except for the faint glow of moonlight seeping through the curtains. The warmth of the tea Lucía left was still on my tongue, but it did nothing to soothe the ache in my chest.

I was so tired.

Tired of fighting.

Tired of losing.

Tired of pretending like I had any control over my life.

Because I never really did.

My entire life had been a carefully caged path, carved out by someone else's will.

First, my father.

He kept me under lock and key, forbidding me from dating, from exploring, from living. I was to remain pure, his words, not mine, until he decided which alpha or beta from another pack would take me as a mate. An alliance. That's what I was to him. A strategic move on a chessboard.

No room for love or my choice.

And now Andrés kidnapping me. Forcing me into this strange home. Into his life.

Another man, deciding what was best for me without asking what I wanted.

I hated that my body reacted to his touch. That my wolf whimpered for him. That sometimes when he looked at me like I was the only thing that mattered, I almost believed him.

I wouldn't be powerless anymore.

And then... the idea came to me.

What if I stopped resisting?

What if I gave him what he wanted—obedience, softness, trust—just long enough to earn his?

Let him believe I was opening up. That I was warming to him.

And when he let his guard down...

I'd finally be free.

No more desperate escapes. No more crashing cars. No more bruises and begging for help.

I'd play the part.

And when he least expected it, I'd disappear from his life like a ghost.

A small, bitter smile crept across my lips as I curled under the covers, the plan forming clearer with every breath.

Let him believe I was falling.

Let him fall harder.

Because this time... I was in control.

And I wouldn't stop until I got my life and my freedom back.

Tomorrow, everything changed.

Tomorrow, the hunter would become the prey.

Chapter 10

MAYA

The morning sun warmed my skin like a gentle balm, soft and golden through the tall windows of the sunroom. I sat curled up on one of the cushioned chairs, legs tucked beneath me, a soft blanket over my lap, and a half-eaten plate of fruit and toast in front of me.

For a moment, it almost felt normal.

Peaceful, even.

But even as the sunlight kissed my skin and the tea soothed my throat, I knew better.

It had been four days since my failed escape. Four days without seeing Andrés. My body had healed, thanks to my wolf and Lucía's gentle care, but he hadn't come near me, not once, since he stormed out that night. True to her word, Lucía promised he'd give me space to recover, and he did.

But today was different.

Today was the first time I'd stepped outside that room. And he noticed.

I didn't have to turn around to know that I could feel him behind me, his presence thick in the air like a storm rolling in. Watching. Waiting.

My wolf stirred instantly, ears perking, body suddenly alert in a way I hated. Her soft whine curled in the back of my mind, and I fought to keep her still.

Calm down, I warned her.

And then he stepped into the room.

Andrés.

His presence filled the space before he even spoke. Tall, broad-shouldered, he wore a white button-up, sleeves rolled to the elbows, the collar loose. His khaki pants clung to his strong legs, his movements slow but purposeful, like he owned the room.

His dark hair was still damp, like he'd just come out of the shower, and the sunlight caught in the angles of his jaw, the honey brown of his eyes locked right on me.

My damn heart skipped.

He didn't say anything at first, just looked at me with that quiet intensity that made me feel like I was being read, like he could see through every layer I wrapped around myself.

My wolf whimpered again.

I took a slow breath and shoved her back down.

Don't get it twisted, wolf. He's still the enemy.

I reached for my tea, pretending not to notice how his gaze followed every movement.

Finally, he spoke.

"Morning," he said, voice low and slightly rough from sleep. "You slept well?"

My fingers tightened around the cup.

There was no growl in his voice today. No edge. Just soft concern. And that, somehow, made it worse.

"I did," I said, quiet but not cold.

His brow lifted slightly, like he hadn't expected that.

"And how are you feeling?"

My eyes flicked up to his. Goddess, he looked unfairly good this morning.

"I'm healing," I said, voice still soft. "My wolf took care of most of the pain."

He nodded slowly, hands slipping into his pockets. "Good. I was..." he clears his throat, "I am glad."

I looked away, hating the small tug in my chest.

This was part of the plan. Pretend. Be calm. Not cold. Let him believe I was softening.

But I had to be careful. He was watching me too closely.

So I offered the smallest smile, tight, polite.

"Thank you... for sending Lucía. She was kind."

His jaw tensed just a little, and I felt the shift in the air between us.

He was waiting. Measuring every word. Probably wondering if this was a trap or a breakthrough.

Let him wonder.

Let him hope.

Because soon... he'd let down his guard.

And when he did, I'd be ready.

Andrés moved slowly, giving me space, but not breaking eye contact. His steps were steady. Careful.

"Can we talk?" he asked, his voice softer than I'd ever heard it.

I tensed for a second, but then gave him a small nod, setting down my tea. He took the seat across from me—close, but not too close. Respecting distance. That was new.

He looked down at his hands for a moment, as if searching for the right words.

"I want to ask you something," he finally said. "And I need you to hear me as a man who knows he did not make the best choices."

I blinked, caught off guard by the raw honesty in his voice.

He met my gaze again. There was no growl in his chest. No command on his tongue.

"Can we start over?" he asked. "Not pretending nothing happened. But just... civil. "

He looked like he was struggling to say the words. He paused, "A truce. You and me, getting to know each other without force."

My lips parted, but the words wouldn't come. So I stayed silent, watching him closely.

"I know you don't believe it," he continued, voice rough now, "but seeing you bleeding...fuck, I thought I was going to lose you before I even had a chance to win you over."

He leaned forward, elbows resting on his knees, gaze locked to mine.

"I want you to see me as something else. Maybe even someday a friend. Or more."

My heart pounded.

He wasn't demanding. He wasn't pushing.

And that made it harder.

Because part of me, a small, traitorous part, wanted to believe him. My wolf stirred again, her soft whine like a breath against my soul. She liked this. She liked him.

But I couldn't forget what he'd done. Not yet.

Still... I could use this.

A truce would let me stay closer.

Gain more trust.

Even as I reminded myself that this was all part of the plan, something about the pain in his eyes twisted inside me. Something real.

I drew in a slow breath and nodded once.

"Okay," I said, quiet but steady. "A truce."

Andrés exhaled like he'd been holding his breath the whole time.

"No expectations," I added quickly. "Just... civility."

He gave me a small, careful smile. "I'll take that."

I nodded again and turned back to my tea, but I could still feel his gaze on me.

"Tell me about your mother?" he asked, his tone soft.

Andrés sat across from me.

"My mother is dead," I said simply, forcing my voice to remain steady.

Andrés stilled, then scooted closer to me, his legs bracketing mine, warm and firm on either side. I instinctively tried to shift back, nerves fluttering in my chest, but he didn't let me. His hands rested on my knees, giving me comfort, and it felt good.

His golden eyes softened. "I'm so sorry. I didn't know," he murmured, his usual teasing confidence replaced with emotion.

I gave him a small smile, one that didn't quite reach my eyes, "It's okay. I have good memories of my mother. She was the best part of my childhood."

He hesitated for a moment, "Do you mind if I ask what happened?" he asked, voice low, cautious.

I took a deep breath, steeling myself against the old ache that never fully went away. "When I turned sixteen, my mother succumbed to cancer," I said quietly.

Cancer is a disease rare among shifters, yet unforgiving when it strikes. For shifters, it is a death sentence, and no amount of healing power or strength could spare my mother.

"I can't imagine how painful that must have been," he said softly.

"Yes, it was," I admitted.

"Leaving you alone with your dad didn't help?" he asked, while moving to sit closer to me and hold my hands.

I looked down at our hands, "He started treating me worse. Cruelly."

I hesitated, debating how much to reveal. The truth was that my father was never kind to me, and once my mother died, he became my worst nightmare.

Andrés's golden eyes flicked toward me, his gaze sharp. "And yet you want to go back to that pack so badly? After everything you've been through?"

"I have good memories there, too," I said firmly, meeting his gaze. "My mother was everything to me. She loved me fiercely, and so did my Nanny Matilda. For the first sixteen years of my life, I knew what love felt like because of them. My pack... it's still my home. It's all I've ever known."

If I were honest, the only reason I survived my father's treatment after my mother died was because Matilda, who threw her body over mine to protect me or hide me from him. She was a ray of sunshine in my nightmare.

Andrés exhaled sharply, running a hand through his dark hair. "I don't understand how you can hold onto a place that's caused you so much pain."

I shrugged, my smile faint. "Because it wasn't all pain. My mother taught me to find light in the darkness, to hold onto the good even when everything feels broken. Matilda showed me some people are worth fighting for."

Andrés was quiet for a long moment, his jaw working as if he wanted to say something but couldn't find the words. Finally, I spoke, "So tell me about your childhood and your pack?"

He told me about his grandparents, the founders of the Luna Stone Pack, who had traveled from Puerto Rico in the 1940s. "It wasn't easy for them," he said. "They faced a lot of hardship because they were Latino. Other packs didn't trust them, and didn't want to accept them. They were seen as outsiders."

I listened intently, drawn in by the story as his golden eyes flicked between me and the window. "So, what did they do?" I asked softly.

"They didn't give up," Andrés said, pride swelling in his voice. "With the help of some witches, they bought a large piece of land in California. It was wild, untamed, and perfect for building something new. They started the Luna Stone Pack from scratch, carving out a place where they could thrive, where others like them could belong."

I could hear the passion in his tone, the deep-rooted pride he carried for his family and their legacy. It was palpable, and for a moment, I found myself envious of the connection he had to his history, to his roots.

"I wish I had something like that," I admitted quietly, my gaze fixed on the scenery out the window. "A connection to my history."

Andrés glanced at me, his brows furrowing. "You don't know much about your pack's origins?"

I shook my head. "No one talks about it. I've never met my grandparents; they died before I was born, on both sides. And as for the pack, it's like its past was erased. No one tells the story of how we came to be."

The words tasted bitter on my tongue. In truth, I had never realized how much I yearned for that connection until now. Listening to Andrés speak about his family with such pride stirred something in me—a longing for something I had never known.

"Your pack doesn't celebrate its history?" he asked, disbelief coloring his tone.

I shrugged. "No. The past doesn't matter to them, only power does." My father made sure of that. I said to myself.

Andrés's jaw flexed at my words, but he didn't press. Instead, he shared more of his own childhood, stories of growing up alongside his siblings. He spoke of his sister and brother with such fondness that it made my chest ache. The love and camaraderie they shared were things I had only dreamed of.

As the conversation flowed, I found myself leaning into the warmth of his presence, the tension between us softening, though it never disappeared entirely. Andrés was still my captor, but with every passing moment, I began to see the man beneath the dominance. For reasons I couldn't fully grasp, I found myself wanting to know more.

I needed to stay focused and not forget the plan. I could not allow his sweet words and my stupid wolf infatuation to derail my plans.

Lucia stepped into the sunroom, her voice gentle, almost hesitant. "Excuse me, Andrés. You have a phone call," she said with a polite smile.

Just like that, the fragile spell around us shattered. I straightened, pulling my gaze from him and turning back to the window, heart thudding. Andrés cleared his throat as he rose, the warmth of his touch still lingering on my skin. But before he stepped out, he paused and looked at me, his golden eyes no longer smoldering with desire, but softened with something deeper.

"Thank you for sharing," he said quietly, then turned and walked away.

I couldn't speak. Could barely move. His words disarmed me more than anything else had. I managed a faint nod, unsure if he even saw it before he disappeared down the hall.

What's happening to me?

This man is not my friend. He's my enemy. He kidnapped me. Drugged me. Spanked me... my body started to react all hot in my core.

No. Stop it. Stop it. Stop it

This isn't real. I have to stay focused. I have a plan.

I closed my eyes and inhaled deeply, trying to steady the storm brewing inside me.

I scoffed under my breath and shook my head.

Get a grip, Maya. He's not your savior. He's not some misunderstood hero from a romance story. He's the enemy. He's dangerous.

This shouldn't be happening. I should hate him. I do hate him... don't I?

I opened my eyes, heart pounding; of course I hate him. I just have to remember the plan.

The scent of sugar and warm bread drifted in the sunroom, feeding my curiosity.

Lucia even stepped fully into the sunroom, balancing a tray with two mugs of café con leche and a tempting assortment of golden pastries. Her smile was soft, motherly.

"I thought you might enjoy something sweet," she said, setting the tray down on the small table beside me. "Andrés will be a while with that call."

The warmth in her voice, the gentle clink of porcelain—everything about her presence eased the tension in my shoulders. I gave her a grateful smile.

"I definitely welcome the distraction," I said, eyeing the flaky little pastries that looked mouth watering.

She sat down beside me, pouring the café and passing me a cup. I inhaled the rich aroma and then pointed curiously to the pastries. "What are these?"

Lucia reached for one of the sweet offerings. "These here," she said, lifting a square dusted with sugar, "are pastelitos de guayaba. Puff pastry filled with guava paste, sweet and a little tart." She handed it to me and I took a bite, my eyes widening at the explosion of flavor.

"Oh my God," I mumbled with a mouthful. "That's amazing."

She grinned, pleased. "This one," she said, pointing to a long-shaped treat, "is a quesito. Cream cheese filling, brushed with syrup. Flaky and soft at the same time."

I tried it next, moaning softly at the creamy texture.

"And these are polvorones," she added, gesturing to the small, crumbly cookies. "Shortbread. They melt in your mouth—very popular around the holidays."

I nibbled one and sighed. "I need to stop before I eat the whole tray. These are better than anything I've had."

Lucia smiled at me with quiet affection. I hesitated, then asked, "Are you married to Manuel?"

She nodded. "*Sí*, I am."

"What was life like in Puerto Rico?" I asked, curiosity blooming in me.

Her smile faltered, just slightly. A shadow passed over her features as she looked out the window, eyes going distant.

"I was born in Ponce," she said quietly. "It was... the place of my greatest happiness and my deepest sorrow."

I stayed silent, letting her speak in her own time.

"I met Manuel there," she continued, her voice growing softer. "We were young and stupid, but so in love. I gave birth to our son there. He was beautiful, with eyes like his father's and a laugh that could light up the street."

Her voice cracked. She blinked quickly and looked down at her hands.

"But it was also where I lost everything. My parents. My son. All in one night."

I swallowed hard. "What happened?"

Her eyes lifted to mine, "There was a massacre. Between rival packs and the government. We were caught in the middle. It was chaos. Blood in the streets. Screams. I'll never forget it."

Her voice trembled but didn't break. "I survived. So did Manuel. But our boy... he didn't."

Silence settled between us like a fragile thread stretched too thin.

"I'm so sorry," I whispered.

Lucia gave a small, bittersweet smile, "After the massacre, we had nothing but each other. Manuel and I were lost... until María reached out."

"María?" I asked gently.

She nodded, her eyes softening with something warmer, something close to gratitude. "María is my cousin. She married Alpha Carlo, Andres's grandfather. After everything that happened in Ponce, she sent for us. Said there was a place for us here, away from the bloodshed. So we came. Started over."

"And you've been here ever since?"

She nodded, the sadness in her eyes dimmed by fondness. "Helping them raise Beto. At first, he was just a little boy. Then Andrés and his siblings. It gave us purpose. Something to hold onto."

I looked at her, seeing her now in a different light, not just the warm housekeeper who brought pastries and coffee, but a woman who had survived so much.

"You've been through so much," I murmured.

Lucia reached out and touched my hand gently, her expression composed, but tired. "We all carry pain, *mija*. But we keep going. We learn to smile again."

She met my gaze, her voice steady. " Look at us, drinking café. Sharing stories. Life has a funny way of finding beauty again, even after the darkest storms."

I didn't say it aloud, but her words stirred something deep inside me, a whisper that maybe, just maybe, even in enemy territory... I wasn't entirely alone.

Chapter 11

ANDRÉS

After wrapping up a long, grueling call with my sibling and father about Luna Enterprise, I found myself sitting in my study thinking about everything that has happened since last night. Her escape, the crash, her injuries, and the conversation we had this morning.

I haven't been the same since the moment I saw her bleeding in that wrecked car, bruised, trembling, barely conscious. The rage I felt when she ran... it was nothing compared to the fear that gripped me when I thought I might lose her. That kind of fear? It changed me. It claws into my chest and won't let go.

Lucía was right. So was my father. I've been acting like she's already mine, like the bond is some shortcut to love and trust. But it's not. She doesn't feel the bond; the pull of this fated bond has me acting like this.

How am I supposed to behave? I never wanted this, before meeting her; I hated the whole concept of fated mates. But now the thought of not having her with me makes me physically ill. My body and wolf desire her. As I get to know more of her, I want her.

I have to control my temper and show her that being with me is good. I have to change. I want her trust. Her laughter. Her fire. Her choice. And if I have to bleed for it, wait for it, prove myself a thousand times over, I will.

With that determination, I stepped into the sunroom, and my chest tightened.

Empty.

The cushion where she'd been sitting still held the indent of her form, a half-finished mug of coffee left behind, steam long faded.

Panic flickered in my chest. No... she wouldn't have.

I spun on my heel, striding toward the main entrance, dread coiling low in my gut. The thought of her escaping, of her out there alone, possibly hurt... No. I couldn't let my mind go there.

Just as I reached for the front door, I heard it. Her laugh. Soft, breathless, unguarded.

My mate.

I froze, breath caught in my throat.

That sound... it wasn't the wary, sharp-edged version of her I was used to. It was something warmer. Lighter. Like sunlight breaking through after a long storm.

I followed the sound, drawn like a wolf to the scent of spring. Her voice led me to the kitchen, and when I stepped through the doorway, the sight hit me square in the chest.

There she was, my little wolf, standing at the island, her sleeves rolled up, hands dusted with flour, smiling. Lucía stood beside her, guiding her through some kind of dessert prep, both of them laughing like old friends.

For a moment, I could only watch.

Her hair was loose, fiery, wild, soft curls bouncing as she moved, lips parted in a grin that made something primal in me ache. My mate, soft, beautiful, and alive in a way I'd never seen before.

I'd stolen her from her world. Taken her by force. And because of that, I had never seen her happy

Until now. There she was. Laughing.

I didn't deserve the warmth curling in my chest... but goddess, I wanted more of it.

Lucia and my mate both noticed me standing in the doorway, though it was Lucia who smiled first, warm and knowing, like she could read the longing etched into my expression.

"Andrés," she called, beckoning me in with a flour-dusted hand, "come try one of our masterpieces. You're just in time."

I stepped forward slowly, careful not to move too fast, not to spook the fragile moment they'd created. But the second my eyes met her eyes, everything in her shifted.

Where just seconds ago she was glowing, laughing, radiant, free, now her shoulders stiffened, her hands drew close to her body, and her smile vanished like it had never existed.

She didn't have to say a word. Her body said it all.

You're the enemy.

Lucia gave me a quiet glance, then returned to shaping the delicate pastries, wisely choosing not to comment.

I moved to the edge of the counter, careful to keep a bit of distance between us. My gaze flicked to my mate's hands, still powdered with flour, fingers twitching slightly as if she was unsure whether to stay or flee.

"You made these?" I asked, voice low, trying to meet her in the space between. "They smell incredible."

She didn't look at me. Instead, she reached for a cloth and wiped her fingers clean with slow, deliberate care. "Lucía did most of the work. I was just helping."

Her tone was clipped, polite. Hollow.

I hated it.

Not because she owed me anything, but because I had seen the real her only moments before. And now she was hiding again.

And it was my fault.

I nodded slowly, keeping my voice gentle. "Well... they look perfect."

She didn't respond.

This was the dance we did—one step forward, two steps back.

And still... I couldn't stop chasing her. Even if she was running from me. Because I was feeling something. I wanted to get to know more of her. My beautiful mate.

Lucía broke the silence with her usual grace, her voice soft but edged with warmth. "Do you remember how you and your siblings used to make these with me when you were little?" She glanced at me fondly as she shaped another pastry. "You'd steal the filling when you thought I wasn't looking. Made more of a mess than the desserts ever did."

I chuckled, the sound low and real, rumbling in my chest like distant thunder. "I remember," I said, the tension in my shoulders loosening just a little. "Manuel would pretend to be the food inspector and fail every single one of mine. Said my *pastelitos* were a crime against Puerto Rico."

Lucía laughed, and for a moment, so did she just a little huff of breath that I am sure she didn't mean to let slip. But I heard it. She knew I did.

Lucía handed her another piece of dough. Slowly, tentatively, she started helping again. She didn't meet my gaze. But I watched her, and worse I could feel her body reacting to it.

We worked in silence for a bit, the kind that wasn't quite comfortable, but no longer hostile.

Then it happened.

We both reached for the same jar of guava filling.

My hand brushed hers.

Tingle passed between our fingers. I froze, eyes lifting to meet her at the same time.

Her pupils were blown wide, and she felt it—goddess, she felt it. The pull. The raw, electric awareness of our bond threading between us, tightening.

I swallowed hard, my breath suddenly too shallow, my heart thudding with traitorous heat. My skin tingled where we'd touched.

I didn't move. My fingers still hovered near hers, close enough that I could feel the heat radiating off her. My voice, when I spoke, was low, meant only for me.

"Did you feel that?"

She didn't answer me.

Didn't have to.

Her breath hitched. Her pupils dilated. That delicious flutter in her chest—I heard it, felt it, savored it. She felt the spark between us when our fingers touched, just like I did. Pretending otherwise didn't change the truth that hung heavy between us.

I wanted to feel it again.

She returned her focus to the pastry in front of her, as if the simple task could shield her from the storm raging inside us both. Her hands small, delicate, dusted in flour worked with such care, rolling the dough, folding the edges just right.

Attempting to follow my father's advice I cleared my throat.

"I was hoping you'd come with me for a tour of the estate," I said carefully, watching her every reaction. "And afterward... we could have a meal outside. Maybe even enjoy one of your *pastelitos*."

It was a peace offering, plain and simple. No chains, no commands, just the hope that she'd see the gesture for what it was.

She turned toward me slowly, one eyebrow arching in challenge. "Are you asking me on a date, Andrés?"

I held her gaze. "Yes. I am."

"Uhm..." she hesitated, shifting her weight, her hands fidgeting in front of her apron. "I don't know if spending time together is a good idea."

"Why not?" I asked, my voice quieter now, "I want to get to know you, little wolf. The real you. And I want you to know me not the man who took you, but the real me."

She studied me, weighing my words like they could tip a scale. Then, slowly, she reached for the cloth and began wiping her hands.

"I guess it wouldn't hurt to see the rest of the house," she said lightly, though the tension in her shoulders betrayed her. "And the surrounding grounds could be... interesting."

Hope stirred in my chest.

"Give me an hour to freshen up," she added, already turning to leave.

I watched her walk away. She said yes. And it was a start.

I waited for her in the foyer, standing just below the grand staircase.

When she descended the stairs, her presence hit me like a stormfront. She hadn't done much—hair pulled back, a fresh change of clothes, that same stubborn fire in her eyes, but goddess, she looked radiant. The mating bond tugged hard at my chest, urging me to reach for her, to pull her close. I didn't.

I simply smiled. "Ready?"

She nodded once, lips pressed in a firm line.

The house tour was short and efficient. A two-story structure with vaulted ceilings, large windows, rooms dressed in the expected elegance of an executive of Luna

Enterprise. She asked questions here and there, mostly about the art. I watched her fingers trace the edges of a carved banister, the way her eyes lingered on a painting longer than necessary. She was taking it in, piece by piece, like she was trying to understand the world I lived in.

But still she kept her distance.

I led her out to the side patio where the golf cart was waiting, already prepped. She hesitated, clearly weighing her options, then slid into the passenger seat beside me with that same stubborn grace.

We drove through the estate, the hum of the cart blending with the wind sweeping across the arid land. The terrain opened up into the wild beauty of the Arizona desert sunbaked earth, low hills, and the soft golden hues of brittle brush blooming between cacti.

"This part here," I said, slowing the cart beside a long stretch of wildflowers, "only blooms a few weeks in spring. But when it does, it's like the desert remembers how to sing."

She glanced at the flowers, then back at me. "Poetic," she murmured, but there was no sarcasm in her tone. Just a quiet sort of wonder.

I told her about the animals we sometimes saw: javelinas, desert hares, coyotes that sometimes followed the scent of the pack. She listened. Asked the names of certain plants. Even knelt once to touch the silvery leaves of a desert lavender bush, her fingers delicate against the rough texture.

She smiled.

Not at me.

At the place.

And goddess, I envied that smile.

She liked it all more than she wanted to admit. I could feel the flickers of genuine interest beneath her effort to stay guarded. But every time our eyes met, she looked away first. Every time my hand drifted a little too close, she stiffened. She wasn't ready.

She was fighting it. Fighting me.

She wasn't some weak-willed girl to fall into my arms because I offered her sunlight and flowers. She was proud, resilient, in her own way. She would come to me only when she chose to.

So I gave her space.

But every look, every breath, every heartbeat between us whispered the truth she was not ready to speak.

She was mine.

And one day, she wouldn't fight it anymore.

As we made our way back toward the house, the tension between us had softened just slightly, like desert stone smoothed over time by wind and sun. I was careful not to push. Let her lead with her curiosity.

When we stepped inside, I gestured toward the hallway on the east wing. "Would you like to see the library?" I asked, watching her reaction carefully.

That caught her interest. Her eyes lit up just for a second before she gave a small shrug, as if pretending it didn't matter that much.

"Sure," she said casually, but the way she stepped ahead of me betrayed her eagerness.

The library was one of the older rooms in the estate. Shelves stretched from floor to ceiling, filled with worn leather spines, gilded titles, and newer paperbacks tucked into corners like hidden treasures. The scent of old pages and cedar filled the air, rich and grounding.

She stepped inside slowly, eyes sweeping the room. Her fingers hovered over the shelves, brushing spines like they were sacred. "Do you actually read all these?"

"Some," I said with a half-smile. "But it's not just mine. My grandfather started the collection, and it's grown over generations."

She turned toward me, curiosity tugging at her features. "What kind of books are in here?"

"Everything, really. History, politics, strategy, mythology. A lot of supernatural lore, some true, some... less so." I watched her, and after a pause, added, "What about you? What kind of books do you like?"

Her eyes darted away, just for a moment. The faintest blush rose to her cheeks.

I tilted my head, intrigued. "Come on, don't hold back now."

She gave me a reluctant smirk, shaking her head before finally admitting, "Romance."

That blush deepened, and I felt my wolf stir, amused and very interested.

"Romance?" I echoed, stepping a little closer. "The steamy kind?"

Her eyes narrowed, but I could see the fluster beneath her mock-glare. "Don't judge. Some of them have really good plots."

I laughed, not mocking, never mocking. It was warm, full, unexpected even to me. "I'm not judging," I said, voice lowering just a touch. "I just didn't expect it."

She arched a brow. "What did you expect?"

"That you'd only read textbooks," I teased.

She rolled her eyes, but the corners of her mouth twitched up. "I like books where the woman wins in the end," she said, quieter now. "Where love doesn't mean giving up who you are."

Goddess.

I felt that. Deep and sharp.

"You'll find those here," I said gently. "If you ever want something to read... the library is yours."

She looked at me, still cautious, still holding herself together like a fortress made of glass, but there was a flicker of something else in her gaze.

After the tour, I led her outside once more, this time toward a shaded courtyard tucked behind the main house. The desert air was warm, softened by the late afternoon sun casting golden light across the sandstone tiles. The scent of blooming desert rose and creosote drifted on the breeze.

A table had been set for two beneath a wooden pergola, its slats laced with climbing vines and strings of soft lights that would glow come dusk. A gentle setup that was intentional. No silver platters or servants hovering. Just us.

My little wolf hesitated for the briefest moment, eyes scanning the scene like she was waiting for the catch. I didn't blame her. I was the enemy, after all.

But still, she stepped forward and took her seat.

"Not what you expected?" I asked, pouring two glasses of cool water infused with mint and citrus.

"I expected shackles," she said plainly, but her tone had softened into something almost dryly amused. "This is... suspiciously civilized."

I gave a low chuckle, settling across from her. "A man can evolve."

She didn't smile, not quite, but the edge of her mouth twitched in the way I'd started to recognize. Her version of interested but pretending not to be.

Lucía had outdone herself. The plates were simple but rich grilled meats, seasoned vegetables, warm bread, and yes, two of the *pastelitos* my little wolf had helped make earlier, waiting at the edge of the table like a secret reward.

We ate in near silence at first. Her every movement fascinated me. The way she tucked her leg beneath her, the flick of her fingers as she swept her hair over her shoulder, the way her lashes lowered when she sipped from her glass.

It wasn't until she took a bite of the pastelito, the flaky crust melting with the sweet guava filling, that her face finally softened.

"Damn," she muttered under her breath. "I'm never going to hear the end of this from Lucía."

I leaned back, smirking. "So you admit it?"

"Don't get cocky." But her voice was lighter, and for a heartbeat, she looked happy. The real kind. Unfiltered. And it knocked the air out of my lungs.

Then she caught me watching her, and just like that, the wall came slamming back up behind her eyes.

She wiped her mouth with the linen napkin, suddenly all composed again. "You keep doing this."

"Doing what?"

"All this. Trying to make me forget that I hate you."

Her words hit sharp, but fair.

I didn't flinch.

Instead, I leaned forward slightly, letting my voice drop into the space between us like a vow. "Then let me keep doing it. Until the day comes you don't want to remember. Until the day you can't."

Her lips parted slightly, but she said nothing. Just looked at me like she wasn't sure whether to run or reach for me.

Goddess, I hoped she'd do both.

Chapter 12

MAYA

First, baking with Lucía—sweet, innocent, almost domestic. Then this surprise outdoor dinner beneath twinkling lights, with laughter just waiting on his tongue and eyes that never stop watching me like I'm something sacred instead of stolen.

If I didn't know better, I'd think he was trying to win me over. But for what? He already has me. I'm here, aren't I? Captured. Kept. A reluctant guest in a gilded cage.

It's maddening.

The same man who bursts into rooms unannounced, who's seen more of me than any man ever should without invitation, now suddenly wants my consent? Now he plays the gentleman?

I grit my teeth, torn between fury and confusion. He's so damned inconsistent. One moment he was a brute with no boundaries, the next he was offering guava pastries and afternoon light like a lover in waiting.

And what's worse... my body is falling for it.

That traitorous ache beneath my skin, the way my wolf stretches inside me every time he's near, every time his voice dips low or his gaze lingers too long on my mouth. It makes no sense. I've been around handsome men before—strong, charming, Alpha-born but none of them stirred me like this. My wolf never purred for them. Never wanted to bare her throat in surrender.

But around Andrés...

I wanted to roll over and serve herself up as Maya à la carte.

It was humiliating.

My body hadn't cared that he was my enemy. That he had kidnapped me. My body had craved him like a drug I had never meant to sample, and now I couldn't stop wondering how it would have felt to give in.

And that... had terrified me.

Now that dinner was over, and he wasn't hovering with that piercing stare that saw far too much, I finally had a sliver of space to breathe. I slipped away from the courtyard, my steps quick, my heart faster, and headed straight for the one place that might give me peace—the library.

Books never judge. Never touch without permission. Never make your wolf moan with need.

Wandering through the rows of shelves, I let my fingers glide across the spines until one catches my attention—a romance novel I haven't read, the kind with a bold heroine and a dark, brooding male who tests her at every turn. And a lot of spice.

Sound familiar?

I settled onto the cushioned window seat, curling into the moonlight, and let the words pull me in. The author's words had been intoxicating—lush with emotion, sharp with tension. And when it came to the spice, she hadn't held back.

One scene in particular had made my pulse race, the way the male character had pressed the heroine against a wall, whispering filth in her ear while worshipping her body like a sacred altar.

I shifted in my seat, warmth pooling low, my thighs pressing together with slow, involuntary need.

And damn me...

I had imagined Andrés doing those things.

I had pictured his voice against my neck, his hands gripping my hips, his mouth murmuring promises and threats alike. I had imagined the way he would have pinned me with his golden eyes, how he would have made me beg before giving me everything I had never known I wanted.

And for a heartbeat, I hadn't fought it.

I had wanted it.

I snap the book shut and press it to my chest, heart pounding like I'd just been caught in the act.

What the hell is wrong with me?

He was the enemy. My captor. My tormentor.

And yet... every day I had spent there, I had been afraid I would stop remembering that.

And worse, I had been afraid I wouldn't care.

I stayed curled in the window seat, the book still open in my lap, though I hadn't read a single word on the last page. My fingers traced the worn edge of the paper, my mind replaying the last scene in vivid detail—his hands, his mouth, the way he whispered the dirtiest promises like sacred oaths.

Heat still simmered low in my belly, and I hated how easy it was to imagine him in the role. Andrés.

Gods, what was wrong with me?

I shifted uncomfortably, trying to shake the feeling... until something colder brushed down my spine.

A prickle of awareness.

That unmistakable sensation of being watched.

I didn't move at first, just slowly lifted my eyes from the page and scanned the library.

That's when I saw him.

In the far corner, half-shadowed by the tall shelves, Andrés sat in one of the leather chairs like he'd been there for a while. Silent. Still. Eyes locked on me with a hunger that stole the breath from my lungs.

His gaze wasn't casual.

It was possessive. Heated.

Dark golden eyes that flickered deeper, pupils dilating until they almost swallowed the light, turning his stare nearly black. His chest rose in slow, controlled breaths, nostrils flared like he was scenting the air between us.

Like he could smell the desire I was trying to bury.

"What are you doing there?" I snapped, hugging the book to my chest like it could hide the furious blush blooming on my cheeks. "You look like a creep."

A slow smirk curled his lips, and when he spoke, his voice was pure, sinful silk. "I was admiring you. You looked so... invested in that book."

I tightened my grip on the pages. "It's nothing. Just a story."

He stood, unhurried, a predator in no rush. "A romance, I'm guessing."

"I didn't say that."

"You didn't have to." He stopped a few feet from me, eyes burning into mine. "Your scent said everything."

I stared at him, mortified. "You're imagining things."

He tilted his head, gaze dragging over me like a caress. "Am I?" His voice dropped to a low murmur. "Your heart's racing. Your cheeks are flushed. Your thighs have been pressed together since page thirty-six."

My mouth parted in shock, no words coming out because he wasn't wrong.

He leaned in slightly, enough to make my wolf tremble with anticipation.

"Hand it over," Andrés said softly, eyes never leaving mine.

I tightened my grip on the book, heart thudding, every instinct screaming no, but not because I feared him. Because I feared what would happen if I did.

Still, something in his voice commanding, but velvet-smooth, compelled me to move. Slowly, like I was handing over something sacred, I extended the book to him.

He took it with a slow curl of his fingers, brushing mine. His gaze dropped briefly to the cover, and that damned smirk curved his mouth.

"Just a story, huh?"

I glared, but I didn't have a single comeback worth saying.

He opened the book to the page I had left off on the one where the heroine was being pinned to the bed, her lover worshipping her with his mouth, drawing her apart one slow, devastating stroke at a time.

And then, to my horror... he started reading.

Out loud.

His voice was low, deliberate, every word dripping with wicked tension.

"She gasped, his tongue sliding over her folds like he was savoring the taste of her, like she was his favorite sin..."

My breath caught.

He didn't laugh or mock the words—he honored them. Every syllable rolled off his tongue with sinful reverence, like he was living it, imagining it, offering it.

My thighs pressed tighter, a pulse awakening low in my belly. My skin felt flushed, alive, too sensitive.

Andrés flipped the page, his eyes never straying from me.

"She writhed beneath him, begging with nothing but breathless moans, her hands buried in his hair, holding on like she was afraid she'd fall apart without him."

I squeezed my eyes shut, as if that would stop the fire.

But it was already burning.

He could smell it. I knew he could. His pupils dilated again, nostrils flaring with a slow inhale that sent a shiver through my spine.

He closed the book gently, voice husky and intimate.

"Would you like me to reenact the scene in the book, little wolf?"

My eyes snapped open, meeting his.

My lips parted, breath trembling, but no words came out.

Because my body was screaming yes.

And my pride... wasn't strong enough to deny it much longer.

"I... I don't know," I whispered, barely able to breathe past the knot in my throat. The admission had hung between us, fragile and trembling like a leaf caught in a storm.

"You don't know," Andrés repeated, tilting his head as he studied me. His voice had been calm, but there had been a heat simmering just beneath it, molten and dangerous. "Or were you just too afraid to say yes?"

My heart had pounded. If I had been honest—truly honest—my body had been burning for his touch since that moment in the woods. Since he had punished me.

But I couldn't say it.

I couldn't admit that my body had been craving the very man who had taken me. My captor. What kind of person felt lust toward someone who should have been the villain in her story?

What had that made me?

"I know what you're doing," I had murmured, clinging to reason like a lifeline.

Andrés had moved closer, slow and deliberate, until I had felt the heat of his body against mine. His lips had found the shell of my ear, and his voice had dipped into that dangerous, intimate tone that slid straight down my spine.

"You're overthinking again," he had whispered. "Why did you always overthink, my wolf? Why couldn't you just... let go?"

Goosebumps had erupted across my skin, a shiver following close behind. My core had tightened, needy, achy, empty. The air around us had thickened with tension, with want, with possibility.

His breath had danced along my jaw. "I could have made that scene real for you. Right here, right now."

I had stiffened, trembling but not from fear. "Let me take off your panties," he had murmured, his voice raw velvet, "and kiss you where it aches the most."

My knees had threatened to give out, and still I hadn't moved. Every instinct had screamed at me to run, but my body? My wolf? She had leaned forward, pressing into him, begging without words.

He hadn't touched me yet.

But the anticipation of it had already been unraveling me.

And I hadn't known how much longer I could have pretended... that I hadn't wanted him to.

His breath was warm against my ear as he whispered, voice low and dark with promise.

"Close your eyes and imagine the scene. Relax... clear your mind. I'll take care of the rest."

I barely nodded, my body no longer mine. My wolf was at the surface now, needy, restless, starving, and all I could do was follow where she led.

He transferred me to the velvet sofa with a gentleness that stole the air from my lungs, like I was something fragile and sacred. Like he wasn't the man who'd taken me by force, but the one offering worship. My heart thundered, but I didn't resist. I couldn't. Every part of me wanted this.

His hands slid down my legs as he knelt between them, parting my thighs until I was completely open to him. His eyes met mine, golden and glowing, fierce with restraint and something deeper. Reverence. Hunger.

He reached for the hem of my shirt and lifted it slowly, dragging it over my head, baring my skin inch by inch. Then he leaned in and pressed a soft, reverent kiss to the center of my stomach.

"Don't overthink, my little wolf," he murmured against my skin, each word brushing heat along my flesh. "For once, let your desire and your wolf guide you."

His voice... Goddess, it curled around me like smoke, warm and rich and devastatingly seductive. My toes curled into the cushions as I exhaled shakily, letting go of the fight. Letting myself feel.

He continued his trail of kisses, slow and unhurried, down to the waistband of my pants. The sound of the button popping open was loud in the quiet room, and the zipper—that delicious little sound—felt like a line being crossed.

There was no going back.

And I didn't want to.

My body arched into his touch, desperate and slick with anticipation, my wolf purring under my skin like we were finally home.

He slid my pants down with agonizing patience, lips brushing over my hips, then lower, soft, teasing kisses along the insides of my thighs that made my breath catch and my whole body tremble.

It wasn't rough. It wasn't rushed. It was delicate. Intimate. The kind of touch meant to unravel me slowly.

He paused just above where I ached the most, his mouth hovering, his voice deep and sinful.

"Your scent…" he said, nose pressing into the soaked fabric between my legs, inhaling deeply, reverently. "It's an aphrodisiac. You make me feral."

A whimper escaped me, helpless and raw.

Warmth pulsed through my core, my panties damp with arousal, throbbing for his mouth, his tongue, him. My thighs trembled. My hands fisted in the cushions.

Goddess, what is this man doing to me?

My breath caught when his hands slid under the last remaining barrier between us. His fingers hooked into the waistband of my panties, tugging them down slowly, torturously, like unwrapping a forbidden gift. The air kissed my soaked folds, and I could feel how open I was for him, how ready.

Andrés let out a low, primal growl, more wolf than man, and it made my thighs press together instinctively.

But he wasn't having that.

"Don't hide from me," he whispered, coaxing my legs apart once more, kissing his way down until his mouth hovered just above my dripping heat. "You're perfect. Let me taste you."

Then he lowered his mouth.

The first slow drag of his tongue from my entrance to my clit made me cry out, my fingers flying to his hair, tangling in the thick, dark strands. His tongue was firm, warm, and precise, licking into me with a rhythm that built slowly, deliberately, like he was savoring every second.

Every flick. Every kiss. Every growl of pleasure against my core.

"Oh, Goddess..." I gasped, hips bucking when he latched onto my clit, sucking it softly, then harder just enough to make my vision blur.

He moaned into me, as if my taste alone could feed him, and I felt it deep in my belly. The way his hands gripped my thighs, strong but gentle. The way his tongue slid inside me, curling with a slow stroke that made me see stars. He wasn't just giving me pleasure, he was devouring me.

My wolf was howling inside me, claws dragging across the inside of my skin.

I was coming undone. Completely. My body quaked, back arching as the pleasure tightened, coiled, snapped.

"Oh, Andrés!"

The orgasm tore through me like wildfire, shattering me in waves. My hips rolled into his mouth, needing more, needing everything, and he gave it to me. He held me steady, licking me through every aftershock until I was trembling and panting beneath him, boneless, ruined.

He pulled back slowly, his mouth slick with me, his pupils still blown wide—predatory and satisfied. He kissed the inside of my thigh before meeting my gaze.

"You taste like honeysuckles," he murmured, voice rough and reverent.

And all I could think, in that haze of bliss and heat and wolf-deep need, was that I'd never be able to look at him the same again.

Because now he'd touched a part of me no one else ever had.

And the scariest part?

I wanted him to do it again.

Chapter 13

MAYA

When I said I would stop at nothing to gain my freedom, I never meant this.

I never imagined the price would be my purity.

Goddess... I thought I'd have to lie to him. Maybe kiss him, flirt with him, smile at the right moments, but I never, never thought it would go this far.

I never thought he'd touch my body with such reverence, such devastating hunger.

And worse, I never thought I'd let him.

Yet here I was. Skin still tingling. Heart still racing. My thighs aching from how tightly they'd clutched his head like salvation.

I knew what that act meant. The other she-wolves in my pack had whispered about it in giggles and hushed tones, long after patrols were over, when the fire crackled low and the moonlight danced over sleeping cabins. A male's mouth on a she-wolf's sex. They called it worship, claiming, devotion.

I always thought that wouldn't happen to me. Not until I was mated. Not until the right alpha came forward and declared his intent.

And now?

Now I wasn't pure.

Now I was... something else. Something less.

What male would want me now?

Especially now that my father was gone, and the Black Stone Pack was barely holding on. I was the only one who could restore it. If I could secure a powerful mating bond with a strong alpha or beta. I could lift us out of the ashes my father left behind.

But this? This ruined everything.

Staring up at the carved ceiling of the library, I tried to piece myself back together. The polished mahogany above me swirled like it was laughing at me, mocking me forever, thinking I could control this.

My body still pulsed with aftershocks, hips tingling with phantom licks and the deep echo of Andrés's voice as he whispered sweet nothings.

Goddess help me.

I let it happen.

Worse... I wanted it. Every second. Every sinful, earth-shattering second.

The deep, gravelly voice of the man responsible for my first orgasm cut through the haze.

"You're overthinking again," Andrés murmured from where he knelt on the rug, lips glistening like he'd just devoured something sacred. His eyes, gold and molten, looked impossibly smug, and the way he licked his bottom lip made heat bloom low in my belly all over again.

I wanted to scream.

At him. At myself. At the way my body still wanted more.

"You're unbelievable," I said through clenched teeth, shoving up onto my elbows.

"I try."

"I wasn't complimenting you," I snapped.

"I know." That damn smirk deepened. "Still sounded like one."

I groaned, dragging a hand down my face. You horny, traitorous whore of a body, stop it. My thighs clenched again without permission, his scent still all over me, branded into my skin.

"I am not overthinking," I said, pushing myself upright, trying to ignore the ache in my core. "This shouldn't have happened. I'm supposed to stay pure. Untouched. I was meant to secure a powerful alliance for my pack."

My voice faltered.

"This..." I gestured between us, my cheeks flushed, "ruins everything."

And then I did what I knew I had to do.

I stood, turning my back to him as quickly as I could, grabbing my panties and jeans. My fingers trembled as I pulled them back up, fabric scraping over still-sensitive skin.

Behind me, I heard him shift, felt his energy change. The heat, the cocky aura of victory... it dimmed.

When I glanced over my shoulder, his face was unreadable.

Except for his eyes.

Wounded.

And I hated that I noticed.

Hated that it mattered.

"I need to go to bed," I muttered, pushing past him, trying to ignore the way my body still buzzed from his touch.

I was nearly past him, almost to freedom, when his hand reached out and caught my wrist. Firm. Unyielding. His heat rushed up my arm, and I froze.

"What if I can secure an alliance for your pack?" he said, his voice low, serious. Deadly serious.

I turned back to him, my heart stuttering. "How could you possibly do that?"

His eyes darkened, pupils swallowing gold until they were endless black. "I'll mate you."

The words struck like thunder in my chest.

I blinked, stunned, searching his face for a joke. A smirk. A cruel twist.

But there was none.

I couldn't help it: I laughed. Loud and a little hysterical. "Are you serious?"

But Andres didn't crack a smile. His expression remained as steady and intense as ever.

"Oh my Goddess, you are serious," I said, blinking in disbelief. "Why in the hell would I ever want to mate with you? I don't trust you... you kidnapped me."

His jaw ticked. "And yet you're willing to choose a complete stranger—someone you know nothing about—for an alliance?"

"That's different," I snapped.

"No, it's not," he replied angrily. "You do know me, little wolf. You know I'd never hurt you. And I can give you a life you'd never have with some power-hungry Alpha's son. You'd be safe. Cared for. Respected."

My eyes narrowed. "I don't know shit. What I do know is that you're a moody, controlling asshole who takes what he wants regardless of anyone else's wishes."

I ripped my wrist from his grip, heart pounding with anger and something far more dangerous. Desire. Goddess help me, the air between us crackled.

He stepped in closer, his chest brushing against me. Firm, unyielding muscle, heat radiating from his covered chest like a temptation I was trying desperately to resist. My wolf stirred restlessly beneath my skin, wanting to rub against him like he was already hers.

"Besides taking you from your pack, what else have I done?" he asked, his voice low and velvety. "I've given you space. I haven't hurt you. I've protected you. I'm offering you everything, especially the one thing you need most: support for your people."

I tried to think of something else anything that could prove he wasn't right. But all that came out was, "You... you spanked me!"

My face flamed red.

He grinned, smug and absolutely infuriating. "That wasn't something bad, little wolf. You earned that punishment... and if I remember correctly, the smell of your arousal says you enjoyed it. So let's call that a good thing."

"Ugh!," trying to summon some dignity. "Even if I considered your offer, how do I know you can actually promise anything? You're not the Alpha; you don't have the authority to forge an alliance."

His gaze darkened, serious again. "I can. In two weeks, we'll return to Luna Stone. You'll meet the Alpha. We'll make it official. Until then..." He stepped even closer, his breath brushing my lips, voice husky. "Stop resisting me."

I placed my hands over his chest, and my heart pounded hard against my ribs as I stared at Andrés.

What did I really have to lose?

I was planning to manipulate him. To earn his trust just enough to slip through his fingers and find my way back home. That was the plan—the only plan.

But now...

Now he was offering me something I hadn't expected. A new path. One that didn't require lies, only to give myself to him. One that could save more than just me.

Become his mate, he said. Not just in name, not just for show, but for real. A union that would tie me to him—and to the Luna Stone Pack. His pack. His sister is the Alpha. That alliance could restore whatever my father destroyed.

Andrés could give them that. I could give them that.

If what he said was true, if this bond between us had the power to forge something strong enough to convince Luna Stone to back us... this could be everything.

I wouldn't have to pretend anymore. I wouldn't have to manipulate or run or fight tooth and claw for freedom.

But at what cost?

My freedom? My pride? My heart?

I let out a shaky breath, the weight of it all pressing down on my chest.

It's not like I had a line of suitors waiting to take my hand and save my pack. So what's stopping me?

"Fine," I said finally, staring him dead in the eye. "If your Alpha agrees to an alliance, then I'll consider making you my chosen mate."

The corner of his lip rose to almost a smile, but I held up a hand.

"And until then, I'll try to get to know you, but I'm not sleeping with you. I have to maintain some purity until my mating night."

A dark smile curved his lips. "Oh, little wolf, there are so many things we can do that don't involve deflowering you."

I rolled my eyes and turned away before my body betrayed me again. "I'm going to bed. It's late."

I strode out of the library, refusing to look back even though I felt his eyes burning into me the whole way. The walk to our room was short, but my thoughts were anything but calm.

Our room. Goddess, it sounded like we were mated already.

I hoped I was doing the right thing.

The next morning, the scent of roasted coffee and toasted bread pulled me into the kitchen, still bleary-eyed and tangled in sleep.

Andrés was already seated at the table, shirtless—of course—with a mug in one hand and a half-eaten croissant in the other, with that irritatingly perfect smirk curved his lips the moment he saw me.

"Morning, little wolf," he purred, setting down his mug.

I rolled my eyes but mumbled a "Morning" back as I slid into the seat across from him.

Lucia, bless her, was already loading the table with more food than a small army could eat.

Once I'd taken a few bites, Andrés reading something on his tablet, casually looking over me.

"I was thinking," he began casually, "we should work out together. Do some conditioning. Physical training is a great way to get to know each other."

I raised an eyebrow, suspicious. "Training?"

He nodded, without breaking contact with his tablet. "Sparring. Combat. Strength drills. We'll sweat. Test limits. Build trust."

"Or you just want to see me in tight clothes," I muttered under my breath before taking another bite of toast.

He stopped looking at his tablet and with a wide grin. "That's a bonus."

I sighed and leaned back, wiping my mouth with a napkin. "I guess I don't see the harm. And with all the food I'm being fed by Lucía, I probably need it."

He tilted his head, voice low and suggestive. "You have nothing to complain about when it comes to your body.

But I wouldn't mind watching you roll around on the mat."

I gave him a hard glare that only made his smile deepen.

Ugh. Why did his arrogance have to be so damn hot?

"Fine," I said, standing and pushing in my chair.

The basement of the house was nothing like I expected.

This was a fully-equipped private training center, sleek and spacious, lit with soft overhead lights that bounced off matte black walls and polished concrete floors. The scent of leather, steel, and something distinctly male filled the air.

Andrés walked ahead of me, shirtless, again. Punching bags hung from thick chains. A weight station sat in one corner. A sparring mat, wide and padded, spread out like a battlefield waiting for us.

"Just sparring," I reminded him again, tightening my ponytail with more force than necessary.

He turned, a lazy smirk pulling at his lips as his golden eyes swept over me.

We started with stretches, slow and methodical. I stayed focused on my breathing, even as I felt his eyes on me with every bend and shift of my body. When I glanced over, he was stretching too, his abs tight and glistening lightly with sweat. My wolf purred with interest.

Down, girl.

After the warm-up, we took our places on the mat.

"Ready?" he asked, his voice low, teasing.

I smirked. "Try to keep up."

We began circling each other, our feet light on the floor. It was slow at first. Dodging, mirrored steps, little taps that tested reflexes but didn't go deeper.

He was smooth, confident, every motion fluid and precise.

I feinted left, spun right, and landed a hand on his side. He looked at me almost impressed.

"Not bad." he said.

I smirked

He lunged in the next moment, not to strike but to test my reflexes. I dodged, twisted, and as I did, our bodies collided. Chest to chest. Breath to breath. My hand slapped against his bare skin to brace myself, and I could feel the heat radiating off him in waves.

His arms came around me instinctively, steadying me.

And suddenly, the sparring was forgotten.

I froze.

"You're holding back," he murmured, his mouth dangerously close to my ear.

I hated that he was right. I hated more how my body responded: eager, flushed, willing.

"Maybe I don't want to bruise your ego," I managed, though my voice sounded breathless even to me.

He chuckled, low and dark. "I'd let you bruise everything."

My heart pounded.

He leaned in just enough that his lips brushed my jaw—not a kiss, but something that made me ache all the same.

"Call it," he whispered.

"Call what?"

"This round. So I can do what I've been wanting to do since you stepped on this mat."

Before I could answer, he dipped closer, his nose tracing the shell of my ear, and every inch of me burned.

But I stepped back, body screaming at me to stay.

"Water break," I said, chest rising and falling with steady, controlled breaths. At least... that's what I hoped it looked like. In reality, my heart was pounding, and not just from the training.

Andrés grabbed a towel and a bottle from the mini fridge tucked into the corner of the basement. He tossed me one without a word, then opened his own bottle and took a long drink, water sliding down the curve of his throat, trailing over his bare chest.

I looked away quickly, taking a sip of my own, trying to cool the fire blazing low in my belly. My leggings felt tighter, my sports bra more suffocating. Damn him. My wolf was practically purring, brushing against the inside of my skin, too pleased by the sound of his voice, the heat rolling off him.

"This basement is impressive," I said, desperate for neutral ground. "You've got everything down here. Who even needs the outside world?"

Andrés leaned back against the wall, wiping his face with the towel before draping it over his shoulder. "Sometimes it's easier to bleed in private," he replied, eyes pinned on me. "Out there, people expect you to hold it all together. In here, you get to fall apart."

The raw honesty in his voice startled me. Was that a glimpse of the real him? The man behind the cocky smirks and arrogant commands?

Before I could figure out how to respond, he stepped closer, holding my gaze.

"You're good," he said. "Your form. Your control. But you're holding back."

"Maybe that's because I don't like being around arrogant, territorial wolves who think they can own people," I snapped, trying to shove down the truth in his words.

He didn't flinch. Just tilted his head, eyes dropping briefly to my lips before meeting mine again. "And yet you're looking at me like you want me to devour you."

My cheeks burned.

I hated that he was right.

Again.

He reached out and gently took the water bottle from my hand, setting it aside before his fingers trailed down the length of my arm. Not possessive. Not rough. Just there. Warm and grounding.

"I don't want to own you," he murmured, "I want to know you. All of you. Even the parts you hide from everyone else. Even the parts you don't think are worthy of being seen."

Goddess, stop looking at me like that.

I took a shaky step back, but his hand caught mine, , not forcing, just anchoring me.

"And if I prove I can give your pack what it needs?" he asked, voice low and rough. "Will you finally stop pretending you don't feel this?"

I swallowed hard. "I said I'd consider the mating bond. Not fall into your bed."

Andrés' expression shifted, not with disappointment, but with something deeper. He stepped closer, closing what little distance remained between us, his presence swallowing me whole. His voice dropped to something softer, more raw.

"I don't need you to fall into bed with me," he said. "I need you to give yourself a real chance... to get to know me."

His hand lifted, fingers brushing along my jaw before resting lightly under my chin. I swallowed hard, eyes darting away.

"It's hard to trust you," I whispered, my voice trembling despite how steady I wanted to sound. "You took me away."

His fingers curled gently, holding my chin still, forcing me to meet his gaze.

"I know," he said, his tone hoarse. "I did it wrong. I'm not a perfect man, little wolf... but I am your man, if you'll let me be."

I opened my mouth to respond, but the words tangled in my throat.

"I don't."

He didn't let me finish.

His hands came up to cradle my face, warm and firm, thumbs brushing the edges of my cheeks. His breath was uneven now, chest rising and falling like he was trying to hold something back—barely succeeding.

"Did it ever cross your mind," he said, voice rough with emotion, "that my wolf and I couldn't stay away from you? That the second I saw you, I was drawn to you? That the idea of you being far from me drove us both mad?"

His jaw clenched, his golden eyes burning with a wild kind of passion that shook something loose in me.

"I didn't plan to take you. But it was the only way I knew how to be close to you. His voice dropped even lower, reverent and aching. "But I'd do it again if it meant keeping you near."

I stared up at him, breath caught somewhere between disbelief and something more dangerous.

Because I believed him.

Every word was etched in his face, painted in the raw lines of his voice, carved into the tension of his hold on me.

And for the first time since he brought me here...

I wasn't sure if I wanted to run.

Chapter 14

MAYA

For the next two weeks, we kept up this strange routine of trying to get to know each other.

Every morning, I woke up in his bed, with his scent still on my skin and the lingering heat of his body beside me. After that night in the library, he started sleeping in his room again with me. No explanation, no conversation about it. It just happened.

And for a few seconds each morning, before I was fully awake, it felt... nice. Comfortable, even.

But then reality always hit.

I was still here.

Still his captive.

Still caught somewhere between wanting to push him away and not hating the way it felt when he was near.

Every morning we sat across from each other over breakfast, the sunlight pouring in, the scent of coffee and fresh bread filling the space between us. He asked about everything, like I was a puzzle he was desperate to solve. My favorite foods, favorite books, songs that made me cry, moments that made me laugh until my stomach ached. He listened to every word like it mattered. Like I mattered.

In return, he shared pieces of his world. The years he spent in college, the reckless nights with his pack, the fierce loyalty between them, the quiet moments with his mother, the stories of his siblings.

I hated how much I loved hearing about it all.

His life sounded full in the ways mine never had been. There was love, yes, but also freedom. Choice. Belonging. I found myself clinging to those stories like lifelines, imagining what it would've been like to grow up surrounded by that kind of warmth, that kind of safety.

With every word, every stolen look, something inside me began to unravel.

I kept telling myself it was strategy learning the enemy, playing the long game.

But the truth?

I was starting to want this. Not the kidnapping. Not the power imbalance. But him. The man who watched me like I was made of starlight, who touched me like I was sacred even when I hated him for it.

And my resistance... was fading.

Day by day, inch by inch, he was becoming the one thing I feared most.

Irresistible.

Then came the part of the day I hated most. The gym.

Andrés was obsessed with being fit, always ready to take on any opponent. He had a warrior's mentality, a need to be stronger, faster, deadlier. I had told him, more than once, that my father had started training me in combat when I was ten years old. But Andrés? He didn't care about words; he wanted proof.

"Andrés, I don't want to fight you," I said, arms crossed over my chest.

He smirked, that cocky, infuriatingly sexy grin curving his lips. "You didn't have an issue fighting me when we first met."

"That was different. I thought you were going to hurt me," I admitted.

His eyes darkened with something dangerous. "I am going to hurt you." He stepped closer, his voice a low, rough growl.

I lifted my chin, standing my ground. "I don't believe you."

And I meant it. Despite him keeping me here, despite his rough edges, Andrés had never truly hurt me. If anything, he had taken care of me in ways that I hadn't expected.

I was so lost in those thoughts that I barely caught the movement from my peripheral vision. Instinct kicked in. I dodged to the side just in time, throwing up my arm to block the punch he aimed at me. The impact vibrated through my bones, but I stood firm, eyes narrowing in disbelief.

"Hey, jerk! What the hell are you doing?" I snapped.

"Sparring with you," he said, rolling his shoulders. "Seeing what you've got."

His muscles flexed, his predatory stance making my blood heat in ways it shouldn't.

Andrés wanted a fight?

Fine.

I'd give him one.

I clenched my fists, rolling my shoulders as I glared at Andrés. His stood there in pure arrogance, his stance loose, almost lazy, like he wasn't even taking this seriously.

"You wanted a fight?" I snapped. "Fine. Let's fight."

He chuckled, the deep sound vibrating through my chest, making my wolf stir. "That's my girl."

Before I could react, he lunged. Fast. Too fast. I barely dodged his swipe, twisting out of reach as I sent a sharp kick toward his side. He caught my ankle easily, his grip firm but controlled.

"Sloppy," he taunted, tossing my leg aside like I weighed nothing.

I growled, heat prickling under my skin. He was toying with me. Again.

"Come on, princess. I thought you said your daddy trained you to fight?"

The way he said daddy made something inside me tighten. I hated how his words, his teasing, always hit somewhere deeper than just my pride.

I struck again, this time faking left before swinging right, my fist aiming for his ribs. He blocked it effortlessly, catching my wrist in one strong hand. His fingers squeezed just enough to make me feel it.

"Better," he admitted, his breath warm against my face. "But still not good enough."

I yanked my arm free and lunged, twisting my body to sweep his legs out from under him. He barely stumbled, shifting his weight to counter the move before grabbing my waist. In a blur, he had me spun around, my back colliding against his hard chest.

"Fuck you," I hissed, trying to elbow him, but he caught my arm, twisting it just enough to trap me against him.

"Not yet," he murmured in my ear.

Then he shoved me forward.

I barely had time to gasp before my chest hit the wall, his big hands pressing into my wrists, pinning them above my head. His body covered mine, heat radiating off him in waves.

And then I felt it.

Big, hard, and pressed right against my lower back.

My breath caught.

"Keep fighting me, little wolf," Andrés growled, his voice thick with dark amusement. "It turns me on."

My entire body tightened, my thighs clenching involuntarily as my breath came out ragged. His words sent a shockwave through me, need curling deep in my core.

I wanted to snap at him, to throw some sharp retort back in his face, but my brain wasn't working properly. Not with his scent surrounding me. Not with the weight of him keeping me caged, keeping me right where I suddenly didn't want to escape from.

For two weeks, we'd been playing this game. Two weeks of stolen touches, of inappropriate whispers against my skin, of him pushing me right to the edge of giving in, and my last-minute sanity stopping me from making the biggest mistake of my life.

I knew he wanted more.

And I didn't know how much longer I could fight it. My body was my worst enemy. A traitor.

Andrés moved away, his body no longer caging me in, but the ghost of his touch lingered, setting my skin ablaze. My heart pounded, my breathing uneven as I stared at him, this man who had taken me, restrained me and promised me the world, yet I could not forget he was my father's enemy and my kidnapper.

Instead, he just walked away, putting distance between us, his body stiff as if he was fighting some internal battle.

"Go shower," he said, his voice rough, controlled. "We leave today for Luna Stone Pack. It's time for you to meet my people."

The shift in energy was like a slap to the face. My mind, still fogged with lust, struggled to process what he was saying.

We were leaving?

I blinked, my back still against the wall as I watched him, waiting for something, anything. Some sign that he was going to come back, press me against the wall again, keep teasing me until I finally broke.

But he didn't.

Without thinking, I reached for him. My fingers just barely brushed against his arm before I realized what I was doing and quickly pulled away, stepping back like I had just been burned.

"Is everything okay?" I asked hesitantly, my voice softer than I wanted it to be.

Andrés caught the motion. His sharp brown eyes flicked to mine. He took a step forward, closing the space between us once more, his fingers grazing my jaw, tilting my chin up so I had no choice but to meet his gaze.

"Little wolf," he murmured, his tone like velvet over steel. "I'm going to be honest with you." His thumb brushed over my bottom lip, making me shiver. "It's getting very, very hard not to pin you against this wall and make you mine."

A sharp breath escaped me, my thighs pressing together as my body betrayed me.

He leaned in, his lips brushing against the corner of my mouth, teasing but not kissing me. "I want you so fucking bad..." His voice was rough now, edged with hunger. His other hand trailed down my arm, slow and deliberate, as if memorizing the feel of me. "But I want you to want me too. So I can't lose control."

His confession sent a rush of heat through me, my stomach twisting in a way I didn't understand.

All I could do was mouth the letter O, feeling my face burn with embarrassment.

Deep down, I did want him.

I knew that if he kept pushing, if he stopped holding himself back, I would cave. I would let him take everything.

My virginity.

The realization hit me like a bolt of lightning. I could not continue to have these intimate moments with him. I was drawn to him not just physically, it's deeper than that, something raw, and it terrified me.

This man—the one who pulled me from my pack and kept me miles away from them is the same man I was considering giving myself to completely.

That was insane.

And yet, my body ached for him.

Now we were leaving. We were going to his pack, to meet his people.

That had to be for the best.

The more people around us, the less risk of giving in to him and his temptation.

At least, that's what I tried to tell myself.

But as I looked up at Andrés, at the way his jaw was clenched, his hands curled into fists at his sides as he fought the same desire I was drowning in, I realized I didn't know how much longer he would fight the desires himself.

Stepping back into the bedroom, I froze.

There were bags everywhere, lined up neatly across the edge of the bed and spilling onto the nearby bench. Designer names I recognized, some I didn't. Sleek boxes. Shimmering tissue paper. Dozens of them.

"Where did all of this come from?" I asked, eyebrows drawn as I turned to Lucía, who was busy fluffing the pillows like nothing was out of the ordinary.

She didn't even glance up. "Andrés brought them. Had them delivered this morning."

My stomach flipped.

"For me?" I asked, unsure if I was annoyed, confused, or... flattered.

She nodded. "Said it was time you had your own wardrobe."

I walked over slowly, tugging one of the bags open. Inside was a soft, deep green dress. I reached in further—more dresses. Jeans, shirts in every color, soft sweaters, casual tops, jackets. Even lingerie.

My face heated.

I moved to the next bag. Shoes: flats, boots, heels, sneakers. Every style. Every shade. Like someone had gone shopping for a woman they actually knew.

I didn't know what to say.

He'd given me an entire wardrobe. For someone who was supposedly just his captive, this felt... personal.

Too personal.

Why would he do this? Why now?

My chest tightened as I stared at the pile of luxury and thought, What the hell is he trying to do?

It felt... thoughtful.

And that only made me more suspicious.

I turned toward Lucía, who was already unpacking the bags and folding things neatly into an open suitcase.

"Why would he do this?" I asked, crossing my arms. "Why spend so much on me?"

Lucía gave me a side glance but didn't stop folding. "Because whether you want to admit it or not, you are his. In Andrés, eyes you are his mate, and providing for you is part of his instinct."

I scoffed. "Right. Providing for the girl he kidnapped."

Lucía didn't rise to the bait. "You need clothes," she said simply. "You're leaving for Luna Stone. You'll be meeting the Alpha and the rest of Andrés' family. You should have something to wear that makes you feel strong. Prepared."

That pulled me up short.

Meeting the Luna Stone Pack.

Andrés's pack. His home. The place where this so-called alliance would either happen... or fall apart.

I sat slowly on the edge of the bed, my fingers curling into the soft fabric of one of the new dresses. "What if they say no?" I asked quietly. "What if they don't want to help Black Stone? My pack has nothing to offer right now. No strength, no leader."

Lucía paused in her packing and looked at me.

Her expression softened.

"That's not true," she said. "You're what your pack has. A Luna-born, strong in ways you don't even realize yet. Andrés knows it. His sister will see it, too."

I swallowed hard. "But what if he doesn't?"

"They will," she said gently. "But don't let fear stop you before you even walk through the door. You're not doing this alone."

I looked down at the clothes again. All these pieces, carefully chosen. Not flashy or loud. Not meant to cage or impress, but to fit.

My chest tightened with something I couldn't name.

Maybe this wasn't just about control or power anymore. Maybe, just maybe, Andrés was trying to help.

I sighed, glancing around the room that had become my strange sanctuary for the past two weeks. It was still a cage, but at least Lucía had made it feel less like one.

"I'm going to miss you," I said softly, my fingers smoothing over a silky blouse.

Lucía paused, looking up at me with warm brown eyes. "Oh, *mija*," she clucked her tongue, placing a hand over her heart. "Don't start with that, or I'll cry."

I smiled, though my chest ached a little. "I'm serious. You've been so good to me. You didn't have to be, but you were."

Lucia scoffed, waving a hand as if brushing away my words. "Of course I did. You're special to Andrés, and that makes you special to me."

I hesitated, biting my lip. "Am I special to him?"

Lucía stopped folding, giving me a knowing look. "Oh, *chiquita*, do you even have to ask?" She reached out, squeezing my hand. "Andrés has never acted this way with anyone. Never."

That sent a strange warmth through me, but I pushed it down. Instead, I focused on what was truly important.

"You've made this whole... situation bearable, Lucía. You didn't have to be so kind, but you were. And your food?" I sighed dramatically. "I'm really going to miss your cooking."

She laughed, patting my cheek. "Now that I do believe."

"I'm serious!" I protested, grinning. "I think I might go into withdrawal without your empanadillas."

Lucía chuckled, shaking her head. "You know, the way to a wolf's heart is through their stomach. Maybe Andrés should be the one worried about you missing my cooking more than him."

My face heated. "Lucia!"

She winked. "What? I'm just saying, mija... You and Andrés, you think you're dancing around this thing between you, but I see it. I smell it. And trust me, so does he."

I swallowed, suddenly feeling too warm. "We should finish packing."

Lucía smirked, but she let it go, humming again as she folded another shirt.

I glanced at the doorway, my heart feeling heavier than I wanted to admit.

I was leaving the strange safety of this room, of Lucía's kindness, of this controlled environment, and going to his pack's territory... the unknown with people that may not be nice to me. Everything was going to change.

Andrés slammed the trunk shut with finality, the sound slicing through the air like a blade. With it came the weight of reality I was leaving. Leaving this place that had become a strange limbo between captivity and comfort.

I swallowed hard, my emotions tangled in a messy knot of fear, excitement, and something deeper I wasn't ready to name.

I had never been to another pack before.

I didn't know what to expect.

Would they welcome me? Hate me? See me as an outsider?

The thoughts swirled in my mind, thick and overwhelming, but before I could sink too deep into them, a pair of warm arms wrapped around me, pulling me into a tight embrace.

Lucía.

Her scent—flour, herbs, something sweet and familiar filled my nose as she held me close. My fingers clung to the back of her sweater, gripping her like she was my anchor.

Oh, how I wished she could come with me.

Tears burned my eyes, spilling over before I could stop them. A quiet sob escaped, and I hated how vulnerable I felt, how much I was going to miss this woman who had shown me nothing but love and kindness.

Lucía pulled back just enough to cup my face, her thumbs wiping away the tears that kept falling.

"*No llores, nena*," she whispered, her voice warm, soothing. "We will see each other again. *Esta es tu casa,* come whenever you want."

Her words cracked something in my chest, making the tears fall faster. I nodded, unable to find my voice.

Home.

How strange that a place I had been taken to against my will had started to feel like something close to that.

A heavy presence lingered behind me, and I knew without looking that it was Andrés. His silence was thick, unreadable. When I turned, his face was serious, his expression unreadable, his usual mask of stoic control.

That look always unsettled me.

It made it hard to tell what he was thinking, what he was feeling.

It made me doubt everything.

"Let's go, little wolf," he said, his voice low, steady. "It's time for us to go home."

Home.

He said it so easily, like it was already decided. Like the Luna Stone Pack was my home, like I had no choice in the matter.

And maybe I didn't.

Lucía hugged me one last time, whispering something soft in Spanish that I was too emotional to process. Then, reluctantly, I pulled away and climbed into the SUV.

The door shut beside me, sealing me inside.

Andrés slid into the driver's seat, his large hands gripping the wheel, his jaw tight.

The air between us felt charged, thick with all the words we weren't saying.

I looked out the window as the car pulled away, watching as Lucía grew smaller in the distance, until she was nothing more than a warm memory.

I didn't know what awaited me at Luna Stone Pack.

Chapter 15

MAYA

We had been on the road for six hours. Six long, silent hours where my mind ran wild with anxiety and unspoken fears. The unknown had always unsettled me, and now it wrapped around me like a suffocating blanket. I hated not knowing what awaited me at Luna Stone Pack. Would they accept me? Reject me? Would I ever be able to leave if I wanted to?

All I had was time. And time was dangerous when it let my thoughts spiral into worst-case scenarios.

"Little wolf, what's going through that brain of yours?" Andrés asked, his deep voice cutting through my storm of thoughts. He didn't look at me, his focus still on the road.

I crossed my arms, sinking into the seat. "Nothing. I'm just here, doing nothing, in a car, heading to an unknown pack," I said, trying and failing to sound indifferent.

Andrés exhaled, a low rumbling sound vibrating through the car, before taking the next exit toward a rest area. My brows pulled together.

Why were we stopping?

We had just fueled up not too long ago. Did he need to pee? It didn't make sense.

But he didn't stop at the main building. Instead, he kept driving, taking us past the rest stop, past the clustered parking spaces, until he reached the back of the lot where the woods stretched out like a dark, endless expanse.

Something inside me tensed.

My hand curled into the seatbelt as I glanced at him. "Where are you taking us?"

"You'll see." His voice was unreadable, firm.

A prickle of unease ran down my spine.

The SUV rolled to a stop in the last parking space, the world around us still and eerily quiet. Andrés unbuckled his seatbelt and stepped out, his movements fluid, controlled. Within seconds, he was at my door, pulling it open.

I hesitated, my pulse kicking up.

Why did this feel... different?

His gaze locked onto mine, intense, unyielding. "Come."

I hesitated, uncertainty coiling in my stomach. "Andrés"

"Now, little wolf."

My breath hitched. The dominant tone in his voice sent an unwilling shiver through me, but there was something else beneath it. Something primal.

Swallowing hard, I reached for his hand. The moment our skin touched, a spark ignited between us, but he didn't react. He just held firm, leading me toward the trees.

The deeper we went, the heavier the silence became. I kept asking where we were going, but he didn't answer. He just kept walking, dragging me further into the woods with unwavering determination.

Panic clawed at my chest. My heart pounded faster, the unfamiliar surroundings making my instincts scream.

"Stop," I said, yanking at his grip. He didn't let go.

I dug my heels into the ground. "Stop!"

With a hard yank, I ripped my hand free, my breath coming out in short, uneven pants.

"Where the fuck are you taking me?" I demanded, my body coiled tight with adrenaline.

Andrés turned slowly, his eyes dark, piercing, his expression unreadable.

"You need to shift."

I blinked, thrown off by the sudden shift in conversation.

"What?"

He crossed his arms, his stance firm. "You think I haven't noticed? In the last two weeks, you've shifted twice. That's not normal. You're wound up, and I can feel it."

My pulse hammered.

I scoffed, folding my arms over my chest. "I'm used to not shifting. It's not a big deal."

Andrés' jaw tightened, his eyes darkening with frustration. He exhaled sharply, running a hand through his hair as he took a step closer.

"That's not how it works, little wolf," he said, voice rough, edged with authority. "You can't just keep ignoring your wolf. She's part of you. Keeping her locked away like that? It's dangerous."

I crossed my arms, my heart still racing from the way he had dragged me into the woods without a word. "I managed just fine in college." I clenched my jaw, looking away. "In college, there was nowhere for me to shift." I exhaled sharply. "So, I got used to keeping my wolf in. She's used to it."

Andrés' nostrils flared. His muscles tensed like a coiled spring.

"You're not supposed to suppress her," he growled. "That's why you're on edge."

I swallowed hard, my fingers curling into fists.

"I'm wound up because I'm scared, Andrés," I snapped, my voice breaking at the end. "I'm scared of going to your pack. I don't know what's waiting for me there."

Andrés took another step closer, his presence over-powering. "You need to let go," he said, voice dropping to something almost coaxing. "Shift. Run. Stop fighting yourself."

Before I could react, he grabbed my wrist and pulled me flush against him, my body colliding with his hard chest. His scent wrapped around me, making my breath hitch.

"You're scared," he murmured, his lips brushing against my ear, sending a shiver down my spine. "You're scared of yourself."

I swallowed hard, my heartbeat thudding against my ribs. "I am not," I whispered, but we both knew it was a lie.

Andrés' fingers trailed down my bare arm, leaving a path of heat in their wake. "You're holding back," he continued, his voice rougher now, almost challenging. "You've been holding back since the moment I met you. But you won't here. Not anymore."

I opened my mouth to argue, but his next words stopped me cold.

"If you don't shift willingly, I'll make you."

A growl rumbled from deep in his chest, and something about it sent a primal thrill through me.

"You wouldn't," I challenged, my chin lifting.

A slow, wicked smirk spread across his lips. "You want to test me, little wolf?"

The way he said it, low and full of dark promise, sent heat pooling between my thighs.

Damn him.

Damn the way he got under my skin.

Damn the way my wolf wanted him to force my hand, to push me past my limits until I had no choice but to give in.

I took a shaky breath, fists clenched. "Fine," I snapped. "I'll shift. But not because you made me. Because I want to."

Andrés just grinned, stepping back and gesturing to the open woods around us.

"Then show me."

I swallowed hard, my pulse hammering in my throat as I reached for the hem of my shirt. Andrés didn't look away, his dark eyes watching my every move, devouring me. His gaze burned over my skin, dragging up and down my body like a touch, making my breath hitch.

I shouldn't feel this way.

I shouldn't be trembling with both fear and desire under his stare.

But I was.

This was the same reaction I had been battling for the last two and a half weeks, ever since he took me away from home. The way my body responded to him without hesitation, without resistance, was something I couldn't control. And I hated it.

And I loved it.

One by one, I stripped off my clothes, my skin prickling with the cool forest air. My heart pounded, my breath shaky as my bare skin was exposed to him, inch by inch.

Andrés didn't move. He just stood there, watching, his jaw tight, his chest rising and falling in a slow, controlled rhythm.

The hunger in his eyes was unmistakable.

I should've felt vulnerable under his stare, but instead, a rush of arousal shot straight to my core, heat pooling low in my belly.

Once I was completely naked, he took a step toward me.

The air between us crackled, thick with something primal and electric.

His large hand lifted, his fingers tracing the curve of my cheek before gliding down to my chin, tilting my face up to his.

"You are beautiful," he murmured, his voice rough, dark.

I shivered.

His touch was deceptively gentle, but there was something dangerous in the way he looked at me, something possessive, something that told me he was barely holding himself back.

"Your body," he rasped, his fingers trailing down my throat, brushing over my collarbone, lower, lower until they reached the swell of my breast, his fingertip circling my nipple with agonizing slowness. "The most delicious temptation."

A gasp slipped past my lips.

My body betrayed me, arching into his touch, my nipples tightening under his teasing fingers. A sharp pang of need twisted low in my stomach, a heat igniting between my legs that I couldn't ignore.

Andrés saw it.

He felt it.

And he liked it.

His smirk was full of dark satisfaction as he leaned in, his breath warm against my ear.

"Shift," he growled, his voice thick with command.

I trembled.

"...And run."

His voice sent a shockwave through me, my wolf rising to the surface, clawing to break free.

I sucked in a sharp breath and let go.

The shift came fast, violent, my wolf surging forward like a dam finally giving way. The crack of bone, the burn of transformation, the fire that spread under my skin—it was freedom and fury all at once.

And then, I ran.

The forest welcomed me like an old lover. The scent of pine, wildflowers, and damp earth filled my lungs as I sprinted beneath the rising moon. My paws tore into the earth, fast and unrelenting. The tension that had been strangling me for days snapped like brittle glass.

But I wasn't alone.

Behind me, a sound rumbled low and dangerous. A growl, not just any growl. His.

Andrés.

He shifted.

That growl tore through the woods, echoing like a promise, like a warning. My wolf pricked her ears, heart racing with something other than fear. She wanted the chase. She wanted him.

I pushed harder, weaving between the trees, breath hot, limbs pumping. I could feel him closing in the ground shook beneath his powerful strides, his massive black wolf a blur of menace in my periphery.

He was faster.

Stronger.

And my wolf? She was drunk on the danger, the thrill of it.

A startled, breathless laugh escaped me as I ducked beneath a low branch only to be ripped off course as a heavy weight slammed into my side. We tumbled together, dirt and leaves flying as he pinned me down. My back hit the ground with a dull thud, his powerful body locking mine beneath him.

His snarl was low, primal, vibrating through my chest as his muzzle nipped at my neck, not deep enough to hurt. Just enough to stake his claim.

My wolf stilled beneath him, trembling in something far more delicious than fear.

Andrés shifted first, and then I followed, the shift pulling a soft gasp from my lips as bare skin met the crisp night air.

Then he was there human, but no less dangerous. His muscles flexed as he hovered over me, heat radiating off him in waves. His hands caught mine, pinning them above my head like shackles of fire. His hips settled between my thighs, and when he ground down, I felt him thick, aching, restrained only by the sliver of control he hadn't yet surrendered.

His eyes, burning, wild, met mine. "Gotcha, little wolf?"

I opened my mouth, but the words died as his lips crashed into mine. His kiss was brutal, starved, like he was devouring every lie we'd told ourselves about not wanting this.

But just as the world began to blur and tilt into something unstoppable, he broke the kiss.

He pressed his forehead to mine, his breath ragged. "You're not ready," he whispered, voice frayed with restraint and something dangerously close to affection.

"Your body wants me... But I won't take you like this. Not until your heart wants me too."

I stared up at him, breathless, trembling. "No," I whispered, though I wasn't sure if it was denial or defiance.

A faint smile ghosted across his lips, dark and knowing. "That 'no' tasted a lot like 'not yet.'"

Then, he pushed off me, rising like a predator bored with the kill. "Come on," he said, already shifting back into his massive wolf. "Let's run."

He took off, a black shadow darting through silver moonlight.

And my traitorous feet followed.

An hour later, we emerged from the trees, bodies humming with spent adrenaline, dirt smudging my skin and tangled leaves clinging to my hair. I was filthy.

But goddess, I was sated.

The run was exactly what I needed, but not what my body wanted. My body wanted the brush of his mouth, the press of his body, just like back in the woods.

Andrés wanted me. But more than that—I wanted him.

Back in the car, I shifted in my seat, forcing myself to focus on the road ahead instead of the delicious ache still lingering in my body. The last thing I needed was for Andres to sniff out just how easily my body still responded to him.

But from the way his fingers flexed on the steering wheel, his knuckles slightly white with tension, I had a feeling he already knew.

The drive stretched on, four more hours of silence thick with unspoken tension. The only sounds filling the SUV were the low hum of the engine and the occasional rustling of trees as we sped past the endless stretch of wilderness.

My body still tingled, sensitive from the way Andrés' touch made me feel, and despite my best efforts, my mind kept drifting back to the way his mouth had felt on mine.

I stole a glance at him from the corner of my eye.

His grip on the steering wheel was tight, his knuckles slightly pale. His jaw was clenched, his expression unreadable, but I knew that look. He was holding himself back.

Why?

I didn't ask.

Instead, I focused on the road ahead, trying to suppress the lingering heat in my body. But it was impossible to ignore the way the air between us felt thick, charged like a storm waiting to break.

And then, finally, we crossed the threshold.

Luna Stone Pack.

The moment we passed the outer perimeter, I felt it: a powerful shift in energy, the distinct weight of pack territory pressing in around me. My wolf stirred restlessly, sensing unfamiliar territory, new wolves.

We slowed as we reached a guarded checkpoint. Two tall, broad-shouldered men stepped forward, their scents radiating dominance, but their eyes instantly flicked to Andrés, recognizing him.

One of them, who had short-cropped brown hair and a jagged scar running down his left cheek, nodded in greeting. "Welcome home, Andres."

The other guard, a younger man with sharp green eyes, gave me a curious once-over but said nothing.

Andrés waved his hand in acknowledgment as he rolled the SUV forward.

The further we drove into his pack's land, the more my anxiety clawed at me. I didn't know what to expect. I have never been in another pack.

The pack house came into view—a sprawling community nestled in the valley, surrounded by forest and greenery. The houses were more rustic but elegant, with winding dirt roads connecting them. There were training grounds, a marketplace, and in the distance, a massive packhouse stood like the heart of it all.

We continued driving past all the buildings, going deeper into pack territory.

Andrés finally slowed to a stop in front of a house, cutting the engine.

For the first time in hours, he turned to look at me. His eyes locked onto mine, steady and unreadable.

"Welcome home, little wolf," he murmured.

Chapter 16

MAYA

I sat frozen in my seat, my body locked in place, my mind racing a hundred miles an hour.

My heart pounded so hard it felt like it was about to rip out of my chest and land in my lap.

"Little wolf," Andrés murmured, his voice low, soothing. "Calm down. There's nobody home except you and me. You're safe."

I swallowed thickly. "O-Okay."

It was the only thing I could manage before he pulled the keys from the ignition and stepped out of the SUV. I watched as he rounded the hood, his movements smooth and confident, coming toward my door.

But before he could reach me, all hell broke loose.

Cars pulled up beside us, doors slamming. The front door of his house swung open, and people started pouring out.

Oh, Goddess.

I could barely process what was happening before my door was wrenched open and a woman—a complete stranger—was pulling me out of the SUV with surprising strength.

"Oh! You must be her!" she gushed, squeezing me into a hug that felt strangely familiar and warm, motherly, like Lucía's. "I'm so happy to finally meet you! I'm sorry, I don't even know your name!"

I was too stunned to respond.

Another voice cut through the chaos, firm yet teasing.

"Mama, you're scaring her. Back off."

The older woman was gently pushed away, and I was faced with a stunning she-wolf with strong, regal features and dark brown eyes that held a mischievous glint.

"Hey," she said, offering a smirk and a handshake. "I'm Sofía, Andrés' older sister and Alpha." She winked at me before glancing at her brother, rolling her eyes at his exasperated expression.

"I'm sorry for the ambush," she continued, her tone playful yet sincere. "*Mama* sometimes forgets that people have boundaries."

Still caught in a whirlwind of overstimulation, I numbly took her hand, shaking it as if I were in some kind of surreal dream.

A flicker of panic clawed its way up my throat.

Andrés must have sensed it because he immediately stepped forward, his presence like a solid wall between me and the overwhelming group of wolves surrounding me.

"Enough," he commanded, his voice deep and full of authority. "We just got here, and we're tired." His tone left no room for argument. "We'll meet you all for breakfast tomorrow. Then we'll talk."

The crowd murmured their disappointment, but slowly retreated.

I glanced at the others, taking them in properly now. But it was the older man who held my attention the most.

He was a mirror image of Andrés, only older, rougher, with streaks of silver in his wavy black hair.

Their resemblance was undeniable.

Andrés' father.

The former Alpha.

"Son," the older man said, his voice heavy, authoritative. "We need to speak. Now."

Andrés didn't flinch. "Let me settle her in first. I'll meet you in my office in a few minutes."

His father gave a stiff nod before walking away, leaving only the scent of dominance and expectation behind.

Andrés turned to me, his hand gripping my wrist not forcefully, but firm, as if he knew I was one wrong move away from bolting.

And he was right.

My wolf was screaming at me to run.

I barely registered the inside of the house as he led me upstairs, guiding me down a long hallway before stopping at a massive wooden door.

He pushed it open, revealing a dimly lit bedroom that smelled unmistakably like him: woodsy, male.

"This is our room," he said, his voice softer now but still edged with that possessive tone. "Get yourself ready for bed. I'll be back in a minute. I need to talk to my dad."

And just like that, he was gone, the door clicking shut behind him.

I stood there for a long moment, staring at the closed door like it might swing back open any second. But it didn't.

I turned in a slow circle, taking it all in. The place was massive: dark walls, warm lighting, a king-sized bed that I definitely wasn't ready to climb into. His scent was everywhere. And infuriatingly comforting.

I hated that I noticed that.

Crossing the room, I found a window and looked out. The forest stretched endlessly, silver under the moonlight. My wolf perked up, itching to run. It'd be so easy. Shift, bolt, vanish into the trees before anyone knew I was gone.

But then what?

Run and lose the only chance I had to actually help my pack? Lose the opportunity to maybe just maybe form an alliance with Andrés and the Luna Stone Pack?

My stomach twisted.

I didn't ask for any of this. I didn't want to be kidnapped, claimed, and dragged across the states to another pack. But if I left now, what would that say about me? What kind of leader just runs?

I sighed, glancing around the massive room, feeling both out of place and a little irritated. He could have at least told me where the damn bathroom was before he left me here.

I tore my gaze away from the bed and moved toward one of the doors, expecting to find the bathroom. Instead, I stepped into a walk-in closet the size of a small boutique.

My mouth fell open.

It was ridiculous row after row of neatly arranged suits in varying shades of black, navy, and gray, each one pressed and hung with precise care. A wall of color-coordinated dress shirts, ties, and expensive shoes completed his side of the closet.

This man likes to dress to impress.

Everything was perfectly organized, no sign of clutter or chaos. Definitely not like me.

Then my gaze drifted to the other side of the closet.

My stomach twisted as I took in the racks of women's clothing. Dresses, jeans, shirts, shorts, workout gear—everything. Even delicate gowns hung there as if waiting for a special occasion. And the shoes... goddess, the shoes: heels, sandals, boots, sneakers.

I stepped forward, running my fingers along the fabrics.

It was all my size.

The realization hit me like a punch to the gut.

Did Andrés buy all of this for me?

I swallowed hard, my chest tightening. Why? Was it his way of making me more comfortable here?

I tried not to dwell on it, instead moving toward the dresser tucked into the back of the closet. The moment I pulled open the first drawer, my cheeks burned.

Lingerie.

Not just any lingerie—delicate, lacy, sinfully sheer sets in deep reds, blacks, and blues. Satin nightgowns, soft pajama shorts, lace-trimmed camisoles... everything meant to tease, to tempt.

My fingers trembled as I traced over the fabric.

Did he expect me to wear these for him?

My body heated at the thought. Damn him.

Shaking my head, I grabbed a pair of soft silk shorts and a matching camisole, deciding I'd rather not think about Andrés watching me in one of those lace sets.

With the sleepwear in hand, I turned back toward the door.

Now, I just needed to find the bathroom before he got back.

And before my mind ran too wild with dangerous, forbidden thoughts.

ANDRES

I walked into my office to find my father already seated in one of the leather chairs across from my desk. His posture was relaxed, but his eyes—those sharp, calculating eyes—were locked on me with quiet intensity. He probably didn't like that I made him wait.

Leaving my little wolf alone in our room had felt like tearing out a piece of my own soul. She'd looked so small, in my big room, fear and confusion still lingering in her eyes. But this conversation couldn't wait.

I exhaled sharply, rolling my shoulders to release the tension coiled beneath my skin. "Alright, Dad. I'm here. What's so important that it couldn't wait until tomorrow?" My voice carried a bite, more irritation than I intended.

He raised a brow at my tone but let it slide. "We need to talk about your future and hers. You've been gone for almost three weeks. Did you come up with a plan to win her over? "

My jaw clenched.

He wasn't wrong.

I dragged a hand down my face, my voice low. "Yes. We've come to an agreement. She'll mate with me in exchange for an alliance between Luna Stone and Black Stone."

The words left a bitter taste in my mouth. This wasn't how I imagined claiming my mate. Well, honestly I never imagined having a mate. But it was the only way she'd let herself be mine for now.

My father studied me for a long, silent moment before finally speaking. "Andrés... why force an agreement? She'll figure out you're fated mates soon enough. When that happens, it'll be over. No more resistance."

I walked to the bar cart in the corner and poured two fingers of whiskey into crystal glasses. The burn steadied my hands as I passed one to him and settled into my chair.

"She was raised differently than us," I said quietly. "Her pack taught her that a woman's duty is to serve the pack. As the daughter of a high-ranking wolf, she thinks she has no choice but to have an arranged mating."

My father swirled the amber liquid in his glass. "And you think offering her help from our pack will convince her?"

"I think," I said, voice tight, "that giving her a way to help her people will ease her guilt. It'll let her accept our bond without feeling like she's betraying them. I want her to see that being with me doesn't mean turning her back on her pack."

He nodded slowly, the respect in his gaze unmistakable. "You've always been a good leader with sound judgment. If this is what it takes to strengthen your bond, you have our support. It might even make her forget you kidnapped her."

A reluctant smirk tugged at my lips. "Goddess knows I'll need all the help I can get with that woman."

He laughed.

"In a few days," I said, setting my glass down, "it'll be her birthday. I want the agreement with Sofía and Black Stone finalized before then. I want her to have peace, something solid she can hold on to. A gift not just of loyalty... but of freedom."

My father's eyes gleamed with pride. "Then let's make it happen. How can I help?"

"You can help me by talking to Sofía," I said, "I know she's still processing everything that Alpha George did to her. She might hate the Black Stone Pack, and she has every right to. But if she could look past that pain and help the ones still trapped there... that would mean everything."

My father's gaze softened, just a flicker. "Alright. I'll see what I can do."

"Thank you." I paused, hesitating before admitting the part that had been clawing at me for days. "There's something else...she doesn't know what a good pack looks like,"

I continued, jaw tightening. "All she's ever known is the hell she grew up in. I need her to see that being part of our pack is good."

My father studied me for a long, silent moment, then set his glass down with finality. "Then we'll show her. We'll treat her like one of us. Like family. Let her feel that our pack is where she truly belongs."

A weight lifted from my chest.

"Thank you, Dad," I murmured, exhaling a breath I hadn't realized I'd been holding.

He clapped a hand on my shoulder, his eyes full of something rare pride. "Make her feel safe, son. And she'll choose you. Not out of obligation or bond... but out of love."

As soon as he left, I wasted no time heading back to my room, already imagining her curled up in bed, smelling like me, wrapped in my scent.

But when I opened the door, the bed was still empty.

Then I heard the soft sound of running water.

A slow smirk stretched across my lips.

My little wolf was in the shower.

Heat flared in my chest, my wolf instantly prowling forward with interest.

The glass shower door was fogged up, but I could still see her silhouette through the haze, her delicate curves, the way she tilted her head back beneath the stream of hot water, fingers working shampoo into her thick, red curls.

She had no idea I was here.

I stepped inside the steamy bathroom without a word, the air thick with the scent of her honeysuckle and heat, wild and clean. The soft hiss of water echoed against the tile, and there she was.

My little wolf.

Her back was to me, water cascading down the gentle arch of her spine. The curve of her waist, the strength in her thighs, the subtle sway of her hips as she moved... my breath caught in my throat. My body reacted before I could stop it, aching with the kind of hunger that had plagued me for weeks now.

I should leave. Should turn around and close the door before she notices me.

But I don't.

My legs moved without permission, drawn to her like gravity. And when I got close enough to see the droplets gliding over her skin, catching in the dip of her lower back, clinging to her rip ass.

I lost all sense of good intentions.

I stepped behind her, close enough that her warmth wrapped around me even through the steam.

She turned slightly, and in that brief second before she could speak, before the shock could twist into fury, I captured her lips.

Soft. Warm.

Not a kiss meant to claim. Just a whisper of a truth I'd denied for too long.

She gasped, jerking back, eyes wide and blazing. "Andrés? Are you are you insane?"

She pressed herself against the tiled wall, wet hair clinging to her shoulders like vines.

I didn't touch her again. Didn't press forward, didn't crowd her the way I wanted to. My hands braced on the wall beside her head, caging her in but barely.

"I didn't mean to scare you," I said, my voice low, rough, still tasting the shape of her lips.

Her chest rose and fell, breaths coming fast. Her eyes flicked to my mouth, then away, like she hated herself for looking.

"You're getting all your clothes wet," she said tightly, her voice trembling with something that wasn't quite anger.

I tilted my head. "Is that an invite to take them off?"

She glared at me, fierce, proud, stunning even when dripping wet. "You shouldn't be here, Andrés."

"No," I murmured, letting my eyes drop to the delicate line of her jaw. "But you want me here."

The silence between us cracked like thunder.

She didn't answer. She didn't have to.

Her body betrayed her just like mine did. The way her thighs clenched. The way her scent shifted, thick with desire. Her wolf called to mine, even when her pride wouldn't let her admit it.

Less than a week, my little wolf, and your body will be mine, but what about your heart?

I stepped back, dragging in a breath, letting the distance cool the fire threatening to consume us both.

Then I left, slamming the door behind me, not because I was angry.

Because if I stayed another second, I wasn't sure I'd survive it.

Chapter 17

MAYA

L ast night's sleeping arrangement?

Same as always. Andrés insisted I sleep in his bed. And just like every night since the day he kidnapped me, I gave in. But last night... last night was different.

It started in the shower.

I was rinsing off the day, minding my own business, when I turned and there he was. Fully dressed, dripping wet, standing under the spray like a damn fever dream brought to life. His clothes clung to every hard line of his body, and his darkened eyes locked onto mine like I was the only thing that existed.

Before I could even form a single thought, his mouth crashed down on mine.

That kiss...

It wasn't rough or demanding like I expected. It was gentle. Devouring. Full of need and something far more dangerous... emotion.

For a heartbeat, I melted into him. Let the warmth, the connection, wash over me. But then instinct roared back to life. I shoved him away, like I always did whenever the line between hatred and hunger blurred too much for comfort.

Only this time... he didn't fight me.

He just stood there, chest heaving, a tortured look flashing across his face before he turned and left, leaving me breathless, burning, aching in ways I didn't want to admit.

Trying to fall asleep after that? Pure torture.

He curled around me like he always did, his body a furnace against my back, breathing slow and steady against the curve of my neck. His arm draped possessively across my waist, pulling me close like I was his. Like I'd always been his.

And the worst part?

The more time I spend tangled up in this twisted fate... the harder it is to pretend I don't feel something when he touches me.

Something real.

Something dangerous.

Something that terrifies me even more than the pull that keeps pulling us closer.

Now, I stood in front of the closet—his closet staring at the obscene amount of new clothes neatly hanging inside. All in my size. All picked with way too much care.

Cranky and overwhelmed didn't even begin to cover it.

"Ugh, I don't know what to wear," I muttered, stepping out of the massive walk-in and into the bedroom, irritation bubbling in my chest.

Andrés leaned lazily against the dresser, arms crossed, his brown eyes tracking my every move like a predator sizing up its prey. That slow, infuriating smirk curved his lips, making me want to punch him... or maybe kiss him. I wasn't sure anymore, and that scared me more than anything.

"You've got hundreds of outfits, all brand new," he said, voice thick with amusement. "Just pick one."

I shot him a glare, crossing my arms tightly under my chest, doing my best to ignore the way his eyes dipped lower for a split second before dragging back up to meet mine.

"I can't just pick something, Andrés," I snapped, my voice sharper than I intended. "I'm meeting your people today. I have to look right. It's not enough that I'm basically your prisoner, I don't want them to hate me too."

The teasing light in his eyes vanished. Just like that.

Gone was the cocky, playboy devil with the lazy grin. In his place stood a man carved from dominance and pure, lethal focus.

He pushed off the dresser with slow, deliberate steps, closing the space between us until I could feel the heat radiating from his skin.

"First of all," he murmured, voice low and rough like gravel, "you're not my prisoner."

He tipped my chin up with two fingers, forcing me to meet his fierce gaze.

"And this house?" His thumb brushed along my jaw, a whisper of a touch that sent my heart into a freefall. "It's not a cage but your home... if you let it be."

My breath caught, chest rising and falling too fast.

"Second," he continued, his voice gentling, but authoritarian, "my people will like you because you matter to me."

His hands skimmed down my arms, fingers brushing bare skin, sending little jolts of electricity crackling along my nerves. I tried to ignore the way my body leaned closer without permission, tried to pretend I wasn't breathing him in like a drug.

"I love how stubborn you are," he murmured, dipping his head lower, his breath teasing the shell of my ear. "I love how you fight me. It turns me the fuck on."

A shiver tore through me, my heart slamming against my ribs as his lips grazed the sensitive spot below my ear, branding me with a heat that made my knees threaten to give out.

Panic clawed up my throat.

I jerked back, putting precious space between us, my hands trembling as I shoved them behind me. "Stop," I rasped, swallowing hard. "Don't say things like that."

Andrés frowned, confusion flashing in those stormy blue depths. "Things like what? The truth?"

I shook my head, wishing I could erase the way his words had sunk deep, wrapping around something fragile inside me.

The drive to the pack house was quick.

I had chosen a sundress that morning, a soft floral piece that felt unfamiliar on my skin. Normally, I hid beneath jeans and sweaters, covering the pale skin I hated, concealing the freckles that littered my body like constellations. But today? Today, my skin was bare, the sun kissing every mark, every flaw. And my red hair? It was the only thing I had managed to control.

Andrés didn't say a word about my outfit, but the heat in his gaze as he helped me out of the car made my stomach flip.

He guided me toward the pack house and into the dining room with a firm hand on the small of my back.

That touch.

I hated the way it made me feel how my body leaned into it, craved it, melted beneath the heat of his palm.

"Oh, they're finally here!" Yolanda, Andrés' mother, exclaimed, her warm voice wrapping around me like a familiar embrace before her arms did the same.

I barely had time to brace myself before she pulled me into a tight hug.

Yolanda had led us into the dining room, where the smell of freshly baked bread, cinnamon, and sizzling bacon had made it feel oddly comforting.

The long table had already been filled with people, their low voices creating a hum of anticipation. But none of it had held my attention like the person sitting at the head of the table.

A striking Latina woman had sat there, her posture regal, her honey-brown eyes scanning me with cool calculation—sharp and assessing, just like Andrés'. His sister, Sofía.

And if the dominant energy pouring off her hadn't been proof enough, the way the others had glanced at her with subtle deference had confirmed that she was the new Alpha of the Luna Stone Pack.

Beside her had sat a man with wavy black hair and eyes like winter storms. He had watched her like she was the sun itself. Her mate.

Andrés had guided me forward, pulling out a chair with a gentleness that had made my pulse stutter. He had been so careful with me, as if I might shatter... or run.

I had sat, trying to hold my spine straight under the weight of so many eyes.

Sofía had spoken first, her voice low but commanding—an Alpha's voice.

"Finally," she had said, a slow, amused smirk curving her lips. "We're allowed to meet her."

The murmur around the table had quieted as her gaze had narrowed on me, not hostile... but not soft either.

"I'm Sofía," she had continued, tilting her head like she was reading secrets in the lines of my face. "Alpha of this pack. This is my mate, Mason."

The man at her side had given me a nod, polite but not overly warm. Protective, I had noted. Just like Andrés.

I had nodded back, forcing a small smile, but my stomach had twisted with nerves.

Sofía had tilted her head, studying me. "What's your name?

My throat had tightened. Shit. I hadn't thought that far ahead. My name could have ruined everything. If they had known who I was—if they had recognized me as Alpha George's daughter—what would they have done to me? Would they have seen me as an enemy? A threat?

I had swallowed hard and forced out, "My name isn't im portant... In the end, I'm just a captive of your brother."

Andrés had stiffened beside me, his jaw tightening. I had known he was pissed, but I hadn't cared. I couldn't risk them knowing the truth.

Sofía's sharp gaze had flicked between us before one perfectly arched brow had risen. "It does matter. I, for one, don't think it's cute for you to be called 'little wolf.' I'll leave that to him." Her lips had curled in amusement before she had sobered, her expression turning serious. "As a guest in my home, on my territory, I ask for your name."

The weight of her gaze had been suffocating, the energy in the room shifting as if the entire pack had been waiting for my response. But I hadn't been able to bring myself to say it. My last name had been a curse in places like this.

Before I had gathered my thoughts, Andrés had spoken, his voice laced with irritation. "Sofía, is this why you wanted to meet her? To interrogate my partner..."

Sofía had cut him off with a sharp look, arching a brow as she had lifted her fingers, mimicking air quotes. "Your partner?" She had scoffed. "Let's not pretend you didn't kidnap this poor girl the same day you came to rescue me."

Andrés had exhaled sharply, his body coiled with frustration. The tension between them had been thick, a silent battle of wills playing out in the space between us.

Before he could argue, Sofía had lifted her hand, stopping him cold. "I will speak with her. Alone. Come with me to my study." Then she had turned to her mate, her expression softening just slightly. "You too, hun." She had winked at him, and his lips had twitched as if amused.

Andrés had instantly tensed. "No." His voice had been a low growl, his protectiveness flaring.

Sofía's honey-brown eyes had flashed with warning. "Andrés, don't forget I am your Alpha before I am your sister. I will not tolerate insubordination. This is a warning."

The authority in her voice had been absolute, leaving no room for argument. My heart had pounded as she had stood, expecting me to follow. Mason had risen beside her, his looming presence like a silent enforcer.

I had taken a shaky breath and risen to my feet. I had felt Andrés' heated glare burning into me, but I hadn't looked back.

The silence had been heavy as I had followed Sofía and Mason down the hallway, my pulse hammering in my ears. The air in the house had felt thick with an energy I couldn't quite name—powerful, commanding, and suffocating all at once.

We had reached a large wooden door, and Sofía had pushed it open, revealing a study lined with dark mahogany bookshelves. The scent of leather-bound tomes and faint traces of incense had filled the air.

Sofía had strode to her desk, settling into the large chair behind it, her posture effortlessly authoritative. Mason had remained standing by the door, his arms crossed over his broad chest, watching, waiting.

I had barely had time to gather my thoughts before Sofía had fixed me with a piercing stare and spoken.

"I know who you are, Maya."

My breath had caught, and my eyes had widened. "If you knew, why didn't you say anything?" My voice had been barely above a whisper, but there had been no mistaking the accusation in it.

Sofía had tilted her head, studying me like a puzzle she had been determined to solve. "I was hoping you would have told me yourself." She had leaned forward, her fingers tapping lightly against the polished wood of her desk. "Tell me, Maya, why didn't you want us to know who you are?"

My hands had clenched at my sides, my nails digging into my palms. "Isn't it obvious?" I had forced the words out, trying to keep my voice steady despite the lump in my throat. "I am the daughter of the man who kidnapped you. The man who hurt you and your Beta."

The weight of my admission had hung in the air, suffocating and undeniable.

Sofía hadn't flinched. Her expression had remained un-readable, her honey-brown eyes locked onto mine. I had exhaled sharply and continued, my voice quieter now, tinged with something close to exhaustion. "As much as I despised what my father did, I didn't want to die for his actions."

Mason had shifted then, a low growl rumbling from his chest, his wolf responding to the tension. His presence alone had been enough to send a shiver down my spine.

Sofía had finally moved, leaning back in her chair. "You think I'd execute you for his sins?" Her lips had curved into something unreadable. "Do I look like a tyrant to you, Maya?"

I had shaken my head quickly, but I hadn't answered. I hadn't trusted my voice not to crack.

Sofía had exhaled through her nose, then glanced at Mason, something silent passing between them. When she had looked back at me, her eyes had softened—but only slightly. "Your bloodline doesn't determine who you are. Your actions do."

Mason had shifted beside her, his gaze still pinned on me, the weight of his scrutiny making my skin prickle.

"So tell me, Maya," Sofia had continued, her voice drop-ping to something almost... intimate. "Were you truly your father's daughter?"

The question had felt like a blade pressed to my throat.

"Of course not." My voice had been firm, but there had been a tremor in my hands as I clasped them together in my lap. "I never believed in the things my father did. I was more like my mother, Luna Donna. She had believed there was light even in the darkest places and had always encouraged me to be that light for our pack."

Sofía had studied me, her sharp honey-brown eyes unreadable. "Then why didn't you become the light?"

I had exhaled slowly, shrugging one shoulder. "It was hard to embrace the light when I had been taught to fear it." I had shaken my head, swallowing the lump forming in my throat. "I was only sixteen when my mother died. I wasn't strong enough to fight back. And the few times I had challenged my father's authority..." I had hesitated, my pulse hammering. "I had paid for it. Dearly."

She had stood suddenly, her movements smooth and deliberate, and perched on the edge of the desk directly in front of me. The space between us had felt almost nonexistent, her powerful presence forcing me to meet her gaze.

"We didn't run our pack like your father ran Black Stone Pack." Her voice had been softer then, but no less commanding. "To prove it, I'll tell you something. Every single person in that dining room tonight already knew who you were."

My breath had caught. "All of them?"

She had nodded. "Yes."

My mind had spun. "So all this time… they knew I was Alpha George's daughter? And they didn't…"

"Say anything?" Sofia had finished for me, a smirk tugging at her lips. "No. They didn't. Because it wasn't their place."

I had shaken my head, still trying to process it. "But… why?"

Sofía had crossed her arms, tilting her head slightly. "Because it wasn't our secret to tell. It was yours. We had all been hoping that you and Andres would actually take the time to get to know each other… and that you'd tell him yourself."

The weight of her words had sunk in, but before I could respond, she had lifted a brow, her smirk widening. "What the hell had you two been doing for almost three weeks?"

A rush of heat had crept up my neck, spreading to my face like wildfire. My body had betrayed me before I could form an answer, my eyes darting away, my lips parting slightly, my breathing hitching just enough for Sofía to notice.

Her knowing gaze had flicked over my expression, and I could have sworn her smirk had deepened into something more wicked.

"Oh."

One simple word, filled with amusement and something dangerously close to approval.

Mason had chuckled from where he leaned against the wall, his deep voice vibrating through the room. "That explains a lot."

"Hm," she had hummed, tapping a finger against her chin. "So that's what you'd been doing instead of talking."

I had wanted to melt into the floor. I hadn't known whether I wanted to scream, deny it, or run, but one thing had been clear...

There had been no more secrets left to hide.

"What should I do?" I had asked, my voice barely above a whisper, as if speaking too loudly would have made the weight of my secret even heavier.

Sofía had watched me closely, her expression softening just enough to remind me that despite her formidable presence, she was still someone who understood. "I think you need to tell him the truth," she had said simply. "One thing I'd learned from my relationship was that good communication was the foundation of everything."

I had swallowed hard. "But what if he got mad at me for hiding it?"

Sofía had exhaled, leaning back slightly on the desk, her fingers drumming against the polished wood. "He'd get over it," she had said matter-of-factly. "And if I knew my brother, he wouldn't just be mad, he'd be hurt. But that wasn't something you could avoid. It was something you had to face."

Her words had settled deep inside me, twisting at something raw and vulnerable. I had known she was right. Andres had given me pieces of himself over those last few weeks—his touch, his trust, the fire in his eyes when he had looked at me. He deserved the truth.

Sofía had straightened then, her sharp gaze pinning me in place. "I'm going to keep your secret for a little while longer," she had said. "I'm giving you the chance to come clean. But if you don't... I will."

Her tone had left no room for argument.

I had nodded, my throat dry. "Understood."

"Now, before we leave, we have to decide what we're to call you, because little wolf is not cutting it," she had said.

"You can call me Mai. It's a nickname that only a few know," I had replied.

She had held my gaze for a moment longer before her smirk had returned. "Good. Now that we've handled that..." She had pushed off the desk, walking toward the door with effortless confidence. "Let's go eat. We've kept them waiting long enough."

I had taken a steadying breath and followed her, but as we had stepped out of the study, my heart had pounded for an entirely different reason.

Chapter 18

ANDRÉS

Sofía taking my girl, my mate, off somewhere and questioning her like she had been some damn criminal?

Yeah, that had pissed me the fuck off.

I wasn't the type to butt heads with authority, especially not family, but having my sister pull rank on me, throwing her Alpha weight around while taking what was mine? Infuriating.

I had paced back and forth near the dining table, fists clenching and unclenching at my sides, the need to go after her and drag my little wolf back to my side pounding through me like a live wire.

"*Mijo*, calm down," my father had said, his voice steady

but firm. "Your sister has responsibilities as Alpha. You, of all people, should understand that. How many background checks did you run on Mason and Darren before you trusted them?"

"Damn, my feelings are hurt," Darren had cut in, flashing a grin as he slid his arm around Estrella, his mate. He had pressed a kiss to her neck, making her giggle and squirm against him.

I had rolled my shoulders, the tension burning hot under my skin. "That was different. We hadn't known Mason was Sofía's mate at first. But everyone here knows what she is to me."

My mother, who had been quiet up until then, had finally spoken, her voice calm but laced with a sharp edge.
"And in a few more days, you'll be able to be open about it. But still, what did you expect when you took her?"
    She had given me a knowing look that had landed harder than any lecture.
"You're lucky your mate's playing nice instead of stabbing you in your sleep."

I had ground my teeth, crossing my arms over my chest. "Playing nice? She'd been stubborn as hell. She wouldn't even tell me her damn name."
    Before anyone could say another word, her scent had hit me—sharp, sweet, unmistakably hers.
My little wolf was back.

I had turned, and there she was, walking into the room. Her steps had been hesitant but steady, Sofía and Mason flanking her like guards.

My gaze had locked onto her immediately, scanning for any sign of distress.

She had looked composed, but I had known her too well already—the slight twitch of her fingers, the way she had pressed her lips together. She had been nervous, forcing herself to hold it together.

What the hell had my sister said to her?

Sofía had slid into her seat, all smooth command as she had addressed the room.

"Before we start breakfast," she had said, her voice cool and steady, "our new guest would like to say something."

She had gestured toward my mate.

My little wolf's pulse had fluttered at her throat, her hands fidgeting as she had stepped forward.

I had sat frozen, tense, fighting the urge to scoop her up and tell her she didn't owe anyone a damn thing.

"Oh, um... yes. Thank you, everyone, for welcoming me into your pack," she had begun, her voice soft but steady enough to cut through the room. "Even though my being here wasn't exactly my choice, it's... nice to see how other packs treat their people."

Her words had sliced into me, sharp and clean.

But I hadn't moved. I hadn't reacted.

I had just sat there, letting her have the space she needed.

She had swallowed, drawing in a breath.

"And you all can call me Mai," she had said. "I'm sorry if I wasn't more open about... other details. But this was as much as I had felt comfortable sharing at that moment. I hoped everyone understood."

The slight tremor in her voice had my wolf snarling beneath my skin.

She shouldn't have had to explain herself. Not to them. Not to anyone.

Without thinking, I had reached for her, sliding my hand into hers.

She had stiffened at first, just a breath of hesitation, but when I had squeezed gently, her fingers had curled around mine.

Relief had crashed through me like a wave.

A small victory.

But a victory all the same.

"Little wolf," I had murmured low, just for her, my thumb brushing over her knuckles, "you didn't have to share anything you weren't ready to. No one here would force you."

After a moment, she had nodded, the tiniest movement, but it had felt huge.

Sofia had leaned forward, her voice taking on that easy, commanding tone. "Mai," she had said, offering a small, reassuring smile, "since you're going to be seeing a lot of us around, let me properly introduce everyone."

She had gestured first to our parents seated at the head of the table.

"You already met our parents last night—Beto and Yolanda, our former Alpha and Luna."

Both had nodded warmly, my father with a respectful tilt

of his head, my mother with a softer smile that had seemed to put even the most anxious wolves at ease.

"And that's our brother, Leo," Sofía had continued. Leo had flashed a crooked grin, lifting his coffee cup in a silent salute.

Sofía's hand had moved to the other end of the table. "That's Xiomara, my Beta and right hand."

Xiomara had offered a small nod, her dark eyes sharp and unreadable. Distant. Quiet. Watching everything without missing a beat. That had been odd; Xiomara had always been so social.

"And finally," Sofía had said, her voice laced with a bit more warmth, "Darren and Estrella."

She had nodded toward the pair sitting closely together. Darren had winked at Mai, all easy charm, while Estrella had given a soft, welcoming smile, her hand tucked possessively into Darren's.

Mai had shifted slightly beside me, and I had felt her relax just a little more, soaking in the names and faces, filing them away.

The tension had slowly bled from the room as the conversation had shifted to lighter topics: Sofía and Mason's wedding, which had happened the week before, the changes happening within the pack, and everything that had gone on since Mai and I had been away.

After breakfast, we had moved to the parlor, where the scent of rich coffee and woodsmoke had still clung to the air. Most of the men had immediately dove into discussions about patrol routes and pack security, while the women had gathered near the hearth, animatedly exchanging training routines and sparring schedules.

At first, I had hated how easily Mai had slipped into their circle.

She had laughed with them. She had listened. She had spoken when spoken to. It had felt too easy. Too natural.

I hadn't wanted her integrating so quickly. I had wanted her for myself. Mine.

But my father had leaned over, his voice low with quiet wisdom. "The sooner she puts down roots, the harder it'll be for her to leave."

And just like that, I had backed down.

Barely.

"So, Mai," Sofía had said, lifting her mug and shooting her that smooth, knowing smile, "will you join us for our daily run? It's something the girls and I do... without the hovering males."

My jaw had tensed at the mere idea of her running through the woods without me. Vulnerable. Exposed. But I had kept my mouth shut. Barely.

Mai had glanced at me, hesitation flickering in those stunning green eyes before she had nodded softly. "That would be nice."

I hadn't said anything, just given her a slow nod that had meant two things: I'd allow it... and I'd be tracking her scent the whole damn time.

Before I could have spiraled into the thought of her running alone in nothing but a sports bra and shorts—goddess help me—Darren had stood, clinking his glass with a fork to get everyone's attention.

"We have an announcement," he had said, grinning from ear to ear. "We've decided to move our mating ceremony date forward. Just family and close friends. In two weeks."

A wave of excitement had exploded through the room. Estrella, practically glowing, had lifted a hand to quiet the noise. "And... I needed to do it now before I can't fit into my mating gown anymore."

The squeals that had followed had been deafening. Women clapping, hugging, congratulating. Even Sofía, who rarely let her walls down, had beamed at Estrella like a proud sister.

Meanwhile, I had sat frozen, caught completely off guard.

Then I had felt her. Mai. She had leaned in close, her breath warm against my neck as she had whispered, "She just announced she's pregnant."

Oh.

That had been all I could manage. But inside?

Inside, something had shifted—something primal. Something feral.

My mind had spiraled, and suddenly I could see it. Her. Mai, belly round with my pup. My scent wrapped around her like a second skin. Her body marked and claimed, full of us. The thought had wrecked me. My fingers had twitched with the need to reach for her. To take her. Again and again until that image became real.

And before I could have stopped myself, the question had come out low, rough, and full of intent.

"What are your thoughts on pups?"

The room had buzzed with celebration, but none of it had registered. The only thing I had seen... was her.

Mai had blinked, startled, her voice softer than before. "I love children... I've always wanted a big family," she had admitted, her eyes flickering with something raw and unguarded. "I guess... to make up for what I never had growing up."

Her words had settled deep in my chest like a brand, hot and unrelenting.

A big family. With me.

I hadn't been able to speak. I had barely been able to breathe.

All I had been able to do was nod, because in that moment, I had known.

After the congratulations had died down, I had pushed back my chair and stood. "I'm heading out," I had said, my voice rougher than intended. "There's still a lot to do at the house. And I haven't even given Mai the full tour yet."

Just as I had been about to stand, my mother's voice had cut through the noise.

"Before you leave, I want to settle one last thing with Mai."

I had tensed slightly, but when I had turned to look at her, she had been smiling in that deceptively soft way that had meant she had already made up her mind.

Mai had shifted beside me, suddenly alert. "Um... okay?"

"It was brought to our attention that in three days, it's your birthday. Is that correct?"

Mai had flushed instantly, the soft pink creeping up her neck, making my wolf rumble in appreciation.

"Yes, ma'am," she had answered, her voice barely above a whisper.

My mother had clapped her hands together, her eyes alight with excitement. "Wonderful! In three days, we'll have a pack gathering to celebrate your birthday and introduce you to the pack properly."

Mai had visibly stiffened, her fingers curling into her lap. "Oh, no... please, you didn't have to do that. There was no need to fuss. It was just a birthday."

My mother had waved her off as if Mai had just said something absurd. "Nonsense. You said you wanted to experience life in a different kind of pack. Well, experience number one: we celebrate milestones. And turning twenty-one? That's a big deal here."

Then she had dropped the bomb.

"Besides," she had added with a teasing smirk, "the pack needs to know why there's a new wolf in our territory who doesn't smell like us yet."

Yet.

Mai's breath had hitched.

And fuck, I had felt it. The truth in my mother's words. She didn't smell like me yet.

But she would.

Mai had swallowed hard, avoiding my gaze as she had forced out, "O-okay. If you insist."

Estrella, ever the chaos-stirrer, had suddenly gasped, her eyes wide with excitement. "Oh, my goddess! You know what this means..."

She had let the suspense hang in the air for a second before screaming, "Shopping!"

Mai had jerked slightly at the outburst, and I had to bite back a smirk.

"We'll talk about all of this after our run," Estrella had continued, "but don't you worry about a thing. We'll handle everything!"

I had glanced at Mai and had immediately seen the restlessness creeping in. The overwhelming attention, the pressure, the way her body had stiffened like she had been preparing for a fight.

That had been enough.

I had slid my hand over her shoulder, grounding her, my fingers pressing firmly against her warm skin. "Okay, that's enough. You're scaring my girl." My voice had been low, commanding, laced with warning.

Mai had exhaled softly, instinctively leaning into my touch.

I had shot my family a look. "See y'all tomorrow."

Leaving my family behind, Mai and I made our way across the packhouse, moving steadily toward the exit.

I kept my focus locked on her, more concerned about getting her out of here than paying attention to anything else around us.

Big mistake.

Out of nowhere, a soft body slammed into me, jarring me enough that I lost my grip on Mai's hand.

I barely had time to react before Rosario, an ex-fling who didn't know when to quit, threw herself at me, her arms winding around my neck and her mouth crashing against mine.

For a stunned second, my body froze.

Then instinct kicked in.

I shoved her away, firm but not rough, wiping the unwanted taste of her off my lips with the back of my hand. My eyes immediately found Mai. She'd stepped back, standing a few feet away, her body stiff, her eyes locked onto me and Rosario, unreadable.

Damn it.

"As soon as I heard you were back, I had to find you!" Rosario gushed, trying to close the distance again. Her voice was sickly sweet, her hands reaching for me like we hadn't been over for months. "Bebé, I missed you so much."

I put a hand out, stopping her before she could get any closer.

"Rosario, what the hell are you doing?" I said, my tone flat and cold. "We haven't been a thing for over six months."

She waved a hand like it was nothing, a bright, almost manic smile stretching across her face.

"Nonsense. You just needed some space. I know I can be a little clingy," she said, reaching out to trail her fingertips along my arm in a move that made my skin crawl.

I stepped back, muscles tense, heart hammering not from Rosario's touch, but from the sight of Mai watching the whole damn thing unfold.

I needed to fix this. Now.

But before I could reach Mai, Rosario caught sight of her and, like a venomous snake, she struck.

"And who is this?" she spat, her voice dripping with venom. "Your next whore?"

A growl ripped from deep in my chest.

"I suggest you shut your mouth," I warned, my voice low and full of lethal promise. "And don't you ever call Mai that. She is my mate."

Before I could say another word, Mai stepped back, pushing my hand away when I tried to reach for her.

"No, I'm not," she said sharply, her voice cutting like ice. Her eyes burned into mine, full of pain I hadn't earned but still somehow owned. "Looks like you don't need a mate. You have plenty of women right here."

"Mai," I rasped, desperation clawing at my throat, "she meant nothing to me. It was just sex, months before I ever met you."

Rosario let out a bitter laugh, the sound shrill and broken.

"I was just sex?" she sneered. "I gave you everything and now I'm nothing? Look at her! She doesn't even want you. She won't even claim you. I would."

She lunged for me again, but I moved around her, closing the distance to Mai, grabbing her hand and pulling her gently but firmly against me, chest to chest

"Mai," I said, my voice rough with emotion, "I told you I want you as my mate. Nobody else."

The moment my lips touched Mai's skin, it must have triggered something inside Rosario. Something dark.

In a flash, she shoved me back with surprising force and lunged straight for Mai, her fingers shifting into claws, her face twisted in rage.

Rosario slapped Mai across the face with a resounding crack that echoed through the stunned courtyard, and then she leapt, aiming straight for Mai's throat.

I scrambled to my feet, blood roaring in my ears, but before I could get to them, Rosario went flying.

She hit the ground hard at my feet, rolling to a stunned stop.

Rosario scrambled back up with a wild, furious look in her eyes. Her claws extended fully now, her lips peeling back in a snarl as she charged at Mai again.

I took two steps forward, ready to tear Rosario, but Sofía's hand clamped down on my arm, stopping me.

"She needs to handle this," Sofía said low and firm, her gaze never leaving the scene unfolding before us. "If you intervene, it'll only make things worse. She has to prove she belongs, right here, right now."

Every instinct I had screamed at me to protect my mate, but I knew Sofía was right.

In our world, respect wasn't given. It was earned.

Rosario lunged at Mai again, her fingers curled into claws, aiming straight for her face.

But Mai wasn't some delicate little flower.

She ducked under Rosario's swipe with a quick, sharp movement, her body coiling like a spring before she drove her shoulder hard into Rosario's gut, knocking the air out of her.

Rosario stumbled back, wheezing, but recovered fast, spinning to slash at Mai again.

This time, Mai grabbed her wrist mid-swing, twisting it cruelly until Rosario cried out in pain.

Without hesitation, Mai yanked her forward and slammed her knee into Rosario's stomach, sending her crumpling to the ground.

Gasps echoed around the room as more pack members gathered, watching the scene unfold with rapt, hungry eyes.

Rosario tried one last desperate lunge, but Mai was ready.

She sidestepped easily, using Rosario's momentum against her. In one fluid motion, Mai grabbed her by the hair, yanked her head back, and forced Rosario onto her knees.

A growl rumbled from Mai's chest, a sound so raw, so primal, it made even my wolf still inside me in stunned awe.

"You will leave me alone. Do not walk near me, do not talk to me, and do not approach Andrés," Mai snarled, her voice sharp as a blade, her body radiating lethal control.

Rosario trembled, her pride visibly warring with her instincts.

But instincts always won.

Slowly, Rosario bared her neck in submission, bowing her head low, exposing her vulnerable throat to Mai.

It was over. But I knew better with Rosario; nothing was ever over.

Mai released her with a shove, stepping back without a single scratch on her, her chest rising and falling heavily as she fought to control the adrenaline coursing through her.

I watched her, my mate standing there fierce, powerful, untouchable, and something inside me snapped tight with pride, with bone-deep want.

Sofía smirked beside me, giving a soft hum of approval.

"She'll be fine," she said under her breath. "She was made for this."

And God help me, she was right.

And she had no idea just how much more dangerous and desirable that made her.

Chapter 19

MAYA

The next morning, I met up with Sofía, Xiomara, and Estrella for a run through the woods. We stayed in human form for most of it, talking, laughing, letting me ease into their rhythm.

Sofía explained that the usual running group was much larger, but for my first time with them, they'd decided to keep it small so I wouldn't feel overwhelmed.

I appreciated that. More than they could ever know.

Because inside, my emotions were still a tangled mess after what had happened yesterday.

I never imagined my introduction to the pack would end like that.

Seeing some tall, gorgeous she-wolf kiss him like he was hers had ripped something jagged inside me. Out of pain and fury, I'd denied him. In front of her. In front of his entire pack. I shoved him away, even though some reckless, traitorous part of me wanted to scream that he was mine.

But he wasn't. Not really.

Even when Andrés swore she meant nothing, the hollow ache in my chest refused to fade.

I had no reason to ache. This mating was convenience, not love. I didn't care what he did, or who claimed his touch. I didn't want him.

At least... that's what I told myself.

Didn't I?

Sofía's voice pulled me out of my spiraling thoughts.

We settled into a steady jog through the woods, our pace smooth enough for conversation.
Sofía spoke easily, telling me about the history of the pack, her voice filled with pride and confidence.

I let her talk, even though Andrés had already shared all this with me.
I nodded at the right times, smiled when she glanced over, but my mind kept drifting back.

Back to yesterday morning.
Back to standing in front of all those strangers, forced to fight for a place I wasn't even sure I wanted.

When Rosario came at me, her claws flashing toward my face, something inside me *snapped*.

It wasn't about Andrés.
It wasn't even about Rosario.

It was about *me*.

I wasn't going to let anyone tear me down again just because they thought they could.

I put up with that crap from my father for too many years.

Never again.

The drive back to his house was silent.

Andrés dramatically swore at everything with Rosario had ended months before he ever met me.

But I just sat there, staring out the window, saying nothing.

Because if I let myself believe him...

If I let myself believe *in* him...

It wouldn't be Rosario who could destroy me.

It would be *him*.

So, I did what I do best.

I hid.

I avoided him all day, making myself scarce around the house.

Andrés must have gotten the message because he kept his distance, giving me space but never too far, always lingering just enough for me to feel him.

Until nightfall.

When the world went quiet, and the walls between us thinned.

That was when he slipped into bed behind me, sliding his strong arm around my waist, tucking me into the warmth of his body.

He nuzzled the back of my neck, breathing me in with a low, rumbling sigh that sent shivers down my spine.

I should've pushed him away.

I should've kept up my walls.

But the truth was...

As much as I wanted to fight it, my body craved his touch. His warmth.

His steady heartbeat against my back.

When Andrés held me like that, the world faded away, and I slept.

Then the conversation had shifted.

Sofía's eyes had softened, and she had started telling me how she had met Mason, her mate.

And wow.

What a story.

Their bond hadn't been instant perfection, not at all. It had been messy and complicated, full of resistance, misunderstandings, and gut-wrenching choices. But listening to her now, hearing the way her voice warmed when she spoke his name, made something inside me ache.

Made me wonder about fated mates.

Back home, fated mates were not celebrated.

Something whispered about, almost shamefully, in private conversations.

My father never spoke of them with reverence or hope. Even though he and my mother shared the rare bond, he dismissed it, choosing instead to believe mates should be selected based on power, alliances on what could be *gained*.

Not love.

Not destiny.

Hearing Sofía speak so differently, so openly, made a thousand doubts swirl in my chest.

What if I find mine?
What if it's Andrés?
What if it's not?

The thought sank its claws into me, and no matter how I tried to shake it off, it clung there, sharp and undeniable.

As much as I hated to admit it...

I was starting to really *like* Andrés.

I know, I'm probably insane.

Liking the man who kidnapped me?

Goddess, there had to be something seriously wrong with me.

But when I stripped away the kidnapping, the chaos, the fear, and looked at the *man* standing behind those actions...

Andrés wasn't cruel.

He wasn't selfish or manipulative like the men I grew up around.

He was...

Protective.

Strong.

Loyal to a fault.

And if I was honest with myself brutally, painfully honest, I liked how he looked at me.

Like I was something rare.

Something precious.

Something worth fighting for.

It felt *good* to be wanted.

To be cherished.

To be someone's *priority*.

Not an obligation.

Not a pawn.

And mating with Andrés... it could help my pack. It could change everything for the people I left behind—the ones still living, the damaged left behind from my father's leadership.

Maybe fate was giving me a chance.

Maybe it was trying to show me that this bond with Andrés could be more than survival.

More than just politics and pain.

But as Sofía's voice faded into the rhythm of the forest around us, that fragile hope inside me wavered.

Because the world we lived in wasn't built on hope.

It was built on blood and survival.

And sometimes, no matter how much you wanted to believe in something better, the past still found a way to drag you back down.

We pushed deeper into the woods, the thick canopy overhead casting long shadows across the forest floor.

The air felt heavier here, thicker. Every step seemed to pull me further from the warmth of my earlier thoughts, replacing them with a growing unease.

And then...

A sharp, metallic scent hit me, slicing through the cool morning air.

Blood.

We all froze instantly, instincts snapping to attention.

A cold shiver raced down my spine.

"Everyone, stay alert," Sofía said, her voice all business now, her Alpha command rolling off her in waves. "I smell blood."

She moved forward cautiously, and the rest of us followed, our bodies tensed, senses stretched thin, searching the trees, the ground, the wind.

The scent grew stronger.

Fouler.

Estrella was the first to break.

She gasped, slapped a hand over her mouth, and stumbled away, barely making it to a tree before she doubled over and vomited.

"What is it, Estrella?" Xiomara asked, stepping closer, her voice clipped with tension.

Estrella didn't answer.

She didn't have to.

Xiomara followed her gaze and I watched the color drain from her face.

"Sofía..." she said, her voice strange and distant. "You need to call the guys. Now."

Dread clawed its way up my throat.

I took a few steps forward, my heart hammering painfully against my ribs.

And then I saw it.

A woman's naked body, sprawled in the dirt.

Bruises, cuts, scratches covering every inch of her battered skin.

The stench of violation clung to the air around her, thick and vile.

I couldn't move.

Couldn't breathe.

I wanted to turn away, to erase the image from my mind, but something, some terrible instinct kept me frozen there.

And that's when it hit me.

Underneath all the blood, all the horror...

A scent.

Faint.

But unmistakable.

Recognition slammed into me so hard I almost stumbled.

No.

No, no, no.

A violent chill spread through my body, locking my limbs in place.

I knew that scent.

I *knew*.

"Sofía..." My voice cracked, small and terrified. "I... I think I know who did this. I can smell him on her."

Sofía's head snapped toward me, her eyes sharp and calculating.

"Who?" she demanded.

I couldn't say it.

Couldn't make myself say the name.

Panic flooded me, my chest constricting until I could barely get the words out.

"Please," I begged, my voice breaking. "Please don't tell Andrés. I beg you."

A sharp inhale came from Xiomara, and then she hissed it out like a curse.

"Oh, Goddess..." she breathed. "*It's him.* Alpha George."

Hearing the name aloud made me flinch like I'd been struck.

A heavy silence fell over the group.

The guilt curled in my stomach like a living thing, making me want to curl into myself and disappear.

Somehow, some way, this felt like it was *my* fault. Like my connection to him tainted me, marked me.

"Sofía, please..." I whispered, tears slipping down my cheeks unchecked.

Sofía stepped forward, her Alpha aura wrapping around me, not crushing, not punishing.

Protective. Solid.

"You are safe here," she said, her voice a lifeline. "We do not punish people for the crimes of their families."

I wanted to believe her.

I *needed* to.

But shame burned through me, blinding and suffocating.

"Is it Alpha George?" she asked again, her tone gentler but still firm.

I couldn't speak.

Couldn't force the word past my throat.

So I just nodded, once, trembling.

Sofía didn't look away.

She reached out, her fingers tipping my chin up, forcing me to meet her unwavering gaze.

"Do not look down," she commanded softly. "You are a strong she-wolf. You had the misfortune of being born to a shitty father, but that does not define you."

I swallowed back another sob, barely holding myself together.

"We won't say you smelled it," she added, her voice lowering into something fierce and protective. "I'll say I did. Understood?"

I nodded, the lump in my throat too big to speak around.

Sofía sighed, her touch softening as her hand brushed against my cheek in a rare, almost maternal gesture.

"But, Maya..."

Her voice sharpened slightly.

I braced myself.

"You cannot keep hiding. We cannot keep lying."

My heart twisted painfully.

"You must tell Andrés the truth."

The words hit me like a blow, stealing the breath from my lungs.

I shook my head weakly, looking away.

"I can't," I whispered.

"You must," Sofía insisted, her voice heavy with the weight of things I didn't want to face.

And deep down, I knew she was right.

Before I could have even formed a response, the wind had shifted, carrying with it the choking stench of magic. It had clung to the air, thick and heavy, coating my tongue like ash.

A flurry of black birds had exploded through the trees,

their screeches splitting the quiet forest, their wings slicing the sky like jagged shadows.

My skin had prickled, instincts screaming at me, every cell in my body lighting up with one chilling truth—something was terribly wrong.

Then... the body had moved.

At first, it had been small.

A twitch.

A grotesque, unnatural jerk of a limb.

And then... it had stood.

My breath had seized in my lungs.

The corpse had stumbled forward, its movements jerky, broken, like a marionette yanked upright by invisible strings.

Not alive.

Sofía hadn't hesitated.

With a snarl that had vibrated through the air, she had lunged, her foot slamming into its chest with brutal force, sending the body sprawling back into the dirt.

But it hadn't stayed down.

Bones had cracked, limbs had snapped unnaturally, and the thing had risen again, its head lolling to the side in a sickening, puppet-like motion.

Its mouth had twisted into something grotesque, a parody of a smile.

And its eyes...

Pure, soulless white.

Then it had spoken.

"Oh, dear Sofía," the corpse had crooned, its voice wrong, slurred, distorted, as if layered with multiple voices, none of them human.

"Did you think we were done with you?"

A violent shudder had rippled down my spine, my hands curling into fists at my sides.

Sofía had remained still, composed, but I had seen the slight tightening of her shoulders, the subtle clench of her jaw.

She had been ready.

Braced.

"You will pay," the thing had hissed, its broken body lurching closer, arms twitching and spasming. "Your pack will pay... I will have my revenge..."

The wind had howled, whipping through the trees with a furious, unnatural force, thickening the very air around us.

"And when all is done..." the voice had crooned, sickly sweet, almost childlike.

The corpse's back had arched, limbs stretched out as if pulled by unseen hands.

"You won't have anything."

The word *nothing* had begun carving itself into its decaying flesh, slashing over and over in blood-red letters, until its body had become a grotesque canvas of pain and rage.

Then...

Silence.

The wind had cut off, the birds had vanished as if they had never been there, and the oppressive magic had lifted like a ripped-away curtain.

The corpse had dropped from midair, landing hard against the ground with a sickening, wet thud.

Silence had pressed down on us, thick and suffocating. No one had moved.

No one had breathed.

The forest had held its breath.

And deep in my bones, I had known.

This had only been the beginning.

I had stood there, shaking, my heart hammering so violently I could hear it in my ears.

"What the fuck was that?" I had whispered, my voice trembling as I had stared at the corpse that should not have moved, should not have spoken, should not have been alive.

"That," Sofía had exhaled, "was dark magic." Her voice had been sharp, laced with something between fury and certainty. "I guess your dear father has made friends with a powerful witch."

My father.

My stomach had twisted.

Of course. Of course, he had.

Before I could have even processed the weight of her words, Estrella had lowered her phone from her ear.

"The guys are coming," she had said, her voice clipped.

A short time had passed before I had heard the pounding of paws against the earth.

And then, they had been there.

Massive wolves had burst through the trees, fur bristling, golden eyes gleaming.

They had moved in unison, radiating authority and dan-

ger, their presence filling the space like a tangible force.
Andres had been among them, his sleek black coat unmistakable.

But even in wolf form, I had felt the rage rolling off him.

They had shifted back quickly, moving with practiced ease, and thank the Goddess they had brought a bag of clothes.

I had refused to spend the rest of the day looking at every man's dick out in the open.

I mean... maybe just one.

But not the rest.

Mason had shifted first, his body tense, already moving toward Sofía before he had even fully stood upright.

"What the hell happened?" he had demanded, his voice urgent, reaching for her, his hands instantly scanning for injuries.

Darren had done the same with Estrella, pulling her close, pressing his lips to her hair, grounding her.

Leo had reached for Xiomara, only for her to step back. I had seen the flash of pain on his face, the quick mask of indifference he had tried to put on, but it had been there.

But then Andrés had been in front of me.

"Little wolf."

His voice had been low, urgent, filled with a desperate need.

His hands had found me instantly, roaming over my body, checking for wounds, for any sign of harm. His touch had been possessive, frantic, warm.

"Were you okay? Were you hurt?"

I had exhaled, finally allowing myself to breathe.
Because no matter how terrifying that moment had been...
he had been there now.
And somehow, that had made everything feel just a little
bit safer.

Chapter 20

MAYA

B ack at the packhouse, an emergency meeting is held in Sofía's study, bringing together the high-ranking officers and several members I haven't yet met via video conference.

On one screen, Jason, Alpha of the Crescent Moon Pack and Mason's brother, watches the discussion with a focused expression. Beside him in another window are two witches, Myriam and Nadya, from a witch coven in New York.

Myriam leans forward, her long fingers adorned with gleaming rings, her voice smooth and rich with authority. "Well, *mi niña*," she begins, her tone affectionate, "for me to give you my full opinion, I need to be there. I need to see it with my own eyes. We'll have to make another trip to your pack."

"Consider it done," Sofía replies, her voice cutting through the tension like a blade. "My father will coordinate with you for the departure time."

I glanced toward where Andrés' father was seated and immediately noticed the man standing beside him.

He looked to be about the same age, but what caught me off guard was the way he was staring—steady, intense.

I didn't know him.

But the way his eyes stayed locked on me made my skin prickle with discomfort.

Why was he looking at me like that?

Trying to shake it off, I turned to Andrés and leaned in slightly.

"Who's the man standing next to your father?" I asked quietly.

Andrés followed my gaze, then smiled easily.

"That's Marcos," he said. "He's my mentor, the former Beta of the pack. Practically like an uncle to us."

I nodded, offering a small smile back, but I couldn't quite shake the feeling that Marcos was still watching me.

Returning my attention to the meeting, Jason had leaned forward, his dark brows drawing together, his jaw tight.

"I'll start reaching out to a few elders and high-ranking officers left in Black Stone Pack," he had offered. "See if they know anything about Alpha George's dealings with witches."

At the mention of my father, my body had tensed instinctively.

My fingers had curled into my palms, my nails biting into

the soft flesh, grounding me against the rising tide of old fear.

Jason had shifted, glancing sideways at the screen. "I was also thinking of contacting Rebecca," he had added thoughtfully. "She might know of witches in the surrounding area."

The moment Rebecca's name had left his mouth, Sofía's entire body had stiffened.

"Be careful how much you tell Rebecca," she had warned, her voice carrying a chilling edge. "At this moment, all witches—except Myriam's coven—were suspects."

"Babe, Rebecca would never—" Mason had started, but he hadn't gotten to finish.

Sofía had cut him a glare so sharp, so deadly, that it had practically ripped the words from his mouth.

I had felt the power in that look, and had even lowered my gaze in second-hand fear.

Mason had cleared his throat, raising his hands in surrender. "Never mind. You're right. Even Rebecca could be a suspect."

Sofía hadn't let it drop so easily.

"It wasn't Rebecca I was worried about," she had stated, her voice firm, unwavering. "It was her sister. She and I hadn't exactly parted on good terms. And neither had you. Did I need to remind you of your scar?"

Mason's jaw had tightened for a second, but then he had simply lifted his hands higher in surrender.

I had frowned, curiosity flickering through me. Later that day, Andrés had filled in the blanks.

Apparently, Mason's pack had a similar alliance with a group of witches near their territory. Years ago, one of them had had a fling with Mason when they had been in college. It had ended badly.

So badly that the witch had lost her damn mind and attacked him.

The situation had escalated to the point that both the Alpha and the coven leader had had to intervene, forcing an agreement that neither Mason nor the witch would ever cross paths again.

But when my father had attacked Mason's pack, they had had no choice but to use those same witches for help.

"What do we do now?" Xiomara had asked, her arms crossed, worry etched into her face.

Sofía had leaned back against the desk, her expression unreadable. "Not much we could do. We informed the pack to stay safe and move in groups, as we had already been asking them to. But life continued."

Her tone had left no argument.

"Life went on."

Yolanda, Sofía's mother, had tilted her head thoughtfully. "Did you still want to have the pack celebration?"

Sofía had straightened, her shoulders squaring, her Alpha presence radiating through the room.

"Absolutely."

She had stepped into the center of the study, her gaze sweeping over everyone, filled with fire and unwavering resolve.

"We could not allow those terrorists to control our lives.

The moment we gave in to fear, they had already won. I would not allow them to win anything."

A murmur of agreement had rippled through the room.

Everyone except me.

Because I hadn't wanted that party.

I hadn't wanted all that attention.

Not when I had still been trying to figure out where I fit into all of this.

As the conversation had shifted to pack security and strategy, Andrés had sent me off with his mother, and honestly, I would have rather been anywhere else.

I would have preferred to stay back, to listen to the security plans, to know how they had intended to protect the pack, to prepare myself for whatever was coming.

But instead... I had been dragged to the damn mall.

Before we could have stepped out, a man had approached me—tall, broad, his dark hair sprinkled with gray at the temples.

"Hello," he said warmly, offering his hand. "I'm Marcos, the former CFO and Beta of Luna Stone. I heard you're from the Black Stone Pack. Welcome to our pack."

I shook his hand cautiously, my wolf bristling slightly at the unfamiliar touch.

"It's nice to meet you," I said, my voice a little stiff.

He smiled, but there was a sadness in his eyes that caught me off guard.

"I apologize for staring," he said, voice softer now. "You look like someone I used to know.

"Oh..." I fidgeted with the hem of my shirt, not sure what to say.

Before the awkwardness could stretch any further, Yolanda swooped in like a saving grace.

"Hey, Marcos," she said cheerfully, slipping an arm around my shoulders in a side hug. "I see you've met Andrés'... friend. Isn't she just lovely?"

Marcos gave a small, sad smile. I glanced up at Yolanda, relieved to have her take over the conversation.

"He said I remind him of someone he used to know," I explained quietly.

Yolanda's expression shifted, a flicker of surprise flashing in her eyes before they softened—and turned misty.

"Oh, Marcos," she murmured, reaching out to pat his shoulder in comfort. "Yes... I can see it. She does resemble her a little. Back when we were all just a bunch of reckless youngsters."

Marcos nodded, his jaw tight with the weight of memories he didn't share.

The moment felt too heavy, too intimate, and I shifted awkwardly, not sure what to do with the emotions suddenly hanging in the air.

Luckily, Yolanda gave my arm a little squeeze and switched gears.

"Come on, *mija*," she said brightly. "We have birthday shopping to do!"

Before I could even think of protesting, Estrella joined her, practically linking arms with Yolanda like a united front.

I tried to protest.

I failed miserably.

Before I could blink, I was being dragged from one boutique to another, their enthusiasm terrifyingly relentless.

Dresses, shoes, lingerie way too much lingerie were thrown at me with dizzying speed, and I had absolutely no business even looking at half of it.

Apparently, my wardrobe was deemed "not birthday party appropriate."

"Why am I even doing this?" I muttered under my breath as they hauled me into yet another store, my arms already loaded down with bags.

Estrella just grinned wickedly, throwing an arm around my shoulders.

"Because, whether you like it or not, your ass is about to be the center of attention," she said, laughing. "And if you're gonna suffer, you might as well look hot while doing it."

I groaned dramatically.

"I hate you."

"No, you don't," she sang, already dragging me toward a rack of dresses that looked dangerously close to lingerie in disguise.

By the time we finally sat down at a restaurant inside the mall, I was starving and exhausted.

I picked at my salad, hoping they'd focus on eating and not... interrogating me.

Of course, I wasn't that lucky.

It didn't take long.

Estrella leaned in, her eyes gleaming with mischief.

"So..." she drawled. "What's going on with you and Andrés?"

I nearly choked on a piece of lettuce.

Yolanda chuckled softly beside me, clearly used to Estrella's complete lack of subtlety.

I swallowed quickly, feeling my cheeks flame.

"It's... complicated," I mumbled, stabbing my fork into my salad like it had personally offended me.

Estrella's grin only grew wider.

"Complicated how? You're staying in his room. He's practically glued to you. Everybody can see he's crazy about you."

I fidgeted with my napkin, heart pounding under the weight of their attention.

"It's just... Andrés wants us to be mates," I said carefully, struggling to find the right words. "But... it's hard to process. He kidnapped me."

Neither Yolanda nor Estrella looked particularly shocked.

They exchanged a knowing glance before Yolanda spoke, her voice gentle.

"He told us he did it for your protection."

I sighed, leaning back in my seat, curling my hands around my glass like it could ground me.

"That's what he says. But still... I'm not supposed to feel things for the man who took me. That's not normal."

"Feel things how?" Estrella pressed, her eyes dancing with curiosity.

I exhaled slowly, struggling to make sense of it all.
"Like... my body and my wolf see him one way, but my mind keeps screaming that I shouldn't."

Yolanda tilted her head thoughtfully.
"Does your wolf like him?" she asked, her voice calm, non-judgmental.

I blinked, caught off guard by the question.
"Yes," I admitted quietly. "She does."

Yolanda gave a small, knowing nod.
"Sometimes," she said softly, "our wolves know things long before we let ourselves see them."

That thought lingers in my mind. Could it be true? Does my wolf like Andrés because she sees something in him that I don't yet understand? The uncertainty coils inside me, unfamiliar and unsettling. I've never been out of sync with her before.

I shifted uncomfortably in my seat, feeling exposed.
"I'm considering it," I said at last, voice barely above a whisper. "But I won't agree to anything until the Alpha herself promises the alliance. I'm not tying myself to anyone without ensuring my people are protected."

Yolanda smiled warmly.
"Spoken like a true leader, *mija*."

Estrella leaned back in her chair, letting out a low whistle.
"Girl, Andres must have crazy willpower," she said, laughing. "Wanting you the way he does and not touching you?"

I nearly dropped my fork again.

I glanced at Yolanda, who calmly sipped her tea, pretending not to hear—but the amused glint in her eyes gave her away.

Clearing my throat, I pushed my salad around my plate, my cheeks burning hotter than ever.

"He's... tried," I admitted reluctantly. "But I made it clear. Nothing's happening until we're properly mated. I'm saving myself for my mating night."

Yolanda only nodded, pride softening her expression.

Estrella leaned in closer, her smile turning downright wicked.

"I was actually hoping you were going to spill how he is in bed."

I choked on my drink, coughing violently.

"What?"

Estrella just rolled her eyes, completely unfazed.

"Oh, come on, Mai. Don't act all innocent. The way Andrés looks at you? Like he's two seconds away from devouring you whole? We all kind of assumed you two were already... you know."

Yolanda gasped, smacking Estrella lightly on the arm.

"Estrella! *Por favor*!"

Estrella just shrugged, flashing a grin that said she wasn't even a little bit sorry.

"What? We're all adults here. Besides," she added, winking, "I just wanted to know if the rumors were true."

I narrowed my eyes at her, suspicious.

"What rumors?"

Estrella leaned in, lowering her voice like she was sharing the juiciest secret.

"You know... the ones the she-wolves whisper about. That Andrés is pure control even in bed. That he's..." She waggled her eyebrows suggestively. "Well-endowed. And that if you ever let him have you..." she grinned wickedly, "you'll be aching for days."

My entire body heated at the memory that instantly flashed through my mind the night in the library.

Andrés between my legs.

The feel of his mouth, his hands, the way he pulled every sound out of me with terrifying ease, like he already owned every part of me.

I cleared my throat, struggling to keep my face neutral.

"Sorry to burst your nosy bubble," I rasped, my voice slightly hoarse, "but we haven't had sex."

Silence.

Then...

Yolanda reached over, squeezing my hand gently, her warmth settling something that had been tight in my chest all day.

"Don't focus on any of that, *mija*," she said, her voice soothing but firm. "Focus on how he treats you. On how he makes you feel. And how he's willing to stand beside you and your pack. That's what truly matters."

I nodded slowly, swallowing around the lump in my throat.

Because deep down... I knew she was right.

Estrella tapped her chin thoughtfully, her mischievous glint softening a little.

"But," she said with a small smile, "if he's waiting, it means he's serious. Otherwise, he wouldn't bother. Trust me."

That thought landed heavy and warm in my chest, stirring something I didn't want to name yet.

Yolanda squeezed my hand again, her next words gentle but full of quiet strength.

"Andrés is a good man, Mai. Mate or not, once he claims someone in his heart... he doesn't let go easily."

I exhaled slowly, the truth of her words sinking deeper into the places I tried so hard to guard.

Because even if I was terrified to admit it...

I already knew that.

⁘

ANDRÉS

My wolf hated leaving Mai's side, but my responsibilities to my pack weighed heavily on my shoulders. Especially now. With Alpha George still at large and the taint of dark magic slithering its way into our lands, I couldn't afford to let my guard down.

After everything that had happened—Sofía's wedding, the attack with dark magic, and the dead body found in our territory, it became clear that our enemies had grown bolder. Our pack needed protection. I needed to keep Mai safe. The thought of anything happening to her while I was away sent a wave of fury through me.

We all sat in Sofía's study, the room heavy with silence. Leo sat to my left, arms crossed, his face hardened with determination. Sofía sat behind her desk, her presence as commanding as ever, despite the trauma she had endured. Several high-ranking warriors and trackers filled the space, their expressions grim.

"We have a serious problem," Sofía began, her voice sharp. "There has been an increase in women from our pack reported missing. It started with two last week, but this week we have a total of five."

A ripple of gasps and murmurs spread across the room. My jaw tightened.

"Why are we just now hearing about this?" I asked, my voice barely above a growl.

Sofía's eyes narrowed. "First of all, your ass was MIA with Mai, so don't come at me with that accusatory tone. Secondly, we initially thought these were isolated incidents until this morning. The dead body found in the northern woods belonged to one of the missing women."

Silence settled over the room as the weight of her words sank in.

Leo cleared his throat. "She disappeared two days ago. We assumed she might have left to visit friends out of state. She was one of our pack members who didn't stay here full-time. But the way she was found..." He hesitated, glancing at Sofía.

"She was marked with dark magic," Sofía finished. "The spells done to her body were similar to the ones used at my wedding."

The room fell into heavy silence. The enemy was getting too close, their methods more ruthless. I clenched my fists, rage surging through me.

"What does this mean for the rest of our pack?" Darren asked. "If this is George's doing."

"It is," Sofía interjected. "I can feel it in my bones. He's working with a powerful dark witch."

A cold dread settled in my chest. I scanned the worried faces of my family and friends. Fear was dangerous. A pack couldn't afford fear; it weakened the bonds that kept us strong.

"What do we do?" Darren asked.

I exhaled sharply. "We set up patrols at every border, double our night guards, and start tracking every missing woman's last known location. If this is dark magic, we find a way to counter it. It's a good thing that the witches from New York are coming to assist us."

Sofía nodded in agreement.

She turned to Leo. "I want you in charge of the trackers. I need full reports on every disappearance and any strange activity near our lands. Andres, you'll lead the patrol teams."

I nodded. "Consider it done."

Mason stepped forward then, his voice firm. "And what about the women? If they're the ones being targeted, we need a way to keep them safe."

He was right. A protective shield wasn't enough. We needed a strategy.

"Curfew," Sofía decided. "Any women traveling outside the packhouse must be accompanied by warriors. We make it clear that no one goes anywhere alone."

A solemn agreement passed through the room. This was war, whether we wanted it or not. Alpha George had declared it the moment he kidnapped our Alpha. He so-lidified it when he used dark magic against our pack.

I thought of Mai. If George thought he could take any-thing else from me, he was sorely mistaken.

He wouldn't touch my pack.

He wouldn't touch my mate.

I'd see to it myself.

Chapter 21

ANDRÉS

As the meeting wrapped up, I turned to leave the study, but Sofia's voice called me back.

"Andrés, can I have a word?" she said, still seated behind her desk, with Mason standing quietly at her side.

I paused, then nodded, curiosity sparking.

"Sure," I said, moving to sit across from them.

Sofía didn't waste time.

"Jason is heading to Black Stone Pack to speak with the elders about Alpha George," she began, her expression unreadable. "While he's there, I've asked him to also gather information about Mai—specifically her role within their pack."

My brows shot up.

"You think my mate had something to do with this?" I asked, a little sharper than I intended. I felt my wolf immediately bristle at the mere suggestion.

Sofía's jaw tightened, but her voice stayed even.

"No," she said firmly. "I'm telling you that as an Alpha, it's my responsibility to investigate every possibility, even the ones I don't believe are likely. As your sister, I'm giving you a heads-up so you don't lose your mind when you hear about it later."

I exhaled sharply, forcing my muscles to relax before my wolf pushed to the surface.

"I guess... thank you for the warning. But for the record, you're wasting your time. Mai's not like that. She's a good person."

Sofía's lips tugged into a faint smirk.

"I know, Andrés. But you taught me to never assume. Always verify," she said, throwing my own old advice right back at me.

Despite everything, a reluctant smile pulled at my mouth.

Touché.

Seeing the tension finally ease, I decided to bring up what had been weighing on me.

"Actually," I said, shifting forward in my seat, "since I have you both here... there's two things I need to ask."

Sofía arched a brow, intrigued.

"Oh?"

I met both of their gazes steadily.

"As you know, Mai comes from Black Stone Pack. Now that things are changing over there, I want to formally ask if, as Alpha of Luna Stone, you would consider an alliance with their new leadership."

I watched their reactions closely, my wolf tense beneath my skin, needing their answer more than I wanted to admit.

Sofía took a slow breath, exchanging a glance with Mason before nodding.

"Considering Crescent Moon Pack is already offering aid, and your union would strengthen ties... I don't see why not," she said with a small, genuine smile.

"In fact," Mason added, chuckling, "your dad already told us about your mate's request. You're just making it official."

Relief flooded my chest. Finally, something was falling into place.

"So what's your other question?" asked Sofía.

I hesitated for a moment, rubbing the back of my neck. "Tomorrow is Maya's twenty-first birthday, and I have no idea what to do about the mate bond."

Sofía's lips curled into a knowing smile. "Dear brother... are you nervous?"

"Stop it," I grumbled. "I'm here for help, not to be made fun of."

She chuckled but held up her hands in surrender. "Alright, alright. So, what exactly do you need help with?"

I exhaled, feeling the weight of my predicament. "The whole damn thing. Should I just go home tonight like nothing's different? Sleep beside her, hope she doesn't wake up past midnight, realize I'm her mate while I'm unconscious, freak out, and leave?" I ran a hand through my hair, overwhelmed. "I mean, what if she panics? What if she needs time?"

Sofía pressed her lips together, considering my words. "Oh yeah, I can see how that could be a problem."

Before she could say more, Mason spoke up, a knowing grin on his face. "If you ask me? Make her miss you."

I turned to him, intrigued. "Go on."

"Don't go home tonight. Stay here. Keep yourself busy. Make her wait until the birthday party to see you. All day long, her wolf will catch hints of your scent, pulling her toward you. She'll have the entire day to come to terms with the bond before she even lays eyes on you. The anticipation will drive her crazy, and by the time she actually sees you, curiosity and instinct will take over." His smirk widened. "She'll come to you."

I stared at him for a beat before breaking into a grin. "You are a fucking genius."

"But what if she texts me?" I asked, suddenly realizing the flaw in the plan. "What do I tell her?"

Sofía leaned back, arms crossed, thinking. "You can't just ignore her. That'll make her panic, and then she'll come looking for you, which defeats the whole purpose."

"Exactly," Mason agreed. "You have to be strategic. Keep your responses vague but reassuring. Something like, 'I've got a lot going on today, may have to stay at the packhouse dealing with pack safety. Can't wait.' That way, she knows you're not avoiding her, but you're also not giving anything away."

Sofía nodded. "Or if she gets insistent, tease her a little. Say something cryptic, like, 'Tomorrow's a big day, just trust me.' Make her curious but don't give her enough to figure it out."

I sighed, running a hand down my face. "So basically, keep her on edge, make her want to see me more?"

Mason smirked. "Exactly. You want her wolf restless, craving your presence before she even realizes why."

Sofía grinned. "It'll make the mate bond hit even harder when she finally sees you. The second she locks eyes with you, all that curiosity, longing, and anticipation will crash down on her like a tidal wave."

I huffed a laugh, shaking my head. "You two are dangerously good at this."

Sofía winked. "That's why you came to us, isn't it?"

I chuckled, feeling a little more confident. "Alright. I'll play it your way. Let's see if my mate can handle it."

Later that night, I crashed at my parents' home, in the same room I had when I was a teenager. The room looked just as I had left it, untouched by time. As I set my bag down and sat on the edge of the bed, my father walked in, his brows raised in curiosity.

"I thought I saw you come in. So, what do I owe this visit?" he asked, leaning against the doorframe.

"Sofía and Mason suggested I stay away from Mai until the actual party," I explained. "They think the anticipation will make her more accepting of the mate bond when she finally sees me."

My father shook his head, rolling his eyes as he walked further into the room. "Since when do we take advice from those two?" he scoffed, sitting beside me on the bed. "They couldn't even figure out their own bond at the beginning. And that was after they both knew they were fated mates."

That thought hadn't even crossed my mind. Sofía had refused her bond for a while, making poor Mason chase after her like a desperate pup. They even tried to hide their connection from the rest of us. Why the hell did I decide to listen to them?

Panic started creeping in. Had I just made a huge mistake?

"So, you think I should go home?" I asked, uncertain.

My father shook his head. "Not necessarily. Let's start with why you sought advice from those two in the first place."

I sighed and ran a hand through my hair before explaining my concerns: how I didn't want to overwhelm Mai, how I feared she might panic or reject me if she found out too soon, and how I thought distance might help her process it better before the bond fully snapped into place.

My father listened patiently, nodding in thought. "Hmm... I see. You have valid concerns. But honestly, son, you can't predict how someone will react to finding their mate. Some people embrace it instantly and live their lives happily ever after. Others... well, some reject it, and no one really knows why. One thing I will say, though, is that you did one thing right. You got to know her first. She already likes you, even without knowing you're her mate."

"You think so?" I asked, hopeful.

"I know so," he said with certainty. "It's the way she looks at you when she doesn't think anyone else is watching."

I exhaled sharply, my chest tightening. "I've never felt so damn weak and insecure," I admitted, frustration lacing my voice. "I hate this feeling."

My father let out a deep laugh and clapped a hand on my back. "Welcome to being in love."

I groaned, shaking my head, but deep down, I knew he was right.

"So, what did you tell that lovely girl you were doing tonight?" he asked, amusement still lingering in his tone.

"Oh, I told her the investigation would keep me out all night and that I'd be crashing here," I admitted. "She doesn't expect to see me until the party."

My father nodded thoughtfully. "Alright, then we stick with that. We keep the story the same, but we have to make it special. You want her to be so overwhelmed with emotion that she'll forgive the lie."

"But Dad, she can't be mad at me for the lie, right? It's against the Council's rules for me to tell her about our bond before she comes of age."

My father chuckled, shaking his head. "Son, women don't care about rules or laws when it comes to their emotions. All she'll care about is that you withheld the truth from her. But..." His smirk widened. "If we plan something unforgettable for her birthday. something unique and special, she'll forgive you."

I stared at him for a moment, then sighed. "And you think this will work?"

"I've been mated for over twenty-five years. Trust me."

So, my father and I got to work, planning something truly special for Mai, something that would make her see just how much she meant to me.

The next morning, I woke up feeling more anxious than I ever had before. My heart pounded, my wolf restless beneath my skin. Today was the day, Maya was twenty-one. I wondered if she had already scented me, if her wolf had recognized the bond between us. Did she figure it out already? Had she woken up in the middle of the night with my scent wrapping around her, pulling her toward me?

I grabbed my phone off the nightstand, my pulse racing as I checked for messages. Nothing.

Good... right?

I hated this, this uncertainty, this mess of emotions swirling in my chest. I was a man who always knew what he wanted, never wasted time second-guessing himself. But with Mai, everything was different. She turned my world inside out, made me feel things I never thought I could.

Running a frustrated hand through my hair, I pushed out of bed and headed for the shower, desperate to clear my head. The bathroom filled with steam as hot water poured over my skin, the heat soothing my tense muscles. But the second I closed my eyes, images of her flooded my mind.

Her soft green eyes, the way they darkened with desire, the way they contrasted so beautifully against her smooth, flawless skin. The way she bites her lip when she gets nervous, that small act so unknowingly seductive, had me wanting to claim her right then and there. And her body....

Her small, perky breasts with rose-pink nipples that hardened at my slightest touch, so perfectly shaped to fit in my hands. Her delicate curves, soft yet firm beneath my touch. The gentle slope of her waist leading to the swell of her hips, the way her toned thighs framed her sweet pussy, pretty and pink. It all drove me to madness.

Her scent, a perfect blend of honeysuckle and citrus, wrapped around me, intoxicating, making my wolf restless with need. These memories were like an aphrodisiac that had me fisting my hard cock up and down, imagining it was Mai's tight pussy. I braced a hand against the tile wall, my breath coming out heavier as I picture it so vividly—her body slick with water, pressed against mine, her heat branding me as her own. The softness of her breasts against my chest, the way her legs would wrap around me as I carried her, pinning her against the cool tiles, water running in rivulets down our bodies.

Her breathy moans echoed in my mind, the sound of her pleasure, the way she would shudder under my touch, desperate for more. I groaned, gripping my shaft, moving my hand up and down, imagining it was her, her warm, wet heat squeezing me just like she did when my fingers were deep inside her.

My wolf growled inside me, as I continued to fuck my hand, squeezing my shaft tighter. I remembered the way she moaned in pleasure, how her body arched into me, begging for more with every thrust, her cries of ecstasy making me lose all control. The way her walls clenched around me, pulling me deeper, her nails clawing at my skin as she surrendered completely to the pleasure only I could give her.

A shudder ripped through me, pleasure tightening my core as I growled her name while I spilled my seed on the tile wall. My body ached for her, my wolf howling for the moment when she would finally be mine, truly and completely.

But not yet.

I took a ragged breath as I let the cold water shock me back to reality. Tonight, she would know. Tonight, she would feel everything I had been holding back. And there wouldn't be a damn thing standing in my way.

Stepping out of the shower, I quickly toweled off and dressed in dark jeans and a fitted black shirt, something simple but clean. I ruffled my hair dry, not bothering to style it.

When I walked into the living area, my father was already sipping on his coffee, watching me with an amused expression.

"Morning, son. Sleep well?" he asked, setting his mug down.

I huffed. "Not really."

He chuckled knowingly. "Figured as much."

I sat down across from him, rubbing the back of my neck. "Where's Mom?"

"She left early to help Mai with something," he said, his lips curling into a smirk. "Seems your mate has a lot on her plate today."

My stomach clenched. The idea of my mother spending time with Mai, fussing over her, making sure she was ready for tonight—it made everything feel more real.

"Good," I muttered. "She deserves a perfect day."

My father nodded, setting his coffee aside. "Speaking of which, we've got work to do. That surprise isn't going to set itself up."

I stood, rolling my shoulders, shaking off the lingering frustration from the morning.

"Then let's get to it."

Because tonight, everything changed. And I was going to make damn sure Mai would never doubt what she meant to me.

Chapter 22

MAYA

After my girls' day out at the mall, I have to admit, I'm glad I went. Shopping might not be my thing, but the girl talk? That was something I didn't know I needed. Even if it meant discussing personal things in front of Andrés' mother. Yolanda's warmth, her motherly wisdom... it made me realize just how much I miss having my own mother near me.

Night came and Andrés did not show up. I sent him a text, hoping to hear from him, but after taking a shower, I passed out immediately. I guess all that shopping wore me out.

The day of my birthday celebration had arrived, and to my surprise, Andrés had never come home the night before. I had known he was caught up with the investigation, that it would be a late night, but I had expected to wake up beside him that morning. I had grown so used to his presence, his warmth against me, the steady rise and fall of his chest as he slept. Now, with his side of the bed cold and empty, there had been a strange ache inside me. A void I had never felt before.

What was happening to me?

I had taken a deep breath, trying to shake the unsettling feeling, but the moment the air had filled my lungs, it had slammed into me. A scent faint yet potent, dark spices and bourbon, rich and intoxicating. My core had clenched, heat coiling low in my stomach. My wolf had stirred, fully alert and desperate. The next thing I had known, I had been on my feet, yanking on clothes with shaky hands, my heart hammering as I had hunted for the source of the scent.

I had searched the house, every room, every hallway, but nothing. And yet, the scent had lingered, teasing me, wrapping around me like an invisible force. My wolf had clawed to be let out, desperate, needy. She had sensed the owner of the scent, but we couldn't find them. It had been as if they had been here... but not here.

Confusion had battled with raw, unfiltered arousal.

Could this have been... my mate?

Oh, God. Had it been someone in the pack?

What if it hadn't been Andrés?

What if it had been Andrés?

Panic and desire had warred inside me, leaving me breathless. I had needed answers, but I had had no one to go to. My father had never prepared me for this—for the way my body was betraying me, for the way my wolf was losing control.

I had grabbed my phone, desperate for a distraction, and had seen a missed text from Andres.

> Andrés: *I'm staying at my parents' tonight. Super busy with the investigation. See you tomorrow at the birthday party.*

Tomorrow. He wouldn't be there until that night at my birthday party.

I had been alone in this.

My wolf had whined, restless and needy, and I had rubbed my temples, trying to will her into submission. *Calm down, girl. Stop acting like a feral beast.* But she hadn't listened; she had been too consumed by the scent, too wrapped up in this hunger neither of us had fully understood.

I had needed guidance. I had needed someone who knew what the hell was happening to me.

Then, an idea had come to mind. I had remembered when Andrés had given me the phone the day before, he had told me he had already saved the numbers of everyone close to him in the pack.

With trembling fingers, I had searched through my contacts and pressed call.

Two rings. Then—

"Good morning, dear, and happy birthday!" Yolanda's voice had been warm and filled with love.

I had swallowed, still breathless. "Hi, Mrs. Yolanda. Good morning."

"For heaven's sake, don't call me that," she had scolded lightly. "Call me Yolanda. Or *Mami,* like all my kids do. Whatever makes you comfortable."

I had hesitated. *Mami.* The word had stirred something in my chest, something deep and longing. My wolf had preened at the idea, but I had shaken my head. I hadn't been taking her opinion into consideration that day—she had been acting feral as it was.

"Okay," I had said softly, but that had been all I could manage. The idea of having someone like Yolanda as a mother figure had been overwhelming.

"To what did I owe this call, sweetheart?" she had asked, her voice warm with concern.

I had swallowed hard, my fingers clenching around the phone. "I... I need help," I had admitted, my voice barely above a whisper. "My wolf and I, something was happening. I didn't understand what was going on with my body, and I had no one to ask. I was sorry to bother her with this, but..."

"Oh, *mamita*," she had interrupted, her voice filled with understanding. "Calm down. I'm glad you called me. I'll help you however I can. Let me come over so we can talk privately. I'll be there soon."

The moment the call had ended, I hadn't been able to sit still. I had paced the living area, talking to myself, to my wolf, trying to make sense of the madness. But then my eyes had landed on something draped over a chair.

A suit jacket.

Andres' suit jacket.

Before I could have stopped myself, I had moved toward it, my fingers brushing over the fabric as my body had acted on pure instinct. I had grabbed it, brought it to my face, and inhaled deeply.

The scent.

That dark, intoxicating scent that had been driving me insane. The one sending my wolf into a frenzy. It had been his.

Andres.

My wolf had howled inside me, the realization crashing down like a tidal wave. The scent had been his all along. But what had it meant?

A shiver had run down my spine as I had clutched the jacket tighter.

I had been desperate for answers.

A sharp knock at the front door had snapped me out of my trance, my fingers still curled tightly around Andrés' suit jacket like it had been the only thing tethering me to reality. My wolf had been pacing, restless, whining for something I couldn't yet grasp.

I had taken a deep breath, trying to calm the storm raging inside me, but it had been no use. My body had felt like it was on fire, my skin too tight, my senses too sharp. Every inhale had been saturated with that intoxicating scent: spices, bourbon, and something distinctly him. It had been like the universe had decided to torment me with a craving I didn't understand.

With shaky hands, I had finally released the jacket, forcing myself to move toward the door. My legs had felt heavy, my heartbeat pounding in my ears.

I had opened it, and there had stood Yolanda, her warm brown eyes filled with concern. She hadn't waited for me to speak, hadn't hesitated for a second. She had stepped inside like she had already known something was wrong, her hands immediately finding my shoulders. The moment her palms had pressed against me, some of the tension in my chest had loosened, just enough for me to breathe properly.

"Come, sit," she had urged softly, guiding me to the couch. "Tell me everything."

I had sunk down, exhaling sharply. "It started this morning," I had murmured, my fingers knotting together in my lap. "I woke up, and Andrés wasn't here. I had already felt... off. But then I caught this scent." My voice had faltered, my pulse kicking up. Heat had crept up my neck as I had forced the words out. "And it did something to me."

Yolanda's eyes had flickered with knowing warmth. "What kind of something, cariño?"

I had swallowed hard, staring at the floor. "It made my wolf go crazy. It was intoxicating. It made me restless, and want something I didn't understand."

Yolanda had studied me for a long moment, and then her gaze had shifted to the suit jacket.

Her expression had softened. A slow smile had pulled at her lips.

"Was that Andrés' jacket?" she had asked.

I had blinked, my breath catching. "Yes."

She had leaned back slightly, watching me closely. "And that scent you were reacting to... it belonged to him?"

The truth had slammed into me so fast I had felt light-headed. My stomach had twisted violently.

"I...I don't understand," I had whispered. "Why would his scent affect me like this? I've been around him for weeks, and this has never happened before!"

Yolanda's smile had grown.

"When we turn twenty-one, our wolves mature," she had explained. "They begin to experience things differently—more intensely. Your wolf has recognized Andrés' scent, but she doesn't know what it means yet."

She had reached for my hand, squeezing gently.

"Mai... I think you need to talk to Andrés."

My breath had shuddered out of me as I had stared at her, my mind spinning so fast it had felt like I was falling.

"But why didn't my wolf know?" I had whispered, desperation creeping into my voice. "She should have known what was happening, shouldn't she?"

Yolanda had shaken her head. "Not necessarily. Every wolf matures differently. Some wolves understand everything, others—especially when there are emotional barriers in the way—need some help." She had given me a pointed look. "And let's be honest, you had plenty of those."

I had swallowed hard. She had been right. I had.

Yolanda had squeezed my hand again, grounding me. "The important thing now is to figure out what this scent means to you and your wolf. You could sit here all day and come up with a hundred different explanations, but there's only one way to know for sure."

I had looked up at her, my throat tight. "How?"

"You go to the source," she had said simply. "You find Andrés."

My chest had tightened. Find him. Face this.

Tears had pricked at my eyes, emotions colliding inside me—fear, anticipation, desire. "I don't know... I'm scared," I had admitted, my voice barely above a whisper.

Yolanda had smiled, soft but firm. She had cupped my cheek, brushing her thumb over my skin with the kind of affection I hadn't felt in years.

"Oh, *mamita*," she had murmured. "Don't be. You are stronger than you think."

I had inhaled sharply, nodding.

It had been time.

I had needed to find Andrés. I had needed to know.

Determined to find Andrés, Yolanda had given me a ride to the packhouse, considering I hadn't had a car or known my way around the territory. With words of encouragement, she had dropped me off at the entrance of the house.

The moment I had stepped into the bustling packhouse, an overwhelming mixture of scents from multiple wolves had engulfed me. The air had thrummed with energy, packmates moving in and out, their wary eyes flicking toward me with a mix of curiosity and suspicion.

I had steeled my nerves, pushing past the weight of their scrutiny, and had focused on what I had come there for: Andrés. His scent, faded but present, had led me toward Sofía's study, but before I could have reached the door, I had been stopped.

"Wait a minute... who is this pretty little thing?"

A deep, unfamiliar voice had dripped with amusement. I had turned, finding myself face-to-face with a tall man, his dark tan skin illuminated by the dim lighting. Piercing green eyes had raked over me.

Unsettled, I had taken a step back, shrugging off his firm grip on my forearm. "I'm looking for Andrés. Excuse me," I had said, my tone even as I had attempted to sidestep him.

He had moved, blocking my path once more. His nostrils had flared as he inhaled, a smirk curling his lips. "You're not a member of this pack," he had mused, his voice laced with curiosity. "But I smell Andrés all over you. No claim mark, though..." He had tilted his head, as if piecing together a puzzle. Then, a slow, knowing grin had spread across his face. "I see. Just a plaything, then."

I had tensed, my fingers curling into fists.

He had leaned in, his voice dropping to a low, velvety murmur. "Didn't know Andrés brought his toys into pack territory. But if he's done with you... maybe you can come play with me instead." His fingers had caressed along the exposed skin of my arm. Disgust had flared hot in my chest, and I had batted his hand away with sharp precision.

My gaze had hardened, my voice like steel. "I belong to no one, and I'm certainly not interested in playing." My lips had pressed into a thin line. "So, no thanks."

The man's smirk had only deepened at my defiance, amusement dancing in his emerald eyes. He had taken a step closer, filling the space between us.

"Oh, feisty," he had purred, his fingers twitching at his sides as if resisting the urge to reach for me again. "I like that."

I had tried once more to slip past him, but he had moved faster, his grip firm as he had seized my wrist. I had jerked my arm, but his strength had been undeniable. My pulse had spiked as he had crowded me, his breath warm over my cheek.

"No need to play hard to get," he had murmured, his free hand brushing against my waist. "I promise, I can be very persuasive."

A shiver of revulsion had rolled down my spine. I had twisted my body, trying to break free, but he had been too strong, too relentless. Before I had summoned the strength to fight him off, a female voice had cut through the tension.

"I suggest you get your filthy hands off her before I rip them off your body."

The voice had been low and lethal.

The man had stilled for half a second, his grip loosening just slightly as he had turned his head.

Xiomara and Estrella.

Xiomara had stepped into view, her onyx curls cascading over her shoulders, sharp brown eyes blazing with fury. Her toned frame had been coiled with barely contained violence, the energy around her practically vibrating with rage.

The man had chuckled, but there had been a nervous edge to it now. "Stay out of this, Xiomara. Just having a little fun."

Her lips had curled, exposing the sharp glint of her canines. "She doesn't look like she's having fun. Javier." Her voice had been eerily calm, but the deadly intent behind it had been clear.

He had turned back to me, his fingers tightening once more. "Don't be like that. You didn't even let her answer."

A sickening crack had echoed through the air.

Xiomara had moved too fast for me to see, but in an instant, the man had been yanked off me with terrifying force. His body had slammed into the opposite wall, the impact sending a deep thud through the packhouse.

He had barely had a moment to recover before Xiomara's booted foot had pressed against his throat, pinning him effortlessly to the ground.

"I warned you," she had said, her voice pure ice. "But since you clearly have trouble understanding words, let me spell it out for you." She had leaned in, her hand gripping his jaw with enough force to make him wince. "She is not interested. Touch her again, and I will tear you apart. Limb by limb."

The man had gasped, his eyes flashing between defiance and fear. He had struggled against her hold, but Xiomara hadn't so much as flinched.

"You think you can just—" he had started, but she had applied more pressure, cutting him off with a strangled sound.

"I don't think," she had growled, leaning down until their noses had nearly touched.

"Do you know who she is? Who she is to Andrés?" Estrella had said.

For a moment, silence had blanketed the room, thick and suffocating. Then, finally, the man had shaken his head. Smiling, Xiomara had lifted her foot from his throat. "Don't worry, you will."

He had coughed, rubbing his neck, glaring up at her.

Xiomara had tilted her head. "Leave."

The man had scrambled to his feet, shooting me one last unreadable glance before slinking away into the packhouse.

My breath had still been unsteady when Xiomara had turned to me, her gaze softening just slightly.
"You okay?"

I had nodded, though my hands had still been trembling.

Estrella had exhaled, then placed a firm, reassuring hand on my shoulder. Her touch had been grounding, a silent promise that I had been safe now. "Next time, don't be afraid to break a few bones if someone touches you without permission," she had said, her voice steady but edged with a playful smirk.

Despite the lingering adrenaline in my veins, I had managed a weak chuckle.

Xiomara's gaze had sharpened with curiosity. "So, what were you doing here anyway? The party's not for a couple more hours."

I had run a hand through my hair, still trying to shake off the unsettling encounter. "I was looking for Andrés. It was really important that I talked to him."

Estrella's smirk had faded into something more apologetic. "Oh, sorry, hun. Andrés left with his dad to run some errands. I was told he wouldn't be back until close to the party."

Damn it. A frustrated sigh had escaped my lips. It had looked like I would have to wait until the party to get the answers I needed.

I had taken a deep breath, willing myself to be patient. "You think you guys can give me a ride back home?"

Estrella's grin had returned, this time more mischievous. "Actually…" She had paused, a glint of excitement flashing in her eyes. "The girls were planning to surprise you at your place and get ready with you."

I had blinked, caught off guard. "Wait, what?"

She had winked. "Yep. So, instead of me just dropping you off, let's stop by my place first. I'll grab my stuff, and then we'll head to your place together. Trust me, it'll be fun."

A small smile had tugged at my lips despite everything that had just happened. A day with the girls, a distraction from my swirling thoughts—maybe that had been exactly what I had needed before facing Andrés.

"Alright," I had said, nodding. "Let's do it."

With that, Estrella had looped her arm through mine, leading me out of the packhouse like nothing had just happened, while Xiomara had rolled her eyes and followed us.

Chapter 23

MAYA

When Estrella said the girls were coming to help me get ready, I hadn't imagined she meant half the she-wolves in the pack. Yet here they were, flooding Andrés' home with their infectious energy, their laughter weaving through the air like a melody. The entire house buzzed with feminine magic, a sacred rite of preparation before the grand celebration.

Every mirror reflected a different scene: eager hands styling hair into cascading waves, shimmering powders being dusted onto collarbones, lips being painted in sultry reds and soft pinks. It was a whirlwind of beauty and sisterhood, a tradition that had existed long before I came into this pack. And yet, here I was, at the heart of it all, feeling both overwhelmed and oddly touched.

I sat in the center of the chaos, my reflection staring back at me, a little unsure, a little breathless. A girl on the brink of something bigger than herself.

Yolanda, Andrés' mother, entered the room just as one of the girls dusted a fine shimmer across my skin, making me glow under the soft lighting. Her presence was grounding, a warmth I hadn't realized I was craving. The maternal kindness in her eyes made me wish, just for a moment, that my own mother was here. But even in her absence, I was grateful for Yolanda's unwavering support.

"Please, Yolanda, save me," I pleaded, my voice laced with desperation as I clutched at the last threads of my patience.

She let out a rich, knowing laugh, her amusement evident. "Oh, no, sweetheart. This is tradition. A rite of passage for all the women in our pack," she said, tucking a stray curl behind my ear with a tender touch. "You get to be pampered and adored tonight. So, suck it up, buttercup."

I groaned dramatically, but the warmth in her voice made it impossible to truly be annoyed.

Then, as if the moment wasn't already overwhelming enough, Yolanda stepped aside with a flourish, revealing what could only be described as a dream.

Two rows of gowns were wheeled into the room, each one more stunning than the last. My breath hitched as I took in the sea of fabrics—silk, lace, velvet, and tulle. Every shade imaginable, from soft pastels to bold, striking hues. Gold embroidery caught the light, delicate pearls glimmered, and the whisper of fine material filled the air as the girls excitedly reached for different options.

I felt like I had just walked into a fairytale, like a lost princess being fitted for her royal debut.

"So many beautiful dresses," I breathed, running my fingers over the luxurious fabrics. My heart pounded. "How am I supposed to choose?"

"Easy," Yolanda said with a playful wink. "Try them on, and we'll take Polaroids of each one. Then you can compare and pick your favorite. It'll be fun!"

The girls cheered in agreement, their excitement contagious.

The first dress I tried on was a deep sapphire blue, the fabric hugging my curves with a sweetheart neckline and a daring thigh-high slit. As soon as I stepped out, the room filled with wolf whistles and a chorus of playful howls.

"Too sexy," one of the older she-wolves tsked, shaking her head. "You'll give the males heart attacks before the night even begins."

I bit my lip to stifle a laugh.

The next dress was a soft blush pink, ethereal and delicate, with floral embroidery scattered across a flowing chiffon skirt. I twirled in front of the mirror, watching the fabric ripple like water, but the reactions were mixed.

"You look like an angel," one of the younger girls sighed dreamily.

"Too innocent," another teased. "You're not a blushing pup anymore, Mai."

I smirked, shaking my head as I moved on.

A rich purple gown followed, regal in its own right. The off-the-shoulder sleeves gave me an air of quiet confidence, and the fabric clung to me like it was made for my body.

Some of the women swooned, murmuring about how it made my skin glow, but something about it didn't feel right. It wasn't the dress.

I cycled through more silver, black, even a bold red that had the younger she-wolves fanning themselves dramatically. Each one was stunning, but none of them felt like mine.

Until I stepped into the dress.

The moment I slid it on, the room fell into an almost eerie silence. A collective breath was held, eyes widening as I turned to face them.

The emerald green fabric molded to my body with effortless grace, the bodice adorned with intricate gold embroidery, swirling in delicate patterns that resembled the enchanted vines of the forest. The off-the-shoulder sleeves draped elegantly, highlighting my collarbones, while layers of soft tulle cascaded like mist rolling through the trees. It was breathtaking. Powerful. It felt like me.

I stepped forward, standing before the mirror, my breath catching in my throat. My reflection stared back, no longer unsure. No longer hesitant.

I looked like I belonged.

Like I was meant for this.

"You look like a goddess," Yolanda whispered, pride shining in her eyes.

"Andrés' Goddess," Estrella added with a smirk, her eyes twinkling with mischief.

Heat rose to my cheeks, but I couldn't deny the warmth blooming in my chest. For the first time, I felt it, the weight of something greater, the significance of this moment.

This night, this celebration... it was more than just a birthday. It was the beginning of something new.

I smiled, turning to face the girls. "This is the one."

The room erupted into cheers, and as I stood there, wrapped in emerald and gold, I knew one thing for certain.

Tonight would be unforgettable.

"Alright, everyone, we've found the dress, so let's get to work!" Yolanda clapped her hands, instantly commanding the room. "We need to adjust her hair and makeup to complement this gown. Tesoro, work your magic on her face. Esmeralda, hair is all yours. Betty, nails. Sarah, toes. We have to be ready by six, so let's move!"

Just like that, the women sprang into action. I barely had time to blink before I was being pulled in different directions, my body no longer my own as hands fussed over me, smoothing, plucking, painting. The hum of chatter filled the air, but all I could do was close my eyes and try to focus on Andrés. It had been three weeks since we met, and this was the longest I had gone without seeing him. The ache of his absence was deeper than I expected, a dull pull in my chest, like a tether stretching between us.

"Uhm... Mai, your eyebrows need some plucking," Tesoro observed, squinting at me. "When was the last time you waxed them?"

"Never," I admitted with a cringe, already knowing that was not the answer she wanted. But the truth was, I'd never cared much for this girly stuff, and even if I had, my father never approved of such things.

"What?" Tesoro's voice shot up an octave.

"Did you just say you've never done your eyebrows?" Estrella echoed, eyes wide with disbelief.

"Yeah, it's not a big deal," I shrugged. "I never really cared about those kinds of things."

Estrella gasped dramatically, placing a hand over her heart as if I had just confessed to a mortal sin. "Oh, goddess above... Mai, do not tell me you're one of those women who don't believe in shaving and just let everything grow wild!"

My face burned under the scrutiny. "Of course I shave my armpits and trim... you know... down there," I said, shifting uncomfortably.

Estrella narrowed her eyes. "Trim? Trim?" She folded her arms and tilted her head like a predator cornering its prey. "Okay, but are we talking neat line, landing strip, or a little Hitler mustache?"

My entire face turned crimson as laughter erupted around the room. "*Dios mío,* Estrella!" Tesoro sputtered. "You seriously have no filter."

"You are a nosy asshole sometimes," Xiomara muttered, shaking her head. "She doesn't have to answer your invasive-ass questions."

Estrella waved her off. "Listen, I'm just looking out for our girl. What if she meets her mate tonight? You want to be prepared for all possible outcomes, right?" She wiggled her eyebrows suggestively.

I groaned. "It's... more like a bikini shave," I admitted hesitantly, hoping that would be enough to end the conversation.

But Estrella recoiled like I had just slapped her. "What? Oh, no, no, no. That simply will not do," she declared before grabbing my arm. "Tesoro, heat up the wax!"

I barely had time to protest before I was being dragged into the bathroom, my fate sealed.

After way too much convincing and thirty minutes of pure, unholy torture, I emerged from the bathroom with the newfound experience of having completely waxed lady parts. The burning sensation was a cruel reminder of why no sane woman would willingly subject herself to this. I couldn't fathom paying someone to do this on a regular basis. The pain was absurd!

"That was barbaric," I muttered, waddling back into the main room.

Estrella only grinned, looking far too pleased with herself. "You'll thank me later, trust me."

The women returned to their tasks, this time focusing on my face. Tesoro shaped my eyebrows with quick, precise motions, and to my surprise, the waxing wasn't nearly as bad as the previous ordeal. Then came the makeup.

Who knew there were so many steps to this? Foundation, highlighter, contouring, blush—my head spun as Tersoro explained each process, her hands working swiftly. She spoke about blending techniques and undertones, but I barely registered the words. At some point, I gave up and simply hoped I wouldn't look like a painted doll by the time she was done.

Finally, Tesoro stepped back, beaming with satisfaction. "Okay, look!"

She handed me a mirror, and I hesitated before lifting it to my face.

My breath caught.

I still looked like me, but different. Ethereal. My features were enhanced in a way that felt effortless, my cheekbones softly sculpted, my lips full with a natural tint, my eyes framed by long, fluttering lashes that made them seem larger, deeper. The overall effect was stunning yet subtle, like I had been kissed by moonlight.

"Oh my," Yolanda murmured, stepping closer. "You look beautiful. Such a natural approach to her beauty—well done, Tesoro."

A warmth spread through my chest at the compliment.

Six o'clock arrived, and I was ready.

My hair was styled in an elegant half-up, half-down arrangement, soft tendrils framing my face in delicate waves. Yolanda had lent me simple gold jewelry, a dainty chain around my neck, small earrings that glinted under the fading sunlight, and a matching bracelet that felt warm against my skin. The emerald-green gown fit like a dream, its intricate gold embroidery catching the light with every movement. The only problem? The towering gold heels that made me feel like I was balancing on stilts. Mental note: bring flats, or risk breaking an ankle before the night is over.

At the foot of the grand steps leading to the entrance, Beto, Andrés' father, stood waiting beside a sleek black limousine. The sight of it felt almost surreal. Everyone else had already gone ahead, their laughter and excitement echoing through the night, while I remained behind with Yolanda, taking what felt like the longest walk of my life.

As I descended, Beto's gaze softened. "You look beautiful, mi *niña*."

I tilted my head. "What does that mean?"

A warm smile spread across his face. "It means my child." His large hands enveloped mine, his touch strong yet gentle. "In our pack, it's tradition for the birthday girl to arrive with her parents. I know you no longer have yours, but... would you give us the honor of taking their place tonight?"

My breath hitched. The weight of his words settled deep in my chest, an unexpected warmth unfurling inside me. They wanted to stand where my parents should have been. The love in their gesture wrapped around me like a shield, making it nearly impossible to fight the tears threatening to spill.

"We can never replace them," Yolanda added softly, stepping closer to lay a reassuring hand on my shoulder. "But we would love to be a part of your life, in any way you'll have us."

I swallowed hard, my voice thick with emotion. "Yes," I whispered. "Of course. I would love that. Thank you so much... for wanting to do this."

Yolanda's eyes glistened as she smiled. "Can we hug you?"

I nodded, unable to speak as I was enveloped in their embrace. The moment their arms wrapped around me, something inside me cracked open—something I hadn't realized had been caged for years. It was the kind of hug that soothed a wound I hadn't even acknowledged, the kind that made me feel safe.

After a long moment, we pulled away, exchanging smiles that carried more meaning than words ever could. With a deep breath, we climbed into the limousine, excitement fluttering through my chest like tiny wings.

The ride felt like a blur, anticipation thrumming through my veins as we made our way deeper into the heart of the Luna Stone Pack territory. And then, the car came to a gentle stop.

When the door opened, my breath left me entirely.

The setting was nothing short of enchanting, a seamless blend of nature's raw beauty and modern elegance.

Towering ancient trees surrounded the clearing, their thick branches stretching high above. Suspended from their limbs, strands of glowing Edison bulbs and soft fairy lights wove through the vines, casting a golden glow that flickered like fireflies against the dusky sky. The entire space felt alive as if the forest itself was humming in harmony with the celebration.

A sleek, transparent canopy was strung between the trees, offering an open-air feel while protecting the space from the elements. Hidden spotlights cast a warm, ambient light, mixing with the cool, silvery beams of the rising moon. Beneath it, round tables with smooth, polished surfaces were draped in soft, earth-toned linens. Each table was adorned with floral arrangements of wildflowers and greenery in glass vases, accented by flickering candles set inside geometric metal lanterns.

The chairs with sleek, black leather cushions, blending rustic charm with contemporary comfort. Nearby, a dance floor had been created from tempered glass overlaid on polished stone, embedded with tiny LED lights that pulsed gently, mimicking the twinkle of stars overhead. A state-of-the-art sound system, cleverly hidden within the landscape, played soft, rhythmic music that built with anticipation.

At the heart of it all stood an opulent banquet table, its surface an artful display of decadence. A fusion of old-world and new-world cuisine lined the expanse, roasted meats laid beside elegantly plated sushi, fresh fruit sculpted into delicate designs, golden pastries stacked beside rich chocolate confections, and sleek glass decanters filled with dark, ruby-colored wine and handcrafted cocktails. Gold-rimmed plates and crystal stemware added a touch of sophistication, a perfect contrast to the raw, untamed beauty of the surrounding forest.

I exhaled slowly, the magic of the moment settling over me. This wasn't just a party, it was a welcome to this pack. A declaration of belonging. A night where I was the guest of honor.

And as the hum of laughter, clinking glasses, and the distant beat of music reached my ears, one thought echoed through my mind.

Tonight was the beginning of something extraordinary

Chapter 24

MAYA

As the night progressed, Sofía and her mate, Mason, guided me through the crowd, introducing me to members of the pack. Their warmth was reassuring, their presence making me feel less like an outsider and more like one of their own. I met elders with wise, knowing eyes, warriors who spoke with fierce loyalty, and young pups who giggled as they ran between tables, stealing bites of dessert when they thought no one was watching.

Yet, despite the friendly faces and endless conversations, my heart remained restless.

I kept glancing around, searching for the one person I wanted to see most. But he was nowhere to be found.

Sofía must have sensed my slipping focus because she gently nudged my arm, pulling me back.

"Mai," she said, her voice warm but firm. "There's a few people I would like for you to meet."

I turned, and standing beside her were four women who instantly shifted the energy around them.

They didn't have to speak for their power to be felt, the witches from New York.

"This is Myriam," Sofía said, inclining her head respectfully. "And her daughters, Nadya, Nelida, and Norma. They're from the New York coven."

Myriam stepped forward first.

Elegant, with long silver-streaked hair and eyes that felt like they could strip you down to your soul.

I offered a small nod.

"Hello, ma'am," I said quietly.

"My *niña*," she replied, her voice rich and smooth with a faint accent that made her words feel almost like a song. "We've heard much about you."

Heat rose to my cheeks under her gaze.

Nadya, tall and serious, gave a single nod.

Nelida offered a soft, easy smile that put me a little more at ease.

Norma, the youngest, winked at me playfully, a mischievous glint in her eye that made me like her immediately.

"Don't let their sweet faces fool you," Mason said under his breath, grinning. "They're more dangerous than half my warriors."

Myriam laughed, the sound rich and low, like she knew exactly how dangerous she was.

"We only use our gifts when necessary," she said, smiling faintly.

For a moment, things settled. The noise of the crowd faded, and the music blurred into the background.

But then Myriam's sharp gaze softened, and she tilted her head slightly, studying me with unsettling accuracy.

"You miss him," she said gently.

I opened my mouth, ready to deny it, to brush it off with some casual comment, but the truth sat too heavy inside me.

So I just nodded, feeling strangely exposed.

Walking away to mingle with other guests, I was stopped by Marcos, who approached me again, that same look of longing and sadness clouding his features.

"Hello, Mai," he said softly, his voice thick with emotion. "You look beautiful tonight. You... you look so much like..."

He stopped, his face crumpling, eyes glistening with unshed tears.

"Marcos, are you okay?" I asked, concern tightening my chest.

Before he could answer, Beto noticed my worried expression and quickly made his way over.

"Everything alright over here?" Beto asked, glancing between us.

"I don't know," I said, my voice uncertain. "He just came over to talk but—"

I didn't get a chance to finish. Marcos suddenly broke, his voice cracking as he turned to Beto.

"Don't you see it, Beto? She looks just like her. Same hair, same eyes..." Marcos said, the words tumbling out in a painful rush.

Beto's eyebrows furrowed, his face shifting from confusion to realization.

Then, his eyes widened in recognition.

"Yes," Beto said quietly. "Now that you mention it... I do see it. Damn, brother, I'm sorry."

He reached out, resting a comforting hand on Marcos' shoulder.

Feeling completely lost, I looked between them.
"Can someone please explain what's happening?" I asked, my voice small. "Who do I look like?"

Before either man could answer, Yolanda appeared at my side. She laid a gentle hand on my arm, her eyes shining with sadness.

"You look just like Marcos' mate," Yolanda said softly. "She passed away... twenty-one years ago. She had the same fiery red hair, the same bright eyes. Back when we were all in college together, you could've been her twin."

I stood there, stunned, not knowing what to say.

It finally made sense why Marcos had been staring at me like that with so much grief and longing.

"Babe, I'm going to take Marcos back to the house," Beto said, his voice heavy. "I think he needs some space."

Yolanda nodded sadly, giving Marcos a kiss on the cheek before Beto led him away.

Still reeling, I turned to Yolanda.
"What happened?" I asked, needing to understand.

Yolanda squeezed my hand, her touch grounding.
"It's a very painful story," she said gently. "One we don't often speak of. But for you to understand Marcos... I'll tell it. Just this once."

I nodded, bracing myself.

"Do you know why our pack and the Black Stone Pack have so much bad blood between us?" she asked.

"Not really," I admitted. "I was just always told you were the enemy that you'd hurt us without remorse."
I gave her a small, sad smile.
"But I know now that was a lie."

She smiled back at me, though it didn't reach her eyes.

"Over twenty years ago, Alpha George approached us with a business proposal, something about a cybersecurity project. Beto and Marcos quickly realized it was a scam. George was planning to use the technology to steal personal information from humans and other packs."

She paused, swallowing hard.

"Beto and Marcos refused to be part of it. They thought that was the end of it. But George saw their refusal as a betrayal... and he swore they would pay."

A tear slid down Yolanda's cheek.

"And he kept that promise," she whispered.

I held my breath, my heart pounding painfully in my chest.

"Delilah, Marcos' mate and my best friend, and I went out for lunch one afternoon. We were ambushed."
Yolanda's voice wavered but she pushed on.
"As Luna, the warriors' first priority was to get me to safety. They pulled me into a car and got me away... but when they went back for Delilah..."
She stopped again, pressing a trembling hand to her mouth.
"George's men had already taken her."

My stomach twisted into a tight, painful knot.

"It took us days to find her," Yolanda said, voice cracking. "They had... they had raped her, beaten her, and..." She closed her eyes, a shudder rolling through her.
"She was eight months pregnant, Mai. They... they ripped her open, trying to destroy the pup, too."

Tears blurred my vision.
"Oh, goddess, Yolanda... I'm so sorry," I whispered, my voice thick with emotion.

She wiped her tears with a shaky breath, composing herself.

"They thought Delilah was the Luna of Luna Stone. They were after me. And my friend... she paid with her life—and her pup's life."

I didn't know what to say. There was no right thing to say.

"After that," Yolanda continued, "Marcos wasn't the same. He went on a blood hunt, killing dozens from Black Stone Pack. We almost lost him to his rage."

A long, heavy silence stretched between us.

"It took the intervention of the Shifter Council to stop the bloodshed," she said. "Eventually, Marcos poured all his grief into protecting the pack, into building the business. He never took another mate. Never even looked at another woman."

She gave a small, broken smile.

"Instead, he helped us raise our children. Loved them like his own. He became family in every way that mattered."

I wiped at my own tears, overwhelmed by the weight of everything she shared.

No wonder Marcos looked at me the way he did.

For him, I was a living ghost of the life he lost.

Yolanda cleared her throat, dabbing the corners of her eyes with a tissue. When she spoke again, her voice was steadier, strong, but gentle.

"Okay, that's enough crying for one day," she said, giving me a watery smile. "Now you know the truth... and we shall not speak of that day again."

I nodded, still overwhelmed, but grateful for her strength and her trust.

She straightened her shoulders, her usual warmth sliding back into place like a shield.

"And you, young lady," she said, pointing at me with mock sternness, "need to dry your face and fix your makeup."

A startled laugh broke from my throat, the heavy sadness lifting just a little.

"You've got a birthday party to enjoy," Yolanda continued, squeezing my hand. "And there are still plenty of people left to meet."

She winked at me, a twinkle in her eye that hadn't been there moments before.

"So let's get moving, *mija*."

I wiped my cheeks quickly, giving her a small but genuine smile.

"Yes, ma'am."

Yolanda hooked her arm through mine, steering me back toward the heart of the gathering, where laughter and music once again filled the air.

Two hours into the party, I had shaken hands, exchanged smiles, and learned more names than I could possibly remember. And still no Andrés.

Where could he be?

Before I could dwell on it further, the murmur of conversation shifted into excited cheers as a massive cake was wheeled in. The soft glow of candles flickered atop it, casting a warm golden hue over the crowd. As if on cue, the entire pack erupted into song, their voices harmonizing into a heartfelt Happy Birthday.

Yolanda and Beto stood beside me, their arms wrapped around me in a warm embrace as they sang alongside the others. I mustered a smile, letting the happiness of the moment wash over me, but deep inside, there was an ache I couldn't ignore.

The one person I truly wanted to share this night with was missing.

As the song ended, the crowd cheered, urging me to make a wish. I stared at the flickering candles, my mind racing with possibilities. There were so many things I could ask for, so many desires whispering to my soul. But in the end, my heart settled on the one thing I had longed for my entire life.

Family. A place to belong. Happiness.

Taking a deep breath, I closed my eyes and exhaled, sending my wish into the universe as I blew out the candles.

The moment my eyes fluttered open, Beto was standing in front of me, a small envelope in his hand.

"Happy birthday, sweetheart," he said warmly, holding it out. "This is from Andrés."

My breath caught. "Andrés?" I asked, snatching the letter with eager hands. "He's here?"

Beto chuckled, stepping aside with a knowing smile. "Open the letter, *mija*. You'll have all your questions answered." With that, he and Yolanda drifted away, leaving me standing there, staring at the envelope.

My fingers trembled slightly as I ripped it open, revealing a simple card inside. The moment my eyes landed on the familiar scrawled handwriting, my heart skipped a beat.

Hey, little wolf,

Have you missed me?

I see you searching through the crowd, those big eyes scanning every face. Who are you looking for?

I hope you're not disappointed by my absence, but I decided our celebration needed to be something different... something just for the two of us.

Come find me at Moonlit Falls.

I promise, it will be worth it.

—A

A sharp inhale left my lips. Moonlit Falls?

I had never ventured beyond Andrés' house alone.

I turned to Sofía, with determination. "Do you know where Moonlit Falls is?"

Sofía's lips curled into a knowing smirk. "Moonlit Falls? Of course I do," she replied smoothly.

"Can you show me the way? I'm supposed to meet Andrés there," I said, gripping the letter tightly.

Instead of answering right away, she simply grinned, her brown eyes flashing mischievously. "I have a better idea. Come with me."

Without hesitation, I followed her as she slipped away from the festivities, her pace quick yet deliberate. The sounds of the party faded into the night, replaced by the rustling of leaves and the soft hum of nocturnal creatures awakening under the moon's watchful gaze.

After a few minutes, we emerged into a small clearing where a four-wheeler rumbled to life, the glow of its headlights cutting through the darkness. Sitting on it, wearing a wicked grin, was Xiomara.

"Come on, girl, we don't have all night!" she called out, her dark curls bouncing as she revved the engine playfully.

I stopped in my tracks, confusion furrowing my brow. "What's going on?"

Sofía just chuckled, crossing her arms. "Stop asking questions and just go with the flow, Mai. Trust me, it'll be so worth it." She pointed toward the four-wheeler, her smirk deepening.

Without another thought, I clutched the letter to my chest and climbed onto the back of Xiomara's ride, trying not to rip my gown in the process. My dress gathered around my thighs, the cool night air kissing my exposed skin as I wrapped my arms around her waist.

With a wild laugh, Xiomara took off, the four-wheeler roaring beneath us as we plunged into the thick embrace of the forest. The scent of pine and damp earth filled my senses as the wind whipped through my hair, heightening the adrenaline already coursing through me.

Deeper and deeper we went, the towering trees standing like silent guardians as the moon cast silver beams across the trail. Then, suddenly, the vehicle slowed, the engine humming to a softer purr. Ahead of us, another four-wheeler stood parked near a massive wooden arrow, its tip glowing faintly with bioluminescent paint.

Xiomara tapped my thigh. "Alright, girly, this is your stop. Just follow the arrows."

I slid off, my heels sinking slightly into the soft moss-covered ground. My heart hammered in my chest, my pulse a steady drum of anticipation. I turned to Xiomara, my face stretching into the biggest smile I'd worn all night.

"Thank you," I breathed, excitement thick in my voice.

She winked before revving the engine. "Have fun." With that, she spun the four-wheeler around and disappeared back into the forest.

I turned toward the arrow and followed its direction, weaving my way through the dense greenery, each step drawing me closer to whatever Andrés had planned. The trees soon parted, revealing a breathtaking sight before me.

A river stretched out like a sheet of obsidian glass, reflecting the moon and stars with ethereal clarity. At its heart, cascading down from towering cliffs, was the waterfall Moonlit Falls.

The water crashed down in a powerful, endless rush, its misty embrace catching the moonlight in a dazzling display of silver and sapphire hues. The roar of the falls echoed through the clearing, a steady, hypnotic hum that resonated deep in my bones. The night air was crisp, thick with the scent of damp moss, wildflowers, and something else, something new, yet intoxicatingly familiar.

Dark spice and bourbon.

A slow shiver down my spine as recognition struck. "I know that scent..." I whispered to myself, my pulse stuttering.

I inhaled deeply, allowing the scent to wrap around me like an invisible tether, guiding me closer. The air vibrated with an unspoken energy, a magnetic pull that made my skin tingle with anticipation. Every step I took over the mossy earth felt like it carried me deeper into something inevitable.

Scattered across the riverbank, large, flat stones formed a natural pathway, each one adorned with flickering lanterns. Their golden light danced across the water's rippling surface, creating an illusion of floating fireflies trapped beneath the water.

Then, my gaze locked onto it.

Another arrow.

It stood near the water's edge, planted firmly in the soft earth, its tip pointing directly behind the waterfall. My heart pounded, excitement coiling in my stomach like a restless serpent.

A hidden cave?

The sound of the rushing water grew louder, its endless cascade both a barrier and an invitation. Andrés had led me here for a reason. This moment, this place, it was meant for us.

I exhaled slowly, steadying myself. Then, with my heart hammering against my ribs, I gathered the hem of my gown, lifting it slightly to keep from tripping, and stepped forward.

Entering the back of the waterfall, the rush of cascading water behind me muffled the world beyond, enclosing me in a cocoon of anticipation. The entrance of a cave came into view, its mouth dark and mysterious, yet another arrow stood firm at its threshold, urging me forward. This is the path.

The moment I stepped inside, the scent enveloped me in a rich, intoxicating mix of dark spice and bourbon. It was stronger now, potent, like a drug my body had been starved for. My wolf stirred violently inside me, a primal restlessness unfurling in my chest. The hairs on my arms prickled, and beneath my skin, I could feel the sharp edge of transformation threatening to take over.

Not now.

I sucked in a deep breath, willing my control to hold. My fingers trembled slightly as I clenched them into fists, my heartbeat a wild, erratic drum against my ribs. The pull was unbearable.

I moved deeper, the dim cavern growing warmer with each step. Then, a soft glow flickered ahead, light, golden and inviting.

Candelabras stood in every crevice of the cave, their flames casting dancing shadows against the stone walls, creating an almost dreamlike atmosphere. A natural hot spring sat at the far end, steam curling in the air. Plush blankets covered a smooth rock surface, layered with an abundance of pillows in deep crimson and gold. A tray sat atop the makeshift bed, filled with an array of fresh fruits, cheeses, and two delicate flutes of champagne.

My lips parted as I took it all in. It was breathtaking. Sensual. Intimate.

"Oh, Goddess... this is beautiful," I whispered, my voice barely audible over the crackle of the candle flames.

Then, the scent hit me again, sharper, deeper, and my wolf surged forward with a possessive growl.

MINE.

Chapter 25

MAYA

The word reverberated through my entire being, not just a thought, but a command. A claim. My body tensed, heat curling in my stomach, my breathing shallow as the full weight of what this meant crashed over me.

Mate.

A deep, masculine voice echoed behind me, rough and teasing.

"Hey, little wolf."

I turned sharply, my breath catching in my throat.

And there he was.

Andrés.

Dressed in a perfectly tailored black suit, the crisp fabric hugged his broad shoulders and muscular frame in a way that made my mouth go dry. The inky color contrasted against his golden skin, his strong jawline freshly shaved, yet his black hair was just perfectly cute, giving him a sinful look. The suit's collar lay open, revealing just a hint of the defined chest beneath, teasing me with the warmth I knew lay underneath.

His piercing dark eyes locked onto mine, a flicker of something primal flashing behind them. His lips curved into that knowing smirk, the one that made my stomach clench and my thighs press together involuntarily.

My wolf whimpered and purred simultaneously, torn between the instinct to lunge and claim him or drop to her knees in submission. The bond between us was no longer a whisper in the back of my mind; it was a deafening roar, a fire igniting in my veins.

I knew what this meant.

This scent, his scent, the way my body responded to him, the way my wolf was clawing to get closer.

Andrés was mine.

And I was his.

A deep, all-consuming heat coiled inside me, something more than attraction, more than lust; it was fate. Destiny. The undeniable call of a mate bond finally recognized.

He took a step toward me, and I shivered as the space between us crackled with electric energy.

"I see you found your way to me," he murmured, his voice low and edged with something dangerous.

My heart pounded. My body begged for him to close the distance.

"You're... you're my mate." The words left my lips in a hushed, breathless whisper as I took a step toward him, my pulse racing.

Andrés didn't hesitate. In two powerful strides, he closed the distance between us, his strong hands reaching for my face, cupping it as if I was something sacred. His touch was warm, grounding, yet searing, like fire licking at my skin.

"Say it again." His voice was rough, edged with both demand and desire, his dark eyes locking onto mine like a predator ready to devour.

"You're my mate," I repeated, my voice stronger this time, conviction lacing my words as I held his gaze, refusing to look away.

A deep, primal growl rumbled from his chest, vibrating through me, sending a pulse of heat straight to my core.

"I have waited three weeks to hear you say those words..." His voice dipped lower, gravelly with need. His thumbs stroked my cheek, his grip firm yet reverent. "Yes, I am your mate, my little wolf... all yours."

My breath hitched at the intensity in his gaze, a storm of hunger and devotion swirling within.

"You've known that long?" I asked, my mind spinning, trying to process the depth of this revelation.

He smirked, dragging his fingers along my jaw before tracing the curve of my lower lip with his thumb. "I have known since I saw you back in Black Stone pack... when you were stepping out of your shower, naked, glistening with water."

Heat flooded my face, my lips parting slightly at the sinful memory I wasn't even aware existed.

He took advantage of the slight parting, pressing his thumb past my lips. Instinct took over, my tongue flicking against the pad of his finger before I wrapped my lips around it, sucking gently.

Andrés let out a deep, low growl, his pupils dilating as his wolf pushed dangerously close to the surface. His breath came out ragged, his chest rising and falling as he watched me, his control slipping.

The scent of arousal and dominance thickened the air, wrapping around us, cocooning us.

His thumb slid free, glistening with my saliva. He dragged it down my chin, my throat, tracing the pulse point that hammered wildly beneath my skin.

"You've known since then?" I gasped, my voice barely a whisper, need coiling inside me, desperate to be released. "Why didn't you tell me?"

His lips brushed against my ear, sending a delicious shiver down my spine. "Babe, I wish I could, but it's forbidden. You had to discover it on your own." His voice was almost reverent, as though he were speaking a sacred truth. "But I'm so glad we're finally here."

His hands slid down to my waist, pulling me flush against him. The heat of his body was intoxicating, his scent flooding my senses like a drug I never wanted to quit. I could feel the hard ridges of his muscles through his suit, the way his chest rose and fell with barely contained restraint.

"And now what?" I whispered, tilting my head back, my lips barely inches from his.

He exhaled heavily, his fingers digging into my hips possessively. "Now? Now I get to claim what's mine."

Then, he crashed his lips against mine.

The kiss was raw, hungry, consuming. It wasn't soft or tentative, it was a claiming, a wildfire set ablaze, burning through every last bit of space between us. His hands roamed my back, gripping me as if he needed to feel every inch of me pressed against him.

I gasped into his mouth, giving him the perfect opening to slip his tongue inside, tasting me, exploring me. My fingers tangled in his hair, tugging just hard enough to make him growl against my lips, the sound vibrating through my body and pooling between my legs.

His hands slid lower, gripping my thighs, lifting me effortlessly until my legs wrapped around his waist. The action was primal, instinctual, right.

"Andrés..." I moaned against his lips, his name falling from my mouth like a plea.

"Mine," he growled, his lips trailing down my jaw, my neck, sucking and nipping as he went, marking me with his desire.

The bond was fully awake now, singing in my blood, demanding more, demanding everything.

"Tell me you want me," he murmured against my skin, his voice dark and edged with restraint.

I arched into him, desperate, aching, needing him to break the space between us completely.

"I don't just want you..." I panted, dragging my nails down his back, feeling his muscles tense beneath my touch.

"I need you."

And that was all he needed to hear.

Andrés slammed me against the rough cave wall, the jagged edges scratching my skin, but neither of us cared.

The heat between us was a wildfire, consuming, obliterating any thought of caution or reason. His mouth crashed against mine in a kiss so fierce, so desperate, it felt like we were breathing each other in. Tongues tangled, teeth grazed, a battle for dominance neither of us wanted to win.

His hands were everywhere, gripping my hips, fisting the fabric of my dress, possessive and demanding. He kissed his way down my jaw, my neck, sucking and biting in a way that made my head spin. Every touch, every searing press of his lips, sent a pulse of aching need straight between my thighs.

I moaned wantonly, threading my fingers through his thick, dark hair, needing more. Needing him.

"Take this dress off," he growled, his voice deep, raw.

My breath hitched as he pulled me away from the wall and led me to the makeshift bed of plush blankets and pillows, the golden candlelight flickering across his hungry expression. He spun me in his arms, his lips pressing against my neck, my shoulders, his hands caressing down my sides as he slowly, torturously unfastened my dress.

The fabric slid down my body like silk, pooling at my feet.

"Your body is exquisite." His voice was softer now, reverent, his fingers tracing my curves, my freckles, memorizing me with every kiss. "Soft, fair, perfect. Every inch of you is mine."

He knelt behind me, his lips trailing lower, lower, following the path of my gown. When he reached the dimples on my lower back, he lingered, his breath hot against my skin.

"Is this for me?" he murmured, tugging at the delicate scrap of lace barely covering me.

I shivered, his deep voice sending a fresh wave of heat through me. "Yes," I whispered, breathless. "Now I understand why Estrella was so persistent that I wear it."

Andrés let out a low, sinful chuckle, pressing a kiss to the curve of my ass. "Remind me to thank her when I see her again." His large hands squeezed my flesh, kneading, teasing, before hooking his fingers under my thong and sliding it down, baring me completely.

He turned me to face him, still kneeling, his heated gaze dropping straight to my core. His eyes darkened, his pupils dilating as his tongue darted out, wetting his lips.

"Is this thanks to Estrella too?" he smirked, arching a knowing brow.

I covered my face with my hands, embarrassment and excitement clashing inside me. "She was very persistent about getting a wax," I admitted, my voice barely above a whisper. "Now it all makes sense."

Andrés laughed, deep and husky, the sound wrapping around me like a caress. He stood, towering over me, his body radiating heat, his scent thick with arousal.

"My love, don't ever be embarrassed with me." He brushed my hair back, cupping my face, his thumb stroking my flushed cheek. "We are mates. Nothing about our bodies should be hidden from each other."

I swallowed hard, my fingers trailing down his still-clothed chest, feeling the rapid thrum of his heartbeat beneath my palm. "Easy for you to say when you're still fully dressed."

His smirk deepened, pure sinful arrogance. "We can fix that real quick." He stepped back, standing tall, his shoulders broad, his dark eyes gleaming with challenge. "Undress me."

My shaky hands moved to his shirt, fumbling slightly as I unbuttoned each clasp, the slow reveal of his perfectly sculpted chest making my breath catch.

Golden tan skin. Hard, defined abs. That devastatingly sexy V leading lower, disappearing beneath his waistband.

My mouth watered.

I worked my way lower, heart hammering against my ribs as I clumsily pushed his pants and boxers down in one swift motion.

My breath hitched when his cock sprang free, thick, hard, and almost intimidating in its sheer size.

I bit my lip, staring in awe, heat pooling low in my belly as I took him in. Goddess. He was... beautiful. Large, girthy, the tip glistening with a bead of moisture that made my mouth go dry, and not from fear.

Andrés let out a ragged breath, his gaze locked on me, reading every sinful, untried thought racing through my mind.

"Do you like what you see?" he asked, voice rough with hunger.

I met his gaze, my body buzzing with anticipation, heat flickering between us like a live, untamed flame.
"Yes," I breathed, unable to tear my eyes away, my tongue darting out to wet my lips instinctively.

His cock twitched slightly at the sight, and his eyes darkened, turning molten.

"Get on your knees, little wolf," he rasped.

I dropped without hesitation, the cave floor cool against my heated skin—but none of it mattered.

All I could focus on was him.

Andrés towered above me, raw power and barely re-strained need rolling off him in waves.

He was pure, devastating masculinity. The kind that made my thighs press together in desperate, inexperienced need.

His cock stood rigid between us, so thick and hard it made my stomach flutter with nervous excitement.

A single bead of pre-cum clung to the tip, gleaming in the dim light.

"Look at you," he murmured, threading his fingers through my hair, tilting my chin up so our eyes locked. His thumb brushed my bottom lip, making me shiver.

"So fucking beautiful on your knees for me."

I swallowed hard, my nerves and arousal tangling to-gether in a dizzying knot.

I'd never been this close to a man before.

Never seen one fully, vulnerably like this.

And yet... all I could think about was wanting him.

"Can I..." I hesitated, breathless, "can I touch it?"

His jaw flexed, nostrils flaring, and he gave a sharp nod. "Anything you want, my little wolf. Anything."

A needy whimper slipped from my lips as I slowly reached out, my hands trembling just slightly.

I trailed my fingers up the thick columns of his thighs, marveling at the strength there, before wrapping one ten-tative hand around his cock.

My fingers barely circled the base; he was so big, so hot in my palm.

I gave a slow, shy stroke, watching his body jolt at the contact, hearing the rough stutter of his breathing.

Encouraged, I dragged my hand up, then down again, mesmerized by the way his cock pulsed in my grip.

"I..." I licked my lips again, my voice small but determined, "I've never done this before. You'll have to teach me."

I kept my eyes on him, innocent yet aching for more, my touch gentle, tentative.

Andrés cursed low under his breath, his fingers tightening slightly in my hair, his whole body shuddering at my confession.

"Fuck," he growled, voice pure need. "I'll show you. I'll teach you everything, little wolf."

And tonight... I realized with a pounding heart...

I wanted to learn.

With him.

Only him.

"Lick the tip," Andrés growled, his voice low and rough, vibrating straight through me.

Heart racing, I leaned in closer, my tongue slipping out to taste him.

I dragged it slowly across the crown of his cock, right where a bead of pre-cum waited for me, salty and hot on my tongue.

The taste was overwhelming and addictive, making my thighs clench as heat flooded my body.

"Good girl," he rasped, his hand tightening slightly in my hair, not harsh, but anchoring me to him. "Just like that."

My breath caught at the praise, and before I could think, I did it again, longer this time, savoring the way he trembled under my tongue.

"Suck it, little wolf," he commanded, voice thick and nearly broken with restraint. "Wrap those pretty lips around me."

I obeyed, nervous but desperate to please him, wrapping my mouth around the thick head of his cock.
He hissed out a curse, his muscles straining above me.

"That's it," he whispered, his voice hoarse. "Take me in... slowly."

I eased down, my jaw stretching wide to accommodate his size.
It wasn't perfect; my teeth grazed him lightly, and I fumbled with the angle, but Andrés didn't seem to care.
He moaned low, a sound that made my whole body ache for him, and gently guided me with his hand at the back of my head.

"Use your tongue," he urged, his thumb brushing soothingly over my cheek. "Swirl it around me... make it messy."

I tried, flicking my tongue around the sensitive crown, tasting him, feeling him pulse against my tongue.
The need to please him outweighed my nervousness, and soon I found a rhythm—slow, wet strokes that had his thighs tensing under my hands.

He cursed again, his control slipping.

"Fuck... you're perfect."

I hollowed my cheeks just like he told me, taking him a little deeper, feeling him hit the back of my throat and pulling back with a wet pop that made him groan gutturally.

"Faster, little one," he growled. "Take more of me."

I sucked harder, moving faster now, feeling him throb inside my mouth, his hips starting to roll gently, matching my pace.

His fingers tightened in my hair as his breathing grew ragged, muscles trembling with restraint.

"Fuck, Mai..." he hissed, pulling back suddenly, his cock slipping from my lips with a sinful pop.

I blinked up at him, my lips swollen, my breathing ragged, a string of saliva still connecting us. He stared down at me like I was the most intoxicating thing he had ever seen, his pupils blown wide, his chest heaving.

"Get up," he ordered, his voice hoarse with need.

I obeyed, my legs shaky as he yanked me against his body, his skin burning against mine, every ridge of his abs pressed into my bare skin.

"I need to taste you. Now."

Before I could do anything but shudder in response, Andrés gripped the backs of my thighs and lifted me effortlessly, walking us toward the plush blankets and pillows. He lowered me slowly, deliberately, letting my body graze against his, ensuring I felt every inch of him before my back met the softness below.

He knelt between my legs, his large hands spreading my thighs apart, his fingers tracing over my heated skin, teasing, exploring.

"Fuck, baby, you're already drenched for me." His voice was low, gravelly, full of raw need as he dragged a single finger through my slick folds, spreading my arousal.

A gasp tore from my throat, my hips bucking instinctively, desperate for more.

"Be still," he ordered, his grip firm on my thighs.

His eyes flicked up to meet mine, dark, hungry, predatory. "I want to enjoy this."

I barely had time to catch my breath before he lowered his head, his hot breath over my core, his tongue flicking out to taste me, slow, deliberate, torturous.

I let out a strangled moan, my fingers immediately tangling in his hair, pulling him closer.

"Patience, little wolf," he murmured against my skin, pressing a kiss against my inner thigh, his tongue tracing lazy circles, making me whimper in frustration.

I could feel him smirk against my flesh before his tongue dove between my folds, a slow, languid stroke that had my back arching off the blankets.

"Andrés—fuck," I gasped, my legs trembling as he devoured me, kissed me like he was starving.

His growl sent vibrations through my core, making me cry out, my thighs trying to clamp around his head, but he held me open with an iron grip.

"So sweet," he murmured, his voice dripping with approval, with possession. "All mine."

His tongue worked me expertly, flicking, circling, stroking over my swollen, aching clit before plunging deep inside me, his nose pressing against the bundle of nerves just right. My body trembled violently, pleasure building so fast it was unbearable.

"I want to hear you, little wolf," he demanded, his voice rough. "Let the woods hear who you belong to."

His words, his mouth, the sheer dominance in his voice, it was all too much.

"Oh, Goddess, Andrés!" My cry was loud, shameless, raw, echoing off the stone walls as the orgasm crashed through me like a tidal wave, sending white-hot pleasure pulsing through my veins.

Andrés didn't stop. He groaned against me, lapping up every drop, his grip bruising, keeping me still as my body convulsed.

Only when my trembling turned to soft, breathy whimpers did he finally lift his head, his lips glistening, his dark eyes burning with satisfaction.

He climbed up my body slowly, sinfully, his mouth finding mine, letting me taste myself on his tongue.

"So fucking perfect," he whispered against my lips, his fingers still teasing, still keeping me on edge.

"And I'm not done with you yet, little wolf."

Chapter 26

MAYA

Andrés hovered over me, his weight delicious yet not overwhelming.

My wolf was pacing within me, restless, hungry, aware of what was coming. She recognized him, our mate, our male, and she urged me to surrender, to give him everything. But beneath that primal need, there was a tinge of uncertainty.

Andrés must have sensed it. His intense, predatory gaze softened, his rough hands that had held me so firmly moments ago now caressed me gently, soothing, coaxing.

"Little wolf," lips pressing against my temple, his voice thick with restraint. "I can feel a change in you. Are you scared?"

A lump formed in my throat. Heat crept up my neck as I turned my face away, but he wouldn't allow me to hide from him. His fingers tilted my chin, forcing me to meet his gaze.

"Yes," I admitted softly. "Will it hurt?"

His jaw clenched, something deep and tender flashing through his eyes.

"The first time can be painful," he confessed, his thumb brushing against my bottom lip, "But I will be as gentle as I can. I cannot promise it will be painless... but I swear I will make it beautiful."

The sincerity in his voice stole my breath.

I nodded, giving him my silent consent.

"I'll take my time. If it's too much, tell me and I will stop."

His lips found mine, slow at first, teasing, coaxing, until heat consumed us both. The kiss was deep, desperate, needy, his tongue sliding against mine, making my body melt beneath him.

He moved lower, trailing open-mouthed kisses down my neck, my collarbone, my chest, his teeth grazing, his tongue soothing.

I gasped when his lips wrapped around my sensitive peak, his tongue swirling, teasing, before moving to the other, his hands kneading, exploring, claiming.

"So damn beautiful," he whispered against my heated skin, his fingers mapping my curves, learning me, worship ing me.

Andrés shifted, his breath warm against my lips. He lifted two fingers to my mouth.

"Andrés..." My voice trembled.

His heated gaze met mine.

"Do you trust me?"

I did. With every fiber of my being.

"Yes."

His lips curved into a slow, knowing smirk.

"Then open your mouth and suck."

My lips parted, my tongue swirling over his fingers, coating them in warmth, in anticipation of what was to come.

Once satisfied, he withdrew, dragging those slick fingers down my body, over my stomach, before pressing them to my entrance.

A sharp inhale left my lips. My core clenched, my body already responding, already craving.

"You're soaked for me," he groaned, his fingers sliding effortlessly through my arousal.

A soft whimper escaped me.

"Relax," he whispered, his free hand caressing my face. "I'll go slow, I promise. But I am not small, and we need to get you ready to take me."

And then, he pushed one finger inside.

A shocked gasp escaped me, my walls fluttering at the unfamiliar sensation.

"That's it, baby," he murmured against my inner thigh, kissing my skin as he let me adjust.

He curled his finger, pressing against a spot deep inside me that made me arch off the blankets, a sharp cry falling from my lips.

"There it is," he growled, pleased with the way I clenched around him.

He moved slowly, carefully, stretching me, coaxing my body to accept more.

A second finger joined the first, his thumb circling my clit in slow, torturous strokes.

He leaned up, his lips capturing mine in a kiss that was deep, sensual, drowning me in him.

"Andrés, please," I gasped, not even sure what I was begging for.

He leaned over me, "I think you're ready," he murmured, his voice rough, his control fraying. "How do you feel?"

I swallowed hard, rolling my hips against his hand, needing more.

"I need you inside me." The words fell from my lips like a confession, a plea.

Andrés shuddered.

"Are you sure?"

"Yes."

His entire body tensed, his breath uneven, his forehead pressing against mine.

He shifted, positioning himself between my thighs. I felt the thick press of his length against my entrance, the heat of him making my breath hitch.

"Look at me, little wolf," he ordered, cupping my cheek, forcing me to meet his gaze.

I did.

And what I saw there made my heart clench.

Lust, yes. But also love. Devotion. A silent promise.

With one slow, careful thrust, he pushed inside.

A sharp pain stole my breath, a cry tearing from my lips.

Andrés froze instantly, his jaw clenched, his hands gripping my thighs.

"Are you okay? Did I hurt you?" he asked, his voice tight with concern, restraint warring with his need.

"It hurts," I admitted, tears pricking my eyes. "But don't stop."

His face twisted with conflict.

"Mai."

"Do it fast, like a bandage," I whispered.

His muscles flexed, his nostrils flaring as he nodded.

"Okay."

And in one smooth, firm thrust, he buried himself completely inside me.

A sharp sting bloomed, a scream leaving my lips, the fullness overwhelming.

"Fuck," Andrés groaned, his body shaking with restraint, his lips whispering praises, apologies, promises.

"You're so tight, ... so fucking perfect."

The pain ebbed away, replaced with something new, something electrifying. Each slow thrust sent a ripple of pleasure through me, a deep warmth unfurling in my belly.

And then, slowly...

Faster," I whispered.

That single word undid him.

Andrés snapped his hips forward, sinking deeper, his pace still slow but filled with purpose. He watched my every reaction, his pupils blown wide, his wolf dangerously close to the surface.

"That's it, baby," he growled, his voice thick with possession. "Take all of me."

His thrusts grew bolder, each one drawing a shocked gasp from my lips, a new sensation blooming inside me, an unfamiliar pressure building.

"You feel that?" he murmured, his thumb finding my clit, teasing in slow, intoxicating circles.

I cried out, my body tightening, my legs trembling.

"That's your body finally giving in to me," he growled, his tone pure dominance, pure need.

I arched into him, whimpering, panting, my body begging for more.

"More," I gasped, not even sure what I was asking for, just knowing I needed it.

Andrés growled, his wolf breaking free in his voice.

"More?" His smirk was pure sin, pure promise.

Andrés' pace became relentless, hungry, every roll of his hips sending fire through my veins. I was burning alive, consumed by him, by us, by the bond that had been simmering between us since the moment our eyes met.

The pressure inside me coiled tighter, sharper, more intense. My wolf whined, her instincts recognizing what was coming, urging me forward, urging me to claim.

"I can feel you," he murmured against my ear, his breath hot, his voice almost shaking with need. "You're close, aren't you?"

"Yes," I sobbed, the pleasure reaching unbearable levels, my body trembling in his hold, desperate for release.

"Let go, little wolf," he commanded, his voice dark, his fingers digging into my hips as he drove into me with a force that sent me spiraling.

I shattered.

Instinct took over. I let my fingers trail up his broad back, feeling the tension coiled beneath his muscles, feeling the wild energy buzzing through our connection.

My mate.

I tilted my head, baring my teeth as I met his gaze—wild, untamed, unbreakable.

And then I bit him.

My canines sank into his flesh, marking him as mine, sealing our bond in blood, in passion, in fate.

Andrés roared, a deep, primal sound that echoed through the cave, through the night, through the very core of me.

"Mai, fuck!"

His release hit, hot and deep, his muscles locking, as he spilled into me.

My wolf howled in satisfaction, in triumph.

But it wasn't enough.

Our wolves howled, their instincts demanding the final step, the ultimate claim.

Andrés pulled back slightly, his darkened, wild gaze locking onto mine, his pupils blown wide, his jaw tight with need. His wolf surged forward, demanding to mark, to bond, to make me his in every way.

His teeth sank into the soft flesh between my neck and shoulder, a sharp sting blooming before it melted into something euphoric.

A gasp tore from my lips, pleasure spiking again as my body reacted, another wave of bliss crashing over me as I clenched around him.

"Fuck," Andrés growled against my skin, his tongue soothing the mark, his body still deep inside me, fully connected in every possible way.

The pleasure was indescribable, raw, overpowering, waves of euphoria coursing between us, feeding off one another, heightening every sensation, every touch, every heartbeat.

And then it settled.

A deep, soul-level peace washed over me, warmth spreading through my chest, my body still intertwined with his, my wolf purring in utter contentment.

We collapsed together, tangled in each other, forever bound.

His lips brushed over my temple, my cheeks, my lips in soft, reverent kisses.

"Mine," he whispered, his voice raw with emotion.

"Yours," I breathed back, feeling it in every fiber of my being.

After lying entangled for what felt like forever, wrapped in his warmth, I sighed in contentment. The bond between us hummed, a comforting, undeniable presence now that our wolves had fully recognized each other.

"Little wolf, are you okay?" he murmured, his fingers lazily tracing circles on my back.

"Yeah... a little sore but okay," I replied, a small smile tugging at my lips.

He shifted onto his side, resting his head on his hand as his eyes roamed over my body.

"Did I hurt you?" His hand reached up, caressing my neck, his thumb brushing over the fresh mate mark.

I tilted my head, touching the spot where his bite had claimed me, a deep warmth spreading through my chest.

"Oh, this?" I smiled softly. "No, actually, it doesn't hurt at all. But..." My fingers trailed over his own mark, still raw against his skin. "I'm sorry I bit you without asking."

His low chuckle sent shivers down my spine. "Don't ever apologize for that." His dark eyes softened as his hand slid from my throat to my jaw, tilting my face toward his. "I wanted to mark you the first time I laid eyes on you. I've been waiting for this moment, for you, for three weeks. I'm just happy we're finally here."

His thumb brushed over my lips, his expression raw with lust and love.

I leaned in, kissing him slowly, sensually, letting my lips express what words couldn't. "I'm glad you're my mate. Deep down, my wolf knew."

Andrés' grin spread across his face, a mix of pride and possession and satisfaction. In one smooth motion, he rolled me onto my back, hovering over me again, his fingers tracing the curves of my body.

"Come," he murmured, his eyes gleaming with mischief. "Let's jump in the hot spring. It'll help with your soreness."

"That sounds amazing," I admitted, my muscles still aching from our first time.

Before I could move, he scooped me up effortlessly, gripping my ass in his large hands, lifting me as if I weighed nothing. My legs instinctively wrapped around his waist, my bare body pressing against his, the water-slick heat of his skin making my pulse stutter.

"Oh, Goddess," I gasped when I felt the unmistakable hardness pressing against me.

"You ready for more?" my voice husky.

I bit my lip, heat curling low in my belly, but I knew he was holding himself back.

"For you? Always." His eyes darkened at my words, but I could sense the hesitation. "But I know you're sore, so let's just bathe."

His control was admirable, intoxicating, infuriating.

I didn't want control.

I wanted him.

He stepped into the steaming water, lowering us both into the natural warmth of the hot spring. My muscles instantly relaxed, the ache between my thighs soothing, but the hollow feeling inside me only grew.

Andrés turned me in his arms, my back now pressed against his chest as he poured water over my shoulders and neck, massaging the soreness from my body. His touch was reverent, gentle, yet teasing, his lips brushing against my ear as he whispered sweet nothings.

For a while, we simply talked about us, our bond, our future. The way he spoke about us made my heart race, made me crave him in an entirely new way.

Then, somehow, we started playing, teasing, laughing. I splashed water at him, and he retaliated by pulling me onto his lap, tickling me until I squirmed in his grasp, panting, breathless.

That was when I felt it again.

Hard. Hot. Pressed against me.

My breath hitched, and my body reacted instantly, a slow, needy ache replacing the playful energy from before. I pressed my palm to his chest, feeling the rapid thud of his heart beneath my fingertips.

I lifted my gaze to his, eyes heavy-lidded, lips slightly parted.

"I want you," I admitted, blushing under his hungry stare.

His smirk deepened, but his fingers remained gentle as they traced my cheek. "But you're sore?"

I swallowed, rolling my hips experimentally against him, feeling the delicious friction.

"We're shifters," I whispered, my voice bold yet breathy. "We heal fast. Show me what I've been missing."

Andrés' low growl vibrated through his chest, and in one swift movement, he spun me around, pressing my front against the smooth rock at the edge of the hot spring.

"Place your hands here," he murmured, his voice dripping with authority.

I obeyed, heat surging through me, anticipation coiling low in my belly.

His fingers traced the length of my spine, caressing every dip, every curve. Then his lips followed, kissing, licking, nipping until he reached my lower back.

His hips pressed against my ass, his thick length teasing my entrance, and I gasped at the sheer intensity of it.

"You okay?" he asked, his voice strained, rough, barely holding himself back.

"Yes... just excited, I guess."

His low chuckle sent a shiver down my spine. "Excited?" His lips brushed against my shoulder, his hands gripping my hips firmly.

Before I could respond, he pushed inside me, slow, deep, filling me completely.

I gasped, the familiar stretch making my body tremble, the dull soreness giving way to something thicker and deeper.

"Oh, fuck" I moaned, clenching around him, adjusting to his size all over again.

"Mai," he groaned, his grip tightening as he stayed still for a moment, letting me take every inch of him. "You feel... perfect."

Then he moved.

Slow at first, rolling his hips in deep, torturous strokes, making me feel every inch of him.

"Fuck, baby, you're gripping me so tight," he growled, his fingers tangling in my hair, gently pulling my head back so he could kiss me.

The pace quickened, the sound of water slapping against our bodies filling the cave, my moans turning higher, needier.

"Andrés," I gasped, arching into him as pleasure built again, coiling tighter, ready to snap.

His growl was pure dominance, pure possession. "Say my name when you come."

His thrusts became relentless, his pace punishing, each stroke sending waves of pleasure crashing through me.

"Andrés!" I screamed, my body shuddering as another orgasm tore through me.

He snarled, his grip tightening as he slammed into me one last time, spilling deep, marking me all over again.

The rest of the night was spent in a blissful haze of passion and discovery, our bodies tangled in ways that left me breathless, boneless, utterly claimed. I had given myself completely to him, and Andrés had taken his time sampling, tasting, worshiping every inch of me.

He had me pressed against the rocky wall, pinned under him, bent over the makeshift bed of plush blankets, even straddling his hips as I rode him into oblivion. There wasn't a spot in this cave he hadn't claimed me in, possessed me in, filled me in.

By the time we finally collapsed, spent, sated, bonded beyond reason, my entire body hummed with exhaustion and the unmistakable satisfaction of being thoroughly, irrevocably his.

"Goddess," I murmured sometime before sleep claimed me, my limbs tangled with his, my cheek resting against his chest. "I don't think I can walk after this."

Andrés chuckled, pressing a lazy kiss to my forehead. "I'll carry you anywhere you need to go."

And with that, I drifted into sleep, wrapped in his warmth, his scent, the mate bond pulsing between us.

I woke up still wrapped in him, our bodies instinctively molded together. His arms were locked around me, holding me close as if he never wanted to let me go.

The day passed in a blissful cocoon of love, spent talking, teasing, touching, simply existing in our perfect little world. Andrés fed me fresh fruit straight from the tray, kissing me between bites, making me laugh, making me moan, making me forget that anything outside of this cave existed.

"I could stay here forever," I whispered, trailing my fingers over the mark on his neck, where I had claimed him.

"We can always return," he murmured, pressing a kiss to my wrist, his voice thick with emotion.

But nothing lasts forever.

As much as I wanted to stay lost in this dream, reality was calling us back.

"We have to go back, my love," he finally said, his voice reluctant but firm.

I sighed, clutching him for a moment longer before nodding. "I know. Reality calls."

As I pulled on my dress, Andrés' phone buzzed against the stone floor. He picked it up, his brows drawing together as he answered.

I could hear Sofía's voice on the other end, but I couldn't make out the words. Still, the tone in her voice set me on edge.

"They found another body."

Chapter 27

MAYA

The journey home felt longer than expected, my body still aching deliciously, my mind spinning with the news that while we were having fun, another body was found.

When we finally arrived at our home, I expected chaos, remnants of the pre-ceremony madness. Instead, the place was immaculate cleaned, restored, as if no dozen women had ever been here.

"Damn," I muttered, taking in the pristine space. "They work fast."

"They know better than to leave a mess in my house," Andrés smirked, but his hands were already on me, his body pressing me toward the bathroom.

I barely had time to step under the warm spray of the shower before Andrés followed me in, his hands already roaming, his lips trailing fire over my wet skin.

"Andrés, we don't have time,"

"We'll make time."

And just like that, I found myself pressed against the tile wall, his mouth devouring mine, his hands lifting me, his body sinking back into mine as if he couldn't stand to be apart for even a moment longer.

By the time we emerged from the shower, damp and breathless, I knew we were very, very late.

When we arrived at the packhouse, Andrés barely had time to press a final kiss to my lips before he was pulled away toward Sofía's study, where the team awaited him.

That left me alone with Yolanda, who was already waiting for me with a knowing smile.

"I take it last night went... well?" she teased, her eyes flicking to the mate mark on my neck.

Heat flushed my cheeks, but I didn't deny it. There was no use.

"I have so many questions," I admitted, crossing my arms. "Like, why did everyone seem to know about Andrés being my mate before I did?"

Yolanda let out a soft laugh, shaking her head. "Oh, mi niña...The way he was behaving from the start and then when he took you from your pack... we knew something was up. You think we were going to be ok with our son taking someone without a reason. He told us. But even if he hadn't, it was obvious. The way his wolf reacted to you, the way you two circled each other..." She waved a hand as if it was the most obvious thing in the world.

I sighed, shaking my head, a mix of frustration and amusement settling in my chest. "And no one thought to tell me?"

"It is against Council Law to tell an underage wolf who their mate is," she said gently, her eyes warm. "You had to figure it out on your own, Mai. The mate bond is about discovery, about feeling it, not just knowing it."

I opened my mouth to argue, but then... stopped.

Because deep down, I knew she was right

"Still, you all could've at least given me a hint," I muttered.

"Would you have believed us?" Yolanda challenged, one brow arched.

I sighed dramatically, making her laugh.

"You're right," I admitted. "I probably would've fought it."

Yolanda smiled, squeezing my hand gently. "And now?"

I met her gaze, felt the warmth in my chest when I thought about Andrés, about everything that had happened, about the unbreakable bond now linking us forever.

"Now," I said softly, "I wouldn't change a thing."

A loud, slow clapping echoed through the clearing, the sharp sound cutting through the air like a blade.

Yolanda and I both turned as footsteps approached, heavy and purposeful.

Rosario stepped into view, her smile venomous, her eyes burning with pure hatred.

She stood there, clapping mockingly, her every movement dripping malice.

"You know," she sneered, her voice loud enough to draw a few curious glances, "I had to come see it for myself. When the girls told me Andres had mated the little outsider whore"

She spat the word like poison as she stalked closer.

I stiffened, feeling the venom in her words lash against my skin, but I refused to look away.

Rosario stopped a few feet in front of me, her arms crossed, her mouth twisted in a sneer.

"I have to hand it to you," she said, her clapping slowing. "You weaseled your way into his bed. Managed to do what no other woman could and catch a Rodriguez son."

The mocking applause died, but the bitter curl of her lip didn't.

"You might think you've won," she hissed, taking another step closer, "but I know a liar when I see one. And you," she jabbed a manicured finger at me, "have a secret. I can smell it. And when I find out what it is, I'll expose you for the fraud you are."

Before I could even open my mouth, Yolanda stepped between us, her voice sharp with authority.

"Rosario, cállate ya," Yolanda snapped. "Have some damn self-respect. When a man doesn't want you, you walk away. You don't tear down the woman he chose."

Rosario scoffed, tossing her hair over her shoulder.
"Easy for you to say, Yolanda. You bagged yourself an Alpha. Some of us have to fight for the men we want."

With one last scathing look my way, she turned on her heel and stormed off, her heels clicking angrily against the stone floor.

The moment she disappeared from sight, Yolanda exhaled heavily and turned to me.

"Don't pay her any mind, mija," she said, her voice softening. She tucked a loose strand of hair behind my ear, a motherly gesture that soothed the sting Rosario's words had left behind.

"She's loca. All talk. She'll get over it."

I nodded weakly, but my heart was pounding too hard, my stomach knotting tighter with every breath.

Because as much as I wanted to believe Yolanda...

Rosario wasn't entirely wrong.

There was a secret.

A terrible one.

The truth that clawed at the back of my mind every single day. The thing that could ruin everything Andres and I were starting to create.

I was the daughter of Alpha George.

The very man everyone in Luna Stone Pack despised.

The man who had caused their deepest scars, who had taken lives, who had torn families apart.

If Andres found out...

Would he still look at me the way he did now?

Would he still want me?

Or would he see me as nothing more than the enemy's blood running through their veins?

A tremor ran through me, and no amount of Yolanda's comfort could chase away the fear that settled deep in my bones.

Because secrets never stayed buried forever.

ANDRÉS

Stepping into Sofía's study, I was immediately met with the familiar scents of my family and our allies from the New York coven. The air inside the room was thick with tension, yet tinged with an underlying warmth.

"Did I miss much?" I asked, shutting the door behind me.

At once, every pair of eyes locked onto me. Then, almost in perfect synchronization, they all took a deep inhale, and that was when the smirks began to spread.

Leo, Mason, and Darren were the first to react. Grinning like idiots, they clapped me on the back, their laughter echoing around the room.

"Finally sealed the deal," Leo teased, his voice full of amusement.

"I assume everything went well?" Dad asked, though his knowing smile said he didn't need an answer.

"Welcome to the group of mated wolves," Mason added, laughing as Darren smirked beside him.

But it was Sofía who had the biggest, most triumphant smile of them all.

She walked toward me with her arms open and a glint of mischief in her eyes. "Now Mom can start nagging you about a grandpup."

The room burst into laughter.

"It was only a matter of time," Mason chuckled.

I rolled my eyes, though a smirk tugged at the corner of my lips. I knew this was coming. The second they smelled Mai's scent mingled with mine, the teasing was inevitable.

Then, a deliberate throat clearing cut through the moment.

"Not to interrupt this touching moment," a smooth but firm voice spoke, "but we rushed here for an emergency, and I would really like to get to it."

All heads turned toward the short, older Latina woman standing at the far end of the room.

She was dressed in a flowing white skirt, her layered beaded necklaces of varying colors standing out against her dark skin. Her silver bangle clinked softly against her wrist as she crossed her arms. Her curly hair was wrapped neatly in a white headscarf, and despite her petite frame, she radiated power.

I straightened slightly, inclining my head toward her. "Sorry, Myriam," I said respectfully.

But before I could say more, my father spoke up, his voice filled with pride.

"My son is finally mated," he announced, his chest puffing up slightly. "In moments like this, we have to celebrate all the good things that happen."

Myriam's stern expression softened, a warm smile touching her lips.

"I agree," she said, her voice rich with wisdom. She turned her gaze to me, her dark eyes holding something nostalgic. "And congratulations, Andrés. You have grown so much."

"Thank you, Myriam," I replied, nodding my head.

Beside her, Nayda, Nelida, and Norma, her daughters, and high-ranking witches.

"Mated? Wow, that's incredible," she said, her tone filled with genuine happiness.

I returned the smile, but the lighthearted moment didn't last long.

Sofía straightened, her expression shifting from amusement to pure business.

"Okay, guys, let's get down to business," she said, folding her arms. "We have two bodies found... and no leads."

The atmosphere immediately darkened.

A frown creased my brow. " When did the second one appear?"

Xiomara, who had been leaning against the window, exhaled heavily.

"Last night, toward the end of the party." Her voice was distant, as if the memory itself unsettled her.

My jaw clenched. "What the hell happened?"

Sofía exchanged glances with Leo before speaking.

"Last night, we were celebrating. Mai and you had already left, but the rest of us stayed to enjoy the party."

Her tone shifted, growing eerily quiet

"Then, out of nowhere... blackbirds, crows, ravens, I don't even know, just like the ones from my wedding, they started swarming toward us. Hundreds of them, screeching."

I stiffened.

"Then," Sofía continued, her voice barely above a whisper, "it happened."

"What?" I demanded, my wolf bristling under my skin, sensing the shift in energy.

"One of the missing women appeared out of thin air."

Myriam and Nayda exchanged looks.

"She was... naked, dead, covered in words." Sofía's voice was flat, but her hands clenched into fists.

A shiver ran down my spine.

"What do you mean?" I asked, my voice dark.

Xiomara turned from the window, her expression grim.

"The words were being carved into her... in real-time. While she was floating mid-air."

The room went utterly silent.

My stomach twisted into knots.

"That is dark magic," Myriam murmured, her silver bangle glinting as she traced a sigil in the air.

"It was terrifying," Sofía admitted. "The way her body twisted... the blood dripping... and then..."

She hesitated.

"And then?" I pressed.

She closed her eyes briefly, then exhaled. "Then, the body... it started talking."

A cold chill ran through me.

Sofía swallowed hard.

Her voice turned strained. "It spoke in a voice that didn't belong to her. Deep, guttural, unnatural. It said things... things that made no sense."

"Like what?" I asked, my wolf pacing restlessly inside me.

She took a shaky breath, then recited, her voice eerily hollow.

"You have what's mine. You will pay with your lives."

The room plunged into a heavy silence.

My wolf bristled, claws itching beneath my skin, sensing something ominous, unnatural. Myriam and Nayda stood frozen, their gazes locked, exchanging silent messages that I couldn't decipher.

"It... sounded personal," Nayda finally said, her voice low, uncertain.

"A warning," Myriam corrected, her eyes sharp as she turned to Sofía.

A warning meant for us.

My grip tightened into fists, my mind already racing through the possibilities.

"Did anyone recognize the woman?" I asked, trying to piece together the horror of last night.

Sofía nodded grimly. "Her name was Camila. She went missing two weeks ago, the same night as the first girl. We searched everywhere... and now she just" She exhaled sharply. "She just showed up like that. Dead. Violated. Used."

"Damn it," I cursed under my breath.

The thought of someone doing this to our pack members, taking our people and using them as vessels for dark magic, made my wolf snarl with barely contained rage.

"What about the first body?" Myriam asked.

Leo answered this time. "Different girl, same ritualistic markings. We found her outside the pack's northern border three days ago. No signs of who put her there. No scent, no tracks, nothing."

Xiomara leaned forward, finally turning away from the window. Her face was pale, serious. "You didn't see it,

Andrés. The way her body twisted, the way the carvings." She swallowed. "It wasn't just magic. It was something... evil."

Evil.

That word sent a chill down my spine.

"We need to find out what they want," Darren said, his usually calm demeanor cracking. "If this is some kind of dark magic, we can't just sit back and wait for another one to show up."

"Agreed," my father chimed in. "But first, we need to understand what we're dealing with."

Myriam stepped forward, her silver bangle clinking softly as she moved.

"This is definitely something personal," she said, her voice slow, deliberate. "Ritualistic killings tied to unnatural magic are not easy to do. Someone with a lot of anger and hate toward someone here is doing this."

"But why?" Sofía asked, crossing her arms, her face grim.

Myriam pursed her lips. "That's what we need to find out."

Nayda stepped closer, lifting a hand, her long fingers tracing an invisible pattern in the air. The temperature in the room seemed to drop, the scent of burning sage suddenly thickening as power hummed around her.

"Dark magic leaves an imprint," she murmured, her voice almost hypnotic. "If we act fast, we might be able to track it before the energy fades."

I nodded sharply. "Then let's move."

But before I could take a step, Sofia's gaze snapped to me.

"Wait."

I stilled.

She frowned, tilting her head slightly, as if sensing something off.

"Not you, Andres." said Sofia

"Why not?" I snapped

"You are newly mated so I want you to go and spend time with your mate. We will keep the traditions of Luna Stone Pack. So go home with your mate for 3 days and do not report a day before," said Sofia with her alpha command.

My face turned up not liking the fact that I was being left out of the investigation. My father noticed my body language. I was not going to be benched to the side while all these threats occurred to my pack.

"Andrés, it's important for you to bond with your new mate. Do your three days and then we can regroup."

Angry, I said, "Fine."

Looking for Mai my mind could not wrap around the thought that my own people pushed me away from this investigation.

Chapter 28

MAYA

Three Months Later

The past three months have felt like living on a knife's edge. Ever since the last body was found, we've been trapped in this unbearable limbo waiting, watching, bracing for the next blow we all know is coming. Two girls are still missing, and with every day that passes without news, it feels like we're inching closer to a ticking time bomb ready to explode.

Thank the Goddess, there haven't been any new abductions... yet. But none of us are naïve enough to think the threat is over. The tension hangs over the pack like a storm cloud heavy, suffocating, darkening even the quietest of moments.

Ever since my birthday party, the entire focus has shifted to one thing: finding whoever's behind these murders and abductions. The witches from New York have thrown themselves into the investigation, using every ounce of their power, weaving spells and poring over both crime scenes. Through shell readings and tarot spreads, they've uncovered fragments of clues but nothing solid enough to lead us to a name, a face, a clear path forward.

What we do know chills me to the bone. A powerful witch is tied to the dark magic behind these killings. Myriam, the head witch, is convinced the culprit must have a connection to someone in the pack. She explained that dark magic like this is usually fueled by deep-rooted hatred, by a sense of betrayal or injustice. Even if we've done nothing wrong, she warned, it only takes one person's twisted perception of being wronged for that hate to fester and spill into something monstrous.

And there's a trace of a shifter. A male wolf, working with the witch, possibly the one dumping the bodies after the killings. No one was surprised to hear that. We'd all suspected it from the beginning. My father's name has been whispered behind closed doors ever since we caught his scent near the first body. And as much as it breaks my heart, I can't deny the truth that's been staring me in the face.

I know my father has wronged people here, hurt them in ways that can never be undone but hearing the hatred firsthand still cuts deeper than I was prepared for. Marco's bitterness. Sofía's anger. Xiomara's icy disgust. And the worst part? Seeing Andrés agree with them. Watching his jaw tighten, his eyes darken with that quiet fury... it makes my blood run cold.

Because as much as I want to believe our bond is unshakable, I can't shake the fear that if my secret ever comes out, if Andrés finds out who my father really is, he'll look at me with that same hatred. He'll see me not as his mate, not as the woman he loves, but as the daughter of the man who shattered his family... the man who hurt his mentor, his uncle, and his sister.

Sofía keeps urging me to come clean. She says secrets have a way of exploding when you least expect them to. But every time I think about telling Andrés the truth, my chest tightens with terror. What if he can't forgive me? What if he looks at me and only sees my bloodline, my father's sins, and not me?

What if loving me... just isn't enough?

Shortly after the witches left, Darren and Estrella decided to hold a quick mating ceremony, making their bond official in the eyes of the entire pack. It was small and intimate, but the love between them was undeniable, a bright moment of joy in the middle of all the darkness we'd been drowning in.

Not long after their ceremony, Darren was called away on an urgent lead about my father's whereabouts. My heart ached for Estrella, watching her try to stay strong as her mate left, especially now that she was expecting. I couldn't even imagine the strain of being separated from your bonded mate while carrying their child. Sofía, ever the fierce protector, wrapped an arm around Estrella and promised her that Darren would be home in time to meet his pup no matter what it took.

Now Estrella is six months pregnant and so ready to be done. She's been a warrior through it all, but it's getting harder for her to move around, and we've all pitched in to help where we can. Cooking, cleaning, running errands, whatever she needs, we're there.

Spending time with her these past few weeks has stirred something deep inside me. Watching her rub her swollen belly, feeling the quiet power of that maternal glow, it's made me think more and more about what it would be like if Andrés and I had a baby of our own.

Not that Yolanda's endless hints are making it any easier to ignore. Every other day, it seems, she drops another playful comment, eyes sparkling with mischief, about how "little grandpups" would complete the pack's circle of love. At first, I'd just smile tightly and change the subject, feeling my nerves twist into knots. Andrés and I had only just begun our life together, and while the idea of kids was beautiful in theory, I wasn't sure I was ready to take that step yet.

But now... things feel different. The more time I spend with Estrella, the more those quiet daydreams sneak up on me. I catch myself imagining tiny little versions of Andrés, wild and free, with his honey-brown eyes and that crooked smile that melts me every single time. The thought of us creating something together, something so pure, so precious... it doesn't seem so terrifying anymore.

In fact, it's starting to feel like something I might actually want. Sooner rather than later.

That night, after a long day of helping Estrella, I curled up on the couch, waiting for Andrés to get home. My hand instinctively drifted to my stomach, my thoughts spinning as I stared at the flickering fire. I didn't even realize I was lost in my own little world until the door creaked open and the familiar scent of woodsy musk and pure male hit me like a punch to the gut.

Andrés stepped inside, eyes finding me immediately, his gaze softening as he kicked off his shoes. "Hey, baby," he murmured, crossing the room in a few long strides.

He leaned down, brushing a slow, lingering kiss against my lips, and just like that, my worries melted away. His fingers slid through my hair, his forehead resting against mine as he sighed, like the tension of the entire day slipped right off his shoulders the second he touched me.

"You've been quiet today," he murmured, thumb brushing my cheek. "What's on that beautiful mind of yours?"

I hesitated, chewing my lip, wondering if now was the right time to bring it up. But with Andrés, it always felt safe to be vulnerable, even when the words felt too big to say out loud.

"Just... thinking," I said softly, my fingers tracing idle circles over his chest. "About the future. About us."

His brow quirked, curiosity sparking in his eyes. "Yeah?" He cupped my jaw gently, eyes locked onto mine with that deep, soul-searing intensity that always made my heart race. "What kind of future are we talking about, my little wolf?"

I swallowed hard, feeling my pulse flutter. And for the first time, I didn't shy away from the thought.

"Maybe... a bigger family," I whispered, my voice barely above a breath. "Someday."

His eyes darkened, a slow, hungry smile spreading across his lips. "Someday," he echoed, his voice low and rough as he leaned in to kiss me again, deeper this time, like he was staking his claim all over again.

That night, wrapped up in Andrés's arms, the firelight flickering across his bare skin, I couldn't stop my mind from wandering back to the conversation we'd left hanging. His breath was steady against my neck, his fingers tracing lazy circles on my hip, but I knew he was awake, just as lost in his own thoughts as I was.

I tilted my head up to look at him, my heart squeezing at the sight of those honey-brown eyes staring down at me, filled with a kind of quiet adoration that always left me breathless.

"We're really building something here, huh?" I whispered, my fingers brushing along his jawline. "A life."

His lips curved in a soft smile, eyes shining in the dim light. "We are," he murmured, kissing my forehead. "And it's only just beginning."

I tucked myself tighter against him, letting his warmth chase away the lingering fears. Despite everything, the danger still lurking, the secrets I kept buried deep, being with Andrés felt like the safest place in the world.

And maybe... just maybe... it was time to let myself breathe, to enjoy the happiness we'd fought so hard for.

For a long time, I'd been so focused on what could go wrong, the fear of my secret coming out, the looming threat hanging over the pack, that I hadn't allowed myself to fully feel the good. But lying there, safe and loved in his arms, I couldn't deny it anymore.

We were building something real. Something lasting.

Because my mating to Andrés has been nothing short of a fairytale, though sometimes it still feels too good to be true, like I'm living in a dream, I'm terrified I might slip through my fingers. From the moment we sealed our bond, everything shifted inside me. There's this tether between us, pulling me closer to him no matter the distance, no matter the noise of the outside world.

It's not just the physical pull, though Goddess knows the physical connection is every bit as wild and consuming as I ever imagined. It's deeper than that. It's in the way he looks at me, like I'm his entire world, his purpose, his most precious prize.

Andrés has slipped seamlessly back into his rhythm at Luna Enterprises, stepping into his role as CFO, confident, sharp, utterly in control. And watching him command a boardroom with that effortless authority? Goddess, it does things to me. There's something intoxicating about seeing him own the world by day, only to come home and surrender to the pull of our bond at night, like nothing and no one else matters.

While he's been conquering his world, I've been carving out my own space too, enrolling in online classes to finally finish my degree. It feels good to have something that's mine, a piece of my life that's separate but still intertwined with his. I love that balance. That freedom. Even though, let's be honest—my heart is always tuned to his, no matter what.

And through it all, Yolanda has been my rock. The mother figure I never realized I needed, stepping in to guide me through the strange, beautiful maze of mated life. There's so much more to being bonded than I ever expected—more layers, more emotions, more challenges. Yolanda's taught me things no one else ever bothered to explain, and she's done it all with love, patience, and that quiet strength she seems to carry so effortlessly.

Lately, she's taken it upon herself to teach me how to cook, something I never thought I'd have the patience for. At first, I joked that Andrés could survive on takeout forever, but Yolanda wasn't having it. There's something peaceful about standing side by side with her in the kitchen, chopping, stirring, seasoning, learning the rhythm of recipes passed down through generations. Her hands guide mine, her voice steady and sure, and what used to feel like a chore has become something... comforting. A new way of showing love.

And every night without fail, Andrés comes home to me. The second I hear his key in the door, my pulse quickens, my wolf stirring with an ache of anticipation. He doesn't have to say a word; one look, dark and hungry, and my knees go weak. He's on me in a heartbeat, his hands rough and desperate, his mouth claiming me like I'm the only thing keeping him alive.

And when he makes love to me, it is slow and deep, fierce and tender. I feel it in every inch of my soul. He touches me like I'm precious, worships me like I'm his salvation. No matter how many times we come together, it always feels new. Always electric.

Afterward, when we're breathless and tangled in the sheets, he holds me close, and we talk in low whispers until sleep claims us. We share everything: our dreams, our fears, the smallest pieces of our days, building a world within these four walls that feels untouchable, like a fortress no one can break through.

And in those quiet moments, with his heartbeat steady beneath my ear, I let myself believe that maybe, just maybe, we really can have it all.

But looking back now, I realize how naïve I'd been, how foolish to think my happiness could last forever. Girls like me? We don't get fairy tales. We get fleeting glimpses of joy before reality comes crashing in to rip it all away.

No matter how much I wanted to believe I could outrun my father's sins, they were always there... lurking in the shadows, waiting to drag me back down.

It was early morning when the illusion shattered. I was wrapped in Andrés's arms, drifting somewhere between sleep and waking, when his phone buzzed sharply on the nightstand. He groaned, pressing a kiss to my temple before reaching for it, his muscles tense beneath my palm as he read the screen.

"Shit," he muttered, sitting up fast, his whole body going rigid.

"What is it?" I asked, my voice thick with sleep but already tinged with dread. My wolf stirred uneasily, catching the sudden shift in the air.

Andrés swung his legs off the bed, rubbing a hand over his jaw. "We need to get to the packhouse. Now."

I pushed up on my elbows, heart pounding. "Why? What's going on?"

He hesitated for a beat too long, his eyes dark and unreadable. "They found another body."

The blood drained from my face, my stomach twisting into a tight, aching knot. I scrambled out of bed without another word, my hands shaking as I yanked on clothes. Andrés moved beside me in tense silence, his jaw clenched, his movements quick and controlled, but I could feel his wolf simmering just beneath the surface, radiating pure, cold fury.

Minutes later, we sped toward the packhouse, neither of us speaking, the silence between us thick with fear and unspoken questions. By the time we arrived, my pulse was a drumbeat in my ears, my palms slick with sweat.

We pushed through the heavy doors and made our way straight to Sofía's study. The room was already packed: Leo, Xiomara, Marco, Sofia, all gathered around the large table, their faces grim.

Sofía's eyes met mine as we entered, her expression unreadable but her energy crackling with tension. Andrés's arm brushed against mine as we stepped closer, a silent comfort even as dread clawed up my throat.

Leo didn't waste any time. "One of the missing girls, the one who was taken two months ago was found early this morning near the southern border," he said, his voice rough with restrained anger. "Patrols spotted her body dumped just inside our territory line."

My stomach dropped, bile rising as I clutched the edge of the table to keep myself grounded.

"She was freshly killed," Leo continued, glancing between all of us, "and left in the same condition as the other victims: mutilated, defiled, beaten. But there's one major difference this time."

Andrés's brows knitted together, his tone sharp. "What difference?"

Leo's jaw flexed. "No trace of dark magic. None. The witches scanned her body and the area around her—nothing. Whatever spellwork was involved before... it's gone now."

A cold chill slid down my spine. "Then what... killed her?" I asked quietly, though part of me wasn't sure I wanted to know.

Leo exhaled, his gaze flicking toward Sofía before answering. "There was a note. Nailed to her forehead."

My breath hitched, horror washing over me in a wave. "A note?" Andrés's voice was hard now, low and dangerous. "What did it say?"

Leo didn't answer right away. Instead, he reached into his jacket pocket and pulled out a folded slip of paper, his fingers gripping it so tightly his knuckles turned white. He handed it to Andrés without a word.

Andrés unfolded the note slowly, his eyes scanning the messy scrawl. I watched his face tighten with every word, his jaw locking so hard I thought it might crack. His hand shook as he passed the note to me, his eyes burning with a mix of rage and disbelief.

I stared down at the words, my vision blurring as the world seemed to tilt beneath me:

> *Daughter of mine,*
> *What a pity that your loyalty was so easily bought by a pretty face with a cock.*
> *Despite your betrayal, I do appreciate everything you've assisted me with.*
> *Love,*
> *Alpha George.*

My hands went numb, the note slipping from my grasp and fluttering to the floor as the weight of his words crushed down on me. My heart stuttered, my breath coming in shallow gasps as I realized the horrifying truth.

He knew. And worse, he wanted everyone else to know too.

Andrés's hand was suddenly on my lower back, grounding me, his eyes locked onto mine with fierce intensity. "What the fuck is this supposed to mean?" His voice was sharp, demanding, but underneath, I could hear the crack, like something inside him was beginning to fracture.

Chapter 29

MAYA

The room was deathly silent, thick with tension as everyone stared at the fallen note. My pulse thundered in my ears, my vision blurring at the edges. Andrés stood frozen beside me, eyes locked on the words, brows furrowed in confusion. His breathing was ragged, his fingers flexing like he was trying to piece it together but coming up empty.

Finally, his voice cut through the silence, low and strained. "Who... who the hell is he talking about?"

The words barely left his mouth when the door swung open, and Rosario sauntered in with that smug, venomous glint in her eyes. She crossed her arms, lips curling in a wicked smile as her gaze swept the room.

"Oh, come on, Andrés," she drawled, her tone dripping with false innocence. "You know who he's talking about. Don't play dumb. Right, Sofía? Right... Mai?"

She let the name hang in the air for a beat too long before her smile sharpened like a blade. "Or should I say... Maya Sinclair?"

I felt the blood drain from my face, my stomach twisting painfully. Andrés's head whipped toward me, his eyes wide, his confusion deepening as he searched my face. "Mai," he said slowly, his voice tight with disbelief, "what is she talking about?"

I opened my mouth to answer, but nothing came out. My throat felt like it was closing in, words tangling and dying before they could reach my lips. The truth sat like a stone in my chest, heavy and suffocating.

Leo stepped forward quickly, placing a steadying hand on Andrés's shoulder. "Brother, breathe," he urged, his tone low and firm. "We need you to calm down."

But Andrés wasn't listening. His eyes were still locked on me, wild and searching, demanding answers.

Suddenly, Xiomara was across the room, grabbing Rosario by the hair and yanking her head back with a vicious growl. "How the fuck do you know that information?" she snarled, her lips brushing Rosario's ear, her wolf flashing just beneath the surface.

I took a shaky step toward Andrés, desperate to close the distance, to explain, to beg. "Andrés, please."

But he moved back, his eyes flashing, his rejection slicing deeper than any blade. His voice was sharp, broken. "Is it true?" His eyes were glassy, almost pleading now. "Is your father... Alpha George?"

Tears welled in my eyes, blurring everything. My heart pounded so hard it hurt. I opened my mouth, my voice trembling as the truth finally spilled out. "You took me from the home of Alpha George. I told you... I told you I wasn't his pet... because I'm his daughter."

The room seemed to stop, everything frozen except the thundering of Andrés's heart, his breathing ragged and sharp. His gaze darted around the room now, wild and betrayed, looking at every face in turn until his eyes landed on Sofía.

"You knew?" His voice was barely a whisper, hoarse and raw.

Sofía's shoulders sagged under the weight of his pain. "Yes," she said softly. "I knew... after you took her and left, the people from Black Stone told me who she was."

Andrés's face twisted, his hands shaking as fury and heartbreak collided in his eyes. His voice rose, sharp and cutting, the betrayal pouring out of him like a wound ripped wide open. "You knew and you said nothing? I am your brother, Sofía! I stood by your side when the Council turned their backs on you. I fought for you when they doubted your place as the next Alpha. I followed you into battle to defend your mate's old pack. I risked my life for you to rescue you!"

Sofía's eyes shimmered with unshed tears, her jaw tight. "And I did what I thought was best for you," she said quietly. "It wasn't my secret to tell."

Andrés turned back to me, his eyes shattered, his voice cracking open. "And you... what the hell was all of this? Was that the plan? Make me fall for you while you handed intel to your fucking father? Hurt my pack from the inside?" His voice broke. "You never loved me. It was all a lie."

"No!" I cried, my voice shaking. "Andrés, please, no! I haven't seen my father since the day you took me. I haven't spoken to him. I swear to you, I would never betray you or your pack. You've all treated me like family. You—"

"Then explain the damn note, Maya!" he roared, his eyes blazing, his chest heaving with raw pain.

Rosario yanked free from Xiomara's grip, smirking as she stepped closer. "She can't explain it," she sneered, her voice laced with poison. "Because there's nothing to explain. She's a traitorous whore who wormed her way into your bed just to hurt your pack. Who knows what kind of witchcraft she used to fool you into thinking she's your mate. She's not your mate, Andrés. Open your eyes."

I shook my head frantically, tears spilling down my cheeks. "That's not true!" I gasped. "I would never."

But my words barely seemed to reach him. Andrés's eyes were locked on mine, filled with so much pain, so much betrayal, that it shattered something deep inside me.

Andrés's ragged breathing filled the tense air as he stared at me, his jaw clenched so tightly it looked like it might snap. His fists were shaking at his sides, eyes wild and dark, the betrayal cutting too deep to contain.

Without another word, he turned and stormed out of the study, shoving the door open so hard it rattled the frame.

"No, wait!" I gasped, scrambling after him. My heart was hammering, breaking apart piece by piece as I caught up, grabbing his arm just before he could disappear down the hall.

"Please," I whispered, my voice trembling. "Don't leave. I didn't betray you. Yes, I kept my identity a secret, but only because at first, I was terrified of what you and your pack would do to me. And then... then I was afraid that you wouldn't want me at all."

He yanked his arm out of my grasp, rolling his eyes with a bitter laugh. "Afraid?" he spat, his voice sharp with disbelief. "Afraid? You think that justifies lying to me? To all of us?"

Tears streamed down my cheeks, my whole body shaking as I choked out, "I swear to you. I have never betrayed you. I love..."

Before I could finish, a savage growl ripped from his throat. His eyes flashed dangerously, and in one harsh move, he tore his hand free and spun away from me.

"No, please!" I sobbed, grabbing at his hand again, desperate to hold him, to keep him from walking away from us, from everything.

He roared then, his voice like thunder cracking through the hallway as he shoved me back with a force that sent me stumbling to the ground.

"Do not fucking touch me!" he bellowed, his face twisted in rage.

I hit the cold floor hard, gasping for breath, my heart shattering into pieces too jagged to pick up. I stared up at him, tears blurring my vision, my wolf whimpering deep inside, broken and lost.

Andrés loomed over me, his chest heaving, eyes burning with fury and something darker, something hollow and bitter. His lips curled in disgust as he stepped closer, towering above me.

"I don't believe a word you say," he hissed, his voice shaking with venom. "You're just like every other she-wolf, using a man until you bleed him dry. I gave you everything, my trust, my heart, and you lied." His voice dropped, cold and final. "I never want to see you again."

My breath caught, my chest caving in as his hand lifted, fist clenched like he was fighting every instinct inside him. He froze, his body rigid, his fist trembling in the air. For a moment, it looked like he might strike, but instead, he snarled and let it fall to his side.

Out of pure instinct, I backed up on the floor, my breath coming in ragged gasps. "Andrés..." I whispered, but the fear tangled with my grief, and my body screamed at me to run.

So I did.

I bolted, my legs barely working beneath me, pushing past the packhouse doors and into the cold night air. I ran blindly, tears streaming down my face, my wolf howling with pain and heartbreak. I ran and ran, the darkness swallowing me whole, until I couldn't even see the lights of Luna Stone territory behind me.

Hours passed; my legs burned, my lungs ached, but I didn't stop. I couldn't stop. I didn't know where I was going, only that I had to get away. Away from Andrés. Away from the betrayal. Away from the heartbreak that threatened to tear me in two.

How could he? I thought wildly, tears blurring my vision. I never gave him a reason to doubt me. Why was he so quick to believe Rosario's lies?

And then the worst thought of all. How the hell did Rosario even know the truth?

None of it mattered now. Andrés had made his choice. He didn't want me. He didn't believe me.

And if that was the case... I had nowhere else to go but back to the Black Stone Pack. Back to the one place I never wanted to return. But without money, without a car, how the hell was I supposed to make it back to Florida?

My legs trembled, my body completely drained, and still I kept running east, toward the only thing I had left.

Night fell, cold and heavy, and when I stumbled across an old, abandoned building, I slipped inside, collapsing to the ground, gasping for air. My body ached, my soul shattered, but I was too tired to keep moving. I tucked my knees to my chest, tears still leaking from my eyes as I slowly drifted into a restless sleep, haunted by Andrés's words.

I didn't know how much time passed before I felt it—rough, calloused hands cupping my face, stroking my hair.

"Andrés?" I whispered groggily, my heart clenching with hope. "You... you found me?"

But a deep, chilling voice answered, one that sent ice straight through my veins.

"No, my child," he said, his face emerging from the shadows with a twisted smile. "It's me."

376

My breath hitched, pure terror flooding my veins as I stared into the cold, familiar eyes of my father.

I scrambled back, my spine pressing against the cold, crumbling wall. "W-What are you doing here?" I whispered, my voice shaking. "How did you even know where I was?"

My father stepped closer, his boots crunching on the broken concrete, his eyes gleaming with something sharp and possessive. He crouched down slowly, reaching out to tuck a strand of hair behind my ear, his touch deceptively gentle.

"Oh, my sweet girl," he murmured, his voice laced with sickening affection. "I've always known where you were. Did you really think I wouldn't keep tabs on my own blood? I've been watching, waiting... ever since that Luna Stone bastard ripped you away from me."

His fingers brushed my cheek like a lover's touch, but the chill it sent down my spine was pure ice. "I've been patient, Maya. So patient. I had to wait for the right moment to bring you home. To rescue you."

My heart pounded so hard it hurt, my instincts screaming that none of this was right. I stared at him, searching his face for a trace of the father I remembered, but all I saw was cold calculation and something darker lurking beneath.

"Rescue me?" I choked out, shaking my head in disbelief. "I didn't need rescuing. I wasn't... I chose to stay. Andrés—he's my mate."

The moment the words left my lips, his entire body stiffened. His eyes darkened, a flicker of pure disgust flashing across his face. His jaw clenched so hard I thought it might snap, but then, in a chillingly smooth move, he pressed a finger to my lips, silencing me.

"Shh," he whispered, shaking his head slowly, his eyes glinting with something dangerous. "It's okay. It's all going to be okay. You've been confused. Misguided. But I'm going to fix it, all of it."

He leaned in closer, his breath warm and heavy against my skin. "We had such high hopes for you, my dear. You were meant for more than this... mess. And yet you threw it all away." His eyes narrowed, his voice hardening. "You gave yourself to that disgusting male from Luna Stone. You tainted yourself."

I flinched, my heart cracking open at his words. "He's my mate," I whispered fiercely, tears burning my eyes. "You can't change that."

But he just smiled, cold and final, his finger still pressed to my lips. "It doesn't matter. At the end of the day, you'll serve me, one way or another."

A cold dread washed over me, my wolf thrashing inside me, screaming to run. I pushed up off the floor, my breath ragged, muscles coiled to bolt, but he was faster.

Before I could even get to my feet, he moved like a striking snake, clamping a rag over my face.

The sharp, bitter scent hit me instantly, chemical and suffocating.

"No!" I gasped, thrashing wildly, clawing at his arms, kicking with everything I had. "Stop, let me go!"

But he was too strong, his grip like iron. His voice, disturbingly calm, slid into my ear as the world started tilting.

"Just breathe, my little wolf," he crooned, holding the rag firm over my mouth and nose. "A little chloroform... and a touch of wolfsbane... does the trick every time."

My limbs grew heavy, my vision blurring and darkening at the edges as I fought to stay awake, to fight back, to do something.

But the darkness swallowed me whole.

The last thing I heard was his voice, far away and echoing, laced with triumph.

"Sleep tight, my darling. We've got a long road ahead."

And then nothing.

Chapter 30

ANDRÉS

I slammed the door behind me so hard the walls trembled. My chest heaved as I stood in the wreckage of silence, fists clenched, hands shaking. The stillness pressed in like a fucking vice, every breath a battle. My wolf paced beneath the surface, snarling, restless, caught between heartbreak and rage.

Maya Sinclair.

The name wouldn't stop echoing. Loud. Relentless. A war drum in my skull.

She lied.

She lied to me.

Rosario's voice—sharp, smug, venomous—kept twisting through my thoughts, poisoning every memory I had of her. Every kiss. Every smile. Every whispered promise in the dark. I could still feel Maya's warmth in my bed, hear her soft laugh, the way she used to say my name like it meant something.

Was it ever real?

"Fuck!" I roared, grabbing the nearest lamp and hurling it across the room. It exploded against the wall, shards raining down like broken truth.

I lost it.

Chairs went flying. Books were torn from shelves. I ripped through the room like a storm, tearing apart everything in my path, but nothing silenced the hollow, jagged ache in my chest.

She lied to me. She let me fall for her, let me mark her, hold her, claim her while she hid who she truly was.

But even in the wreckage, even in the betrayal, I still wanted her.

Goddess help me, I still fucking wanted her.

My wolf cried out for her, howled for the mate he couldn't forget. No matter how much my head screamed, my soul still ached for her.

I stumbled into the bedroom, out of breath, blood roaring in my ears. And then I saw it

Her sweater.

The one she wore on chilly mornings when she made coffee barefoot. The one I'd pulled off her body too many times to count. It was draped over the edge of the bed like she'd never left.

My feet moved before my brain did. I dropped to my knees and grabbed it with both hands, dragging it to my face and inhaling deep, desperate for something that still felt like her.

Honeysuckle. Citrus. That soft warmth that was mine. I broke.

My knees gave out, and I collapsed onto the cold floor, clutching that damn sweater like it could hold me together. My chest convulsed with ragged, choking sobs, hot tears burning down my cheeks as everything I'd been holding in came crashing down.

I hated her.

No, I missed her. Goddess, I missed her.

Her laugh. Her mouth. The way she curled against me at night like she belonged there.

But every time my heart reached for her, my mind slammed the door shut. She lied. She used me. Played the long game and played it well.

I growled low in my throat, my hands trembling as I clutched the fabric tighter. "Why?" I rasped into the silence. "Why the fuck didn't you just tell me?"

If she'd told me from the beginning, hell, even after I brought her here. I could've protected her. Could've understood.

But instead... she hid the truth like a dagger behind her back. Let me love her with blind trust. Let me fall for a fantasy while she guarded a secret that had the power to burn down everything.

Alpha George's daughter.

The words tasted like ash.

How could she be related to him? That man was a monster. He destroyed lives. Ripped families apart. He hurt my sister and my pack.

And yet... she was nothing like him.

Her eyes were soft. Her voice, warm. Her heart... it had felt honest.

Hadn't it?

I dragged my hands through my hair and let my head fall back against the wall. I wanted to scream. To shift and rip something apart. But instead, I just sat there, broken.

Because the truth I hated most was that I still loved her.

I don't know how long I stayed there, crumpled on the cold floor, drowning in guilt, rage, and everything in between. The shattered glass, overturned furniture, and broken pieces of my life surrounded me, silent witnesses to the storm inside me.

The room was chaos. And so was I.

It was hours later, just as the moon began to rise, that the front door slammed open with a heavy thud.

I barely looked up at first until I heard the footsteps. Heavy, urgent. Familiar.

My father's voice hit first, sharp and reprimanding. "Andrés," he snapped, his tone full of disapproval, "this is how you handle things now? Destroying your home like some feral pup in a tantrum?"

I pushed to my feet, slowly, fury building all over again. My chest heaved, my claws pricking at the edges of my skin, ready to break through.

"Don't come in here and lecture me like you know what the fuck I'm going through," I snarled, my voice raw. "You have no idea what it feels like to finally have something, someone that completes you... only to find out it was all a lie."

Behind him, my mother stood next to Leo and Sofía with heartbreak in her eyes. Xiomara trailed in last, dragging Rosario by the arm, bruised, bloodied, and limp like a ragdoll.

But I couldn't focus on any of that. I was too far gone.

"She didn't deny it," I bit out, pacing the room, hands clenching and unclenching. "She is Alpha George's daughter. That wasn't just a mistake. That was a secret. A dangerous one. If she had nothing to hide, why didn't she tell me? Why did all of you keep it from me?"

My eyes burned as I spun around to face them all. "She put all of us at risk. Every warrior, every elder, every pup in this territory. Why didn't you tell me anything, Sofía?"

With a low voice, Sofía said, "I did what I believe was right. She told me she was going to tell you. She was just scared of your reaction, which based on what you are doing, I don't blame her."

I dragged a hand through my hair, pacing like I was one breath away from shifting. My voice cracked. "Did you not read the note? She has been spying for her father, helping him with the kidnappings and who knows what else."

I turned and pointed to Xiomara. "Her father is the reason why Xiomara has become distant and never smiles."

Xiomara looked down as if she was embarrassed. I hate calling her out after all she went through, but I am so angry, I am trying to prove a point regardless of who I hurt.

I stopped in the center of the room, my whole body trembling. "What the hell was I supposed to think?"

My body was heavy, every muscle tight with the weight of everything I'd just said. My gaze drifted across the room, landing on Rosario.

Her face was wrecked—swollen cheek, split lip, eyes bloodshot from crying. She looked like a shadow of herself, and yet... I didn't feel pity. I felt dread.

"What the hell is this?" I asked, my voice low and rough. "Why does she look like that?" My eyes cut to Xiomara. "What are you doing?"

Xiomara didn't flinch. She narrowed her eyes and yanked Rosario forward by the arm, dragging her into the center of the room like a captured traitor. Then she kicked the back of Rosario's knee.

Rosario buckled with a cry and fell to the floor.

"Go on," Xiomara said coldly. "Tell him what you told us."

Rosario kept her mouth shut, trembling, her jaw locked like she could will the truth away if she just stayed silent.

"Tell him," Xiomara snapped.

Still nothing.

I stepped forward, instincts coiled tight beneath my skin. "Enough," I growled. "Leave her alone."

Xiomara slowly turned to me with a look that could skin flesh from bone. "Are you actually defending her? After what she did? After what you did?"

Before I could answer, Leo stepped up beside her, his voice cutting through the tension like a blade.

"You've always been a fucking hothead," he bit out. "Acting like you're the one with control, like you've got your emotions all locked up. But the second things get messy, the second it stops going your way," He pointed to the wreckage around me, to the storm still burning in my eyes. "You lose your damn head."

My jaw flexed hard. "What the hell are you trying to say?"

Leo's expression darkened. He pointed straight at Rosario. "Did it ever cross your mind that she was lying? That you tore apart the woman you love because you were too blinded by your own pain and pride to see it?"

Xiomara's voice followed, smooth and sharp like polished steel. "And how convenient," she added, "that Rosario just happened to show up right when we found the note. And even more convenient that she just knew Maya was Alpha George's daughter—on the same damn day a body was dumped at our border?"

She folded her arms, her gaze slicing through me. "I don't believe in coincidences. So I remembered the training I got at Luna Enterprises. And I interrogated her."

Her lips curled, deadly. "Now she's going to tell you what she told us."

I turned slowly to Rosario. The room was thick with silence, every heartbeat like thunder in my ears.

I stepped forward until I towered over her, my voice a low growl. "If you've got something to say... say it now. Because if I have to hear it from them." My claws threatened to break through. "I swear to the Goddess, I will kill you."

Rosario's eyes widened in fear, and her lower lip began to tremble. When she spoke, her voice was hoarse, broken, like someone who'd been crying for hours.

"A few days ago..." she began slowly, "I overheard Alpha Sofía and Maya talking. Maya said she wanted to tell you the truth. That she was scared. Your sister encouraged her, told her you wouldn't care that she was Alpha George's daughter."

She looked up at me, tears glistening in her swollen eyes. "But I knew she was lying. She was manipulating everyone. Just like she manipulated you."

My blood roared in my ears, but I didn't move. I let her speak.

"So I did what I had to. I asked around. Found out Alpha George does have a daughter. Maya Sinclair." She sniffled. "During patrol, I caught the scent of an unknown wolf and followed it. Before he ran off... I told him I knew where his daughter was. That she was with you."

Her voice cracked. "It was him. Alpha George. He listened."

My heart sank. Rage burned.

"I told him everything about you, about her. I made a deal. I told him I'd get her to run. That I'd make you hate her."

She swallowed hard. "But I didn't know about the body, I swear. He just told me I'd know when it was time to play my part. And to keep listening in case I learned something useful."

She reached for me then, her voice trembling with emotion. "But Andrés, I did it for us. She doesn't deserve you. She lied to you. She never loved you like I do."

Her hand brushed mine.

"I love you. I've always loved you."

I looked at her, really looked, and all I saw was everything I'd destroyed. Everything I'd thrown away because I'd listened to her.

I pulled my hand back slowly, revulsion curling through me like venom.

My mother stepped forward, her voice soft but firm, the kind of strength only a Luna carried. "You see now," she said, placing her hand gently on my arm. "Maya wasn't lying. She never was. You need to go to her, mijo. You need to find your mate."

Something inside me clicked back into place at her words like the fog finally cleared. The guilt, the grief, the rage. They were still there, but underneath it all burned something stronger.

Resolve.

I was going to find her. Whatever it took, wherever she was—I'd bring her back.

I turned toward the door, ready to run. Ready to tear through the world if I had to.

But laughter stopped me cold.

Rosario.

She chuckled from the floor, the sound brittle and cracked but still filled with spite. "I can't believe this," she spat, lip curled. "After everything, after she lied to you, endangered this entire pack, probably used witchcraft to fool your senses, you're still running after her?"

Her laughter turned to a giggle, high-pitched and hysterical. "Well, too late. She's gone. I saw her leave the territory hours ago."

The smugness in her voice was the last straw.

Without hesitation, Xiomara stepped forward and drove her knee straight into Rosario's face. A sickening crack followed, and Rosario collapsed to the floor, unconscious.

"Shut the fuck up already," Xiomara growled, shaking her hand and glaring down at her like she was filth.

I didn't even flinch.

"Leo," I said, voice hard as steel, "take her to the dungeon. Post a warrior at the door. She doesn't breathe without someone knowing about it."

He nodded, already pulling her limp body up by the arm.

I turned back to the others, mind racing. "If what she said is true... if Maya ran, then where the hell would she go?"

Everyone fell silent.

My gaze shifted to my father. His jaw tightened. I saw it the second the thought hit him.

And at the same time, we both said it out loud.

"*Black Stone Pack.*"

Chapter 31

ANDRÉS

I barged into Sofía's study, my heart pounding like a war drum in my chest. "I need you to connect me with Alpha Jason," I said without preamble. "I need to go to Black Stone Pack."

Sofía and Mason looked up from where they were seated, both blinking in confusion.

"Wait—what?" Sofía asked, brows pulling together. "Why the hell do you want to go to Black Stone Pack?"

I started pacing, too wired to sit still, adrenaline thrumming through me like wildfire. "I'm not sure if you've heard what happened..."

Sofía stood slowly, crossing her arms. "We know. About Rosario. About the confession."

My steps faltered. "You knew?"

She nodded, her expression flat. "Yes. I know what she did. I stayed because I was too angry to look at you. If I had followed you home after you shoved your mate and accused her of betrayal, we would've ended up fighting. And that wouldn't have helped anyone."

That hit hard, but I deserved it.

"Yeah," I muttered, running a hand over my face. "That makes sense."

Estrella, glowing and very pregnant, shifted uncomfortably on the couch. "So... why do you need to go to Florida?" she asked.

I turned to her, chest tightening. "Rosario said she saw Maya leaving the pack territory. If she ran... there's only one place she'd go."

Sofía's eyes widened. "Her old pack."

"Exactly," I said. "Black Stone is the only place she knows outside of here. I have to go. I have to find her. And when I do, I have to beg her to forgive me."

There was a moment of silence before both Estrella and Sofía let out a long, knowing "Ohhhh..."

Sofía immediately turned to the tech on her desk. "Give me a second. I'll set up a secure channel to Alpha Jason."

Mason moved beside her, helping her align the camera and patch into the private pack line. Within moments, the screen glowed to life, ringing.

On the third chime, Jason's face filled the screen, looking relaxed as ever.

"Hey," he said, smirking. "Miss me already?"

"Not really," Mason replied dryly.

Jason chuckled. "Fair enough. What's going on?"

Sofía stepped aside so I could take the lead. I cleared my throat. "Alpha Jason... I need your permission to enter your territory."

Jason's smirk faded. "And, why is that?"

"It's Maya," I said. "She's missing. She ran after..." My voice caught. "I need to find her, and I am pretty sure she returned back to her own pack."

Jason frowningly asks, "Wait? You talking about the girl you took for Black Stone Pack?"

"Yes, she is my mate, and I found out she's George's daughter. She kept it from me. Even after we... mated. I did not handle that discovery well. And now...she's run away."

"She ran," Leo muttered under his breath. "Or did you push her away?"

"Leo," Estrella warned softly.

"She ran," I admitted, voice low. "She ran because I hurt her."

Jason leaned back, eyes narrowing as he took it in. "Do you know where she is now?"

I shook my head. "No. But I know her. The only place she might feel safe is the home she left behind."

Jason was quiet for a long moment.

Finally, he nodded once. "As the Black Stone Pack temporary Alpha, I will give you permission to come and look for your mate. I will meet you there and help you with all I can."

"Thank you, your support will not go unnoticed," I had replied.

After a couple more minutes of conversation, during which we had coordinated logistics, the screen had gone dark.

"I want to leave as soon as possible," I had said.

"Do you want me to go with you?" Leo had asked.

Shaking my head, I had answered, "No, Leo. Stay here, help Sofía protect the pack. I will be fine with Alpha Jason's help. If I find myself needing more help, I will call Darren."

Leo had nodded his head, understanding.

Estrella had gotten up and hugged me. "Andrés, be safe, and if you drag my husband to help you, make sure you keep him safe. There is a baby that he needs to meet," she had said with a smile.

Looking at her large belly, I had smiled, and my thoughts had gone to imagining Maya swollen with my pup in her belly. My heart had filled with hope that one day we could have a family.

The next morning, after a very restless night, I had quickly packed all my essentials into an overnight bag, and before the sun had risen, I had been in Leo's car, being driven to the airport. The flight to Florida had been quick, and Alpha Jason had been waiting for me at the airport, ready to take me to Black Stone Pack territory.

"Thanks, Jason, for assisting me in this," I had said while in the car.

"Of course. You guys were there for us when we needed y'all the most. This is what allies do," Jason had replied.

We crossed into Black Stone Pack territory just as the sun began to rise behind the treeline, casting long shadows over the land. But even in the fading light, it was clear—this place looked nothing like I remembered.

New structures had sprung up, sleek and modern alongside the older ones. Several houses were mid-renovation, their frames lined with scaffolding and fresh lumber. There was life here—order, progress. A sharp contrast to the dark reputation this place used to carry under George's rule.

"Wow," I muttered, my eyes sweeping the landscape. "The pack looks so different."

Jason smirked from the driver's seat beside me. "You'd be surprised what good leadership can accomplish."

There was a quiet pride in his voice, one I didn't miss.

We drove deeper into the heart of the pack until the car slowed in front of a house that stopped me cold.

I knew this place.

The old Alpha's house.

The place I'd first found her.

Before Jason even killed the engine, I opened the door and stepped out, my gaze locked on the two-story home. My boots crunched on gravel, but I barely heard it. My breath caught in my throat as memories slammed into me, vivid, consuming.

That night. Her scent. Her lips.

The fire in her eyes when she stood her ground despite having no idea who I was or what I'd come for.

The pull of the bond that had snapped into place the moment I laid eyes on her.

She had no idea she was mine. But I had known.

Jason stepped beside me, his voice lower now, more cautious. "This is the Alpha's house. Where Maya used to live."

I didn't speak. Couldn't. My throat was tight, and my chest ached with the weight of everything I'd lost. I could only nod, eyes still fixed on the door like she might walk through it at any moment.

Jason glanced at me, then gestured toward the porch. "While I waited for your arrival, I did some digging," he said. "And I found a few things I think you need to see. Things that might help you understand Maya a little better."

He didn't wait for my reply just turned and walked toward the house.

I followed, the scent of old wood and faint lingering wolf musk flooding my senses the moment we stepped inside. Jason led me down a narrow hallway, stopping in front of a door I recognized as hers.

But before I could reach for the handle, he turned and held up a hand.

"There's someone I want you to meet first," he said. "A couple from Black Stone. The wife used to work here when she was a maid for the old Alpha. And based on what she told me..."

He trailed off, his jaw tight, eyes suddenly stormy.

"It might change everything you think you know about Maya."

My pulse quickened. The wolf inside me growled low, restless, uneasy. Something told me this visit was about to rip open wounds I hadn't even realized were there.

But I nodded once, bracing myself.

Jason led me into the living room of Maya's old home, and the second I stepped inside, the air felt heavier, like the walls themselves held onto pain, whispering the memories of a girl who had suffered here in silence.

We didn't sit.

I stood near the fireplace, arms crossed tightly over my chest as Jason walked toward the front door and opened it. An older couple stepped inside—his posture straight and protective, hers slightly hunched—but her eyes... sharp. Observant. Wary.

"This is Matilda," Jason said, placing a hand on the woman's shoulder. "She served as Alpha George's housemaid... and later, became something much more important."

Matilda nodded politely to me. "Hello, sir," she greeted softly. Her mate, John, stood quietly at her side, one hand resting on the small of her back.

Jason continued, "And this is her mate, John. Both are highly respected in the pack. They've seen things most people haven't. And I thought you should hear it... from someone who knew Maya before you ever met her."

I nodded, stiffly. "Thank you for coming."

Matilda took a seat on the edge of the couch, her hands folded neatly in her lap. Her eyes swept the room like she, too, was reliving ghosts.

"Maya," she said, her voice gentle, "was a bright soul born into a cruel world. Life under Alpha George... it was no life at all. But she tried to find joy in the small things. In books, in music, in fleeting moments with her mother."

I swallowed hard, my voice rough as I spoke. "She told me she was happy here. That her mother made this place feel safe."

Matilda nodded, a sad smile tugging at her lips. "That's true. Luna Donna was the only light in this dark pack. She was everything George was not kind: warm, gentle. She shielded Maya from him as best she could."

She paused, her voice thinning. "But when Luna Donna died... Maya lost that protection. And George... he turned all his anger, all his twisted obsession with control, onto her."

I clenched my fists at my sides. "What kind of abuse?"

"Mostly physical. Emotional, too," Matilda said quietly, not flinching. "It wasn't always obvious. He knew how to strike where it wouldn't show. Knew how to break her down with words. He wanted her obedient. Molded into what he thought a daughter of an Alpha should be. Not free, not loved, just useful."

John reached for his mate's hand, holding it as her voice trembled.

"When Maya was sixteen," Matilda continued, "I was promoted, or rather, reassigned, as her nanny. She didn't need a nanny by that age, of course. But it was just George's way of keeping watch on her."

Matilda looked up at me, and the pain in her eyes nearly undid me.

"I tried to protect her," she said. "As best I could. If I heard him shouting, I'd go in first. Step between them. Try to calm him, lie, take blame for things she hadn't done. One night, when she snuck out to visit the infirmary to help a wounded pup... George found out. I told him I ordered her to do it. He beat me within an inch of my life."

John's jaw clenched, eyes flashing with the kind of rage that comes from being helpless too long. "She nursed Matilda after the beating. Still a child herself... and already taking care of others."

My chest burned. Every breath felt heavier.

This wasn't just about a girl who kept a secret.

This was about a girl who survived.

Alone.

And I turned my back on her.

"I didn't know," I murmured, voice rough. "Why did George hate his own flesh and blood?"

Matilda and John exchanged a look. Something passed between them, fear, hesitation... and something heavier.

Then Matilda's voice came, low and trembling. "There's something no one in the pack knows," she said. "Not even Maya."

I froze. "What do you mean?"

She swallowed hard, glancing at her mate again. "Maya... Maya was not Alpha George and Luna Donna's biological daughter."

The world tilted.

I couldn't speak.

Jason was the one to step forward, his Alpha instincts kicking in. "Wait, what are you talking about?" he demanded. "Not their daughter? You need to explain. Start from the beginning."

Matilda looked pale, her eyes brimming with old ghosts. "Go on, love," John whispered gently, rubbing her back.

"You've carried it long enough. This might help Maya now."

Matilda nodded slowly, and with a deep breath, she began.

"It was almost twenty-one years ago. I was still working as a maid in the Alpha's house. One of George's many 'business deals' had gone sideways, we all knew when he came back bloodied and laughing that something horrific had happened. But none of us expected what came next."

She clasped her hands tightly, her voice distant now, as though she were watching it unfold all over again.

"I didn't even know she was down there... in the dungeons," she whispered. "Not until we heard it. A cry. A woman's scream."

My heart slammed against my ribs.

"Luna Donna and I went to investigate. What we found..." Her voice cracked. "It was a beautiful she-wolf, covered in bruises, barely conscious, her belly huge with child. She was in labor. She was dying."

Matilda's jaw tightened, and tears shimmered in her eyes. "Donna rushed forward to help, but before she could even touch her, George appeared shirtless, pants undone. There was blood on his hands. And we knew." Her voice broke. "We knew what he'd done to that woman."

I felt my stomach turn, rage clawing at the edges of my control.

"Luna Donna tried to reach her anyway, tried to offer comfort, but before her hand even touched the woman's face, George kicked her across the room like she was nothing. And that poor woman… she just laid there, trembling, in pain."

John's face was tight, his hands clenched. Matilda went on.

"Donna begged him to stop. So did I. But he only laughed and called us weak." Her voice dropped to a bitter whisper. "That man loved no one but himself. He didn't care who he broke to prove his power."

Tears rolled silently down Matilda's cheeks now. "But Luna Donna, she was clever. She knew his pride was his weakness. Years before, George had visited a shifter doctor, trying to figure out why his mate couldn't get pregnant. What he never told anyone… was that it wasn't Donna. It was him. He was sterile."

Jason sucked in a breath. I stood there, frozen, fists trembling at my sides.

"Donna threw it in his face that day," Matilda continued. "Told him he was no real Alpha if he couldn't give his pack an heir. She knew it would push him, but she used it. She said if he couldn't give her a child, then maybe he could at least let her keep this one."

Matilda closed her eyes. "And to our shock… he agreed. On one condition. That she never again mention his sterility. That she would claim the baby as her own—say it came early in secret. That no one would ever know the truth."

The room felt like it was holding its breath.

"He made me swear silence," she said. "Said he'd rip my tongue out if I ever spoke of it."

"What happened to the woman?" I asked hoarsely, though I already feared the answer.

Matilda's hands trembled. "She was too weak. Donna tried to help her, to clean her wounds, to ease her pain. But George..." Her voice shook with rage and grief. "He grabbed a butcher knife from the kitchen. Right in front of us. And he cut that woman open while she was still alive. Ripped the baby from her body."

I staggered back a step, bile rising in my throat.

"She screamed," Matilda choked out. "And then he... slit her throat. Smiling."

John looked away, his jaw tight with fury.

"I wrapped the baby in the towel," Matilda continued. "She was tiny. Crying. Bloody. But perfect. And Luna Donna swore she would raise that child as her own. That she would protect her, love her, no matter what."

She looked up at me, her voice strong despite the tears. "That baby... was Maya."

A silence fell so thick I could barely breathe.

Matilda sniffed, brushing tears from her face. "Donna introduced her to the pack as her daughter. Said she had kept the pregnancy quiet to avoid any outside threats. She poured every bit of her soul into loving that little girl."

"But George?" Jason asked softly.

Matilda's expression hardened. "George only tolerated Maya because Donna loved her. But he was never a father to her. And when he saw Donna giving that child more attention than him... that's when his hatred toward Maya started. He even tried to convince Donna to get rid of the baby. But she refused. Told him if he ever laid a hand on Maya, she'd leave him."

She looked down, her voice hollow now. "He didn't believe she meant it, and for years they lived in a house full of hate and love. Alpha George would use the excuse of training to abuse Maya while Luna Donna would console her after training."

My heart cracked.

"This got really bad after Luna Donna heard him talking about using Maya as chosen mate to gain alliance with some pack from Canada. He was going to ship her to this older alpha in a couple of weeks because she was already sixteen and old enough to have pups."

My knees nearly buckled.

"Luna Donna instructed me to find Maya and get her ready, but we were too late. Before I left the house, I heard Alpha George yelling. He found her packing. Luna Donna had planned to run with Maya. She never made it. George shifted into his wolf... and killed her." Matilde said, crying.

"Wait a minute, Maya told me her mother died of cancer," said Andres

Wiping the tears from her eyes, Matilde said, "She did have cancer, but she was getting better and stronger. She did not die of cancer; she was murdered by Alpha George."

Chapter 32

MAYA

A sharp ache pulsed at the base of my skull as consciousness crept in like an unwanted guest. My eyelids felt like bricks, heavy and uncooperative. Every breath I took filled my lungs with the damp, rotting scent of mold and decay. The air was thick, choking. I coughed, instinctively turning my head to the side, but even that small movement made my body scream in protest.

I was tied up. Arms wrenched behind the back of a wooden chair, legs spread and bound to each of the chair's legs with rough rope. The abrasive fibers bit into my skin, stinging with every twitch. My wolf stirred, weak but alert, and I knew it wasn't just any rope. It was laced with something poison or wolfsbane, because no matter how hard I pushed, I couldn't shift, couldn't tap into my strength.

Panic flirted at the edge of my thoughts, but I shoved it back down. If I was going to survive this, I needed to stay quiet, sharp. My ears perked at the sound of voices—two of them.

One was unmistakable. My father.

The other, a woman. Her voice was sharp, defiant. A Southern drawl wrapped in venom. Texan, maybe... but I couldn't place her.

I held my breath and focused, straining to hear.

"I do not care about who the fuck she is and what she can do for you," the woman snapped, fury in every syllable. "We did not agree to bring your stupid daughter to our safe house."

Safe house. My blood ran cold.

A low growl rumbled from my father, one I knew too well, the same one he used when someone challenged his authority.

"Watch your tongue, witch. I do not take kindly to people disrespecting me."

The woman laughed. A cold, mocking sound that sent a chill down my spine.

"Do I look like one of your fucking mutts? Don't twist our agreement just because you suddenly think you run shit. You run nothing, George. You will never be my Alpha."

Another growl. This time louder. More violent.

"Did you not learn from Mike?" she continued, unbothered. "He took Sofía instead of killing her. Y'all dumbasses kept her prisoner, hoping for some miracle info on Luna Stone. What did that get you? Mike's head rolling in the mud and your pack scattered like fleas."

The room went silent. I could practically hear my father grinding his teeth.

"I wasn't about to give up the opportunity to take my daughter back," he said finally, the smugness returning to his voice. "She can give me information on the Luna Stone Pack, on her mate, Alpha Sofía's brother. And when I am done, I'll sell her off to the Alpha in Canada. That bastard is desperate for a she-wolf who can give him an heir. Win-win."

My stomach churned. He was going to sell me. Like cattle. Like some breeding prize.

But the woman wasn't impressed.

"I fail to see the win/win for me. Why the fuck would I care about your twisted deals or your clueless daughter?" Her voice dipped, almost feral now. "All I want is him back. He belongs with me. Like he always has."

My breath hitched.

"So," she said, her voice sharpening with command, "we stick to the original plan. Especially now that Rosario's dumb she-wolf mouth gave us everything we need to take down Luna Stone."

Rosario betrayed them. My thoughts reeled.

My pulse pounded. My throat was dry. I was trapped in a room with monsters, one of them my blood, and my only weapon was the silence I kept while they schemed.

I stayed still, barely breathing, hoping they wouldn't hear the storm raging inside of me.

But my time was running out.

And if they were planning to attack Luna Stone...

Andres... Sofía... everyone I cared about...

They were in danger.

And I had no idea how to warn them.

The sound of footsteps echoed through the hallway, measured, deliberate, predatory. My body tensed as they drew closer, but I kept my eyes shut and my breathing slow, forcing my chest to rise in a steady rhythm. It took everything in me to ignore the panic clawing up my throat like wildfire.

I couldn't let them know I was awake.

The door creaked open, and the musty air shifted around me. Their scents hit me hard—bitter wolfsbane laced with the sickly sweetness of dark magic.

"She still unconscious? Damn, "the woman said with irritation. Her voice was closer now, sharp and smooth like silk hiding a dagger. "How much wolfsbane did you give her?

"Not that much," my father growled, "But I am not surprised. She's weak."

That cut deep. Not because it was true—but because I knew he wanted it to be.

I could hear the rustle of fabric, footsteps shifting around me. The uncertainty of what they were doing—what they might do—sent anxiety spiking in my chest. I focused on keeping calm, on the image of Andrés' arms around me, of Luna Stone's warmth, of safety. But I felt like prey, tied and vulnerable.

Then cold.

A splash of icy water crashed against my skin, hitting my face and chest. I gasped on reflex, choking as water rushed up my nose and down my throat. Coughing violently, I blinked against the sting, my cover blown.

"Rise and shine, your little whore of a daughter," my father sneered.

Blinking rapidly, I looked up, my vision adjusting just enough to make out two figures. My father loomed, furious and unhinged. But the woman next to him was new. Raven-haired, dressed in dark clothes that hugged her curves, she stared at me like I was something on the bottom of her shoe.

"She's a little pretty thing," she drawled, smirking as she walked closer. "Not sure how something so pretty came out of you, George."

Her pale fingers brushed my cheek. I jerked my head away, but the ropes burned tighter. The pain was immediate and sharp. I bit back a wince.

"Father... what are you doing?" I croaked, my voice raw and shaking.

"I should ask you that," he spat. "Our pack gets attacked and you run off with the enemy?"

"Andrés isn't my enemy," I said, my voice gaining strength with every word. "He's my mate."

His lip curled in disgust.

"And what a mate he is, throws you out like garbage, and who has to come pick up the pieces? Me, again. You are nothing without me."

He began circling me, slow and deliberate. Like a wolf playing with its food.

"But," he said, stopping just behind me. I could feel his breath at my ear. "I'm willing to forgive your traitorous behavior... if you give me something worth forgiving."

My skin crawled at the heat of his breath on my neck.

"Like what?" I asked, already knowing I wouldn't give it.

"I don't know. Maybe something that will help me take over Luna Stone. Maybe....something that will finally let me bury Beto and his smug family six feet under."

I swallowed hard.

"But Father, I don't know anything," I whispered. "And Beto's family, they're my family now. They are good people. They don't deserve to die."

The blow came fast.

His fist slammed into my face before I could finish, my head snapping to the side. Stars exploded in my vision. A sharp sting lit up my lip and I tasted hot, metallic blood.

"You ungrateful little bitch!" he roared. "You think you belong with them? They'll never accept you. You're mine. You'll always be mine."

I don't know how long it lasted. Minutes? Hours? Time lost all meaning after the first punch turned into a blow, after the first insult turned into a scream. My father, Alpha George, beat me like I was his enemy. And maybe to him, I was.

Because I loved his enemy.

Because I defied him.

Because I was no longer under his control.

He wanted information about Andrés, about Luna Stone, about their defenses, their numbers, their weaknesses. I gave him nothing. Not even a name. Not even a lie.

So he used his fists, then his belt. The back of his hand. The heel of his boot. And when he realized he couldn't get what he wanted, he spit on me and told me I was worthless. Finally he said something I never thought I would hear, but I wished for so long. He said I wasn't his real daughter.

"You ungrateful little bitch," he spat, his voice filled with hate, a twisted satisfaction curling at the edges. "You're just like her. Stubborn. Filthy. A whore, just like your mother."

His words sliced deeper than the belt ever could. But it was what he said next that truly shattered me.

"And you know what?" he sneered. "You're not even my daughter." My breath caught in my throat.

"That woman you called 'Mother,' she begged me to keep you alive. BEGGED." He laughed, cold and humorless.

"Said I should raise you as my own. I should've shoved a blade into your chest before you ever took your first breath. But no, I let you live."

I froze.

"I gave you a life, Maya. You owe me everything."

The room spun around me, nausea rising so fast I thought I'd throw up. But not from the pain.

From the truth.

The woman I thought was my mother, wasn't. My real mother... someone I never even had a chance to meet, had died before ever meeting me. And this man, this monster who raised me with beatings and fear, who demanded loyalty and obedience, wasn't my father.

We are not related. I am not his blood and never will be.

And instead of heartbreak, something else cracked open in me.

Relief.

A cold, sharp kind of relief that curled into the corners of my soul. I wasn't his. Not by blood. Not by fate.

Whatever poison ran through Alpha George's veins didn't flow in mine.

But still, beneath that, buried deep, I mourned the woman I never met. The mother who tried. Who sacrificed. Who had loved me enough to fight for my life before I was even born. Who died at the hands of the man I now wished I could kill with my bare hands.

She was real.

And she died so I could live.

The tears that leaked from my eyes weren't from the pain of broken skin or bruised bones. They were from the ache of not knowing her. From the cruelty of being raised in a house where love was a weapon, and survival was the only language spoken.

When Alpha George stormed out, shouting to the witch about needing to "clean up the fucking mess," I let myself go limp again. Unmoving. Bleeding. Breathing faint and shallow.

"She's probably dead," he muttered. "Useless girl."

Then the door slammed.

Moments later, the low rumble of a car engine growled to life and faded into the distance.

Silence.

I waited. Counted each breath. Ten seconds. Twenty. Thirty.

No footsteps. No voices. Nothing but the drip of water from a pipe above and the dull ache in every part of my body.

Now. It had to be now.

If he came back... I wouldn't survive it.

With a sharp inhale, I forced myself to shift my weight forward. The ropes burned, reopening the fresh welts on my arms, but I didn't stop. I leaned as far as I could, shifting awkwardly to my feet while still tied to the goddamn chair.

Sweat and blood clung to my skin. My legs were tied wide to the chair's legs, the rope soaked and digging in deeper with every movement.

"Come on," I hissed, gritting my teeth.

Summoning every ounce of strength I had left, I braced myself, bent low... and shoved.

With a sickening crack, I hit the ground on my back. The old wooden chair splintered beneath me, the backrest snapping clean off. I coughed at the impact, stars flashing in my vision, but the sudden freedom of movement lit a spark in me.

Still tangled in the ropes, I twisted and kicked until I could slip one wrist free, then the other. My fingers fumbled, trembling with pain, as I yanked at the knots on my ankles. The skin was raw, bloody—but I was free.

Barely able to stand, I staggered to a nearby table littered with weapons—his weapons.

"You picked the wrong daughter to try to break," I whispered.

My hand closed around a silver-handled blade, small but sharp. I sheathed it and took another, sliding one into each ankle strap and the last across my waist beneath my shirt.

Three blades. One shot at survival.

I limped toward the heavy metal door, adrenaline fueling me past the pain. My mind screamed to move faster, but my body dragged behind, exhausted and battered.

I turned the handle slowly. No alarm. No spell. Just the eerie creak of rusted hinges.

The hallway beyond was dim and unfamiliar, made of stone and cold shadows. No windows. No markers.

I didn't know where I was. The stone walls around me offered no clues. No map. No sense of direction.

But one thing was clear.

I wasn't Alpha George's daughter.

And I would not die here.

Not before I made it back to Luna Stone and made him pay.

Branches slapped my face. Thorns tore at my skin. My lungs burned like fire as I ran, not stopping, not daring to look back. The forest around me blurred into streaks of shadow and moonlight. I didn't know if I was heading toward Luna Stone or deeper into hell, but I kept running anyway.

Every breath came with a stab of pain. My ribs throbbed. My legs threatened to collapse beneath me. But I couldn't stop.

I wouldn't stop.

Leaves crunched beneath my bare feet, roots threatened to trip me, but I didn't slow down. All I had were the blades strapped to me and the bitter truth of who I really was. A girl born from tragedy, raised by a monster, and now hunted like prey.

Night fell fast, and the temperature dropped with it. The cold bit into my torn clothes and bloodied skin. My body trembled, but I pushed forward, chasing a freedom I wasn't even sure I could reach.

Suddenly, the trees opened to a clearing, and I broke through the brush and onto an empty road. Asphalt scraped my feet raw, but I didn't care. I stumbled into the middle, panting, barely upright.

And then.

BAM.

A flash of black. The thunderous roar of a motor. And pain.

Blinding, crushing pain.

My body flew through the air like a rag doll. I hit the pavement hard, my head bouncing off the ground, my vision exploding into a shower of sparks. The air was knocked from my lungs. Blood gushed from my arm, maybe my leg, I couldn't tell anymore. Everything hurt.

I tried to breathe, but each inhale was agony.

Then I heard footsteps. A low hum of an engine still purring nearby. The click of boots. Slow. Purposeful.

Panic surged.

I pushed against the pavement, crawling backward, every movement setting fire to my nerves.

Then he appeared. Tall. Broad-shouldered. A black helmet concealed his face. He walked toward me with unhurried grace, a predator's ease. But it wasn't his pace that froze my blood.

It was the scent.

He didn't smell like a human.

Or a shifter.

Or a witch.

He didn't smell alive.

He stopped just in front of me and slowly removed his helmet.

Blonde hair tousled from the wind. Eyes like polished silver in the moonlight. Skin pale and smooth, beautiful in that terrifying, unnatural way.

A vampire.

A cold, ancient kind of power radiated from him. My wolf whimpered inside me, pulling back instinctively.

I tried to scramble farther away, but my body wouldn't cooperate.

He crouched in front of me, surprisingly gentle in his movement.

"Calm down, calm down," he said, voice smooth and calm. "I mean you no harm. Just want to see if you're okay."

He tilted his head, assessing me with a strange sort of curiosity.

"I didn't see you out there. You came out of nowhere. What are you running from, little wolf?"

I stared at him, trembling, torn between the urge to scream and the hope that just maybe he wasn't like the stories I'd heard.

Because if he was...

I was too broken to fight. Too lost to run.

"I don't want any trouble, vampire," I rasped, trying to sound brave despite the raw fear twisting in my gut. My body ached, my blood was still drying on my skin, and now this, a vampire.

"I'm just trying to get home."

He tilted his head slightly, the moonlight catching the edges of his silver eyes. There wasn't mockery in his expression, just curiosity.

"So where did you come from that left you looking so beat up?" he asked, his tone calm, conversational, like we were two strangers meeting at a bar instead of a predator crouched over a wounded wolf.

I lowered my eyes and stayed silent. Trust wasn't something I had to give, not after what I'd just escaped. And definitely not to someone like him.

"Like I said," he continued, his voice softer now, "I don't mean you harm. I know... my people have created a bad reputation. Most of it's deserved." He gave a small, sheepish shrug. "But some of us are trying to change that. If you're in trouble, I could help you."

There was something sincere in his voice, something that made my wolf stir not with warning... but consideration. Still, I wasn't sure. I'd never seen a vampire in real life until tonight, only heard the stories. And none of those stories ended well for shifters like me.

Then he took a slow breath and spoke again.

"I get it. You don't trust me. But if I wanted to hurt you, little wolf... I could've done it already. There's nothing stopping me."

My head snapped up. His words slammed into me like a punch, and he saw it instantly, fear flashing across my face. My entire body tensed.

He raised both hands in surrender, his voice quick and gentle. "I'm not going to hurt you. I meant that to reassure you, not scare you. Look, I'm trying to help. Who knows? Maybe I'll make a friend out of this. A shifter ally wouldn't be the worst thing in the world."

He gave a half-smile. Charming. Disarming.

"So tell me," he added, "where are you going?"

I hesitated, the words sticking to my dry tongue. Then finally, I whispered hoarsely, "California."

His lips twitched up into a smile.

"Well, that's a good thing. Because you are in California. Where exactly?"

"Santa Cruz," I said.

He nodded thoughtfully. "Mhm. You're a couple of hours off. We're near L.A. right now."

I didn't know what else to say. I just... nodded, slowly, and tried to get up. My legs trembled beneath me, but I pushed through the pain. He stepped toward me to help, and instinctively, I recoiled from his touch.

He froze. Hands still raised. Not offended, just understanding.

"I promise you, I'm not here to hurt you. If anything, I'd like to help. I can take you to Santa Cruz. Drop you off wherever you need to go. A pack? Family? You tell me."

I hesitated. The doubt was still there... but so was the urgency.

There's no way I'll make it in time on foot. Not to warn the Luna Stone Pack. Not before Alpha George moves.

I didn't have a choice. What else did I have left to lose?

"Okay," I whispered. "I'm part of the Luna Stone Pack."

His eyes lit with recognition. "Alpha Beto's pack?"

I blinked at him, surprised. "You know Alpha Beto?"

He grinned, full of boyish charm.

"Who doesn't know the famous Luna Stone Alpha and CEO of Luna Enterprises? I don't know him personally, but I'd love to."

I couldn't help; it despite the exhaustion weighing on my soul, I snorted.

"Oh," I said weakly, "he's my father-in-law."

He let out a low, impressed whistle. "Now that is something. Tell you what, little wolf, how about we make a deal?"

I arched a brow at him, wary but curious.

"I take you to him safely," he said, "and you introduce me. Please?"

I eyed him carefully. "And how do I know you won't hurt them?"

He laughed, the sound low and warm.

"Come on. I'm one vampire. One. You think I can take on the largest pack on the West Coast? You should be worried about me, not the other way around."

That made me... smile. Just a little. It was unexpected. And it felt strange and foreign to smile at all after what I'd just endured.

But I nodded. "Deal. You get me to Luna Stone, I'll make sure Alpha Beto meets the vampire that helped me back home."

And just like that, he turned and walked toward his motorcycle, tossed me his helmet, and helped me onto the back.

Moments later, the wind was rushing past me, the engine purring like a beast beneath us. The vampire whose name I still didn't know drove fast and smooth, weaving through the highway curves like the night was his to command.

I clung to his back, the road blurring beneath us.

I was heading home.

Broken. Bruised. Battered.

But alive.

And Alpha George had no idea what was coming.

Chapter 33

ANDRÉS

My thoughts were spinning.

Finding out that Maya wasn't actually Alpha George's daughter, that she was the product of one of his sick, twisted crimes, had unsettled something deep inside me. But what haunted me more was this nagging feeling in my chest, like I'd heard this story before. Not all of it, but enough for something to tug at the edges of my memory.

After a restless night of tossing and pacing, I finally called the one person who might help me piece this puzzle together, my father.

He answered almost immediately. "Andrés?"

"I found out something," I said, rubbing the back of my neck. "It's about Maya."

There was a pause, his voice turning serious. "Go on."

"She's not George's real daughter. She was born from something much worse. He kidnapped a pregnant she-wolf, beat her, kept her locked up. When she tried to escape... he killed her. But he kept the baby. That baby was Maya."

There was a long silence before he spoke again.

"Damn. I didn't see that coming. So... she's not his blood at all?" he asked, still processing.

"Yeah." I exhaled. "But here's the thing, when the maid told us the full story, something about it felt too familiar. Like I've heard it before. It's been bugging me. That's why I called you."

"All right," he said. "Start from the beginning."

So I did. Word for word, I retold the story exactly how Matilda had shared it. I didn't hold back, even when it turned dark and brutal. When I finished, the line went quiet.

"Papa?" I asked.

His voice came low, almost a whisper. "Did you say... he kidnapped a pregnant she-wolf?"

"Yeah. Why?"

"Did Matilda tell you what happened to her body?" he asked.

I shook my head, even though he couldn't see me. "No. We were focused on Maya. Why?"

"I need to speak with Matilda," he said suddenly. "Face-to-face. Can you get her on a video call?"

"I'll try. I don't know where she lives, but I'll find her," I said, already heading for the door.

A short while later, after grabbing a quick breakfast and tracking down Jason, I found him in the courtyard with a woman who immediately had my senses on alert. She was tall, raven-haired, and definitely not a wolf.

A witch.

"Alpha Jason," I said, raising a brow. "Didn't know Crescent Moon was still on speaking terms with witches after what happened with Mason."

Jason smirked. "We kept an alliance with that coven. That drama with Mason was a one-off with a unhinged witch. Right, Rachel?"

She stepped forward with a warm smile. "Our coven has honored our alliance with Crescent Moon for generations. We don't break our bonds."

Her tone was confident, her energy calm but strong. I didn't trust her fully. Witches rarely came without strings, but right now, I had other things on my mind.

"I need to find Matilda," I said to Jason. "My father wants to speak to her. He thinks he might know something about this mysterious pregnant she-wolf."

Jason's expression turned serious, and he nodded. "Come on. She lives just beyond the orchard."

We walked together, Rachel trailing behind silently, until we reached a modest ranch-style home nestled in the trees. Jason knocked, and Matilda answered a few moments later, wiping her hands on her apron, her brows knitting in confusion.

"Matilda," I said gently, "my father wants to speak with you about the story you told us. He... he thinks he's heard it before. Would you mind doing a quick video chat with him?"

Her eyes widened a bit, but she nodded. "Of course. If it helps Maya."

I pulled out my phone and called my father. When he picked up, I held the screen so they could see each other.

"Papa, this is Matilda."

She gave a timid smile. "Hello, sir."

"Hello, Matilda," my father said kindly. "Thank you for sharing your story. I want you to know how brave you are for coming forward. It's not easy to carry something like that."

She dipped her head slightly, eyes misting.

"My pack lost a pregnant she-wolf twenty-one years ago," my father continued. "She vanished without a trace. The story you told sounds eerily similar."

All of us—me, Jason, even Rachel—stood frozen as the weight of his words settled over us.

"Do you remember the name of the she-wolf George kidnapped?" he asked.

Matilda shook her head. "No... I was never told. He kept her locked up. She was barely alive when we found her."

"Do you know what pack she came from?"

Again, she shook her head, guilt flashing across her face.

"What happened to her body?" he asked, quieter this time.

Matilda swallowed. "All I know is what I overheard. George... he used her death to send a message to the other packs. Said this is what happens when you don't respect him."

My father went silent, then excused himself from the screen. A few minutes passed before he returned—holding a photo.

I recognized it immediately. It was one I'd seen since I was a boy. An old picture of a woman with soft eyes and a warm smile. Someone my father always said was a dear friend.

"Matilda," he said. "Was this her?"

Matilda stared at the screen. Her lips parted, and a soft gasp escaped her. "It's her," she whispered, her voice cracking. "That's her."

Tears spilled down her cheeks as she broke down.

I pulled her gently into my arms, trying to comfort her. "It's okay. You did the right thing. You did."

"Papa," I said, looking back at the screen. "What does this mean?"

But he shook his head. "Not yet. I think I know who she was, but I need to be sure. Right now, the priority is getting Maya home."

I wanted to push. I wanted answers. But I knew my father; once he made up his mind, nothing moved him.

So I nodded. "Okay. We'll focus on getting her back."

The call ended, and Matilda, still visibly shaken, whispered a soft thank you before retreating back into her small home.

Jason exhaled beside me, scrubbing a hand over his jaw. "Well," he muttered, "that wasn't weird and secretive at all."

I shot him a look, but I couldn't help the tight, grim smile that pulled at the corner of my mouth. "You're not wrong."

As we walked back to the packhouse, my mind buzzed with questions, too many answers still hanging in the air like a storm cloud about to burst.

Once inside, I glanced over at Rachel, the quiet witch with the all-too-calm energy. "So, how much do you know about what's going on in my pack? And about my mate missing?"

She stopped, turned toward me, her expression unreadable. "About your mate... nothing until today," she said honestly. "But the attacks? The dark magic being used against your people? That I know plenty about."

We entered the study, the tension following us like a shadow. Jason rounded the desk and sat behind it while Rachel and I took seats across from him.

"This is why she's here," Jason explained, folding his arms. "I asked her to come and speak with you. She's been tracking this magic longer than any of us."

I leaned back in the chair, arms crossed. "All right. Let's hear it."

Rachel smiled softly, almost apologetically. "Alpha Jason told me about the patterns wolves found with their life essence drained, signs of necromancy. I'm concerned," she said, her tone turning serious. "Not all witches dabble in that kind of magic, and even fewer master it. But the one working with Alpha George... she's powerful. Ruthless. My coven has seen her work before."

My jaw clenched. "Then why couldn't our New York coven detect or block her? They've been with us for years."

Rachel met my gaze without flinching. "Because most covens don't want to deal with necromancers. But mine? Many of the most powerful necromancer witches came from my coven."

That answer landed like a stone in my gut.

Before I could respond, my phone rang.

My sister.

A chill crawled up my spine as I answered. "Hello?" My voice cracked, hopeful, but braced for the worst.

Her voice came in a frantic rush. "She's here. We have her. She needs you. Come home, now."

I blinked. "Wait... Maya's home? You found her?"

"More like she found us," she breathed. "But I'll explain everything once you get here. Just hurry."

The call dropped before I could speak again.

I stood frozen for a heartbeat, a mix of relief and adrenaline crashing through me. Then I turned to Jason with a grin I couldn't contain. "You heard her. Time to go. My mate's home."

I barely made it a few steps before Rachel reached out and gently touched my hand. I froze.

Her eyes rolled back.

Jason and I watched in stunned silence as her body stilled, her expression going blank and her eyes turning pure white. Magic swirled around her like a whisper, thickening the air.

After a long, tense moment, her eyes fluttered open. She was pale and troubled. A single tear slid down her cheek.

"Andrés..." Her voice trembled. "Please be careful. I saw darkness. Real darkness. That witch, she's furious. She's coming for Luna Stone, and she's not alone."

I stepped closer, heart hammering. "How soon?"

Rachel took a shaky breath, then sank into the chair again. "A day. Maybe less. Call your allies. Prepare your defenses. What's coming is more than just another attack, it's war."

My blood ran cold.

Without thinking, I pulled my phone back out and re-dialed my sister. But as soon as her voice came through the speaker, Rachel gently plucked the phone from my hand and began speaking softly.

I blinked in confusion until I remembered.

Rachel and my sister already knew each other.

Back when Jason's pack was under attack and their territory was bombed, Crescent Moon came to Luna Stone for help. That alliance had been forged decades ago, back when both packs were led by old alphas who understood the value of loyalty over pride.

During that time, my sister had found her mate... and crossed paths with Rachel, the witch who helped them uncover the traitor. And now here she was again, brought back into our lives, just in time.

She brought the phone to her ear. "Sofía," she said, her voice calm but firm, carrying the weight of a warning. "You need to prepare. I had a vision that dark magic is coming. It's already circling your territory."

There was a pause, and I could barely make out my sister's voice through the receiver, sharp, alert, but laced with fear.

Rachel's gaze sharpened. "I saw the Luna Stone pack covered in shadow. Your pack is at risk and your people will die if you do not prepare."

Jason and I exchanged a look, our bodies tensing with the same shared instinct: war was coming.

Rachel continued, steady as ever. "If you're ready, and I mean truly ready, there's still a chance to stop it before it takes hold. But you don't have much time."

She paused, her voice softening just slightly. "My coven specializes in handling magic like this. Many of the witches who've mastered dark arts but chose to walk the path of balance came from us. We know how to dismantle it, how to strip it at the roots."

She glanced over at me and added, "I'll fly in with Andres tonight. I'll help in whatever way I can."

Another pause.

Then Rachel smiled faintly. "Good. I'm glad you feel the same, Alpha Sofía. Gather your warriors. Prepare your wolves. If it comes to battle, I want your people armed not just with claws, but with knowledge. With light."

She handed the phone back to me.

On the other end, my sister's voice was fierce and unwavering. "We'll be ready," she said. "I'll rally everyone, every warrior, every healer, every witch still loyal to us. I don't know what's coming, but if that bastard George thinks he can strike us again, he's going to learn what real hell looks like."

A surge of pride swelled in my chest. "I'll be there soon," I said. "And Maya...?"

"She's resting," Sofía said gently. "Bruised, exhausted, but she's safe. She hasn't spoken much, but when she opened her eyes, the first name she whispered was yours."

Fuck.

My throat tightened. Every part of me ached to be beside her.

"I'm on my way," I said, then ended the call.

Rachel was already gathering her things, preparing to leave. Jason stood behind his desk, tension rippling through his shoulders.

"I'll leave my second here to run things," he said. "Whatever's coming... the Crescent Moon Pack will fulfill their duties as allies to the pack."

The sky was still ink-black when we boarded Jason's private jet bound for Texas. There wasn't time to waste, not when dark magic was hovering over Luna Stone like a blade waiting to drop.

Jason needed warriors, his most elite fighters. And Rachel had to connect with her coven, pulling in any witches trained in countering necromancy and protective warding. I called Darren to call him back home. Once updating him of the latest, he started making his way to meet us back at Black Stone Pack. Every second felt like it stretched forever, and still, it took almost a full day and a half to coordinate, to gather supplies, to make sure we had every weapon and magical defense we could carry.

It was agony.

Two days after the call from Sofía—two whole days—we were finally flying back, the jet vibrating beneath us with every mile that brought me closer to my mate. I barely spoke the entire flight, sitting at the window, staring out into the endless dark sky, silently praying that Maya was still safe.

"We will make it on time," Darren reassured me.

All I could do was nod my head and hope that he was right.

By the time we landed and loaded into the convoy of black vans, the air was heavy with tension. Every warrior was alert, armed, and ready. Jason's wolves radiated a barely-leashed aggression, and the witches Rachel had brought with her were silent, fingers twitching with restrained magic.

I sat at the front of the lead van, Rachel beside me. Her aura pulsed with calm energy, but even she seemed on edge.

Then we reached the gates of Luna Stone.

Or... what used to be the gates.

My breath caught in my throat.

The towering cast iron structure that had once stood tall and strong now lay mangled and bent, one side twisted inward like a giant had slammed through it. Blood stained the dirt. The scent hit me hard: shifter blood. And it was fresh.

Dead guards littered the ground, their eyes wide and lifeless, claw marks and magical burns scarring their bodies.

One of the warriors in the van behind us whispered, "Oh no... we're too late."

"No," I snapped, jumping out of the vehicle, my body already beginning to shift.

But before the wolf could break free, Rachel grabbed my arm.

Her touch was firm, commanding. "Andrés—wait."

I growled low in my throat, every part of me fighting to take off, to tear through the woods, to find her.

"Look around," Rachel said calmly, her voice cutting through the haze. "Do you feel that?"

I stilled.

The air was thick—unnatural. Cold despite the warm breeze. Magic clung to the trees like frost, invisible threads pulsing just beneath the surface of reality.

"Dark magic is everywhere," she said, eyes scanning the treetops. "The wards are cracked, and the land is soaked in power that doesn't belong. If you run in without a plan, you could trigger something worse."

I clenched my fists, my wolf howling beneath my skin.

"Then what?" I ground out. "We sit here while my mate could be fighting for her life?"

"No." Her voice softened, but her eyes didn't waver. "We move together. We fight smart."

She turned to me then, expression serious. "Where should we go?"

I swallowed the panic clawing at my throat. "The pack-house," I said, my voice hoarse. "If they're holding the line, that's where they'll be."

Rachel nodded and turned back to the convoy. "Drive slow. Magic traps could be hidden anywhere."

As we moved forward, weaving through familiar forest roads now littered with bodies, scorch marks, and smoke, I prayed.

I prayed to the Moon Goddess.

Please let my little wolf still be alive.

Chapter 34

MAYA

The drive to Luna Stone Pack felt endless every minute stretched into an eternity as I replayed the horrifying words spoken by George and that witch over and over in my head. My only prayer to the Moon Goddess was that we'd make it in time. That I could warn Alpha Sofía before it was too late. Before whatever darkness was coming swallowed everything.

My heart raced as the main gates came into view. Relief and panic clashed in my chest. The moment the bike skidded to a stop, I jumped off my vampire companion's back, still not knowing his name, which felt ridiculous considering he'd just carried me across territory lines. But there was no time to think about that now.

I yanked the helmet off and stepped toward the gate guard.

"It's me, Maya. Mate of Andrés Rodriguez. I need to speak with Alpha Sofía immediately. It's urgent," I said, breathless but determined.

The warrior's eyes widened slightly at the mention of Andrés, and without hesitation, he nodded. "Go on in."

Grateful, I climbed back onto the bike and we sped off through the open gates. Thankfully, my memory didn't fail me. I still remembered the path to the packhouse.

When it finally came into view, my breath caught in my throat. Standing outside were familiar faces—my family. All of them... except Andrés.

That ache I tried to suppress cracked wide open in my chest.

I hated how easily my heart dropped at his absence. A part of me hoped he'd be the first one waiting for me. That he'd be here to pull me into his arms, to prove I wasn't the only one drowning in this bond. But maybe I was.

Maybe he was still angry. Maybe his love wasn't as deep... or as consuming as mine.

But it didn't matter.

Not right now.

Because this wasn't just about us. This was about the lives of hundreds. About my pack. My home. My people.

As soon as the bike rolled to a stop in front of the packhouse, I didn't wait. I jumped off, ignoring the ache in my thighs and the bruises screaming under my skin. My feet barely touched the ground before I rushed forward, straight into the arms of Yolanda and Beto. They held me tight, their warmth grounding me as emotion swelled in my chest.

They weren't just Andrés' parents—they were mine too in every way that mattered. And I hadn't realized how badly I needed to feel safe until I was in their arms again.

"Oh, *mi niña*," Yolanda whispered, stroking my hair. "You had us worried sick."

Beto kissed the top of my head. "You've been gone too long, Maya."

I closed my eyes against the tears burning behind my lids. "I'm so sorry... I'll explain everything. But we need to go inside. Somewhere private. I don't have much time."

Sofía's voice cut through the heavy silence. "Where have you been? We've all been going crazy looking for you."

I turned to her, my voice soft but urgent. "I swear I'll tell you everything. Just... not out here."

We began to move toward the packhouse when a throat cleared behind me.

Shit.

I spun around to see the vampire, my unexpected savior, standing a few feet back, arms casually crossed, a faint smirk tugging at the corners of his mouth. Clearly, he wasn't going to let me forget our little deal.

"Oh! I almost forgot..." I turned toward the others, gesturing between them. "This is—"

But he stepped forward before I could finish, extending a hand toward Beto.

"Hello," he said smoothly, voice like velvet over steel. "I'm Ascelin."

Beto's eyes narrowed. "A vampire... there's a vampire on Luna Stone territory?"

"Yes," I said quickly, stepping between them before any tension could flare. "But before anyone freaks out, he helped me. He found me when I was lost, and if it wasn't for him, I wouldn't have made it back alive. He got me here in time. I owe him everything."

I looked back at Ascelin, giving him a grateful smile. He dipped his head slightly in return, eyes never leaving Beto's.

The air was thick with tension. Estrella shifted uncomfortably, her sharp gaze flicking between us. Leo was already standing in a subtle defensive stance, just in case. Xiomara's brows rose, curious but calm as ever.

Sofía crossed her arms, assessing Ascelin with that fierce alpha energy of hers. "You brought her back. That earns you a sliver of trust," she said coolly. "But step out of line even once..."

"You'll tear my heart out through my throat?" Ascelin finished with a smirk. "Noted. I'd expect nothing less from an Alpha."

"I like him," Estrella said with a smile.

I exhaled, nerves settling just a bit. "Please... can we go inside now? There's something you all need to hear. Something coming... something dark. And we don't have much time."

They all nodded, silently falling into step as we made our way into the packhouse.

As soon as we stepped into the packhouse, a wave of dizziness crashed over me. My vision blurred, and the warmth of the room tilted sideways. I heard someone call my name—maybe Sofía, maybe Yolanda—but everything faded too fast. The last thing I felt was the strength leaving my legs and the ground rushing up to meet me.

Darkness.

When I came to, the air was cool, the sheets beneath me soft and familiar. The scent of the packhouse, of home, wrapped around me like a fragile comfort.

"Maya?" a soft voice said beside me.

I blinked my eyes open and turned my head to find Estrella sitting in a chair near the bed, her hand resting protectively over her round belly.

"You fainted, honey," she said gently. "You're in one of the guest rooms. Don't move too fast."

But I was already trying to sit up, the urgency in my chest pushing me forward.

"I need to talk to Sofía... and Beto," I said, forcing my body upward even as my head spun slightly. "It's important."

Estrella shot up or tried to, but her large belly slowed her usual quick movements. She grunted softly, frustrated, then finally made it to my side to help steady me.

"Maya, stop it. You're weak. Your body's been through hell and you need to rest," she scolded, her hands firm on my shoulders. "If it's that serious, I'll get them to come here. You're not going anywhere."

I nodded slowly, my body relenting even if my soul was still racing. "Please... get them. And call Leo and Xiomara, too. They need to hear this."

Estrella sighed but pulled her phone from the nightstand, her frown deepening as she typed out a message. "You're going to be the death of me, girl," she muttered.

Minutes passed in a haze until the door creaked open.

First in was Sofía, followed by Leo, then Xiomara and a wide-eyed Yolanda slipped in behind them. Finally, Beto entered the room—his expression a mixture of concern and command.

Right beside him was Ascelin.

No... Ace. I decided then and there that I'd call him that. It suited him better. Less formal, and easier for me to pronounce.

Everyone gathered around the bed, their presence heavy with anticipation.

Sofía stepped closer, her voice calm but firm. "We're all here, Maya. What's going on?"

I took a shaky breath, glancing at each of them. My heart thundered in my chest as the weight of what I had to say settled over the room like a storm waiting to break.

"It's Alpha George," I said quietly. "He's coming. And he's not coming alone."

I took another breath, steadying my nerves as every pair of eyes in the room stayed locked on me.

"When I ran away from here, I was trying to go back to Black Stone... but if I am honest, I had no sense of direction and I found myself just running for hours until I found an abandoned building where I rested there. In the middle of the night, I heard footsteps. I thought maybe Andres came to get me, but when I realized who it was, it was too late and Alpha George had sedated me."

Everyone tensed.

"When I woke up, I was tied up to a chair. While they thought I was sedated, I heard Alpha George talking with a witch. I did not recognize her, but her scent was definitely one of a witch. She had black hair, light complexion, very pretty. They were discussing their plans to invade the pack. They said that thanks to Rosario, they knew the weakness of the pack." I stopped talking, overwhelmed with tears.

Estrella came to my side to soothe me and hold my hand.

"He's not planning just a physical attack. He's using dark magic to reanimate the dead. I heard it. The witch he is partnered with is very powerful. I could taste the dark magic coming out of her pores. She is very angry; she claims that we have what's hers. Alpha George believes that with her power behind him, he can destroy everything and claim our lands."

The air grew thick. A few of them glanced at each other, but no one interrupted.

My voice cracked.

"But that's not all." My hand gripped the blanket, knuckles turning white. "There's something I never expected to learn…"

I looked down, afraid to see their faces when I said the next words aloud.

"Alpha George… isn't my real father."

Gasps filled the room.

"No," Beto muttered, stepping forward like the floor had just shifted beneath him. "Maya, are you sure?"

I looked up at him, tears glossing my eyes. "I overheard him saying it to the witch before I was able to escape.

Yolanda brought her hand to her mouth, and Leo cursed softly under his breath.

438

"I think... I think he only kept me close to use me. As a pawn to obtain alliances. He never loved me, which makes sense."

No one said anything for a beat. Just the silence of revelation.

I cleared my throat, trying to gather myself.

"That's why I was in such a rush to get here," I said, my voice firmer now. "To warn you. To warn everyone. Whatever he's planning, it's unnatural. And it's dangerous. We need to be ready because he is on his way."

Sofía nodded slowly, her expression grave but steady. "We know, Maya, and will be ready."

Ace leaned casually against the wall, watching but not saying a word. His presence was a silent reminder of the strange path I'd taken to get here—and the strange allies I'd found along the way.

"I'm scared," I whispered, finally letting it out.

Beto walked to my side and placed a strong hand on my shoulder. "It's okay to be scared. But you're strong and we are all stronger together. We'll face whatever comes—together."

Nodding, I turned slowly to Sofía, my voice barely above a whisper. "You said you knew... how? How did you know?"

Sofía's expression softened, a small, knowing smile curving her lips. "While you were resting after fainting, I called Andrés. I told him you were home... safe. He'd gone to Black Stone Pack, Maya. To find you."

My breath caught in my throat. "He went to look for me?"

The knot that had been forming in my chest twisted tighter, rising up to my throat like a swell of emotion I could barely keep down.

Yolanda sat beside me on the bed, brushing a strand of hair gently from my face. "Of course he did, *mi amor*," she said, her voice warm and full of affection. "He loves you. He's a dumbass sometimes, but one who loves you deeply."

A wet laugh escaped me, the kind that came with a tight chest and blurry eyes. We both giggled through our tears, and for a moment, the weight of everything felt a little lighter.

Sofía moved closer, her gaze steady on mine. "He was ready to move heaven and earth to find you," she said, her tone laced with both pride and amusement. "He didn't care what he had to do to get you back."

My throat ached. Goddess, why did hearing that hurt and heal all at once?

Before the silence could stretch too long, Ace stepped forward from where he stood near the door, arms casually crossed over his chest. "If I may," he said, voice smooth but deliberate. "I'd like to offer my help. And not just mine. I have two brothers, Dorian and Aldric. We're willing to fight with you."

Sofía turned toward him, brows arching. "Why?" she asked, her tone not unkind, but firm. "What's in it for you?"

Ace's gaze didn't waver. "Because we're tired of being feared, hated, and distrusted for centuries. But not all of us crave blood and chaos. Some of us... want more."

His voice dipped lower, more serious now.

"We believe alliances are the way forward. Camaraderie. Unity between the supernatural races. Fighting alone has only led to isolation and hate. And let's be honest..." He smirked, but it didn't quite reach his eyes. "Even wealth gets old when all you're surrounded by is resentment. No mansion or treasure can buy peace. Or purpose."

The room fell into a thoughtful hush.

Sofía studied him for a moment, then nodded slowly. "We'll talk more. But... thank you, Ace."

He inclined his head. "You're welcome."

I sank back against the pillow, my body finally giving in to the exhaustion.

My limbs felt heavy, my head dizzy, and a hint of nausea twisted low in my stomach, but I welcomed it. It was the kind of fatigue that only came after your body had been beaten, and mine was definitely beaten. I let myself melt into the soft mattress, comforted by the scent of clean sheets and the distant sounds of the packhouse. I was home. Safe. And soon... I'd be with Andrés again.

Just the thought of him—his voice, his touch, the way he looked at me—was enough to send a warm flutter down my spine.

My eyes drifted shut.

I don't know how many hours passed, but something pulled me awake. A cold whisper at the base of my neck. The hairs on my arms stood on end.

"Maya."

I blinked, squinting into the dark. Estrella was standing by my bed, her brows drawn tight, her voice low and urgent.

"Wake up. Something's wrong."

I sat up slowly, still groggy. "What is it?"

"I don't know… but the energy shifted. I felt it. Like something foul just crossed into our territory."

My heart skipped. I swallowed the lump in my throat and forced my legs over the side of the bed. "Where's Sofía?"

"In the war room with Mason and the others. Come on."

I followed Estrella, knowing that this something wrong had a name and it was Alpha George.

Chapter 35

MAYA

The moon, once full and radiant, looked pale and distant behind a shroud of eerie mist. And the night... it didn't sound like night.

No owls.

No rustling wind.

Just silence.

And dread.

Then I caught the scent.

Rot.

Not the natural kind, but something twisted, a stench of death laced with bitter, unnatural magic. My wolf stirred beneath my skin, snarling in warning.

From the edge of the forest, a howl ripped through the stillness. It wasn't one of ours. It was low, guttural and wrong.

Estrella gripped my hand tightly, yanking me forward. "They've crossed the outer border."

My heart kicked into overdrive as we sprinted toward the front of the packhouse. The moment we reached the front, I spotted her.

Sofia stood like a goddess of war, her back straight, golden eyes burning with fury, her aura pulsing with pure Alpha dominance. Mason stood to her left, shirtless and already half-shifted, muscles taut like a spring ready to snap.

She didn't have to say a word.

Her stance spoke for her.

This was war.

To Sofía's right stood Beto and Marcos, both grim-faced and battle-ready. And beside them, impossibly calm, dressed in all black with his long blond hair, was Ace.

The vampire's silver eyes gleamed under the muted moonlight. There was something hauntingly beautiful about him. Cold. Dangerous. Loyal.

His voice was quiet, but it cut through the tension like a blade. "They're close. I can smell the decay from here."

Just then, movement stirred to the left. Shadows broke apart as the witches from New York stepped into the clearing. Myriam led the group, her usual polished appearance gone. Her sleek bun was undone, long earrings swaying with each breathless step.

Her eyes found Sofía. Wide. Unsettled. "It's dark magic," she panted. "Necromancy. The witch is with him."

Sofía's jaw tightened, though her voice remained level. "I'm glad you made it. I was starting to think we'd be facing this with just teeth and claws."

Myriam gave a breathless, humorless chuckle. "It was close. JFK tried to shut us down. Thankfully, a little witchy persuasion went a long way."

Beto stepped forward, flanked by Marcos. "Who did you bring?"

"My three daughters," Myriam replied. "And most of my senior santeras y brujas. A total of twenty."

Beto exhaled slowly, the weight of the moment thick in the air. "Let's hope that's enough."

Marcos shook his head. "We make it enough. We don't have a choice."

I stepped forward, trying to keep the tremble out of my voice. "When does Andrés arrive?"

Marcos stared at me like he does every time I am near him. How sad that even in moment of life and death, I have to remind him of his dead wife.

Sofía shook her head. "Not sure. He didn't say. I just hope it's soon."

I swallowed hard, nodding. The words were meant to be comforting, but they only made the unease in my chest grow heavier.

Sofía turned sharply, refocusing her energy. She began organizing our warriors with swift, precise commands. Some witches followed the patrol groups, their spell work blending with wolf instincts as they prepared to hold the line. Others, led by Yolanda, disappeared toward the school grounds, there, they would lead the elderly, the children, and the she-wolves who weren't trained to fight into the underground safe room.

I look at Estrella and say, "Go with Yolanda. Keep yourself and your baby safe."

Estrella rolled her eyes, "I am a warrior before a mother. My pup will know that while others hide, his mother fought for her future. I cannot go hide while others fight my battles."

I tried to argue more with her about the safety and that of her baby, and she refused to listen to me or to stop getting herself ready for war.

The energy shifted again.

Thicker. Darker. The kind of pressure that made it hard to breathe.

My stomach churned.

Estrella stood close to me, her hand brushing mine. She didn't speak, but her presence was steady, anchoring me in the chaos. I didn't realize how badly I needed someone until I felt her there, solid, warm, alive.

Around me, people moved, prepared, braced. But I couldn't shake the feeling of being watched. Not just by someone, but by something. My fingers clenched at my sides, the cold biting into my skin.

"They're coming," Estrella whispered.

And then we heard it.

A low, bone-deep rumble like the earth groaning in pain. From the treeline, shapes began to emerge. Not fast. Not loud.

Just wrong.

Dozens of corpses staggered from the treeline: wolves, men, women. Some still wore scraps of clothing clinging to their half-decayed bodies. Others were barely more than brittle bone and shriveled flesh, their mouths slack, their movements jerky, eyes hollow like their souls had been ripped away.

A deep, guttural growl rolled across the battlefield.

Sofía stepped forward, her Alpha aura slamming into us like a wave. "George."

He emerged from behind the sea of undead like a nightmare given flesh, his cloak billowing, body etched with glowing crimson runes that pulsed with sickening energy. He looked calm. Cold. A man who knew he was standing on the edge of destruction and wanted it.

But he wasn't alone.

The witch beside him hovered inches off the ground, her crimson robes writhing around her like they were alive. Her black hair spiraled in invisible wind. She locked her eyes on Sofía like prey.

I felt bile rise in my throat.

Sofía's voice was razor sharp between clenched teeth. "It's you."

She snarled and lifted her hand. "Attack!"

The warriors launched forward like lightning, their howls splitting the sky. Bodies shifted midair, bones snapping, fur erupting from skin. Witches spread out, flanking them with glowing palms and ancient chants.

Claws tore through bone. Teeth sank into cold, undead flesh. Some corpses exploded into ash from the strength of a wolf's bite or a well-placed spell but others reformed. Re-assembled like puppets from hell, refusing to stay down.

We were surrounded.

And then Ace.

A blur of black leather and pale skin, he was everywhere and nowhere. One moment slicing through an enemy wolf with supernatural speed, the next tearing the head from a reanimated corpse like it was paper.

Blood splattered across his face as he grinned, fangs gleaming in the pale moonlight. "You boys really should've stayed dead," he muttered, driving his fist into the chest of another corpse.

But even with his power, he was only one vampire.

One very fast, very lethal vampire, but still outnumbered.

He fought like he enjoyed it, until he skidded to a stop near Nadya, barely dodging a spell meant to impale her. Without missing a beat, he grabbed her waist and spun her out of harm's way, dipping her like a lover mid-dance.

"Well, well," he murmured, eyes glowing silver. "Maya never said they was going to be beautiful brujita here."

Nadya huffed, cheeks flushed. "Let go of me, *sanguijuela*."

"Oh, I don't know," he smirked, slicing through another enemy. "Near-death experiences make me need some TLC."

I could not help but smirk.

Blood soaked the dirt around us, soaking into the soil like the land itself was bleeding. Sofía had shifted her massive white wolf charging through the chaos like divine vengeance. She moved like fire and fury, tearing through flesh, bones snapping beneath her jaws.

Mason was beside her, a blur of black fur and gold-eyed wrath, taking down anything that dared touch her flank.

I barely had time to react before a corpse lunged for me, Estrella yanked me back, and a burst of spell fire from Myriam turned it to ash.

"Stay sharp!" she barked, already casting again.

This wasn't a battle. It was a massacre.

And George? That bastard just stood behind the waves of carnage, watching us fight like it amused him. His witch kept summoning more of the dead, each one worse than the last.

I was scanning the field when Sofía—now naked and back in human form, her body smeared in blood and dirt—shouted out commands, her voice slicing through the madness. Mason shifted mid-sprint and charged once again, crashing into a cluster of undead like a wrecking ball of fur and fang.

That's when Marcos appeared beside me.

He grabbed my arm, steady and grounding, his eyes locked on mine. "Stay behind Nadya. Both of you."

"And you?" I asked, breathless, heart hammering against my ribs.

He looked to where Beto was calling. "We'll be where we need to be, killing whatever we can get our hands on."

Then he was gone, already shifting midair, his body exploding into his wolf form as he and Beto dove into the fray.

I obeyed, I followed Nadya, shielding her as she clutched a glowing crystal, whispering her final spell.

She drove it into the earth with a cry.

A pulse of blinding white light burst out from the center, surging over the battlefield like a shockwave.

The undead screamed a sound that wasn't human and then collapsed. Dozens of them dropped like broken toys, lifeless, limbs twitching once before stilling. The witch screamed in agony, falling to her knees as her spell was ripped away.

Then came George... He stepped forward. Calm. Composed. Smirking.

His eyes locked on Nadya like she was already bleeding, like he could taste her downfall.

"Nice little trick there, you white witch," Alpha George hissed, voice dripping with venom. "But I not leaving here until I get what I'm not leaving here until I get what I came for."

Mason stepped forward, shifting smoothly back into human form, his tall frame bare and glistening with blood and sweat. A massive wolf, one of our best warriors, stood at his side, teeth bared and growling low.

"And what is it you want?" Mason asked coldly, his voice steady even as tension vibrated off of him like a taut wire.

George's lips curled into a smirk. "Isn't it obvious? I want Sofía dead. Her family buried. And Luna Stone Pack mine." His tone dropped into something almost gleeful.

The shadows stirred beside him, and the witch stepped forward.

Slowly, she pulled back her hood—and my stomach dropped.

That face. Pale skin, sharp cheekbones, raven-black hair. The haunting, soulless eyes.

Her.

The witch who watched me while I was tied up in George's home. The one who never blinked, never looked away. The one who made my skin crawl with just a glance.

Judging by the way Sofía and Mason froze, they knew her.

"Hello, Mason..." Her voice was sickly sweet. "Missed me?"

"Fucking Rebecca," Sofía spat, her jaw clenching hard enough to crack. "I should've known. Only a lunatic like you would go this far for a man who doesn't even want you."

Rebecca's wicked smile dropped, her nostrils flaring. Her aura pulsed with dangerous magic, sharp and cold like broken glass.

"You always did have such a filthy mouth, Sofía," she sneered, turning her attention toward the Alpha.

"Still desperate for a man that doesn't belong to you," Xiomara called out, stepping forward with a raised brow and a gleam of disgust in her eyes. "Pathetic."

Rebecca snarled, lifting her hand, magic swirling around her fingers like a storm of black lightning.

Before I could even gasp, she launched it straight at Sofía no warning, no spell words, just raw power meant to kill.

But she never made contact.

A golden light flared between them, and with a flick of her wrist, Myriam stepped into the blast's path and deflected it. The spell shattered midair in a clash of sparks and sound, scattering ash into the wind.

"You'll have to go through me first," Myriam said, her voice rich and commanding, her eyes glowing with ancestral power.

She flicked her fingers again, murmuring an incantation, and a whip of energy surged from her palm, striking Rebecca dead in the chest. The witch flew back like a rag doll, crashing into a twisted tree trunk with a screech of pain and fury.

The earth shook beneath her impact.

Chaos rippled outward.

Wolves howled. The witches readied their next spells. Warriors braced for another wave of undead. But I couldn't stop staring at Rebecca as she slowly pulled herself to her feet, eyes filled with hatred, lip bleeding.

"You dare..." she hissed.

"I protect what is mine," Myriam replied, stepping in front of Sofía. "And Luna Stone is under my protection tonight."

George stepped forward again, unbothered by Rebecca's rage or the spell still sizzling in the air. His eyes swept across the crowd until they landed on me.

His smile twisted cruelly.

"And you," he said, voice lowering. "Maya. Don't think I've forgotten about you. You will pay for your betrayal."

And then... he started walking toward us.

Every instinct inside me screamed danger. Estrella stiffened beside me, and I immediately stepped in front of her, my body trembling with rage and fear, the heat of my wolf rising beneath my skin.

"You thought you could escape me?" George growled, his voice thick with madness. "You thought you could run, whore? That there wouldn't be a price to pay?"

His gaze flicked to Estrella, and the malice in his face twisted into something even darker. "Your friend will bleed for your betrayal." He pointed a clawed finger directly at her belly. "I'll make you scream so loud that your child will claw its way out just to escape the sound. And when it does..." His lips curled into a sickening grin. "I'll gift the little thing to Rebecca. She's been dying to taste newborn blood."

Estrella gasped, hand flying to her swollen belly, eyes wild with terror.

I snapped.

"Touch her," I snarled, my voice vibrating with fury as my bones began to burn, the shift surging through me. "And I'll rip your fucking throat out."

Before George could take another step, a fireball exploded from the side, slamming into his shoulder and knocking him back with a roar of pain.

I turned, heart catching.

"Nadya!"

She stood barely upright, leaning against a crumbling wall, blood trickling from her mouth. Her hands still glowed from the blast she'd thrown, her face pale and glistening with sweat.

"You twisted fuck," she spat, coughing violently. "Stay the fuck away from them."

Suddenly, movement came too fast.

George dropped to one knee, ripped a dagger from his boot, and threw.

"No!" I screamed.

The blade cut through the air like lightning and struck Nadya in the chest with a sickening thud. She staggered back against the wall, breath hitching as she slumped to the ground, the hilt of the blade trembling with every ragged breath she took.

"NADYA!" I shrieked, my vision blurring with tears.

But I wasn't the only one moving.

Ace flashed across the battlefield in a blur of black and silver, racing toward Nadya with supernatural speed, fangs bared, eyes wide with panic.

"No no no!" he called out, shoving through two corpses in his path.

But just as he reached her.

Rebecca turned, eyes black, and flung a bolt of jagged purple magic straight at him.

It hit Ace mid-charge.

He let out a sharp grunt as the spell struck his back, sending him flying forward through the air like a rag doll. He vanished in a cloud of smoke and crackling light, his body gone.

"No!" I screamed from behind us, eyes wide with horror. "Ace!"

For a moment, it felt like the world stopped.

My body shook with fury, and my screaming turning into a growl that echoed across the battlefield

Before I knew it, I was already shifting.

My bones snapped, skin tore, and fire spread through me as my auburn wolf exploded outward. I didn't think. I launched.

George shifted mid-lunge, his massive black wolf snarling, eyes blazing with fury.

We collided midair, a whirlwind of blood, fur, and claws. He was older, heavier, but I was faster, my rage sharpening every movement. We tore across the battlefield in a brutal clash of teeth and muscle. He landed a deep slash across my ribs, and I bit down hard on his leg, twisting until I felt bone crack beneath my jaws.

His yelp of pain only enraged him.

He slammed me with his shoulder, then clamped his massive jaws around my neck and threw me like a rag doll.

I crashed against a tree, a sharp crack echoing from my spine. My wolf whimpered, and I shifted back midair from the pain, hitting the ground naked and breathless. Mud clung to my skin. My vision blurred

Everything hurt.

And George, he wasn't done.

He stalked forward, his giant form towering as he turned toward Estrella.

"No..." I gasped, trying to move. "Please..."

Estrella pulled a silver blade from her boot, her hands shaking.

And just as George loomed over her—she leapt.

With a feral cry, she drove the knife between his shoulder blades. He howled in rage, thrashing as the blade sank in deep.

But he was too strong.

He bucked her off with a violent jerk. Her body flew through the air and hit the ground hard, her head cracking against a rock with a dull, wet thud.

"ESTRELLA!" I cried, crawling forward through blood and dirt.

George turned, his eyes on her limp form.

He crouched, then bit down.

Her scream tore through the air, raw and shattering.

Blood sprayed. His jaws clamped around her shoulder and neck, shaking her like prey. Her scream faltered into gurgles.

"NO!" I sobbed, screaming through the pain. "STOP! Leave her alone! Please—STOP!"

I clawed at the ground, trying to get to her—but my body wouldn't move fast enough.

I was too slow.

Too broken.

Too helpless.

And the man I hated more than anything... was going to kill the woman I swore I'd protect.

Then, out of the trees, a massive gray wolf came barreling out of the shadows and tackled George off her.

The force of it cracked the ground as the two wolves rolled across the field, biting, tearing, snarling like two demons from hell.

I fell to Estrella's side, hands slipping in blood.

"Estrella... no, please goddess, no!" I pressed both palms to her wounds, trying to stop the bleeding, sobbing so hard I could barely see. "Please don't leave me. Please."

Everyone else was fighting. Sofía, Mason, Myriam, they were locked in battle with Rebecca and a dozen of the undead. Screams, howls, spells—it was all chaos around us.

"Help!" I cried out. "Somebody please!"

That's when I heard the shuffle of movement and looked up to see Nadya staggering toward me.

Her face was gray, the dagger still embedded in her chest. Her lips trembled, but she reached for her skirt and tore off a large strip of fabric.

"Use this," she whispered, falling to her knees beside me. "Push here just above the artery. Yeah, that's it."

"Nadya, you're hurt!"

She gave a weak smile, her lips trembling. "Didn't hit any vitals... hurts like a bitch, though."

I sobbed, pressing the makeshift gauze into Estrella's wound. "Stay with me, Estrella, please. You're strong. You've got that baby to fight for."

Estrella opened her eyes slightly, barely conscious.

Her lips parted in a whisper.

"That's... my man," she said faintly, a tear sliding down her bloodied cheek. "He came for me... came to protect me and our baby..."

Then her eyes fluttered shut again.

Chapter 36

MAYA

Estrella was in and out of conscious, trembling as the adrenaline faded. Nadya kept one hand pressed to her dagger wound, the other cradling Estrella's stomach.

Darren and George were still tearing into each other, fangs, claws, blood soaking the ground beneath them. It was savage, primal... and far from over.

Suddenly, a familiar voice cut through the air.

"MAYA!"

I spun around, heart catching in my throat.

Andres.

He was running toward me, covered in dirt and blood, wild with desperation. I didn't care how much everything hurt—I ran. We collided in a bruising, breathless embrace. His lips crashed into mine, frantic and raw. The moment we broke apart, he pressed his forehead to mine and whispered, gravel in his voice, "I was going mad without you, my little wolf. I—"

I cut him off, gripping his face. "Grovel later, mate. Right now, go finish that bastard off."

His eyes flared with renewed fire. He kissed me again hard and deep, then turned and ran toward Darren and George, shifting mid-stride in a glorious explosion of fur and muscle. His wolf joined the fray, tackling George with Darren in a savage dance of vengeance.

I was about to follow when I heard it: a scream.

Whipping around, I found Nadya's face pale with panic. I sprinted to her side just as she knelt beside Estrella, who was panting, her face twisted in pain.

"My water just broke," Estrella whispered, tears in her eyes. "No... no, it's too early..."

"How is this happening?" I gasped, kneeling beside her and lifting her head onto my lap.

"The stress," Nadya's said, moving between Estrella's legs. "Trauma like this can trigger labor. And yes, this quick."

Another witch, Naomi, Nadya sister, appeared, limping toward us with a black eye and a bloodied cheek. "We need to move her," she said firmly.

The three of us dragged Estrella beneath a thick tree, far enough from the core of battle but not so far that we were out of protection. Two wolves took position, snarling at anything that moved.

Naomi dropped beside Nadya and peeled off her torn skirt, revealing leggings beneath. "I'm the one with midwife experience," she muttered. "Let me take it from here."

They switched places seamlessly. Naomi's hands moved fast and sure. "Oh, Moon Goddess, the baby's crowning."

Estrella whimpered, her nails digging into my arm. "I don't want to do this alone... I need him. I need my mate."

Her cry shattered something in me.

"I'll get him," I swore.

I bolted.

I found Darren mid-fight, his gray fur soaked in blood. He and Andres were locked in a brutal rhythm with George and half a dozen undead. I waited, watching for my opening—then I shouted, "DARREN! You need to go! Estrella's having the baby!"

His wolf's eyes widened in horror.

He turned to Andrés, nuzzled him once like a brother, then bolted toward the trees without a second thought.

I stepped forward to help Andrés, but a hand gripped my shoulder.

I turned, startled. Marcos.

"Go help Estrella," he said darkly. "George and I have unfinished business."

"Marcos, what?"

But George's cruel laughter cut us both off.

"Oh, how precious," he sneered. "Coming to avenge your wife? Or are you here to thank me... for taking care of your bitchy little daughter?"

I blinked.

What?

Marcos turned to me, just as confused, but Andrés didn't wait.

"You fucking bastard!" he roared, shifting back to human long enough to drive his boot into George's chest, sending him crashing into a tree.

Before he could strike again, a bolt of magic slammed into Andrés, knocking him to the ground.

Rebecca.

She raised her arms, laughing as another dozen undead clawed their way from the dirt, surrounding George like a barrier.

Before I could leap in, Marcos was already in the middle, joined by Beto, both of them hacking through the undead, trying to reach George.

Then—

Rebecca turned back to Sofía.

She unleashed a flurry of spells: fire, ice, shadow. Sofía dodged as best she could, but two blasts caught her hard—one to the shoulder, one to the ribs.

She hit the ground hard. Mason was on the ground, unconscious and bleeding.

She tried to get up, but her legs failed her. Crawling backward, dirt caked in her mouth and blood pouring from her side, she stared up at Rebecca.

"Do you think I was going to let you come between us?" Rebecca snarled, approaching like a demon queen. "Mason loved me first. I was meant to be his mate. Your precious little wolf bond ruined everything."

She was shaking, magic leaking from her pores in dark threads.

"I would have had him," she continued, voice trembling, "if you hadn't whored your way into his life. But I'll fix it. I'll kill every last one of you and he'll have no one left to love but me!"

Her eyes turned pitch-black. Black veins burst along her arms and throat, pulsing with twisted magic.

She raised her hands.

I screamed Sofia's name

But then, a white orb of pure magic streaked out of the forest, striking Rebecca square in the chest.

She screamed and stumbled, falling to her knees, clutching her sternum.

From the shadows stepped a woman I hadn't ever seen.

Sofia whispered her name. "Rachel."

Her presence was calm, powerful, terrifyingly focused.

"How could you, Rebecca?" Rachel said as she walked toward her. "You risked everything. Our coven. Our alliance with the shifters. For a man who doesn't love you."

Rebecca looked up, tears mixing with rage. "You attacked me?! You're my sister. Blood of my blood!"

Rachel's eyes didn't waver. "And how many sisters have you slaughtered trying to get to one woman? You think we don't know what you've done? You can't outrun fate, Rebecca. You can't fight the Moon Goddess. Sofía is Mason's fated mate."

"NO! NO! SHE'S WRONG! HE'S MINE!" Rebecca screamed, throwing a bolt of magic at Rachel.

But Rachel simply lifted her hand.

And stopped it mid-air.

Rebecca's eyes widened in horror.

"No," Rachel said softly.

"You're not!" Rebecca spat. "I'm more powerful than you. I always was!"

"No," Rachel replied. "You were hungry. I was patient. That's why Mother chose me as her successor."

She stepped closer. "She must have known what you'd become. That this... madness... was inside you."

"Necromancy?" Rachel spat. "How low will you fall?"

Rebecca trembled. "You've never shown greater power, how?!"

"I didn't want to break you," Rachel said quietly. "I didn't want to humiliate you. But now I see why Mother made the choices she did. She prepared me... to stop you."

She lifted both hands and whispered a spell in a foreign language. Rebecca surged forward, but Rachel struck first.

A wave of magic lifted Rebecca off her feet and slammed her against a tree, pinning her in place.

"No more," Rachel whispered, and with a powerful incantation, she began stripping her sister of magic.

One by one, the black veins receded. Rebecca screamed. Her connection to the earth shattered. Her power broke like glass.

And when it was over... she collapsed to the ground. Unconscious.

For a breathless moment... everything was still.

Then, all at once, the remaining undead fell.

Like puppets with their strings cut, they dropped wherever they stood. Bones cracked, rotted limbs twisted. Dozens of corpses, mid-swing, mid-growl now lifeless, unmoving. The battlefield turned from chaos to eerie calm in a heartbeat.

Silence spread.

No spells.

No snarls.

Just breathing. Shocked, heavy breathing.

Then

A voice shattered it all.

"ESTRELLA!"

Darren's scream ripped through the quiet like a knife.

My heart seized.

We ran me, Sofía, Rachel, Leo, everyone who could move. My body felt like it barely held together, but I ran until my legs ached and my lungs burned.

The scene stopped us cold.

Naomi was kneeling in the grass, her hands bloodied as she gently cleaned a tiny, crying newborn wrapped in her skirt.

Beside her, Darren cradled Estrella's limp, pale body in his arms.

"Please," he choked, tears running down his cheeks. "Please, baby... wake up. Please, don't do this. We just got our child. You can't leave now. Please."

Estrella's face was peaceful. Too peaceful. Her skin had gone gray, her lips tinged blue. Blood soaked the ground beneath her—too much blood.

"No..." Myriam whispered, dropping to her knees beside them.

She reached for Estrella's wrist, checking for a pulse. Her face fell.

"I'm sorry," she whispered, eyes shining. "She's gone."

Sofía collapsed beside them, her face contorting as she clutched Estrella's body. "No. No, no, no—please, Estrella," she cried, her voice breaking apart. "You were supposed to survive. You were supposed to meet your daughter…"

Darren let out a strangled sob and pressed his forehead to Estrella's.

"She fought so hard," Naomi said softly, holding the baby close. "She held on long enough to give her life… for her."

Suddenly, footsteps thundered behind us.

"What's going on?" Xiomara's voice rang out, frantic. She pushed through the crowd, her braid flying behind her, eyes wide.

"Xiomara, wait," Leo said, trying to block her path. "Let us explain"

But she shoved him out of the way, her breath catching as she looked down.

Her sister's body.

Her niece in Naomi's arms.

"No…" she whispered. Her face twisted, and she dropped to her knees, screaming, "NO!"

She crawled to Estrella's side, trembling as she touched her cold hand.

"No, Estrella, please," she begged. "Come back. You can't leave me, *hermanita de mi alma*."

Sobs broke from her chest as she pressed her forehead to her sister's arm, refusing to let go.

The only sound that followed was the soft, newborn wail of a baby who would never know the warmth of the woman who gave her life.

The battlefield had gone quiet, but grief clung to the air like smoke.

We stayed near Estrella's body, not ready to move. Not ready to let go.

Then Naomi's voice broke through the silence. "Darren."

He looked up slowly, eyes glassy, as Naomi stepped closer, gently cradling the newborn wrapped in her torn, blood-stained skirt. "You should hold your daughter."

He blinked. "I can't."

Sofía moved to his side, placing a steadying hand on his shoulder. "You can."

Mason crouched beside him, his voice low but firm. "She needs you now more than ever."

Darren looked frozen, his hands shaking.

Beto stepped forward, eyes dark with emotion. "Take her, *hermano*. Let all the love you had for Estrella pour into that little bundle of life. That's her gift to you."

With trembling hands, Darren reached out.

Naomi gently placed the baby in his arms.

He held her like she was made of moonlight and glass.

"She looks just like her," he whispered, eyes flooding with fresh tears. He leaned down and kissed her soft, wrinkled forehead. "You're the last piece of her I'll ever have."

Just then, a whoosh of air rushed behind us, followed by heavy, staggered breathing.

We turned in time to see Ace materialize out of nothing, dirt-covered and shirt torn, his blonde hair a mess and his silver eyes wide.

"Goddess," I gasped, sprinting toward him. "I thought she killed you!"

"Nah," he said, panting. "I'm a vampire. Pretty hard to kill me." He leaned on his knees, catching his breath. "Though she did fucking launch me to Alaska. Sorry it took me so long to crawl back."

Then his eyes darted around frantically. "Where is she?"

Before I could respond, a weak voice called from near the trees. "I'm here..."

We turned.

Nadya was slumped against the trunk of a tree, the dagger still embedded in her chest. Her shirt was soaked through with blood, her skin pale, too pale.

Ace blurred to her side in seconds, catching her as she tried to move and nearly collapsed.

"Don't you fucking move!" he snapped, holding her like she was already fading. "Why hasn't anyone treated her?!" he growled, his voice breaking.

Naomi tried to speak. "There were too many people, too much—"

"No." Ace cut her off, voice raw.

Nadya blinked up at him, her lips trembling. "Ace..."

"Shh," he whispered, cradling her against his chest.

Myriam appeared, her steps slow as she approached her youngest daughter. Her face crumbled the second she saw Nadya's condition.

"*Oh, mi cielo*," she whispered, tears slipping down her face. Her fingers trembled as she reached for Nadya's bloodied wrist to check her pulse. She didn't say anything, but the look in her eyes told us everything.

She wasn't sure if her daughter would survive the night.

Sofia cleared her throat, voice steady despite the tears staining her cheeks. "Let's get everyone inside."

She turned to Mason and Leo. "Can you carry Estrella?"

Mason nodded, eyes filled with pain. Together, he and Leo carefully lifted Estrella's body.

"Ace," Sofía said gently, "bring Nadya to one of the guest room. Maya, can you show him the way?"

I nodded. "Of course."

Ace scooped Nadya into his arms like she weighed nothing and followed me silently toward the packhouse, his eyes never leaving her face.

⁂

The heavy scent of smoke, blood, and grief lingered in the air as we gathered in the study.

Sofía sat at the head of the room, her posture straight but her expression shattered. Around her were Mason, Leo, Xiomara, Marcos, Beto, Andrés... and me. All of us worn, bruised, and emotionally wrecked.

She exhaled deeply. "Does anyone know what happened to George?"

Everyone looked around, tense.

Marcos growled. "He vanished during the chaos. While we were all rushing to help Estrella... he slipped away."

Beto cursed under his breath. "Always two steps ahead, that bastard."

Sofía's jaw clenched. "We will find him. No matter how long it takes."

She swallowed hard, then turned to the next bitter task. "What about Estrella's funeral arrangements?"

Before anyone could answer, Xiomara stood, her lip trembling.

"I can't," she whispered, tears spilling over as she stumbled toward the door.

Leo tried to stop her. "Xio, wait."

She pushed past him and disappeared into the hallway, her sob echoing down the corridor.

Leo rubbed his face with both hands. "She's taking it hard. Too many bad things for one person to handle."

Sofía nodded, her voice quieter now. "And Darren?"

"He's with the baby," Leo said. "He hasn't left her side. Naomi's helping him with feedings and care. They named her Esperanza."

A silence fell across the room, both comforting and unbearable.

Then Sofia looked at me. "Nadya?"

I swallowed, the words clawing in my throat. "Between the blood loss and the witch's spell... her body isn't healing. The magic isn't holding like it should."

Mason's brows drew together. "You mean..."

"She might not make it through the night," I whispered.

Sofía closed her eyes. Andres gripped my hand. And none of us said anything for a long time.

Because what could you say... when it felt like George was still stealing pieces of the people you cared about?

Chapter 37
ASCELIN (ACE)

The moment I hit the snow-covered ridge and saw nothing but pine and silence, I knew something had gone wrong.

Alaska. That insane witch actually blasted me across continents.

One second I was sprinting for Nadya, and the next, I was buried in ice and snow with nothing but rage to keep me warm.

I didn't pause. I didn't think.

I ran.

Through dark forests and across empty mountain valleys, moving faster than any creature should, guided by nothing but instinct and the unshakable pull in my chest.

I had to get back to her.

I'd stopped believing centuries ago, But when I found her... when I scented her magic... everything in me knew.

I had given up on ever finding her.

But I had her now.

And she was in danger.

When I finally made it back to Luna Stone, everything was too quiet. The smell of blood and death lingered in the air.

So much death.

I slowed, chest rising and falling with heavy, unnecessary breaths as I took a few careful steps forward.

That's when the scent hit me sharp, coppery, and utterly hers.

Her blood.

I panicked.

"Where is she?!" I shouted.

I didn't care who heard. I didn't care what had just happened. I needed to see her.

And then...

"I'm here..."

Her voice so soft, it could've been a breath of wind.

I turned toward it and saw her slumped against a tree, her body barely upright, as if she were holding herself together with sheer will. Her skin was ghostly pale. Her top was soaked with blood. And in her chest...

A fucking dagger.

No one was doing anything. No one was helping her.

Rage exploded in my chest like a star.

"Why hasn't anyone treated her?!" I snarled, my voice low and lethal, a growl that shook the damn leaves on the trees.

If someone answered, I didn't hear it.

I only saw her, bleeding out, alone, shaking.

I knelt beside her, scooping her into my arms like she was the most fragile thing in existence.

"No... not now," I whispered, pressing my forehead to hers. "I just found you."

They escorted us into the packhouse and gave me a guest room. Like hell I was leaving.

Her mother and sister were there. They helped clean her wounds, changed her bloody clothes. Even as I held her in my arms, they asked me to leave.

I didn't.

Not once.

And when their healing spells failed to stick... when her pulse weakened again... I knew what I had to do.

The truth couldn't stay hidden anymore.

I sat beside her, ignoring the glare from Myriam and the panic in Naomi's eyes. Without a word, I slashed my wrist and lifted it to Nadya's lips.

She didn't resist.

She drank.

Naomi lunged forward. "Stop! What are you doing?!"

I growled deep, guttural. A sound that made the walls tremble.

"Do not interrupt me," I said, eyes locked on Nadya as her color slowly began to return.

She sighed softly against me. Her breathing eased. The flush returned to her cheeks. Her body, once stiff and dying, relaxed as life flowed back into her.

When I saw enough, I pulled my wrist away, licking the wound closed with a hiss. I cleaned her lips and jaw gently, the way I'd cradle something precious.

"I didn't know vampire blood could do that," Naomi whispered.

Before I could answer, Myriam beat me to it.

"It normally doesn't...."

Naomi turned, confused. "*Mamá, ¿qué estás diciendo?*"

Nadya was finally breathing normally.

Her pulse had stabilized. The color had returned to her face. The bleeding had stopped.

But the air in the room hadn't softened.

It tightened.

I could feel it in the way Myriam stood across from me, arms crossed over her chest, chin high, fury hidden just beneath the surface of her grief. Rachel stood silently at the door, unsure whether to step in or step away.

Myriam's voice was quiet at first, but sharp. Cutting.

"You should not have done that," she said. "You had no right to give her your blood."

I met her eyes. Calm. Unapologetic. "She would have died if I hadn't."

She took a step forward. "And if she had? Then she would have passed in peace, surrounded by her family, with her soul untainted."

I stood slowly from the bedside, blood still drying on my hands, Nadya's heartbeat pulsing gently behind me.

"I saved her," I said evenly. "You're welcome."

Myriam's face twisted. "You didn't save her. You tethered her. You've anchored her to you. You've changed the course of her path without her consent."

My jaw tightened, and I fought the beast in me that wanted to rise at those words.

"My fated match. You think I planned this?" I growled.

Myriam's expression faltered but only for a breath.

"She is my youngest child," she hissed. "She still has so much to learn. Her magic is barely stable. She belongs with her coven, with her sisters."

I stepped forward. "I would protect her with my life. My people, those closest to me, we want change. We want connection. Peace."

"Your people?" she scoffed. "You're a vampire, Ace. There will always be those who see witches as threats. I have spent all my life keeping my daughters safe. I will not watch my baby get destroyed because of a vampire."

I let out a breath. "You think I don't want to protect her?"

"Then leave her," Myriam said. Her voice cracked just once. "Let her heal. Let her learn. Let her live with her family before she's swept into something she's not ready for."

I stared at her for a long time. The monster in me, the man in me it all rebelled against the idea of leaving Nadya. Against keeping our connection a secret. Against denying what we were.

But this wasn't about me.

It was about her.

The soft rise and fall of her chest. The slow rhythm of her pulse.

She had nearly died. She needed rest. Time.

"I will agree," I said finally, my voice low. "I won't tell her. I won't tell anyone. Not yet."

Myriam exhaled, a slow nod following.

"But listen to me, *bruja*," I said, stepping closer, my fangs barely restrained behind clenched teeth. "I may step back, but I will not be kept from her, and when the time comes, I will claim her."

Myriam didn't answer. Her silence was thick with warning, but I didn't care.

Because I had waited too long for this.

And now that I had found her?

There was no force strong enough to take her from me.

Not even her mother.

I didn't look back.

Not once.

If I had, I would've said fuck it all, the coven, her overprotective mother, this delicate alliance with the shifters. I would've snatched her from that bed and run. Far. Where the bond between us could breathe without being smothered by fear.

But as little as I knew about Nadya... one thing was painfully clear.

Family was everything to her.

And I couldn't be the monster that ripped her away from the people she loved, no matter how much I wanted to keep her.

So I walked.

Found an empty hallway and dropped down on one of the ridiculous carved benches this castle of a house was littered with. Head down. Elbows on my knees. My hands raking through my hair.

I sat there, still soaked with her scent, my wrist sore from where I fed her, my soul screaming for the one woman who didn't even know she was mine.

What the fuck am I supposed to do?

I barely had time to spiral before I heard it.

Her voice.

Soft. Raspy. The sound of her waking up.

To someone else.

Vampire hearing is a gift. Until it isn't. Until you're forced to sit outside a room, invisible, listening to your other half speak like you don't even exist.

"*Mamá... ¿dónde él está*?" Nadya asked weakly.

"*¿Quién?*" Myriam answered, too damn calm.

"*El vampiro*," she said. "*El que... me salvó.*"

"Outside. Why?" Naomi added, her voice casual. Dismissive.

Then came the knife.

"*¿Él me cargó hasta aquí? ¿Él... me salvó?*" Nadya's voice was hesitant, curious... hopeful.

There was a pause. A very calculated pause.

Then Myriam cleared her throat. "Yes. He helped bring you here. Your sister and I saved you."

That last part? She made sure to drive it in.

My hands curled into fists on my knees.

"I swear I heard his voice..." Nadya whispered. "So weird."

Her words gutted me.

"Under distress, a lot of things can happen," Myriam said quickly, brushing it off. "Don't read too much into it."

No one said anything else.

But I heard enough.

More than enough.

She felt me. Even if she didn't remember the details. Even if she didn't understand why.

The bond was there.

Buried, but alive.

And that gave me just enough strength to stay seated. Just enough to not storm back in and claim her the way every part of me was begging to.

I'd wait.

I'd be patient.

But the day would come when she'd remember.

When she'd feel it.

And when that moment arrived... I would be there waiting for her.

Despite all my centuries of control, despite all the ancient strength I had pulsing through my veins... I wasn't a damn masochist.

I couldn't sit outside that room any longer, pretending her voice didn't twist something inside my chest. Pretending it didn't gut me to hear her question whether I was even real.

I stood from that cursed bench and walked.

The packhouse was too quiet, too clean. All that polished wood and warm light couldn't mask the heaviness of what had been lost here.

I needed to leave before I lost the thread of restraint I was barely hanging onto.

But just as I rounded the hall toward the back door, I heard voices.

Raised ones.

"Andres, I'm mad at you. I do not want to talk to you." Maya's voice. Sharp. Hurt. She was walking fast right toward me.

A male voice followed, desperate and stumbling behind her. "I know you're mad, but can we just talk about this? Can you hear me out?"

"Hear you out," Maya snapped, stopping short. "Wouldn't that be nice? To be heard."

The crack in her voice was subtle, but I heard it.

I stepped forward.

"Is everything alright, Maya?" I asked, keeping my tone neutral as I approached.

She turned toward me quickly, her eyes glassy, shining with unshed tears, but her expression softened when she saw me.

"Oh, hey, Ace." She tried to smile, brushing at her cheek. "I was actually heading to find you. How's Nadya?"

I kept my expression flat. "She's fine. Completely recovered. She's a strong woman."

Maya's brows lifted. "That quickly?"

"Yes. Miracle, right?" I said, glancing to the male beside her.

He was tall. Broad. His energy screamed alpha-in-the-making, but right now, he looked more like a kicked pup.

"And who are you?" I asked.

His mouth opened, then closed.

Maya answered for him. "This is Andrés. My mate."

I gave him a slow once-over. "The one who kicked you out without listening to your side of the story?"

Andrés flinched, his gaze dropping for a beat. I saw the guilt flash across his face before he forced it down.

"Yes," Maya said, a little smile curling her lips. "That one."

"Well," I said, extending my hand with a faint smirk, "nice to meet you... and you're welcome."

He looked at my hand like he wasn't sure if it was a trap. Then, slowly, he took it, his grip firm.

"Welcome?" he asked, confusion creasing his brow.

I leaned in slightly, just enough for my voice to drop with that dry, razor-sharp edge. "Yeah. You're welcome for finding your girl half-dead and instead of draining her dry like any other vampire would've done, I brought her here. To your pack. She risked everything to warn you of the coming attack. So yeah... you're welcome."

His jaw flexed, and I saw the tension in his shoulders rise but he didn't say anything.

Smart.

Maya elbowed him gently. "Play nice," she murmured, but her lips twitched like she was enjoying this far more than she should.

"I'm always nice," I said smoothly, stepping back and folding my arms. "Especially with the people I almost died for."

Andrés looked at me then, really looked, probably trying to figure out what my angle was. I didn't bother explaining myself. He'd learn, eventually.

"So... is Nadya awake?" Maya asked, her voice softening with curiosity.

I nodded once. "Yes. She's with her mother and sister. I was just leaving."

Maya blinked. "Wow. She recovered fast. I mean. I'm glad, but I didn't know witches could heal like us."

"They can't," Andrés chimed in beside her, his brows drawn tight. "I've known Nadya since she was a kid. She's never had any quick-healing abilities."

"Her mother and sister did... something," I said, shrugging with a hint of casual arrogance I didn't really feel. "Some healing spell. I don't know. Witchy stuff."

But that wasn't what brought her back.

Not entirely.

Maya tilted her head. "Do you think she's up to visitors?"

I hesitated for a second too long.

"She's still weak," I said. "Maybe tomorrow."

I shifted my stance, ready to move.

I needed to move.

Before I said something I shouldn't.

Before I turned around and went back to her bed just to hear her say my name again, even if she didn't understand why it pulled at my soul.

I took a step back.

"Wait, where are you going?" Maya asked, her brows lifting in surprise.

"I'm leaving," I said simply, with that crooked smile I used to keep people at arm's length. "I came here to help you and your pack. And that? I did. Now it's time to get back to my world."

Maya frowned. "Just like that?"

"Just like that," I said, turning slightly, the smirk never fully reaching my eyes. "Rehabilitating the vampire image isn't exactly a part-time gig. Someone's got to show the supernatural world we aren't monsters."

And gods help me, if I stayed any longer, I would go back on my agreement with Myriam, just to keep her by my side.

On my way out of the packhouse, I nearly made it to the door when I ran into Alpha Sofía.

We both paused, our eyes meeting hers steady and sharp, but warmer than I expected.

"Leaving already?" she asked, tilting her head.

"Yeah," I said, offering a faint smile. "Alpha, I've got an image to fix. Can't let the world keep thinking all vampires are soulless bloodsuckers."

She chuckled lightly. "Could've fooled me."

Her presence alone carried that rare blend of power and poise most leaders could only pretend to have. She stepped forward and offered her hand, no hesitation.

"I want you to know we appreciate everything you did for us, Ace. You came through when it mattered. That doesn't go unnoticed."

I shook her hand, firm and respectful.

"You can count on us if you ever need anything," she added. "Let's meet next week at Luna Enterprises. Talk business. See what kind of collaborations we can stir up between vampires and wolves."

My brow lifted slightly. "That would be... surprisingly great. Thank you."

Mason came up behind her, giving me a nod. I shook his hand too, firm grip, Alpha's tension beneath it, but no hostility. Just mutual understanding.

After that, I made my way down the steps and across the front lot, the cool wind brushing against my face as I approached my bike.

The engine purred the second I turned the key.

I didn't look back.

Just slid onto the seat and revved the throttle.

The road back to L.A. would be long, and the guys at home.

They weren't going to believe a damn word of this story.

Witches. Shifters. Necromancy.

Yeah.

Not a word.

Chapter 38

ANDRÉS

I followed quietly behind Maya as she walked ahead of me, the soft echo of her bare feet on the wooden floor the only sound between us. We'd just come from the war room, where we had funeral plans and status updates.

Since the moment Estrella died, I hadn't had a second alone with Maya. And I needed it, I needed her. To talk, to apologize, to hold her the way I'd wanted to since the second I realized how badly I'd fucked everything up.

She stepped into our room in the packhouse and didn't look back.

I closed the door behind me, twisting the lock—barely a breath of silence passed before bam.

A fist cracked across my cheek.

"Shit," I muttered, grabbing my face and stumbling back. "What the hell was that for?"

Maya's eyes blazed with fury and tears. "That's for being a total jerk and believing Rosario over me, you asshole!"

I blinked, stunned but not surprised. Not even a little.

"I'm sorry," I said, the words rough in my throat. "You're right. I fucked up. And for the rest of my life, I'm going to regret it."

I took a step toward her, but she held up her hand.

"Do you even know how much it hurt?" she demanded, her voice cracking. "Hearing you say that I was using you? That I was part of my father's sick plan? When all I've done since day one is fight the pull toward you, deny what this bond wanted, just to keep control of my life."

She started punching me again, not hard, just enough to make a point. Over and over, against my chest.

"I hate you," she cried. "I hate you, I hate you, I hate"

I didn't let her finish.

I wrapped my arms around her and held her tight. Her fists thudded against me until they didn't. Until all that was left were muffled sobs pressed into my chest, and the way her fingers curled into the back of my shirt like she didn't know whether to shove me away or never let me go again.

I let her have it all. The pain. The anger. The heartbreak.

She deserved every second of it.

When her body finally sagged into mine, trembling and quiet, I pulled back just enough to see her face. Her cheeks were streaked with tears, lips trembling, eyes filled with more emotion than I could take.

I cupped her face with both hands, gently, reverently.

"I'm an asshole," I said softly, forehead touching hers. "And stupid. And blind. And any other word you want to throw at me. But I will never, ever, stop loving you."

Then I kissed her.

Not to erase the pain. Not to pretend everything was suddenly okay.

I kissed her because I meant it.

It was slow. Desperate. Passionate. Like we were putting all the broken pieces back together, one breath at a time.

Her mouth was soft and demanding against mine, her hands gripping my shirt like she was still deciding whether to pull me closer or push me away. I let her choose every second, every kiss, every breath.

And she kissed me back.

Fierce. Desperate.

Like maybe she still hated me.

Like maybe she needed to feel how much I loved her.

"Maya," I whispered between kisses, my lips brushing her jaw, her cheek, the corner of her mouth. "I love you."

She tensed.

But I didn't stop.

"I love you more than my pride. More than the pack. More than the bond. I love you as you. Stubborn. Sharp-tongued and strong as hell."

Her hands slid beneath my shirt, fingers skating across my ribs.

"I'll spend the rest of my life making it up to you," I breathed against her skin. "I'll protect you. Worship you. Fight for you. Whatever you need—I'm yours."

She pulled back slightly, panting, her eyes dark with heat and unshed emotion.

"Then show me," she said, her voice low, commanding. "No more holding back. No more doubts. If you're going to love me, do it like you mean it."

I stared at her for a long moment, chest heaving, then nodded.

"I mean every damn word."

My hands slid to the hem of her shirt. She raised her arms slowly, and I peeled it over her head. The second her skin was exposed, I stilled just to look at her.

Like I was seeing her for the first time.

My mouth parted. "Goddess..."

I traced my fingers gently across her shoulder, down the line of her collarbone.

"Your skin...," I whispered, dragging my fingers across her bare shoulder. "soft like porcelain, made to be admired... and made for me to break."

She bit her bottom lip as I leaned in and pressed a kiss to her bare shoulder, then lower.

I pulled her sports bra over her head, watching it fall to the floor.

Her breasts rose and fell with each breath, her nipples already tight from the cool air—and maybe from the heat between us.

"You're perfect," I murmured, brushing the back of my knuckles across the swell of one. She gasped.

Her lips parted, her eyes gleaming with mischief and hunger.

"You're staring."

I met her gaze, my voice rough. "Yeah. And I'm not stopping."

She licked her lips slowly, purposefully. "Then I want to see you too."

I tugged my shirt over my head and dropped it between us. Her eyes moved across my chest, and when her hands followed, my breath caught.

Her fingers explored like she'd never touched me before. She ran her nails over the lines of my stomach, then down to the edge of my jeans.

I hooked my thumbs into the waistband of my jeans and boxers, stripping them both off in one fluid motion. I let them fall to the floor behind me as Maya's eyes immediately dropped.

Her lips parted with a smirk. "Well... someone is ready to make up."

I chuckled, voice low and rough as I stepped closer. "Always. Especially for you."

Her smile turned coy, playful, and my chest tightened watching her fingers move to the button of her pants. But I wasn't going to let her do this alone.

I dropped to my knees in front of her, pressing a kiss to her bare stomach before looking up. "Let me."

Her breath caught as I slowly tugged her pants down over her hips. Her arousal hit me hard.

"Fuck," I breathed, eyes trailing over her like a prayer. "You smell so fucking good."

Her cheeks flushed as I took her in, bare, stunning, mine.

I leaned in and pressed an open-mouth kiss to her inner thigh, letting my lips linger. Then another... and another. Each one closer, deeper, wetter, my tongue flicking softly, teasing her skin, tasting her.

She whimpered, her hand gripping my hair.

I groaned against her. "You smell like everything I never knew I needed."

Then I licked her.

One long, thick, deliberate stroke of my tongue between her folds, slow enough to savor, hard enough to make her feel it.

Her knees buckled, and a loud, raw moan escaped her lips before she could stop it.

"Shit," she gasped, eyes fluttering. "Andrés..."

I grinned against her, my voice vibrating against her skin. "I'm just getting started."

My palms slid up her thighs, resting at her hips as I stared up at her completely bare, glowing with power and desire and emotion.

"I've never wanted anything more than I want you right now," I said. "You're everything."

She exhaled sharply, cheeks flushed, chest rising fast.

"I'm yours," she whispered.

I rose slowly, my hands never leaving her body, and guided her to the shower to wash all the death and sadness of the day.

Steam wrapped around her like mist clinging to the moon, her back to me, water pouring over her skin, soaking those wild red curls. Her shoulders were tense, her breath uneven.

I moved closer, slowly, placing my hands on her waist like I was afraid she might disappear again.

She didn't move away.

That was all I needed.

I pressed myself to her back, burying my face in the curve of her neck. She smelled like soap and rain and us. I stood there, holding her under the heat, and for the first time in days, I felt like I could breathe again.

"I'm sorry," I whispered, lips brushing her wet skin. "For not believing you. For not listening to you first."

She turned around slowly, her chest pressed against mine, her eyes wide and shining not with tears, but fire.

She kissed me.

And I let her take everything from my mouth—anger, pain, guilt—and return it with hunger. Her lips were frantic, her hands grabbing at my shoulders, my hair, my chest.

It wasn't just a kiss. It was a demand. Don't fuck this up again.

I wasn't planning to.

I lifted her easily, gripping that perfect ass in my hands as she wrapped her legs around my waist. Her back hit the cold tile and she gasped, her eyes meeting mine, wild and wanting.

"Sorry for running," she said, breathless. "For not fighting for us. I should've made you listen."

I kissed her again, rougher this time, more desperate. My cock was already hard between us, grinding against her slick heat. I could barely think.

But I needed her to hear it.

"You're mine, Maya. Forever. I'll never doubt this again. Never doubt you. From now on, I'll listen to you first."

And then I thrust into her.

She cried out, her head falling back against the tile, and I nearly lost it right then and there.

"Shit," I breathed, closing my eyes. "You're so fucking tight, give me a second…"

She clenched around me like she already knew I was hanging by a thread.

Our foreheads touched. Her breath hitched. Mine was shallow.

"I need more," she whispered, voice like smoke curling into my ears.

"Yeah?" I growled, pulling back slowly, letting her feel every inch.

I drove into her again. And again.

Her hands clawed at my back, her moans mixing with the sound of water crashing around us. I held her in place, fucking her deep, the slickness between us only adding to the filthy rhythm we found.

I kissed every inch I could reach her mouth, her neck, the swell of her breasts. Her legs tightened around me, her body trembling with each thrust.

I wasn't just making love to her.

I was claiming her all over again.

For every moment I failed her, I gave her this. My body. My promise. My forever.

I stepped out of the shower, still buried deep inside her, our slick bodies pressed together, water dripping from our skin. She clung to me, her arms wrapped tight around my shoulders, breath hot against my neck.

I didn't bother with a towel.

Didn't care that we were soaked, that we'd soak the sheets.

I carried her straight to our bed, still hard, still inside her, and laid her back against the duvet. Water pooled beneath her, dampening the covers, but I didn't give a damn. All I cared about was the way her eyes darkened as I hovered over her, the way her body welcomed me back with no resistance, only need.

I thrust into her again, low, deep, watching her body arch, her slick curves glistening in the low light.

She was gorgeous like this.

Mine.

"Fuck, Maya..." I groaned, watching the way her breasts bounced with every hard stroke, how her lashes fluttered, her lips parted in pleasure, breathy moans escaping with every movement.

Her hands gripped the sheets, her hips rising to meet me. Her body knew me. Matched me.

"Yes," she cried. "Harder... oh goddess, yes!"

I growled deep in my chest, gripping her thigh and hooking one leg over my shoulder. Her breath caught as I adjusted the angle deeper, harder, my cock slamming into her with smooth, relentless rhythm.

She gasped, her hands flying to her breasts as if trying to hold herself together.

But I was unraveling her.

Her walls clenched around me, tighter with every thrust, and I could feel her getting closer, her body trembling beneath me, her moans turning into broken cries of bliss.

"That's it," I rasped. "Come for me, my little wolf. Give it to me."

Her entire body arched, her head thrown back, and then she cried out high, wild, mine as her pussy clamped around my cock with pulsing waves.

The second I felt that tight squeeze, I lost it.

I gritted my teeth and thrust deeper, harder once, twice before spilling myself inside her with a groan that sounded more like a vow.

I buried my face into her neck, breathing hard, holding her tight as her legs wrapped around my waist and locked me in place.

Her fingers tangled in my hair, her voice a whisper against my ear.

"I love you."

I pulled back just enough to look at her flushed, glowing, pcrfcct.

"I love you more," I said, kissing her slowly, reverently.

Because there wasn't a single part of her that didn't belong to me.

And I would never let her go again.

Maya's body was still warm beneath mine, her breath finally beginning to slow, her arms wrapped tight around my back like she wasn't ready to let go.

I wasn't either.

I kissed the sweat-damp skin between her breasts, then her collarbone, then finally her lips, soft, lazy, lingering.

She sighed into my mouth, her fingers threading through my hair, keeping me close.

The storm between us had passed. And what was left felt like home.

Eventually, I pulled out gently, earning a soft whimper, and left the bed. I grabbed the towel draped over the nightstand, thank the goddess we'd left one, and began wiping her down with care. Between her thighs. Her hips. Her belly.

She watched me through heavy lids, her cheeks still flushed. "You keep doing that and I might start thinking you're sweet."

I chuckled low, brushing my thumb across her lips. "Don't let it get around. I have a reputation to protect."

She gave me a sleepy smile, then reached for the blanket I pulled up around her. I slid in beside her, curling around her from behind, her body snug against my chest, our legs tangled together.

For a while, there was only silence. Our heartbeats. The rhythm of shared breath.

Then, softly, I said, "I want to know everything."

She turned in my arms to face me, her expression a little more serious now, but not guarded. Not with me. Not anymore.

"What happened... after you ran?" I asked gently, brushing a damp strand of hair from her cheek.

Maya exhaled, eyes searching mine. "I didn't think you wanted me anymore. I did not know where to go, so I ran to the Black Stone Pack. But I got caught."

My body tensed, but I stayed quiet.

"I was taken to my father," she continued, her voice steady but low. "He locked me up. Kept me tied up to a chair. He beat me, demanding I gave him any useful information that he can use against Luna Stone Pack. I didn't..."

I place my finger on her lips. "Shush...I believe you."

She paused, then smiled faintly. "My father left me alone and I was able to break out of my restraints and I ran. Thank Goddness I ran into Ace."

I blinked. "That's the vampire?"

She nodded. "Meeting was scary at first. I had never met a vampire in person, but he helped me. He saw I needed help, and without asking any questions, he drove me here."

I raised a brow. "He helped you just like that?"

She hesitated, then said, "It's... more complicated than that. But yes. He saved my life."

I processed that in silence. A vampire helping a shifter? My mate?

"You trust him?" I asked.

"I do," she said softly. "He's different. And I think he's got more at stake than he lets on."

I nodded slowly, then leaned forward to press a kiss to her forehead.

"I don't care who helped you, as long as you're here. Safe. With me."

"I'm not going anywhere," she whispered, her hand curling over my chest. "Not again."

I wrapped my arms tighter around her, tucking her against me like I could shield her from every threat in the world.

Because I would.

Because she was mine.

Chapter 39

MAYA

The next couple of days passed in a blur.

Grief hit like a slow-rolling storm, heavy and unrelenting. Every morning, I woke up sick to my stomach, no appetite, no energy. Just a hollow ache in my chest that refused to fade. Even brushing my teeth felt like a chore, like moving through wet cement.

Poor Andrés was out of his mind trying to help, hovering with worried eyes and silent hands that didn't know where to rest.

"I'm fine," I said one morning, my voice flat as I stood in front of the bathroom mirror, toothbrush in hand.

"You're not," he replied gently, standing in the doorway.

I spit out the foam and rinsed before turning to him. "Andrés, calm down. I'm just... sad. My friend died and left her newborn daughter motherless. We lost wolves. People I fought beside. And it's all because of me."

His arms wrapped around me before I could say anything else.

Andrés pulled me close, pressing his face into the curve of my neck and breathing me in like I was the only air he trusted.

"Look at me," he murmured against my skin. "Nothing that happened was your fault. The only people to blame are a power-hungry alpha and a fucking psycho witch."

He kissed my neck, slow, grounding, reverent.

I exhaled, letting his warmth soak through the ache for just a moment.

Estrella's funeral was quiet, and it moved quickly. She was cremated and her ashes scattered in the sacred glade behind the packhouse, where the moonlight touched the ground first, as our shifter traditions required. It was beautiful.

We celebrated her life afterward in a small gathering behind the packhouse. Plates of food sat untouched while people shared memories that made us laugh, cry, or both at once. It felt strange... but therapeutic.

Darren didn't speak much. He just held Baby Esperanza to his chest, rocking her gently, his eyes far away but dry. The baby was becoming his whole world now. Little Esperanza was the spitting image of her mother, same hair and same tiny nose. Every time someone looked at her, they smiled through tears.

Xiomara, on the other hand, was... distant. Cold, almost. She stayed on the edges of every room, avoided conversations, avoided touch. Even Leo couldn't reach her, but not for lack of trying. He'd hover nearby, sit with her, bring her a plate of food... but she wouldn't even look at him.

Losing her sister broke something in her.

As I stood to the side, quietly watching, I felt eyes on me. I glanced up.

Marcos was staring.

His expression wasn't pity, it was something else. Something sharp. Unreadable. He didn't look away when I met his gaze.

He just watched me.

Like he was trying to figure something out.

When the event ended and the last candle was snuffed, we stayed behind to clean up. Then we all ended up lingering in the kitchen, no one speaking, just sitting in silence, sipping tea, letting the quiet comfort us like a warm blanket.

Until Leo burst in.

"She's gone," he said, frantic.

Sofia stood immediately. "Who?"

"Xiomara," he breathed. "I checked her house. Her clothes... her car. They're both gone."

My chest tightened. "Where could she have gone?"

Before I could stand, Andrés was already behind me, arms wrapping around my waist, lifting me gently and setting me down on his lap. His touch was grounding, but the panic was already curling in my chest.

Leo ran his hands through his hair, pacing. "I knew she was up to something. I felt it."

"Maybe..." Sofía said cautiously, "maybe she just needs time. Space. To grieve in her own way."

"No," Leo snapped, eyes wild. "She's turning twenty-one soon. She's my mate, Sofía. She can't leave without knowing what she means to me."

"You think she hasn't figured it out?" Andrés muttered. "You haven't left her side in days."

Leo turned sharply. "Did she tell you that?"

Andrés stilled.

Then shook his head. "No."

"Then you don't know," Leo bit out, his voice cracking.

No one spoke after that. The silence was heavier this time, drenched in worry and the dread that Xiomara had left not just the pack... but maybe Leo, too.

And if that was true...

She wouldn't be easy to find.

"I'm going after her," Leo said suddenly, voice sharp and full of fire.

Andrés straightened beside me. "Do you really think that's a wise idea?"

Leo didn't even blink. "I don't care if it's wise. I have to go. I'm leaving."

"Stop." Sofía's voice rang out, calm but firm. She stepped forward, the weight of her Alpha presence wrapping around the room like a storm about to break. "Xiomara is my friend as much as she's your mate. I love her like a sister. But chasing after her right now? It won't bring her back."

Leo's jaw tightened.

"She's been through hell, Leo. Losing her sister... nearly losing the pack... let her breathe."

For a moment, I thought her words had reached him.

But then he lifted his head.

And the pain in his eyes cut deeper than anger ever could.

"I'm not taking advice from someone who denied her mate," he said, voice laced with hurt as he stared directly at Sofía.

Then he turned to Andrés. "Or from someone who didn't even believe his."

The silence that followed was suffocating.

And then he turned on his heel and walked away.

Sofía made a move to follow, but Mason stepped in front of her, wrapping an arm gently around her waist.

"Let him go," he said softly. "This is his journey... and his mate. He needs to do it his way."

Sofía's face crumpled as she turned into Mason's arms, resting her head against his chest. Her shoulders shook as the tears finally came.

"Why does it feel like everything is falling apart?" she whispered.

"Because it is," said a calm voice from behind us.

We all turned to see Myriam standing at the threshold, her daughters at her side.

"But like the phoenix," Myriam continued, her gaze locking with Sofía's, "you will rise from this. All of you will. Stronger. Wiser. And more united."

Sofía sniffled as Myriam approached her. The elder witch pressed a kiss to Sofía's cheek and embraced her.

"Take this time to rebuild your pack," Myriam whispered. "And build stronger alliances. You're not alone anymore." She pulled back with a small smile. "We're just a jet away."

With that, Myriam gave her a final squeeze and turned, leaving the packhouse with her daughter beside her.

I was still reeling from the funeral, still walking through grief like fog, when Beto called me into the study.

Andrés came with me, his hand brushing against mine as we followed behind. The study was dimly lit, the air heavy with quiet tension. Marcos was already there, pacing near the window. Sofía was sitting behind her desk while Mason stood off to the side, watching with unreadable expressions.

"Sit," she said softly.

We obeyed, glancing at each other with subtle tension coiled between us. The air in the room felt heavier than usual.

"I got a call from Alpha Jason," Sofía began. "His pack is spread thin between helping us during the attack, lending warriors, and trying to rebuild what's left of Black Stone… he's running out of resources, and fast."

Andrés nodded. "That makes sense. He's done more than enough."

"We agree," she said. "So we spoke thoroughly and came to a decision."

She looked at Andrés, "It's time, brother."

Andrés's body stiffened beside me.

Sofia stood from behind the desk and walked toward us. "You need to embrace your alpha wolf, Andrés. You've always been a leader—strong, protective, relentless. The reason you and I bumped heads so often wasn't because we didn't see eye to eye. It was because you were never meant to follow. You were meant to lead."

My heart caught in my throat.

"And so," she continued, "by the power granted to Alpha Jason and me by the Shifter Council, we officially appoint you as Alpha of the Black Stone Pack."

She looked at me next and my breath stilled.

"And you, Maya... as his Luna."

The words hit like thunder and left silence in their wake.

Andrés slowly stood. "I've never wanted to lead," he said quietly, his voice raw. "I've always been happy serving you as my Alpha. This pack is my home."

Beto stepped forward, his voice warm and filled with conviction. "And that's exactly what makes you ready. A good Alpha doesn't crave power—he earns it through loyalty, through sacrifice. Your people will follow you, Andrés. They already do. You just haven't accepted it yet."

Andrés turned to me then, his jaw clenched, his eyes filled with vulnerability.

I stood and reached up to cradle his cheek. "I know this is scary. I see the doubt in your eyes. But I believe in you, Andrés. Completely."

He closed his eyes, leaning into my touch.

"I'm afraid I won't be enough for them," he murmured. "That pack is broken... abused. Maybe someone more experienced—"

"No, son," Beto cut in gently. "You are enough. Marcos and I will guide you—just as we do for Sofía. You'll never lead alone."

Andrés nodded slowly, the weight of his new title settling over him.

Then I remembered something else.

"So... we're moving to the Black Stone Pack?" I asked.

Sofía nodded. "You leave tomorrow. Take what you need. The rest will be sent with the movers."

Andrés and I looked at each other, everything unspoken written across our faces. This was happening.

But Beto hadn't finished.

He stepped closer, his eyes falling on me. "Before you go... there's something else we need to talk about."

He placed a comforting hand over mine.

"Andrés discovered something after his visit to Black Stone," he said gently.

I frowned. "What did he discover?"

Beto glanced toward Andrés, giving him the space to speak.

"Your nanny, Matilda," Andrés said. "She told me something... about your birth. About what really happened in Alpha George's dungeon."

My stomach twisted.

"She said she and Luna Donna found a pregnant woman locked up," Andrés explained, voice rough. "Beaten. Weak. They tried to help her... but George he..." He swallowed. "He cut the baby out of her. Handed that baby to Luna Donna, and then... killed the woman."

I felt like the air had been knocked out of me. "What does that have to do with me?"

Andrés looked at me, his gaze haunted. "You were that baby, Maya. Luna Donna couldn't have children. George was sterile. So he made a deal: her silence in exchange for a child. You."

I felt my head spinning, and I clutched to Andrés to steady myself.

"So I'm truly..." My voice broke. "I'm... an orphan?"

"Not necessarily," Beto said, his voice steady but soft. "After Andrés told me that story, I had a feeling. Something didn't sit right. So I looked into old Luna Stone and Black Stone files."

Beto's eyes shifted toward Marcos.

He stood frozen in the corner, shoulders tense, staring at the floor like the truth had been sitting in his chest all along.

"Maya..." Beto said carefully. "We believe Marcos is your biological father."

The room went still.

I couldn't speak. Couldn't breathe.

"It all makes sense now," I whispered.

Sofía stepped forward, eyes wide. "What makes sense?"

I looked around the room, heart racing. "What George said during the fight. He looked at Marcos and said... 'Are you here to avenge your wife, or to thank me for taking such good care of your daughter?'"

Gasps echoed around me.

Marcos finally lifted his head. His eyes locked on mine, and I saw it—clear as day.

Love.

"I knew," he said, voice thick with emotion. "From the moment I saw you. At first, I thought it was just how much you looked like Delilah, your mother. But your scent... the familiarity. My wolf recognized you. Even when I couldn't admit it."

Tears slipped down my cheeks. "But... George always said—"

"He lied," Marcos said, stepping forward. "He killed Delilah. And I thought he killed you, too. For years, I thought I had lost everything. But he kept you. I don't know why. But it doesn't matter now."

I trembled. "But what if it's another manipulation? George says anything to confuse us."

Andrés wrapped an arm around me. "Do you believe he's your father?"

I shook my head. "No. I heard him say I wasn't. But that still doesn't prove anything."

Beto reached into his jacket and pulled out a sealed envelope. "That's why I brought this. While Andrés was looking for you, I used your toothbrush and Marco's to send out a DNA test and I have the results."

I stared at it, breath catching in my throat.

"I... I can't open it," I whispered. "I'm too scared."

Beto nodded gently. "Then I will."

He tore it open slowly, carefully unfolding the paper.

His eyes scanned the page.

Then he looked up, voice calm but firm.

"There's no doubt. Marcos is your father."

The silence was deafening.

Marcos stepped forward, eyes full of tears. "You're... my daughter."

Something inside me shattered and then healed all at once.

I crossed the room and fell into his arms, sobbing.

He held me like he'd never let go.

"I missed everything," Marcos whispered, his voice thick with emotion. "Your first word. Your first birthday. I should've been there. I should've protected you."

Tears streamed down my face as I clung to him, arms wrapped tight around his back like I could make up for the years we'd lost in a single hug.

"But you're here now," I choked. "And that's enough."

And it was.

For the first time in my life, I knew what it felt like to belong to someone by blood. My heart felt full in a way I didn't know it had been empty.

Marcos pulled back slightly, brushing a tear from my cheek. "I don't want to waste another second. I want to go with you."

I blinked up at him. "Go... with us?"

"To the Black Stone Pack," he said with certainty. "I want to help Andrés rebuild, and more than that... I want to be near you. To make up for the time we lost. To watch you grow into everything I missed."

My breath caught. I looked to Andrés, who turned his gaze from Marcos to me, his expression soft with understanding.

"I love that idea," I said, smiling through fresh tears. "I want that too."

Andrés nodded, eyes still on my father. "I'm more than okay with it. I'll need all the help I can get... especially from my mentor."

Sofía, who had remained respectfully quiet during the moment, finally stepped forward, smiling.

"I think that's an excellent idea," she said warmly. "But you do understand what this means, Marcos. You'll no longer be part of Luna Stone Pack. You'd be joining Black Stone as one of its own."

Marcos looked at me again. And in his eyes, I saw the weight of his decision, how much this meant, how real this was.

"I'll go to any pack," he said, voice unwavering, "as long as I'm with my family."

He pulled me close again, pressing a kiss to the top of my head.

And for the first time in what felt like forever, I felt whole.

We were leaving behind everything we knew.

But we were doing it together.

And that made all the difference when you did it with your family.

Epilogue

MAYA

It's been a year since we moved to Black Stone Pack... and somehow, everything was different, and yet so right.

Taking over as Alpha and Luna wasn't smooth, but not as bad as we expected. The truth? The bar wasn't exactly high to begin with. Most of the pack had lived under Alpha George's reign of fear and control for so long that they were just relieved to finally breathe. Some welcomed us instantly. Others... took time. And a few still glare at me like I walked in here swinging a sword. But that's fine; I've always known how to earn my place.

There were rough patches. Lots of them. Restructuring ranks. Establishing new systems. Trying to figure out how to run a pack that had been broken for years. At first, we didn't even know what to do with all the land we inherited.

None of us knew the first thing about working a damn field.

Then Luna Enterprises stepped in.

They partnered with us and decided to use Black Stone Pack as the headquarters for their elite custom security and protection services. Black Stone Security became a thing focused on high-end private jobs, VIP events, celebrity contracts... the works.

Andrés took to it like a wolf to the moon. Watching him step into his alpha role, confident and commanding it still makes me weak in the knees. He's found his rhythm. His power. And I couldn't be prouder to stand at his side.

While he focused on building the security division, I focused on something just as important: the women.

Our she-wolves had been treated like background noise for decades, pushed aside, undervalued, told they were only as useful as their wombs or kitchen skills. Not anymore.

I found artists. Creators. Women with skills in jewelry-making, candle crafting, aromatherapy, even leather work. And together? We transformed one of George's old warehouses into something ours. A production hub. A space for creation, business, and independence. We gave leadership roles to the women who never had a voice.

And with a little help from my favorite vampire friend, Ace, we launched multiple Etsy shops. They exploded. Turns out the world was more than ready for she-wolf handmade goods.

And now?

We're opening our first boutique in a nearby town.

Yeah. That's right.

Black Stone Boutique is officially becoming real.

I was packing up for the grand opening, carefully folding one of our handmade leather jackets into a travel garment bag, when I heard that annoyingly familiar voice behind me.

"Who would've known that being Luna would look so damn good on you?"

I smirked. "Right? If you'd told me two years ago this would be my life, I would've laughed in your face—and probably slapped you for good measure."

Ace chuckled, leaning casually in the doorway like he owned the place. Still dressed in black-on-black, silver eyes gleaming like the smug immortal he was.

"Where have you been?" I asked. "You've practically disappeared the last few months. Still sneaking off to NYC?"

He gave me that smirk—the one that said he was up to something. "You know I have some very... valuable assets in the city that require regular attention."

I narrowed my eyes at him. "Is that a euphemism?"

"Could be," he said, grinning. "But you'll just have to wonder."

I shook my head, laughing, then walked over and hugged him tight. "Thank you, Ace. For helping us. For believing in us."

He hugged me back, firm and warm, and murmured into my ear, "You were born for this, Maya. You just needed the right storm to rise from."

As I pulled away, I caught the way his eyes flicked—just for a second—toward the far window where the moonlight was pouring through the trees.

And I knew.

He was thinking about her.

"You ever going to tell her?" I asked softly.

Ace's smile didn't reach his eyes this time. "When she's ready."

I nodded.

"I thought I heard a man flirting with my mate," came that deep, possessive voice I could recognize anywhere.

I didn't even have time to turn before Andrés was on me—his lips crashing into mine with a kiss so fierce and passionate it made my toes curl. His body pressed against mine like it always belonged there, like he was claiming every inch of me all over again.

"Get a room," Ace muttered behind us.

Andrés pulled back just enough to smirk at him. "Don't watch."

He sealed the comment with one more heated kiss before whispering, "You're being summoned to the big house."

I grinned, breathless. "Duty calls."

I left what I was doing and headed across the field to the packhouse, smiling the whole way. We'd chosen to live here to keep close to our people and stay connected to their daily needs. It was important. They'd been neglected for so long. We wanted them to know we were here. Present. Committed.

Also... Andrés wanted me close to my father. And the pack doctor.

Because, as it turned out, my fatigue and nausea from last year wasn't just stress or mourning.

I'd been pregnant.

"Finally. I swear, he only wants you," my father grumbled affectionately as I stepped into the living room.

There he was—Marcos, my dad—cradling my baby boy like he was made of glass.

I still had days where it didn't feel real. That I had him. A father who loved me unconditionally. A grandfather who doted on my son with more joy than I thought possible.

The Moon Goddess really outdid herself with this one. A fated mate I once tried to deny, a son I never knew I needed, and a father I thought I'd lost forever. My heart was full in a way that made my past pain finally make sense.

"There's my little monster," I said with a giggle, reaching for the baby in his arms.

Marcos handed him. "He's been fussing for his mama."

I scooped my son into my arms, breathing in his sweet, warm scent. Goddess, he smelled like peace. "Hello, Diego. Are you hungry, my love?"

He blinked up at me with those sage green eyes, my eyes set in a face that looked far too much like his father's. Wavy black hair, tanned skin, and a strong, brooding expression even in sleep. He was a little Andrés clone, and yes, I was completely obsessed.

After we arrived at Black Stone, the symptoms hit hard: constant exhaustion, nausea, and unpredictable emotions. I thought I was falling apart.

"I'm just adjusting," I kept insisting.

But Andrés and my father weren't buying it. Eventually, they teamed up and dragged me to the pack doctor.

And there it was.

Two pink lines and a heartbeat that changed everything.

At first, I was terrified. How could I tell Andrés, with the weight of a crumbling pack on his shoulders, that we were bringing a baby into this chaos?

But the second I told him, his entire face lit up. He smiled—truly smiled—with the kind of joy that made my knees weak. It was the biggest grin I'd ever seen on my grumpy wolf.

"Seriously?" he whispered, pulling me into his arms. "You're giving me everything, Maya."

And when we told my father... he cried.

He'd missed everything with me, every first, every milestone. But now? He had the chance to do it all with his grandson. And watching him rock Diego to sleep or whisper stories about my mother, Delilah, filled something in me I hadn't even realized was broken.

Seven months later, after a surprisingly fast labor, a lot of cursing, and Andrés nearly passing out when he saw just how big his son was, I gave birth to a healthy, chunky baby boy.

Eight pounds, three ounces. Twenty-three inches long.

This mama was wrecked... but I'd do it again in a heartbeat.

Now, with Diego four months old, my heart sometimes feels like it might burst from how much I love him. He coos. He kicks. He smiles when he hears his dad's voice.

And when he nurses, tucked against me in the quiet of the nursery, I swear I feel the whole world fall into place.

As I cradled my son to my chest and rocked him in the nursery rocker, I brushed a kiss against his downy hair. My chest swelled; this, I thought, this is everything.

A soft knock sounded against the doorframe. I looked up to see Andrés standing there, arms crossed, his usual intensity softened by the sight of our son in my arms.

Andrés stood there, arms crossed, watching us with that fierce love he never quite put into words.

"You look good like that," he said softly. "Like a goddess with our cub."

I smiled. "That's because I am."

He chuckled, then walked toward me, pressing a kiss to the top of my head.

"How's my little warrior?" he asked.

"He's asleep," I whispered, smiling. "Just finished feeding."

Andrés leaned down to press a kiss to Diego's cheek.

"I hate to interrupt," he said gently, "but Ace's still here. He said he needed to talk to us."

I nodded, carefully rising from the rocker and placing Diego into his crib. He stirred but didn't wake.

I followed Andrés back into the kitchen, where my father sat with Ace. They both looked up as we entered.

Ace was already mid-sip from his wine glass. "Perfect timing," he said, setting it down. "I've got a story."

Andrés and I exchanged a glance as we took our seats.

"Have you heard from your brother, Leo?" Ace asked.

Andrés shook his head. "No. Not in over six months."

Ace exhaled through his nose. "Well... I saw him. About two weeks ago. In New York."

My stomach tightened.

Ace continued. "I was walking through the Lower East Side, one of the places vampires don't get hassled too much—when I saw two shifters fighting in the alley behind a bar. At first, I thought it was an attack... some asshole male going after a female."

He paused. "But when I got closer, I saw it wasn't that at all. It was Leo and Xiomara."

My breath caught. Andrés tensed beside me.

"She was hitting him," Ace added. "And he... wasn't fighting back. Just blocking her blows. Wild look in his eyes. Desperate. Obsessed."

"What happened?" Andrés asked, his voice tight.

"I called his name. He turned to me. Xio used the moment to run." Ace's jaw flexed. "He came at me, feral. I had to subdue him. He looked awful. Dirty. Thin. Not right in the head. Whatever happened between them... it broke him."

I blinked back the sting in my eyes.

"And then he shifted," Ace said. "Ran after her. I let him go."

Silence stretched thick across the room.

But none of us were surprised.

After Estrella's funeral, Xiomara left without a word. Leo left immediately to find her.

That was the last time we saw either of them.

Every now and then, Leo mailed a postcard to their mother. No return address. No detail. Just a few words: I'm alive. I am okay.

After a long silence, conversation turned to business. Rebuilding plans. Upcoming contracts. Pack logistics.

Eventually, Ace stood. "I'll see you both soon."

And as he disappeared into the twilight, Darren entered—his daughter, little Esperanza, perched on his hip.

He was quiet, like always. But his eyes still told the truth.

He missed her.

Estrella.

My father, who had quietly taken to mentoring Darren, often reminded him: There's no wrong way to mourn the one you love.

He was healing.

Slowly.

And Esperanza? She was thriving. Full of light. Mischievous and wild. She loved being around Diego, helping change his diaper and feeding him.

I loved her like she was my own. I had to. Because she deserved to grow up surrounded by love.

Despite the heartbreak. Despite the loss. We were whole. Not because life was perfect, but because we had each other.

One of the kitchen staff entered, holding a stack of envelopes. "Excuse me, Luna. Sorry it's late. Here's today's mail."

"Thank you," I said, distracted as I shuffled through the stack.

Bills. Flyers. A baby store catalog. A letter from Luna Enterprises.

And then... a single white envelope.

No return address.

No postmark.

Just my name written in tight, deliberate handwriting I hadn't seen in over a year.

My blood went cold.

I tore it open with trembling fingers

And I didn't even need to finish reading it.

I already knew who it was from.

Alpha George.

The words, written in smooth black ink, felt like poison:

Hello, Daughter.

You didn't really think it was over, did you?

I let you play Alpha. Let you build your little home, raise your pretty boy, love your broken father...

But I'm coming back.

For what's mine.

And this time... I'm taking everything.

Especially that child.

My breath hitched.

The letter slipped from my fingers.

And everything around me—my family, my peace, my future—shook.

Because he was alive.

And he was coming.

The end for now....